F
Low

Lowenthal, Michael.

The same embrace.

DATE			
MAR 7 1999			
AUG 0 4 1999			
NOV 21 1999			

The Same Embrace

The Same Embrace

Michael Lowenthal

A DUTTON BOOK

DUTTON
Published by the Penguin Group
Penguin Putnam Inc., 375 Hudson Street, New York, New York 10014, U.S.A.
Penguin Books Ltd, 27 Wrights Lane, London W8 5TZ, England
Penguin Books Australia Ltd, Ringwood, Victoria, Australia
Penguin Books Canada Ltd, 10 Alcorn Avenue, Toronto, Ontario, Canada M4V 3B2
Penguin Books (N.Z.) Ltd, 182–190 Wairau Road, Auckland 10, New Zealand

Penguin Books Ltd, Registered Offices: Harmondsworth, Middlesex, England

First published by Dutton, an imprint of Dutton NAL,
a member of Penguin Putnam Inc.

First Printing, September, 1998
10 9 8 7 6 5 4 3 2 1

 REGISTERED TRADEMARK–MARCA REGISTRADA

Library of Congress Cataloging-in-Publication Data

Lowenthal, Michael.
    The same embrace / Michael Lowenthal.
        p.   cm.
    ISBN 0-525-94416-8
    I. Title.
    PS3562.0894S26   1998
    813'.54—dc21   98-10171
                                                                        CIP

Printed in the United States of America
Set in Transitional 521

PUBLISHER'S NOTE
This is a work of fiction. Names, characters, places, and incidents either are the products
of the author's imagination or are used fictitiously, and any resemblance to actual per-
sons, living or dead, events, or locales is entirely coincidental.

This book is printed on acid-free paper.

In memory of my grandparents
Eric I. Lowenthal and Suzanne S. Lowenthal,
and also Peter Achmed Yehuda Loewenthal

CONTENTS

Part Three: April 1993

Charge the angel who has redeemed me from all harm to bless the lads; in them be my name recalled, and the names of my fathers.

—Genesis 48:16

Every single angel is terrible.

—Rainer Maria Rilke, *Duino Elegies*

The Secret

Papa Isaac let him in on a secret. Once. The only one he ever shared.

"Just between you and me?" he asked Jacob in his cornhusk voice. It was a question but not a question. Jacob knew he could never tell.

They stood together in the kitchen. Jacob wondered where Nana Jenny was, why she had deserted them so close to the end of Shabbos. In the steel sink, faucet drips boomed like depth charges detonating. The gas burner left on for the holiday roared from the stove, its dragon's breath of flame taunted by the window's leak. The second hand of the clock was a schoolteacher's scolding finger: *not, not, not.*

The secret was this:

Sundown arrived officially at 6:43. It said so right on the Jewish-year calendar. And here it was, only 6:25. But Papa Isaac had run out of cigars. He needed to visit the shop in Kenmore Square that stocked his brand. He had to take the T. He had to handle money. These things you couldn't do till Shabbos ended.

"Just between you and me," Papa Isaac said as he reached for the clock. The motion made his sports jacket bunch and fold on itself at the shoulders, the way skin wrinkled around his eyes when he winked. He fumbled for the knob on the mechanism. Arthritic fingers and maybe guilt slowed him for an instant. Then he returned the clock to the wall. Six forty-five, it read, and the second hand resumed its chiding.

They rode the Green Line to Kenmore. As the old trolley bucked and shuddered its way down Beacon Street, Jacob understood what the real secret was. It was that a grandfather could do what Papa Isaac did. He could change time, turn day into night. A flick of the wrist, the twist of a knob, a simple statement: Just between you and me.

PART I

September and October
1992

A Moving Target

One by one the men sprouted in the gray calm of the airplane cabin. They rose tentatively at first, limbs stiff with hours of sitting, then burst to life like flowers blooming in a time-lapse nature film.

It was one of those impossibly calm flights, the 747 so solid under their feet that Jacob wondered if they'd ever left the runway. He imagined the pilot and copilot smirking to each other, then taxiing to a deserted hangar, parking, and breaking out a bottle of Johnnie Walker Black. The dappled clouds outside the windows were just a backdrop projected by some high-tech Spielberg toy. They could do wonders with holograms these days.

Marty would say it was just the irony of modern life: Everything seems more stable at a height of thirty thousand feet.

No, Jacob reminded himself. Marty *would have said*.

Bag-eyed passengers clutched blankets in fitful last attempts at sleep, tiny pillows slipping from their cricked necks. Even the flight attendants had taken their seats, recouping energy before the breakfast service. The one Jacob had his eye on—the name tag said "Yoni"—stared forward in a glassy gaze. They were still almost two hours from Israel.

Once vertical, the men migrated to the aisles, trying not to disturb their sleeping rowmates. In the grainy light their tiptoeing was a silent film comedy. Overhead bins were opened and small velvet bags removed. Lengths of cloth were unfurled, the fabric kissed with reverent lips.

It wasn't until he recognized the stripes and knotted fringes of tallises that Jacob knew the men were preparing for morning prayers. This was no longer your ordinary jumbo jet, he thought, it was a steel-and-rivets synagogue on wings.

He didn't know how the men could determine the precise moment of daybreak when they were six miles above the earth, and hurtling ever closer to dawn at five-hundred-something miles an hour. Surely there were no provisions for this in the Talmud. The ancient thinkers had not considered the possibility of morning as a moving target.

He tried not to gape at the man closest to his left. Bearded and balding, the man wrapped the thin leather straps of tefillin around his doughy forearm so tight that flesh bulged in the spiral's empty spaces. Then he started in on his prayers, bobbing and weaving as if on the verge of a faint. The other men rocked too, some in slow, pious arcs, others with jerky nods, mumbling under their breath the way autistic kids commune with themselves.

Jacob tried to recall the last time he had witnessed this archaic display. It would be scary if you didn't know what you were seeing: grown men tied up, strange tumors jutting hornlike from their heads.

Then he remembered: Papa Isaac's funeral.

They went to synagogue for early-morning services while his mother stayed home with Nana Jenny, waiting for a phone call from some "aunt" he'd never heard of. It was just his father, his brother Jonathan, and him—the three remaining Rosenbaum men. They grabbed yarmulkes from the basket in the lobby, paper-thin freebies of black polyester. Inside each moon of fabric, words were stamped in gold: *Bat Mitzvah of Rachel Cohen, September 12, 1981,* and *Marriage of Samuel Schwartz to Mira Cantor, June 9, 1978.* Jacob wondered if they made commemorative yarmulkes for funerals, too.

They lifted tallises from the rack and walked down the corridor to the small weekday chapel. Rabbi Dinnerstein greeted them as they hunched into the silky prayer shawls.

"Is it Eugene?" the rabbi whispered to his father. "Yes, Eugene. I'm so glad you came."

Jacob hadn't known a rabbi could be fat. With his mounded belly, chipmunk cheeks, and dark beard, Rabbi Dinnerstein looked like the Jewish Pavarotti.

"It's good to pray now," the rabbi said, "as a family. It's more private than during the funeral. May I ask? Do you lay tefillin?"

"Yes," his father answered, though Jacob couldn't remember him ever performing the morning ritual. "I . . ." He paused, adjusting the yarmulke on the peak of his skull. "I forgot to bring mine."

Rabbi Dinnerstein rested a pudgy hand on his father's shoulder. "Don't worry. Anyone would be frazzled. I'm sure we have an extra set to lend."

He shuffled two soft steps before he turned. "And the boys? Should I get three pairs?"

Jacob and Jonathan glanced up, each daring the other to say yes, or to have the guts not to. Papa Isaac had given the twins tefillin sets for their bar mitzvahs the previous year, but neither one had learned the complicated protocol. The bags were gathering dust in the cedar closet at home, where their father insisted they remain.

"No," his father told the rabbi. "Not the boys."

Rabbi Dinnerstein strode away, then returned a minute later with a single worn velvet bag. Once obviously a bright purple, it was now the muddy shade of dried blood.

Jacob's father unzipped the bag. The jumble of straps and boxes resembled a spider's web with two large bugs trapped in the weave. He untangled the leather and held it before his face, then stood for what seemed minutes, saying nothing, his hand fluttering like a leaf in a sudden squall.

The dozen men in the chapel, their bald heads adorned with thick-rimmed glasses and hearing aids, turned, hunting for the rabbi. Jacob avoided their rheumy eyes.

When his father finally spoke, it was without opening his mouth, a pathetic Tin Man's plea: "I don't remember."

At first, the rabbi didn't understand. He gestured with his hands, encouraging Jacob's father to go ahead and wrap the tefillin. He seemed impatient to get back to the congregation.

His father breathed the words again. "I don't remember."

Now Rabbi Dinnerstein understood. He wrested the tefillin from his father's hands and spoke in hushed platitudes. "Quite understandable. Death is a breach of meaning. Even the most routine things become foreign."

The rabbi stood over Jacob's father and wound the straps around his arm, as if dressing a boy too young to tie his shoes. His fat hands worked rapidly and with some force, leaving reddish fingerprints on Jacob's father's skin. Jacob had never thought of his father as especially thin, but now he saw that his arms were barely more than bones. He could blow over without warning, shatter like a rose dipped in liquid nitrogen.

Yoni appeared, unbeckoned, with a stack of El Al napkins, and mimed a wiping motion below his eyes. Jacob hadn't even noticed the tears. He accepted the flight attendant's gift and, swabbing his cheeks, mouthed one of the few Hebrew words he knew: "*Todah.*"

Yoni placed his hand on top of Jacob's and let it linger a moment too long—or not long enough. "You're welcome," he said, then walked off to prepare the breakfast trays.

Jacob played with the button on his armrest, tilting the seat back to a steeper recline. He imagined his grief as a liquid bubbling up his throat; if he changed position, he might keep it from spilling out.

But he wasn't certain which sorrow was sinking him. He should be mourning Marty, his best friend, ashes barely cooled, not his grandfather, dead a full ten years. Dwelling on Papa Isaac now felt disloyal, an adultery of grief.

And what of his brother? Was it premature to mourn that loss? Only in their father's hyperbolic rants was Jonathan's leaving akin to death, but perhaps, being freely chosen, his was an even greater abandonment.

Papa Isaac. Marty. Jonathan. The three disappearing acts converged into a single gaping absence. It was like those terrible game-show episodes when the host asks a question just as the out-of-time buzzer blares. The challenge dangles, unanswered, haunting living rooms across America.

For months, his parents had begged Jacob to accept a ticket to Israel. Having made the trip themselves last March to no avail, they were holding out for the chance that he could convince his brother to come home.

Jonathan's drug phase they had handled, his Grateful Dead period, too, even his brief flirtation with Scientology. But his fanatical embrace of the religion in which they themselves had been raised sent them into spasms of parental hysteria. Jacob's father in particular chafed at the mere mention of Jonathan's having joined the ranks of the "observant." "Yeah, right! That's the last thing they are. All they see is their own goddamned noses." Whenever the subject was raised, he rubbed his hands uncomfortably, as if trying to wipe off the residue of being a rabbi's son.

Three weeks after Marty's funeral, Jacob had finally accepted the ticket. Without Marty to care for, his lack of purpose was incapacitating. There were no doses of AZT to administer, no TPN drips to infuse. He shrugged off post-work plans with friends, keeping himself free in case of crisis, then sat home alone each night because the crisis had ended.

He tried logging extra hours at the Common Press, the small publisher where he was publicist and sub-rights manager. But even there his futility overwhelmed him. How could he inspire enthusiasm in others when he himself was so despondent? How could he pretend books would change the world?

Chantelle, his editor buddy at work, urged him to take the trip. "It's like a rescue mission," she said. "It'll make you feel useful." She recounted her own trip to Chicago two years ago, when her sister Sherry was being battered by her boyfriend. "I told her she had to ditch the creep, and I even changed the locks on her door to keep him out. She didn't want to admit there was a problem. She yelled all sorts of shit, said I couldn't understand, I was just a dyke. But now that she's away from him? Now she tells everyone I saved her."

Jacob consented to a week at the yeshiva. But he harbored no ambitions of "saving" Jonathan. For starters, he didn't know enough about these Orthodox recruiting centers, or what they taught, to devise any convincing counterarguments. Besides, he and Jonathan had hardly been best pals before this craziness. They were twenty-four now, long past the childhood fantasy of spending their lives together. Even if Jonathan came to his senses and left Israel, Jacob had little hope for a heartwarming, swell-of-music reconciliation.

When Jacob told people he had an identical twin, they always oohed and aahed and asked a million questions. It must be wonderful to have someone so close to you, they would say. Do you tell each other everything? Just the other day someone had launched into a fawning speech about a recent *Oprah* episode: "There were these twins? And the one told how he was having his appendix out in New York. His brother in California had no clue about the surgery, but he had a splitting stomach ache that whole day. All the way across the country. Isn't that incredible?"

Sure, incredible. Amazing stuff, twins. Jacob usually went along, smiling, not wanting to shatter people's illusions.

Yes, he and Jonathan had enjoyed their share of ESP moments: the phone calls picked up before a single ring, the uncanny parallel dreams. At seven, when they came down with chicken pox, the pustules manifested in matching patterns on their freckled backs, exact mirror images in the rough shape of question marks.

But what no one seemed to consider was the flip side of such closeness: the disproportionate pain of life apart. No one wanted to hear the story of twins who went their separate ways, who ended up not really liking each other. No one wanted to know the disquiet of being almost two, yet not quite one.

Jacob had no consciousness without his brother. His first memory was of being nudged awake by an arm—Jonathan's arm—and though he knew rationally that the scene must have occurred in the crib they shared, Jacob sometimes let himself believe it was an even earlier recollection. An Amherst friend now at Harvard Medical School reported that some ultrasounds showed twin fetuses embracing. She'd even witnessed an intrauterine kiss.

Of course, Jacob thought when she told him. That's why the rest of life seemed such a grab at empty air. How could he ever reclaim that first amniotic hug? Sometimes—still—he woke in the night, thinking he'd felt the urgent prodding of his twin; but when he opened his eyes, he was alone.

Marty had been one of the few singletons who understood what it really meant to be twinned. Jacob remembered what Marty said after the one and only time they slept together, before they realized they'd fare much better as just friends. Marty wiped himself off and then rolled over on the bed, coming face to face with the photographs on Jacob's nightstand. He focused on the one showing Jacob and Jonathan as six-year-olds, straddling the neck of the giant dinosaur outside the Museum of Natural History. They sported the same bowl haircuts, identical rugby shirts and cut-off denim shorts; most people wouldn't have been able to tell them apart. But even in this early snapshot Jacob could discern their differences. His own face was stricken with a serious smile, intent on pleasing their father behind the camera. Jonathan's features were blurry because he had been distracted by something off to the side, and Jacob had tapped his shoulder for attention.

Marty stared too long at the photo, longer than was polite, studying its details under the lamp.

"It's just a picture," Jacob said. He patted the pillow to lure Marty back.

"In a sec," Marty stalled. "I'm trying to figure out what parts of you are just your genes, and what parts are, you know, really *you*."

That was precisely what Jacob wondered, too. Most outsiders fixated on twins' being identical. But to him, it was the discrepancies that were meaningful. Jonathan was a gauge, a standard of comparison by which Jacob could measure who he himself—and only he—truly was.

Israel had never been high on his list of places to visit—in fact, it had never occurred to him—but now that he was going, Jacob was determined to make the most of the trip. He had browsed Barnes & Noble's supply of guidebooks and amassed a quirky roster of must-see attractions.

Number one was the Mount of Olives. He'd always hated olives, sickened at the mere smell of their rotten brine, but he spun a fantasy that if he picked one fresh from a tree, it would become his favorite food. One of the guidebooks said that on the Day of Judgment, the dead will rise from the Mount of Olives cemetery. God will make tunnels from all the world's graveyards, converging on the Mount, gathering humanity immemorial to ascend to heaven. Jacob remembered the ending scene from *Longtime Companion*, when all the AIDS dead return for a party at Fire Island. Maybe the Mount of Olives would be the same way, he thought. Marty would be there. Papa Isaac, too.

Swimming in the Dead Sea was another must. The salt water was supposed to steal years from your face, erase acne scars in minutes. It was the one place on earth where you couldn't drown.

Jacob wanted to feel what it was like to float with no fear of going under.

He had also toyed with the idea of a day trip to Sodom, just so he could say he'd been. Marty would have loved that. He would have done some Jewboy right next to a pillar of salt—daring God, just daring Him. Jacob wondered if they sold T-shirts: I WAS SODOMIZED IN SODOM.

Marty had always brought Jacob souvenirs from his trips. There was the GOD IS MY COPILOT license plate from Memphis, the miniature shoofly-pie paperweight from Amish country. Marty adored travel, especially airplanes. By now he would have cornered Yoni in the bathroom, pressing him up against the stainless-steel sink, the toilet freshener's fumes filling their nostrils like some antiseptic brand of poppers.

Jacob leaned back, gauging the nervousness that simmered in his veins whenever he pondered sex. It shouldn't be so difficult. It couldn't be. Marty and a million other guys blinked their eyes and got their wish.

But sex was a tightrope Jacob couldn't quite balance on. He found himself unable to fuck without emotion, but equally unable to forge any meaningful connections. Most of his trysts were famously disastrous, like Hannes on his trip to Germany. Misery loves company, he learned, and so does sexual neurosis.

When Jacob's father scoffed at his activism, claiming that gay rights was just an excuse for easy sex, Jacob always challenged him: "That's what *you* focus on, not us. For us, it's about the freedom to define ourselves." But secretly—when he wasn't spokesperson for anything—Jacob couldn't help agreeing. Being gay *was* about sex, and that's why he was bad at it. He'd never had a real boyfriend; he couldn't even turn a simple trick. He was a fraud.

What he hadn't told his parents, or even Chantelle, was that he hoped this trip might be the chance to change. Maybe, far away from everything, he could finally earn his fairy wings. He conjured Palestinian falafel boys, their fingers greasy with deep-fry oil as they groped his chest. And Israeli soldiers, stomachs as hard as the Uzis they never surrendered, not even in bed.

He adjusted the seat-belt buckle to cover his burgeoning erection. Maybe, he thought. Maybe this time.

*   *   *

Breakfast was bagels and lox—no wonder the tickets cost so much. But what did he care? His parents were paying. Jacob scarfed the meal, then tipped back and dozed dreamlessly.

He woke what seemed only minutes later to trays scraping, cabinet doors banging shut. The doughy man to his left—Michelinski, he'd decided to call him: the Jewish Michelin Man—still displayed plum-colored marks on his arms where the tefillin straps had dug in. But now he paged through a *Sports Illustrated*, moving his lips with the same meditative determination he had shown murmuring his prayers.

The captain's voice crackled on the intercom, instructing them to prepare for landing. Jacob had never seen such a compliant group of passengers. All around the cabin, people locked tray tables and brought seat backs to full upright position with the fervor of children downing vegetables to expedite dessert.

The changing air pressure was excruciating, but these passengers happily endured the suffering. A middle-aged woman two seats to Jacob's right pinched her nose, then, like a sixties high-school girl doing the Swim, blew hard to pop the pressure from her ears. Air squealed from her nostrils, and the old man between them burst into giggles.

The cabin's gray light glimmered, flared, then washed with tie-dyed streaks of yellow-blue. Jacob craned his neck to the windows. He was too far from the tiny ovals to see, but he could tell they had punched through the clouds. The plane jounced like a body surfer at the mercy of surging waves.

And finally they touched down—two gentle bumps, then another jarring one—and the tires spun on solid ground. A cheer erupted spontaneously throughout the cabin. A Muzak version of "Havah Negilah" pumped through the intercom and was immediately amplified by dozens of singing, clapping passengers. The man in front of Jacob, so solemn two hours earlier with his tallis and tefillin, now bounced in his seat like a child on a Ferris wheel.

Jacob was a confirmed nonclapper. Even as a child, he did not sing along on the chorus when Peter, Paul, and Mary beseeched him to. He never stood when the Wave reached his section of the grandstand. Yet even Jacob found himself swept up in this excitement. Everyone's joy seemed so genuine and unself-conscious. There were tears in some passengers' eyes.

He kept telling himself not to get carried away; Israel was not *his* promised land. But he couldn't help thinking of all those Passover seders when he was a kid, each concluded with the words "Next year in Jerusalem." How many thousands would have given anything to fulfill the pledge? Papa Isaac's father, sent to his death at Bergen-Belsen just three weeks before his visa was to arrive. Nana Jenny's brother Walter, also killed in the camps. And Nana Jenny herself, who had never been to Israel and said she was too old now for the trip, who asked Jacob to go for her, to carry her heart in his own. All those eager would-be pilgrims, and now unbelieving Jacob was the only one who'd made it.

The plane rolled to a halt and the seat-belt sign flashed off. Jacob prepared for the usual scuffling in the aisle. But the passengers around him kept deferring to one another, gesturing *No, you first*. Michelinski retrieved the jacket and tote bag of the woman who had performed the Swim. The man in front of him asked if somebody could help him reach, and a horsey teenage girl opened the overhead bin. It was a spontaneous conspiracy of cooperation, something Jacob knew could never happen in America, except at a car accident or emergency.

He accepted his windbreaker from Michelinski with a grateful nod and joined the line inching forward to the door. He was trying to think of something to say to Yoni on the way out. Maybe he could ask Yoni's schedule and see if he'd be working the return flight. They could exchange home addresses, make a date.

He saw the flight attendant ahead, framed in the harsh light of the open door, a big-toothed smile locked on his face. As he walked closer, Jacob could hear Yoni singsonging his way through the file of passengers: "*Sha-lom. Sha-lom.* Bye. Bye-bye. *Sha-lom.*"

Jacob's face was singed with the shame of another failure. The napkins, the special attention—it hadn't been special at all, he admitted. Yoni had only been doing what he was paid to do.

"Bye-bye. *Sha-lom. Sha-lom.*"

Jacob imagined Yoni had composed the little ditty just to mock him. Just to tell him their connection was nothing a hundred other passengers hadn't also shared. He shuffled onward, eyes pointed to the floor.

He was about to step out and onto the stairs when, like a tiny bird, a hand landed on his shoulder. Yoni squeezed the shoulder and winked. "Take care of yourself," he said. "No more frowning. I will think of you."

Before Jacob could say anything back, he was urged out by one of the other flight attendants. "Bye now," she said. "Watch your step." She grabbed his elbow and pushed him along.

He turned to look for Yoni in the doorway, but the sunlight glancing off the white plane blinded him. A magician's trick, a flash of magnesium, and Yoni was gone.

Jacob walked down the stairs and was blasted with a gust of dry heat that turned the world gauzy and slow. He balanced himself on the railing, the metal so hot it stuck to his palm. At the bottom of the stairs an old woman fell to her knees and kissed the ground. Jacob saw other passengers doing the same. They pressed their lips to the hot tarmac, not caring about the oil and grime.

He had the urge to kiss the ground, too; but what could he ever believe in so thoroughly? His own *lack* of faith? The tingle of Yoni's touch, already faded? He walked past the prostrate forms and into the terminal.

After customs Jacob strapped himself into his big internal-frame backpack and walked to the passenger greeting area. This was his least favorite part of traveling. It always seemed a competition, one more means for ranking humans in the hierarchy of loved and unloved. Did you have friends and family who cared enough to be waiting when you arrived? Or did you have to linger ten, fifteen, twenty minutes before anyone bothered to find you? Perhaps no one cared at all, and you hailed a taxi alone.

He watched the multinational chaos of the terminal. Israelis in shorts and sandals gestured largely to one another, taking up two and three times their needed body space. Palestinian men greeted each other with kisses on both cheeks, then turned quickly away, their kaffiyehs rippling in the breeze of their own motion. The display shocked Jacob. Why was it that in cultures rumored to be intolerant, two men could kiss and hug with impunity; but back in Boston, a seconds-too-long glance at a stranger could get you pummeled?

He scanned the crowd constantly for Jonathan. Jacob was at a distinct disadvantage, because he hadn't changed since college, but who knew what Holy Jonathan was going to look like? His parents had told him Jonathan didn't wear a long black coat and black hat, or have earlocks at the sides of his head. Still, every time a Hasidic man entered the greeting area, Jacob squinted in search of family resemblance.

And then he saw him: stepping around an Arab woman and her young child, almost knocking the child over, but not apologizing. He wore a plain white button-down shirt and dark blue slacks that, even from this distance, Jacob could tell were polyester. Dangling from his waist like scrawny tentacles were the knotted strings of his tzitzis, the fringes that marked him Orthodox.

Jonathan hadn't seen him yet. He didn't appear to be particularly searching. He walked with even steps, expressionless, as if on any errand, a trip to the grocery store.

Jacob was about to wave, but he held back and watched Jonathan. It was like seeing himself in a mirror, only with a few crucial parts rearranged. Jonathan still shared his eagle-beak nose, of course, with the odd leftward crook at the tip. He had Jacob's same eyes that waxed and waned in their blueness depending on clothing choice or weather; the same burnt-looking brown hair beset by cowlicks. Jacob recognized in his twin's shoulders the broadness for which strangers often complimented him. But there were differences, too: the scar through Jonathan's right eyebrow from an early bike accident; the never-pierced ears; and, most notably now, a beard.

He had never seen Jonathan with a beard, not a real one. The last time Jonathan had tried was at seventeen—the height of his pothead period—when the hair sprouted only in sparse patches below his jawbone. It had made him look ridiculous, a catfish out of water, but he wore it like a boast proving his selfhood. This new beard was actually quite handsome, full and dark, red tinges sparkling like tinsel in the duller brown. If Jonathan trimmed it a little, and exchanged his polyester pants and Oxford cloth for jeans and a T-shirt, he would attract plenty of attention at Paradise or the Ramrod. I might cruise him, Jacob thought. I might ask him home.

Now he raised his hand—first like a student not wanting to anger the teacher with interruption, only to shoulder level; then all the way above his head. Jonathan noticed him, nodded once, and turned.

It had been almost two years since they'd seen each other, probably twice that since they'd engaged in meaningful conversation. Still, the affection surfaced instinctively as breath, so essential and familiar it was barely distinguishable from simply being alive. Jacob thought, as he often had when they were kids, of the fact that they'd begun life as the same single cell. And though it made no sense, he missed Jonathan suddenly now more than ever, *this instant*, even though his brother was just yards away.

Then Jonathan was within an arm's length. What Jacob wanted was to hug his brother the way they used to, squeezing as hard as they could until one of them called uncle. But he would settle for a plain old hug. He took half a step, starting to open his arms. Jonathan didn't respond. He didn't flinch or turn away, nothing so forcefully rejecting; he just seemed closed to the possibility.

Jacob caught himself midstep and regained his balance. Good manners brought his right hand automatically forward to shake Jonathan's, but he willed himself to lift it all the way to his face, and scratched his chin instead.

"I thought it was just women you weren't allowed to touch," he said, stuffing his hands into his pockets.

Jonathan locked his jaw. "We're *not* not allowed to touch women. Anyway, that doesn't apply to family."

"Jon, I'm kidding," Jacob said. "I was kidding."

Silence swirled almost visibly between them, like some theatrical effect, wisps of dry ice.

Jacob couldn't tell if it was the industrial lighting or what, but through the beard Jonathan's face glared shockingly, sickly pale, the fragile white of denim scarred with bleach. As kids, Jonathan had been a shade or two darker than Jacob, a rugged complexion Jacob wished he could steal. Now he felt guilty for his secret jealousy. He wanted to lend Jonathan some color.

It wasn't just the beard or the pale skin. There was a change in Jonathan's eyes, a darkening of the blue, a wariness. He stood unbendingly, turned his entire torso when he glanced to the side. Jacob thought how much it would please Mr. Stipple, their eighth-grade algebra teacher, who always berated Jonathan for his terrible posture. "You're not an invertebrate!" he would shout as he kicked Jonathan's chair. "You're not a jellyfish. Sit up!"

Jacob considered making a joke about Mr. Stipple, but he wasn't sure if Jonathan wanted to hear about his past, his preobservant life. Eighth grade had been when Jonathan began slipping into the disaffection that sparked their steady drift.

He caught his brother's vacant, unblinking stare. "Nana Jenny says hi," he offered, hoping their grandmother could provide a safely neutral topic.

"She's all right?" Jonathan asked.

"Sure, I guess."

"Good, good. When we talked on Friday, she seemed a little . . . I don't know, fuzzy. Maybe she was just nervous about your trip. She doesn't trust airplanes."

"Maybe," Jacob said. "That could be it." He realized now the ludicrousness of his reporting to Jonathan on their grandmother's well-being. Since Jonathan had become Orthodox, he had taken to calling Nana Jenny every Friday afternoon before Shabbos. Jacob, on the other hand, though he lived just a couple of miles from her, spoke with Nana Jenny only every month or two. What could they talk about without stumbling into the Forbidden Topic?

"Oh," he said. "Listen. Don't let me forget this. Nana Jenny wants me to get her a mezuzah."

"She can't buy one in Brookline?"

"It's some special commemorative thing they only sell here. Another lady at her synagogue apparently brought one back. I've got the pamphlet somewhere in my pack."

"Fine," Jonathan said. "Show it to me later. We'll figure out where to buy it."

Jacob nodded. At least they were talking now. At least Jonathan was treating him like a human.

"There's also a care package buried in here," he said. He patted the bottom of his bulging backpack.

Jonathan looked confused; he clearly hadn't expected a gift.

"From Mom," Jacob clarified. "She thinks you can't buy soap or toothpaste in Israel."

Jonathan's eyes lightened a shade around the rims. "She sent underwear for the first three months," he admitted. "I had to get the rosh yeshiva to write her and say they do in fact have laundry here."

"And she actually listened?"

"She did, believe it or not. No more packages from Lord & Taylor. Now Israeli customs has to spend their time on all the old boring stuff again—arms shipments, letter bombs."

Jacob turned his head both ways, as if spying for eavesdroppers. "Promise not to tell something?" he asked.

"Uh-huh."

"Really promise?"

Jonathan made a zipper motion across his lips.

"She still sends me stuff, too, but I give it all to Goodwill. I don't even open the packages anymore. I bring them right to the donation center."

A wet bubble of laughter popped from Jonathan's throat, and Jacob laughed too. They shook their heads at their mother's well-meaning lunacy. Jacob watched dimples claim their posts on his brother's face, two on each side at the upper edge of his beard. Jacob had the exact ones, a genetic match.

Still smiling, Jonathan checked his watch. "Let's head out front," he said. "The bus leaves in five minutes."

When Jonathan turned, Jacob could see for the first time the knitted yarmulke pinned to the back of his brother's head. He waited and walked purposely a step behind Jonathan, examining the Hebrew writing around the small cloth circle's edge. It had been ages since he'd attempted to decipher the alien alphabet, and even at the height of his Hebrew knowledge he'd never been able to read without the vowels. He stumbled from character to character, trying to recall the individual sounds of the letters. Then he relaxed his eyes, letting them absorb the whole word, and the shape was immediately familiar. It was his own name. Their name. Rosenbaum.

The Grip

The first time they had to wrestle, it was Chanukah. He and Jonathan were ten years old.

Jacob remembered it was Chanukah because as soon as they entered their grandparents' apartment building, the greasy odor of latkes seeped like skin lotion into his pores. Almost everyone who lived there was old and Jewish.

The cab ride from Logan Airport to Brookline had taken almost as long as the flight up from Washington. Jacob was a spring-loaded alarm clock, ticking toward a rattling explosion. When the foyer door buzzed open he bolted through, neck-and-neck with Jonathan.

He kept his head down as he double-timed the stairs, the way his baseball coach had taught him to steal second base. All he could see were his own feet and Jonathan's beside them, in identical green suede Adidas. Two steps below the landing, just as he was about to ease up, he slammed into something hard and fell.

Then he was being lifted to his feet, his chin upturned by calloused fingers. "Always so eager," Papa Isaac said, massaging his own kneecap with his other hand. "Even if a sore skull is your only reward."

By then Papa Isaac was seventy-six and his shoulders were stooped, but you could tell how tall he had been. Everything about him was magnified: his nearly bald head burdening his ropy neck; his ears cavernous folds of flesh that could have been models for the elephant-ear pastries at Kupel's Bakery.

Papa Isaac coughed a ratchety laugh and, like a rusty crane being lowered, bent to kiss first Jacob and then Jonathan on the lips. Jacob always waited for this greeting with a mixture of excitement and disgust. No one else made him kiss on the lips, not Nana Jenny, or even his own mother. Papa Isaac's lips were wrinkled as fruit forgotten in the refrigerator. Stained muddy from his cigars, they left a tingling sensation on Jacob's mouth.

Papa Isaac stepped aside to allow room for Jacob's parents, who had trudged the three flights with adult sluggishnesss. "Sarah?" he said before kissing Jacob's mother—as though, after more than a decade as her father-in-law, still unsure that he would get her name right. Jacob's father drifted forward and the men shook hands silently.

When Papa Isaac broke the grasp, he teased his hand into his left jacket pocket. Jacob jockeyed closer, in front of Jonathan, staking position for the first choice of prizes. His grandfather must have had a dozen blue and brown sports coats, all identical in style. They had been tailored for a younger, larger Papa Isaac, so that now the sleeves threatened to swallow his arms. Yet somehow this made him seem even more impressive. When he reached into the bottomless pockets the treasure might be anything: a piece of candy, a shining coin, the paper ring from one of his cigars. Jacob wouldn't have been surprised by a white-feathered dove.

This time Papa Isaac's hand emerged with only a cruddy handkerchief. He blew his nose in a single blast like a basketball game's ending honk.

Smoke suffocated the kitchen. Cookie sheets lined with paper towels filled every inch of counter space, piled high with latkes in their greasy haloes. Jacob watched Nana Jenny bustle about the room. His grandmother's face was contracted into an unusually severe pout, deepening the wrinkles around her mouth to mini-canyons. A thin white strand had pulled loose from her carefully shaped hairdo; it flapped like a distress signal, the waving kerchief of an endangered movie heroine.

She was already dressed for dinner, in a calf-length, silky aqua dress, but she had covered it to protect against stains with the WORLD'S GREATEST GRANDMA apron Jacob and Jonathan had given her last Chanukah. Actually, their mother had picked the present.

She had paid for and wrapped it, and he and Jonathan had only signed the card. Jacob blushed at the sight of the stupid thing, guilty that Nana Jenny felt obliged to wear it. The apron was a gift for someone else's grandmother, some other family; they would never call Nana Jenny "Grandma."

He kissed his grandmother on the cheek, the side without the moles and their tufts of old-lady hair. She hugged him with her elbows, greasy hands held safely aloft to keep from getting fingerprints on his starched holiday shirt.

Jacob enjoyed helping Nana Jenny in the kitchen. Sometimes she let him dunk matzah balls into the boiling chicken broth and watch them swell like dandelion puffs. His other favorite job was to pick grapes off their stems for the fruit compote. Later, when dessert was served, she always gave him credit. "Jacob made the grapes," she would say, lifting one on her spoon for everyone to see. It never impressed Papa Isaac. He would shake his head, muttering, "*God* made the grapes."

Jacob started to roll up his sleeves so the cuffs wouldn't get messy. But his grandmother shook her head. "I was late shopping," she explained. "I'm too much behind schedule."

He didn't understand. Together couldn't they cook twice as fast? But she tilted her head to the door, shooing him with her gaze. Just then Jacob's mother appeared, her dress hidden behind Nana Jenny's fraying everyday apron. "Listen to your Nana," she said. "We have cooking to do."

In the living room, Jacob's father sat on the couch. He had picked through the coffee table's clutter, strewing aside copies of the *Jewish Advocate* and the *Jerusalem Post* to find the last three issues of *Time*—the only non-Jewish periodical in the apartment. The subscription was in fact his yearly gift to Papa Isaac, guaranteeing he'd have something to read when they visited.

Jonathan knelt on the floor, sketching geometric designs on graph paper. It was his recent obsession: meticulously symmetrical abstractions, often diamonds inside of diamonds inside of diamonds, every minuscule stroke accounted for. Their teachers urged Jonathan to try more free-form drawings, maybe landscapes or even cartoons, but he wouldn't be swayed from his patterns. The only person he would let tamper with the diagrams was Jacob, whom he sometimes asked to add colored highlights in Magic

Marker. Only Jacob, he explained, understood where things belonged.

Jonathan looked up now and without having to say anything invited Jacob to join him. But Jacob wasn't in the mood. He loved his brother, but the routine of their play sometimes bored him. He frowned at the paucity of his options: he didn't want to be with Jonathan or his father; Nana Jenny and his mother had rebuffed him. Sometimes Jacob fantasized other family members to choose from: at the very least an aunt and uncle, perhaps a cousin or two. He imagined a man arriving in a pinstriped suit, his arms laden with shiny gifts. He would regale them with stories of the exotic city where he lived, and invite Jacob to visit for an intoxicating summer.

Once, he made the mistake of telling the fantasy to his father. "Careful," his father warned. "Ask too much and you might get what you ask for." Jacob pressed his father to explain himself, wondering what it could mean to ask "too much," but his father wouldn't say anything more.

He was about to find a deck of cards to play solitaire when Papa Isaac entered the room.

"Jacob, Jonathan. Come," he said, waving his hand once as if snatching a fly.

Papa Isaac spoke in a deep grating rasp. Jacob had never had the guts to ask, but he imagined his grandfather's voice had been wrecked by a childhood of German consonants. He and Nana Jenny had been in America half their lives now—since 1942, when by some miracle they had escaped—and as far as Jacob knew, they hadn't spoken a word of German since. But the growl of an accent stayed with them, his grandfather especially, unavoidable as a disfiguring birthmark. Emerging from Papa Isaac's throat, even Jacob's own name could sound unfamiliar, a secret code word, full of foreboding.

"Come," Papa Isaac beckoned again, and Jacob and Jonathan jumped to their feet. They marched behind their grandfather down the hall and into his study. It was his private room, thick with cigar smell and the mustiness of old books. There were no windows, just a single dim overhead bulb.

Papa Isaac closed the door and sat in his bentwood rocking chair, feet flat on the floor, perfectly motionless, as if in a battle of will against gravity. He lifted his right hand from the rocker's smooth arm and pointed to the floor. "Let's see which is stronger," he said.

Jacob followed an invisible line extending from Papa Isaac's finger, searching for the objects to which he had referred. There was nothing but the bare oak floorboards.

"Wrestle with your arms," his grandfather commanded. "No one is really identical. Let's see which of you wins best."

Jacob looked at Jonathan, waiting to see if he would drop to the floor. Terror paled his brother's face, making his red, trembling lips conspicuous as a bleeding gash.

Jacob was terrified too. He had never contradicted Papa Isaac. But to obey him now would be to directly disobey their mother. She had told them that being twins was a unique opportunity. They would always have a companion their own age; they would always have two-is-better-than-one. But it would be easy to spoil it, she warned. That was why when they played Wiffle Ball in the summer, the game always ended in a "Rosenbaum tie." That was why they didn't keep score in Scrabble, but simply stopped when someone ran out of tiles.

"Come," Papa Isaac insisted. "On the floor."

Jacob knelt, then lay flat on his belly. Jonathan did the same, facing him. Jacob shivered when the floorboards touched his stomach. There was dust everywhere, wispy balls of lint and hair.

He wanted to get up and brush himself off. He worried about dirtying his holiday shirt. But he could tell from Papa Isaac's voice that this wasn't a game you could decide to quit. He pushed his shirt sleeve past his elbow, then propped his right arm in front of him, the wrist curved over, a question mark. Jonathan answered with his own hand. He curled his thumb around Jacob's and closed his fingers one by one. For balance, they linked left hands below the angle of their wrestling arms.

They held each other like that, their four arms in a sturdy X, the kind of grip you might choose to rescue someone fallen overboard. Jacob found his brother's eyes, hoping to send a private message. They could speak without words—in fact, hadn't learned to speak at all till they were two years old, the incentive dulled by their silent understanding. But Jonathan's eyes were hollow with fear, inaccessible.

Then Jacob felt the sweat oozing from his brother's palms. It was a sticky and embarrassing dampness, like wetting your pants. He sickened with claustrophobia. He yearned to let go his hand, to wipe himself dry. Jonathan wouldn't loosen his hold.

"Ready?" Papa Isaac asked.

Acid surged in Jacob's stomach. He answered a breathless yes for both of them.

"I will start you to make it fair. On your marks . . . set . . . go!"

Jacob tensed his forearm and felt Jonathan do the same. They both pushed, testing the resistance. Like a tree in a shifting breeze, their joined arms swayed.

Despite their mother's warnings, there had been inevitable competitions. But the previous skirmishes had been private, the stakes devised by and known only to the two of them. They had never been pitted against each other by another person. They had never had a witness, a judge.

Jacob adjusted his grip to keep from slipping on Jonathan's sweaty palm. He wanted to win for his grandfather. He wanted Papa Isaac to see that he could be stronger. He wanted to grind Jonathan into the ground.

He eased up for just a second. The strategy worked; his brother was thrown off balance. Jacob cranked from the elbow, his arm a powerful lever, and Jonathan crumpled under him.

He had done it. He had proven he was the worthy one.

Jacob released his grasp, sure he'd won a piece of candy, at least, and maybe something bigger. He looked up for his grandfather's smile.

Papa Isaac's eyes were pinched as if in pain, his mouth bunched in a complicated frown.

"Now," he said softly, "the left arm."

In the Shadow

They had barely entered the main yeshiva building when a jubilant voice cried, "Hey, Yoni!"

Jacob's heart quickened. He blinked in the hallway's sudden darkness, searching for the sympathetic flight attendant whose touch was a soft memory on his shoulder blade.

"Yoni," the voice called again. "We missed you this morning."

Someone materialized from the shadows and clasped a hand on Jonathan's neck, then tousled his hair, skewing his yarmulke's bobby pins. Only then did Jacob realize that "Yoni" referred to Jonathan. It was the diminutive of his Hebrew name, Yonatan.

"This is your visitor?" the student asked with one eyebrow hoisted. "You never said you had a twin."

"This is Jacob," Jonathan said.

The student pumped his hand. "Yaakov—very good. I'm Ari. Welcome to Etz Chaim."

Nobody had called Jacob by his own Hebrew name since his bar mitzvah. Under normal circumstances it might have made him spit up laughing. But he repeated the name silently, trying it on.

Ari introduced himself as Jonathan's study partner. He had a rosy face that, along with his dishwater-blond hair, could have passed for Irish if he weren't wearing a yarmulke. He must have been twenty-two or twenty-three, but he was four inches shorter than Jacob, and thin in an adolescent way that meant he would still get carded in a bar.

"Your brother's a great guy," Ari said. "Very *frum*. I bet it runs in the family?"

Jacob had never heard the Yiddish word for "observant" used positively. "Well," he said, "we're not identical in everything."

He caught Jonathan's gaze as it dropped to the floor. He had assumed his brother must bad-mouth him all the time, but it was clear Jonathan hadn't so much as mentioned his existence.

Ari didn't seem to notice the tension. He bounced on his toes. "How long do we have you?" he asked.

"Just a week."

"Well, if you need anything . . ." Ari placed his hand on Jacob's neck and gave a more-than-friendly squeeze. "Off to *beit midrash*. Study, study." He took off, humming, down the hall.

Jacob stood with his brother, reeling from the warmth of Ari's touch. How strange to have traveled halfway across the globe to be reunited with Jonathan, and then to be more intimate with someone he'd only known two minutes.

"I'll show you the room," Jonathan said. "I'm missing class."

Jonathan lived by himself, a perk reserved for students who lasted at Etz Chaim six months or more. It was your better basic dorm room: thin green carpet stretching wall-to-wall like Astroturf, an overvarnished wooden dresser guarding the door. Above a rusty sink, mildew stains peppered a blurry mirror. Jacob detected the ripeness of dirty socks.

"Why don't you catch some sleep?" Jonathan said. "I'll check in before dinner to see if you're up." And before Jacob could even ask where the bathroom was, he disappeared.

Jacob felt powerful in a way, inducing such discomfort in his own brother. It was like having pinkeye as a kid, being able to fend off even the most hated schoolyard bully with the threat of contamination. The problem was, the people whose attention you craved had to keep their distance too.

He remembered when they were juniors in high school. For their birthday, their mother had provided tickets to the Dead show at RFK Stadium, with the stipulation that they go together. She hated the band, and she knew Jacob couldn't stand them either, but she overlooked these facts in an attempt to facilitate détente.

In the parking lot's maze of VW campers, the old-shoe smell of pot blurred the air with enticement. When people did double takes—identical twins were an endless fascination—Jonathan shadowed his face the way criminals hide from courtroom cameras. He was clearly as embarrassed to be associated with nerdy Jacob as Jacob was to be seen at a Dead show.

But once they were inside the stadium and the eerie music began, Jonathan loosened—the Scarecrow unhitched from his wooden perch. He wiggled to the hypnotic rhythms, eyes rolled back in their lids. Jacob realized how long it had been since he'd seen his brother happy. And as much as he hated the music, the sweaty crowd, the clouds of suffocating smoke, he was glad to be there, to witness Jonathan's release.

Half an hour into the show, Jonathan tripped during a particularly energetic spin. He fell to the ground laughing, and as he was getting up, he caught Jacob's eye. The look of bliss that had radiated from his face for the previous thirty minutes dissolved into disappointment. "Oh," he said, "I, like, totally spaced the fact that you were here."

Jacob had to make excuses about all the smoke to explain why his eyes began to tear. It was the first time the thought had crystallized: Maybe Jonathan could only be happy apart from him.

There was only a single bed, which Jonathan had not offered, so Jacob unfurled his sleeping bag on the floor. He was exhausted from the overnight flight. His back felt as though it might snap if he twisted wrong. But even with the window open, the heat was too intense to fall asleep. He lay there, trying not to let any body part touch another, wincing when flesh accidentally adhered in a kiss of sweat. With a sickened cringe, he remembered Marty: miserable with fever, breaking into sobs because no aspirin, no fan, nothing could allay his dying body's burn.

He ditched his sleeping bag and sprawled on the carpet.

When Jonathan finally reappeared, evening obscured the window's swatch of sky. Jacob had been up for an hour, reading the proofs of a book he had to promote when he returned to Boston. It was a gay inspirational quote book, which the Common Press would publish on National Coming Out Day in hopes of subsidizing more substantive titles.

At the sound of the door opening, Jacob whipped the galleys

shut and stashed them inside his sleeping bag. He suffered an instant's guilt for his self-censorship, then realized it wasn't the gayness he was hiding from Jonathan, only the banality of this manifestation.

"I thought you'd never come back," he said, starting to put on his shoes. "Is it dinnertime yet? I'm completely starved."

"Oh," Jonathan said. He sat on the bed, then slouched against the wall. "I forgot. I already ate."

In the morning, while Jonathan studied with Ari, Jacob sat in on the Beginning Talmud class. The rabbi interrupted his lecture to shake Jacob's hand and encourage him to participate. He was thirtysomething, with a beard sculpted along angular lines. He wore a dark sports coat and a white shirt without a tie.

"Maybe the cow already gave birth to the calf before she was gored," he said, resuming the lesson, "and it would have been a stillbirth anyway. Maybe it's the ox's fault, maybe not."

He paused, seeming to revel in the dilemma. He raised and lowered his palm-up hands, first the left and then the right, the tipping scales of a balance.

"So the question is: If the ox has gored the cow, and its newborn calf is also found dead, does the owner of the ox have to pay damages for the calf as well as for the cow?"

Jacob sat in the last row, trying not to laugh. But the other students stared at the rabbi as if at some magician's illusion, a wax figure come to life. Many were still dressed in nonobservant civvies: T-shirts and jeans, some even in shorts. Their faces radiated an artificial peachy cast, like the hand-tinted antique photographs Jacob had collected when he was twelve. It was the same coloring, he realized, that marked certain kids after spring break in college. They would have traveled to Aruba or Cancun, whatever resort was "in" that year, and bronzed themselves to perfection. But back in gray Amherst their skin appeared synthetic and gaudily out of place.

Jonathan, too, must have looked this way newly arrived at the yeshiva, still sporting the rugged tan from his months of trekking in Nepal. How long had it taken before his face drained to its current vampirish pallor? Maybe with a little practice, Jacob thought, you could observe the shade of a yeshiva student's skin and judge how many weeks he had been cooped at the school.

"Listen now," the rabbi said, "and learn a crucial concept in Judaism." He squinted one eye on the word *crucial*, exactly the way Dan Rather always winced on key phrases from his TelePrompTer.

"First," he continued, "look at the law. The text specifies that we're talking about a *shor tam*, an ox with no reputation for goring animals. So the law says, give the owner the benefit of the doubt. He only has to pay half the value of the cow.

"But the Talmud goes a step further. Because while we know the ox is responsible for the cow's death, we can't be sure it killed the calf. So again we give the benefit of the doubt, and the two owners split things down the middle. That's the principle here: When in doubt, split evenly. And half of half is a quarter. So now you see why the owner of the ox reimburses for half the cow's value, but only *one-quarter* the value of the calf."

The rabbi paused, making sure everyone had followed the logic. Then he smiled and ducked his hands into his pockets with a fashion model's studied nonchalance.

"Now, you may wonder, what do a couple of farm animals have to do with anything? But you will come to see that Judaism is not so much concerned with a mystical kind of belief as with the way one should live and treat others. Jews get a pretty bad rep in history for being greedy, right? Think of Shylock. But you can see here just how generous and fair-minded a religion it is."

As a publicist himself, Jacob was impressed by the rabbi's spin-doctoring. In a different outfit, he thought, this man could run for office. Or sell pasta machines on an infomercial.

Jacob tried to imagine Jonathan succumbing to this same initiation. He remembered the first letter Jonathan had sent their parents:

> *You won't believe it but I'm writing this from a yeshiva. You know, a school for Orthodox types. Only this one is especially for kids who weren't raised that way, then decide to convert. Ba'al teshuvah, it's called (I'm not sure I spelled that right).*
>
> *Don't freak out, I haven't like joined a cult or something. I'm just checking it out for a couple of days since my plane tickets*

were extendable. I was at the Western Wall and this guy comes up to me, dressed all in black like you see people in New York. "Give it a try," he said. "You came here for adventure, right? How can you say you've seen Israel if you haven't seen a yeshiva?" I totally knew what he was up to, but I've got to say he had a good point.

They let you stay for free and eat meals and everything if you check out their classes. It's not at all what I was expecting. Actually, I don't know what I expected. I guess I've always thought of religion as being about God and miracles and stuff. But I've been learning that Judaism is all about ethics and morals, the way to lead a holy life. Or maybe that's not a good word, because it's more like a pious life. You're always supposed to be aware of what you're doing, and give thanks for everything. When you wake up in the morning, you say a prayer of thanks for being alive. That's the first thing you do. Isn't that cool? It's like all the mitzvahs (sp?) make you take the time to enjoy what we have. Every action you do means something.

They even tell you there's a Jewish way to put on your shoes. You put on the right shoe first, and then the left. But you tie the left shoe first, and then the right. That way you're not favoring one over the other. It sounds silly, I know. Tying your shoes. But when you think about it, it's really a great philosophy. Compare that to Christianity or something, where they're always telling people they're no good and condemning them to hell.

They must not have given the condemnation lecture yet, Jacob thought. When did that come—two weeks into the program? Two months? Jonathan's subsequent letters had been laden with biblical injunctions and hateful rhetoric. Jacob wasn't supposed to have seen them, but he'd stumbled across the envelopes in his mother's sewing box on a weekend visit when a button popped off his shirt. One line in particular stuck in his memory: "It's a commandment to honor your parents, so despite the things we see differently I will work hard to do that. But there's no commandment about honoring a brother."

Jacob stole the letter and crushed it in the trash compactor.

How had Jonathan, his twin, who shared his very cells, calcified into such intolerance? Jacob wanted to blame Etz Chaim and its insidious indoctrination. But he knew Orthodoxy wasn't entirely culpable. Orthodoxy had only provided this more persuasive language for a long-brewing resentment.

Jacob had come out to Jonathan during his freshman winter at Amherst. Jonathan wasn't in college yet. He was taking a year off to travel and "find himself," and passed through town en route to the Kripalu meditation center in Lenox.

Jacob struggled with how to raise the subject. He didn't think Jonathan would be hostile; his Buddhist and Deadhead buddies prided themselves on open-mindedness. Still, the news would shock. As preteens, he and Jonathan had talked of living together always, finding a set of identical twin girls to marry. We could swap, they'd joked; maybe our kids would turn out alike. In the gradual disseverance of their teenage years such dreams had been abandoned, but now Jacob's announcement would foreclose the possibility.

He settled on a sidewise approach. There was a flier on the bulletin board in the gay students' association office. A geneticist at the University of Massachusetts was seeking twins for a study of homosexuality. Both monozygotic and dizygotic pairs were eligible. A stipend of two hundred dollars would be paid.

Jacob brought Jonathan with him to dinner, then toured him through the snowbound campus. They were in front of Frost Library when he began.

"How're you doing for cash?" he asked. He knew Jonathan had been flitting from odd job to odd job since the summer.

"Kind of low," Jonathan conceded. "I'm worried I'm going to have to ask Mom and Dad."

"Well, if you can stick around a day, there's this really easy way we could make some dough. It's a study over at U-Mass."

"Cool," Jonathan said. "What kind of study?"

"Um, about sexuality. Homosexuality? They're looking at twins where at least one of them is gay, and, you know, seeing what part's maybe genetic."

Jonathan appeared to flinch, as if touched by an icy hand.

"It's no big deal," Jacob continued. "I think they take some blood and you fill out a survey form. It takes like two hours at most."

Now Jonathan stopped, the way he might in a room where someone had doused the lights. He scooped a mound of snow. "What are you saying?" he asked.

"That I'm—I mean, we're eligible. I'm gay."

Jonathan slapped a snowball into shape with his bare, reddening hands. "Since when?"

"For a long time. Since we were kids. But I didn't really figure it out—not enough to say anything—until a couple months ago. Don't tell Mom and Dad, okay? I want to myself."

Jacob felt as though a wasp had stung his heart; only Jonathan's assurance could salve the tender muscle. They hadn't spent much time together recently, but they were still brothers. Jacob couldn't think of losing him.

Jonathan's face was unreadable in the flickering light of a distant lamppost. He tossed his snowball from palm to palm until it crumbled, and he reached for another handful.

"This is bullshit," he finally said.

"What?" Jacob said, losing his breath.

"I mean, aren't we different enough yet? Are you still worried people think we're identical? I thought I was doing a pretty good job being the freakish one, but no, I guess like always you've got to one-up me."

"It's not about one-upping, Jon. I'm just finally coming to terms with myself. I'm gay."

"So what does that make me?"

"Nothing. You're my brother."

"Well, I'm not gay," Jonathan said, pounding what was now almost ice in his trembling hand.

"I never said you were."

Jonathan windmilled his arm and hurled his ammunition at a maple tree. "And I'm *not* doing your stupid study." The snowball whipped into the upper trunk, rattling the frozen branches like bones.

They trudged back to Jacob's dorm without speaking, and Jacob fell asleep wishing he could rewind time. When he woke the next morning, Jonathan was gone.

The rabbi dismissed his awestruck Talmud class, and Jacob hurried to his brother's room. He wanted time to change before they headed into town.

Jonathan had balked at first when Jacob asked to be taken to the Western Wall, but Jacob had manipulated commandment number five to his advantage: "Mom said you promised. She even gave me a prayer to leave in one of those cracks in the stone." Jonathan still hemmed half-heartedly about not being able to cut class. "Consider it a religious field trip," Jacob told him. "Missionary work. Maybe they'll even give you extra credit."

Jacob stripped his stiff Oxford button-down—which he'd worn for the class, not knowing some kids here dressed normally—and reached for a plain white T-shirt. Jonathan walked in just as he was pulling the shirt over his head, and looked quickly away, as if to deflect any suspicion of interest in his queer brother's naked chest.

"One more sec," Jacob said, tucking himself in. "I just want to put on some sunblock."

He squeezed a cold line of lotion onto each of his forearms. Massaging the cream into his skin, he studied Jonathan's wooden presence. He had started thinking of his brother as some kind of alien, like Mr. Spock on *Star Trek*, emotionally devoid.

"So Jon," he said, trying to provoke attention. "You've got some creative teachers here."

"The method is traditional," Jonathan said without inflection.

"No, really, I was pleasantly surprised. I mean, I thought this was a yeshiva, not an ag school."

"What are you talking about?"

"Stillborn calves? Good oxen and bad oxen?"

For a moment, Jonathan's face creased with confusion. Then understanding brought a sheepish smile. "Oh," he said. "I remember that lecture. You picked a good day to sit in."

"It *was* good," Jacob said, daubing sunscreen onto his cheeks. "The rabbi—what's his name? Selman?"

"Seligman."

"Rabbi Seligman's a smooth talker. Anyway, his point was nice: You're supposed to give people the benefit of the doubt."

Jonathan took the tube of sunscreen from Jacob and squeezed way too much onto his hand, like a child who hasn't learned yet about amounts. "It's really more of a technical passage," he said, "about evenhandedness in financial matters. But believe me"— he paused to apply the lotion to his face—"I'm trying."

"What?" Jacob asked.

Jonathan didn't rub long enough, and the sunscreen left a milky film on his nose and cheeks. Patches of skin peeked through in a dappled pentimento. "To give you the benefit of the doubt."

Jacob congratulated himself silently. So, his brother was trying, too.

Jonathan hoisted a small backpack onto his shoulders and opened the door for Jacob. "Ready?" he asked.

"Wait, that reminds me." Jacob rummaged through his own backpack's top pouch and found the folded piece of paper tucked in his address book. He transferred it to the hip pocket of his jeans. "Okay," he said. "Now I'm ready."

Technically, he wasn't supposed to have looked at the paper, but his mother must have known he would. "Dear God," she had written in her precise script, "let Jake and Jon find some common ground. Let them see that blood is thicker." It was her quintessential mothering style, melodramatically optimistic and meticulously careful to avoid taking sides. It also conformed to her annoying habit of reciting only the first part of a cliché and leaving the rest to implication.

During yesterday's flight Jacob had reread the prayer. Its plaintive, unfinished tone had been more than he could take. He didn't have a pen with the same color ink, but he completed the sentence anyway with his own handwriting: "than water."

Outside, everything reeked like the stale morning sweat of someone who ate too much garlic the night before. Jacob didn't know if the odor was in fact perspiration—a city's worth of bodies as overheated as his own—or spices wafting from the apartments above the street.

He had expected Jerusalem to be different from anything he'd ever seen, with people in togas astride gray-muzzled donkeys. Even the new parts of the city would be zoned to look ancient, he imagined, along the lines of Colonial Williamsburg. Disappointingly, the streets were filled with normal people doing normal things.

Women in cotton dresses clustered in doorways, loudly chattering. Men shouted to people standing right next to them, waving their arms in flourishing interruptions like rival talk-show guests. The rapid-fire Hebrew was a flow of liquidy vowels interspersed with sharp syllables that sounded like *Jake, Jake, Jake*. He kept turning his head, thinking Jonathan was addressing him. But Jonathan, walking swiftly onward, was close-mouthed.

A neon sign captured Jacob's attention: a string of Hebrew letters and an arrow pointing down an alley. The glass tubes flashed pink against the sober yellow of a Jerusalem-stone building.

"What's that say?" he asked, intrigued by the sign's trashiness. It looked like something that belonged in Amsterdam's red-light district, not here, the birthplace of world religion.

"What?" Jonathan said. "Oh, the pink?"

"Yeah."

It took him a second to translate. "Fax. Or faxing, I guess. They're advertising their service."

"Faxing?" Jacob laughed. "I thought it was—well, never mind." He studied the sign again, its indecipherable twists and curls. "You can really read that?"

"We take *ulpan* in the afternoons. Hebrew lessons."

"But you must be pretty advanced to know the word for 'fax.' "

"Not really. It's just *facsimile* transliterated."

"Are you kidding? That's great!" Jacob jumped at the chance to go off on one of his standard riffs—anything to keep the conversation going. "Can you believe how Americanized everything is getting? It's disgusting. And the worst part is, when other people borrow our culture they make it even more abysmal than the original. Like, have you heard what the big new holiday is in Japan? Guys will save up months' worth of salary so they can take out their girlfriends and party on 'Ku-leesmas Ee-bu.' "

Jonathan's face remained blank, so Jacob repeated it. " 'Ku-leesmas Ee-bu.' Christmas Eve. Isn't that terrible?"

Jonathan still didn't laugh. Jacob couldn't understand it. Everyone loved his Japanese jokes. He could put Chantelle on the floor just by reciting toothpaste names in Japanese: *Coru-gate-u, Aku-wa-fu-lesh.*

Jonathan didn't look at him when he finally spoke. "Your Hebrew was always better." It wasn't said with bitterness, but neither was it a compliment. It was simply a statement of fact.

"You're crazy," Jacob said. "All I can remember from Hebrew school is that weird list of translations Mrs. Greenberg used to drill us with: 'Me is who, who is he, he is she, and dog is fish.' Three years of Wednesday nights and I swear that's all I got."

Jonathan squinted in the slicing sun. "No," he said. "You were better. I wanted to be as good as you. I wanted to learn it, but I couldn't, so I just gave up. It was like the wrestling. After a while there was no point even trying."

They had never spoken of the arm wrestling. Not during the years when Papa Isaac had forced them to compete, and not in the decade since he'd died. Jacob had wanted to talk about it for so long, wanted to apologize for beating Jonathan every time, for not having the guts to say no to their grandfather. But now with the opportunity abruptly in front of him, it was too monumental, a cliff that looks scalable until you're standing at its base, staring at a cold slab of stone.

"Well," he said, "you certainly know more Hebrew now. How'd you become so diligent all of a sudden?"

Jonathan shrugged. "It's different when it's something you, like, need for your life. It doesn't feel like work."

"So you really feel comfortable here? It's good?"

"Yes," Jonathan said. Then softer, "Yeah. It mostly is."

"Mostly?" Jacob studied Jonathan's face for signs of weakness. He hadn't thought the Orthodox were allowed "mostly."

"It's just—" Jonathan started, then seemed to think better of something. "It's hard because so many people come and go."

"Most people don't stay as long as you?"

"There's a lot who only come for a week, or less," Jonathan admitted. "More than half, actually. Just about all my friends from when I came are gone already."

Jacob thought of Marty: the first friend he'd met in Boston. They'd stood side by side at dance clubs and demonstrations, collaborated in planning countless events. National Coming Out Day—their signature show—would be a couple of weeks after he'd get home; Jacob dreaded the prospect of this year's rally, alone.

"So you're the veteran, I guess," he said to Jonathan.

"Yeah," Jonathan said. "Me and Ari. I think there's only two others who've been here longer."

"Well, Ari seems like a good guy." Jacob pictured Ari's schoolboy looks, the bouncy way he had walked off to the study hall. "Is it just me," he asked, "or does Ari look like a goy?"

A laugh erupted burplike from Jonathan. "It's true. We kid him all the time. Ari says he's brought Etz Chaim into the age of multiculturalism: our token blond."

"Look out!"

A teenager hurtled recklessly at them on a moped. Jacob grabbed Jonathan and pulled him from the bike's path. In the dodge to safety they bumped. Their arms exchanged ovals of sweat.

After the moped passed, Jonathan stayed close—no longer touching, but near enough that Jacob could feel his brother's heat. They walked a gauntlet of strangers' stares: *Are they twins?* the faces seemed to ask. *Yes, look—if the one didn't have a beard. . .* Silence encased them, but the lack of conversation didn't bother Jacob. This wasn't the muteness of antagonism, but of understanding, the bond they'd shared as infants, before speech.

They entered a large plaza. Jacob recognized the Wall at the far side, but from this distance it looked the same as the other old buildings they had passed. Tour groups hovered like herds of buffalo. The tangy, foreign odor of the previous neighborhood gave way to the astringent scent of underarm deodorant.

Families milled in matching T-shirts and baseball caps. One young boy, about seven or eight, peeled a Jaffa orange twice the size of his fist and dropped the spongy curls of skin on the ground. "Pick that up!" his father yelled, shaking the kid's arm. "Do you have any idea where we are?"

They walked toward the Wall, navigating eddies in the crowd, defending themselves with elbows akimbo. Without warning, a uniformed guard seized Jacob's shoulder.

"Kippah?" the man demanded.

In his alarm, Jacob didn't comprehend the word. He reached involuntarily for Jonathan's arm, seeking protection against the accusation.

The stern-faced guard raised his jaw. "Kippah?"

"Take one," Jonathan said. "You need it to go any further."

Only then did Jacob see the yarmulke in the guard's hand. There was a large box of them: thin cardboard cones, warped from use. He accepted the disposable skullcap and balanced it sheepishly on his head, wishing he had a real yarmulke like Jonathan's.

"So this is where they—um—?" He was about to say "recruited," but held it back; that was the word their father had used when he learned Jacob was gay.

"Over there." Jonathan pointed to an entrance at a different corner of the plaza, where a group of college kids huddled, dwarfed by their bulging, travel-battered backpacks.

Jonathan must have read the revulsion on Jacob's face. "Jake, come on," he said. "It's not the Moonies. It's a guy in a black hat and beard, and he invites you to come see the yeshiva. Everything's up front. No one has to say yes."

"It's not that simple, Jon. The kids are vulnerable, away from home. It's unfair to prey on them."

"Maybe they're vulnerable," Jonathan said, "because they need something in their lives. Maybe they *want* to find something."

"That's just the problem. It could have been anything. What if it *was* the Moonies?"

Jonathan stomped his foot on the dusty plaza. "You just don't get it, do you? It wasn't, like, some radical, strange idea for me to go to a yeshiva. I'm Jewish, Jake, remember? You are too. Or supposed to be."

Jacob blinked against the gritty cloud that his brother's stomp had fomented. He remembered Chantelle's rescue mission to her sister, and his own insistence that he wouldn't try to "save" Jonathan. He hadn't considered that Jonathan might try to save *him.*

"Let's please not make a scene," he said.

"Fine," Jonathan said. "Fine, let's go to the Wall."

They approached the boundary of the area set aside for prayer. Jacob was surprised to see so many people who were not tourists. There were middle-aged professionals in business suits, young soldiers in their washed-out uniforms, ancient caftaned men like figures from a medieval painting. It was the middle of a weekday—how did they have time to come here and pray?

They pushed ahead, careful not to disturb the supplicants. Some stood in small groups, others randomly alone. Those closest to the wall looked the most pious, their heads and faces concealed by huge white-and-black tallises. They bobbed and bowed, each according to his own rhythm. Against the faded yellow of the ancient stones, they looked like sandpipers flitting on a blond stretch of sandbar.

The sight was moving in its quiet exoticism, but also in its familiarity; Papa Isaac had prayed this way, too. Jacob remembered his grandfather's precise movements when the old man prepared to worship. He would wrap his tallis around his head, cross the wool cloth under his chin, then rock as if enduring a frigid wind. Jacob's earliest idea of God had come from watching Papa Isaac: God as a breeze chilling enough to make his grandfather shiver.

With the tallis around his head, Papa Isaac looked to Jacob like an aged shepherd woman in a shawl. But his white goatee stuck out comically. One day during the Amidah, the silent devotion, when he was a year too old to be forgiven for giggling, Jacob looked at Papa Isaac and saw him as a circus freak show's bearded lady. He laughed out loud and had to bite his hand to stop.

Papa Isaac, lost in prayer, said nothing. But as they walked back to the apartment after services, he told Jacob it was not right to laugh. Someday he, too, would seek the comfort of the tallis. He would seek refuge in the shadow of His wings.

Jacob had tried to picture a God with wings large enough to embrace a man his grandfather's size. All that came to mind was the pterodactyl skeleton at the Museum of Natural History. The fossil was sharp and gray in his memory, a menacing heap of bones.

But Jacob understood the shadow. The shadow meant be quiet, do not disturb. It meant there was a secret no one should tell. Papa Isaac didn't need his tallis to submit to its darkness.

He wrapped himself in the shadow sometimes when there was an argument at the dinner table and he didn't want to respond. Or when Nana Jenny spoke certain names Jacob didn't recognize—Ingrid and Opa and Oma. Or when the word Germany was mentioned. Other times it happened with no apparent reason. His grandfather would be sitting with them on the couch, stroking his beard, and Jacob would see the darkness descend, the look in his eyes that sucked light and didn't let go. Papa Isaac would drop out of the conversation, stiffly silent, then rejoin after a while with a question that had been answered minutes ago.

Once, Jacob found him standing in the kitchen, staring at the blue flame on the stove. When Papa Isaac noticed him, his grandfather rushed to turn off the burner, but he twisted the wrong way. Fire leapt at his eyebrows, singeing him before he could reverse the knob. The smell of burned hair snaked through the room.

"Cook," he answered, even though Jacob hadn't questioned him. "I was going to cook something."

*   *   *

"Let's go all the way up," Jonathan proposed.

"Are you sure we're allowed?" Jacob asked. "I mean, me?"

Jonathan clucked his tongue. "Jake, this is *our* Wall. It belongs to us."

As they approached, Jacob marveled at the enormity of the blocks of stone. He flashed to scenes from *The Ten Commandments*: sweaty slaves hauling car-sized bricks to the top of a pyramid. The bricks here were just as massive, a looming challenge to disbelief. Jacob squinted against the intensifying brightness, wishing he'd brought sunglasses. The sunblock heated until his arms sizzled greasily as grilling hot dogs.

Jonathan stepped forward and tenderly touched the Wall, then brought his hand to his mouth and kissed his fingertips. Jacob followed his brother's lead. Yellow dust flaked off onto his fingers, and he thrust his hand to the Wall again, trying to replace what he had rubbed off.

His cardboard yarmulke floated on his head, a disconcerting aura, as though he were in a room with a too-low ceiling. He felt the giddy disorientation of having stepped into a fairy tale. That's what the Bible had always been to him—an amusing bunch of stories, no more real than "Goldilocks" or "Jack and the Beanstalk." The difference was that there was no actual house in which three bears had lived. There was no garden with a gargantuan beanstalk. But this Wall before him was the real thing.

Even if the religious part didn't mean anything, it was amazing to stand at the epicenter of Judaism. Jews all around the world faced Israel when they prayed. Jews in Israel faced Jerusalem. And Jews in Jerusalem faced this spot. But he was here; the world was facing him.

Jacob stepped back and closed his eyes, pausing to absorb the confusing grandeur of the place. The reflected sun was so bright, he could still see daylight. It created a universe on the insides of his eyelids, glittering stars and tiny comets streaking near his nose. Gravity loosened its grip. His body seemed to levitate.

He listened to the buzz of men around him. More than grunts, less than fully articulated speech, their collective murmur cast magic like a snake charmer's incantations. He floated higher. He couldn't feel his feet.

And for a moment Jacob forgot all the bigoted aspects of the religion, the hatred it instilled. He forgot that this was what had pulled his brother farther away from him. In the reflecting oven of these ancient stones, he smiled with the thought that if Jonathan's Orthodoxy felt anything like this warm buoyancy, it must be a happy conversion. After all these years of anxious drifting, Jonathan might finally be content. How could he begrudge his brother that?

Jacob opened his eyes and turned to Jonathan. His brother was bent down, unzipping his backpack. He still looked sickly, his limbs rigid and thin. But the yolky light gilded his face. Reddish strands sparked in his beard.

Then Jonathan pulled something from the pack. The tallis bag was bluer than Jacob remembered, the gem-bright blue of the Mediterranean from the plane window yesterday. Tinsel embroidery skirted the edges, glittering, almost alive.

He hadn't seen the bag since the day of his grandfather's funeral. They had buried Papa Isaac in his beautiful, fraying tallis, but kept this velvet pouch, the one Papa Isaac's father had passed down to him upon his ordination as a rabbi. It was the sole remnant Jacob's grandparents had managed to save in their flight from Germany, the only evidence of the family the Nazis tried to erase.

Jacob wondered how Jonathan had gotten the bag. The old jealousy pressed in like a fist squeezing his heart. He wanted to lunge at his brother, to snatch Papa Isaac's bag away. Wasn't he at least as deserving?

Then Jonathan unzipped the pouch and removed his own tallis, identical to the one Jacob had received for his bar mitzvah, now buried at the bottom of some drawer. Jonathan recited a prayer, kissed two corners of the cloth. And as he draped the shawl around his shoulders, Jacob at last understood: His brother's late-blooming Jewishness, this supposedly spiritual awakening, was in fact a coldly calculated trump card. If Jonathan lived as strictly as Papa Isaac had, if he followed all the tedious commandments, how could anyone question his claim to the legacy?

Jacob had sensed this before, but only as a shapeless skepticism, murky and indistinct as fog. Now, as he watched Jonathan's display, the hollowness of his brother's observance struck him as a gift-wrapped gag: You untie the bow and scour the box for a promised treasure, pulling handfuls of tissue paper until you reach the empty bottom.

Jacob found himself ready to step up, here in front of all these people, and confront Jonathan with this new understanding. Jonathan seemed suddenly an easy target, his claim of authenticity such an obvious deception. Who could believe that this suburban drifter had found God at a tourist attraction?

But as he looked again at his brother, Jacob's bubble of conviction burst as quickly as it had formed. Jonathan stood by the towering Wall, his tallis pulled tight around his head. Trembling, he whispered words from memory, his face twisted in rapt concentration.

Jacob was shocked by the vision's clarity: Jonathan was standing in the shadow.

Shame rose into his tightened throat. Who was he to question his brother's faith? Jacob imagined how foolish *he* must look standing here next to Jonathan—he in his jeans and T-shirt, the idiotic cardboard yarmulke on his head. If anyone in this scene was a fraud, it was he.

Around him, the crowd pressed in, thieving the air with their Hebrew chants. He needed oxygen. He needed space to breathe.

He pushed through the men as fast as he could, avoiding Jonathan, whose eyes were still shut in some private ecstasy. He ran past the gate and up onto the main plaza, dodging tourists and Israeli soldiers. People glared at his rudeness but he refused to acknowledge them.

As he passed the guard who had scared him earlier, Jacob grabbed the cheap skullcap from his head. The cardboard crumpled in his angry grip and he tossed it into the box. The crinkling sound reminded him of the slip of paper in his back pocket, the prayer he had carried all the way here for his mother. He was supposed to have left it in a crack of the ancient wall.

The paper was damp and fragile from sweat. The ink had begun to smudge, blurring his and his mother's handwriting to an indecipherable stain. He squeezed the paper in his palm, condensing it into a tiny ball, and dumped it in the pile of yarmulkes.

Last One Out

The fact that they were twins didn't mean he and Jonathan were exactly the same age. By the first day of kindergarten, Jonathan was proclaiming to the teacher that he was actually older.

"I was ready sixteen minutes before him," Jonathan announced, as if they had been casseroles cooking in the same oven. "We're twins, but *I* was first."

Most of the time, Jacob couldn't have cared less about being second from the womb. It wasn't as though birth was some kind of playground game: Last one out is a rotten egg! Sometimes at night, while Jonathan slept in the next bed, Jacob lay awake staring at the clock and counting sixteen-minute intervals to remind himself how insignificant a gap it was.

The only time it made a real difference was Passover, when the youngest child was supposed to sing the Four Questions.

Singing the Four Questions was one of the truly terrible things about being Jewish. Jacob was sure the tune had been composed by some sadistic boy-hater, like the black-hatted child catcher in *Chitty Chitty Bang Bang*. The melody rose and fell through an impossible range of notes. If you picked a medium-high key, hoping to put the tune's low notes in reach, there was no way you could screech out the higher parts. But start lower in anticipation of the high notes, and you croaked like the Cookie Monster when the melody dipped down.

If the Talmud said anything about who should sing the Four Questions in the event that the only children were identical twins, none of the Rosenbaums had found the relevant passage. Every year there was a battle. In the days before the holiday, Jacob and Jonathan both refused to practice the tune. They would interject seeming non sequiturs during family meals—"I'm not going to," or *"He* should be the one"—and everyone knew what they were referring to.

Nana Jenny, always the conciliator, tried any number of plans to mediate. Once, she suggested that Jacob and Jonathan split the task, two questions each. "Even Steven," she said, her German accent turning the v's into f's. Another year, she gave a big speech about what an honor it was to chant the questions, the most important part of the entire seder. Thus, both boys should have the opportunity. They both should sing, one after the other.

The year she gave the speech about honor was the year of the birth certificate joke.

Jonathan would have nothing of their grandmother's proposal. "But Jacob's younger," he protested. "He's younger. You told us so. Dad?"

Jacob's father cleaned under his thumbnail with the tine of a special-for-Passover fork. He spent these visits to Brookline sulking and passive, incapable of fathering in his own father's presence. When he'd garnered his bounty, a grayish blob of grime, he pinched it between his fingers and hid it beneath the table.

Jacob and Jonathan both turned expectantly to their mother. She bit her lip with indecision, as if calculating how much capital she had left in each of her various accounts: mother, wife, daughter-in-law. How much would it cost her to intervene, and on whose behalf?

Jacob was hopeful. His mother's track record in these cases was to urge equity. She was a seventies mom, coached by *Sesame Street* and Dr. Spock. But when it came to the Jewish stuff, Jacob knew she felt out of her league. She'd been raised only a High Holiday Jew, with no training in the arcane rituals that Jacob's father had been drilled with by Papa Isaac.

So when Jacob and Jonathan appealed to her at the seder table, each counting on her to demonstrate her unadulterated love for him and him alone, she failed them both. She didn't say anything, not even the beginning of a cliché. She just nodded a "this is a tough one" nod, the way stumped game-show contestants signal the host to move on, because no amount of extra time will help.

Nana Jenny tried to intercede again. "I don't see why it's such an issue," she said. "It's not meant to be a burden."

Jacob smiled at his grandmother, sorry that her opinion always seemed to be ignored. He thought maybe the two of them should secede from the rest of the family and conduct their own private seder in the kitchen. He was sure she would let him skip the religious parts and just eat *haroset* and macaroons.

Jonathan was still bent on lobbying their mother. "I'm older," he whined, clutching the tablecloth, his knuckles as white as the fabric. "I *am*. There's a difference."

In his fervor, Jonathan jerked the tablecloth. Everything danced on the brink of collapse.

Papa Isaac had been sitting at the head of the table, immobile but attentive, like George Washington in the famous portrait, whose eyes followed no matter which vantage point you chose. Now he leaned forward. He stroked his pointed goatee, even whiter than his head's remaining ring of hair. The beard gave his whole face an angular quality. Jacob thought of him sometimes as an arrowhead, sharp and ever ready to attack.

"It is true," Papa Isaac intoned in his King Solomon-dividing-the-baby voice. Everybody at the table stopped breathing. Even Jacob's father looked up from his fingernail-cleaning project. "Jonathan is older. If we had the birth certificates, this is what they would show."

There was silence. Jacob swallowed hard against the coppery taste of defeat.

Jonathan must have worried he hadn't quite clinched the victory. In the way children have of repeating what adults have said, he blurted, "Do I need to bring out the birth certificates?"

It wasn't so much what he said as how he said it, in the exact tone their father used quarreling with their mother. Jonathan even threw in their father's patented gesture, slapping the back of one hand in the palm of the other three or four times.

Their mother was the first to laugh, mocking Jonathan's imitation of her husband. Then his father joined; between self-deprecating chuckles he muttered "birth certificate" over and over, as though it were a secret dirty joke. Papa Isaac laughed so hard that the table shook again. Wine sloshed over the edges of the kiddush cups, staining the tablecloth like a used bandage.

It became a catch phrase for the whole family, always good for a gag. "Do I need to bring out the birth certificates?" someone would say, and whatever argument they were in the midst of would lose momentum. Nobody but Jacob seemed to remember that in the end, he had still been forced to sing.

Contact High

That's it. Come on. Suck it down." Ari grasped Jacob's wrist, forcing the glass against his lips. "It doesn't count," he said, "unless you do the whole shot."

The lukewarm liquid burned tastelessly in Jacob's throat and stung his nostrils like doctor's-office antiseptic. A shiver pushed sound from his lungs, something between a sexual grunt and the gasp of being sucker-punched.

Ari loosened his fingers, letting go of Jacob's hand. "It's better chilled," he apologized. "But we're not allowed to keep personal stuff in the kitchen."

Jonathan, sitting on Jacob's other side, took the empty shot glass and lifted it to his nose. He inhaled deeply, as if sniffing glue. "Right to your head, huh?"

Jacob's throat convulsed with ripples of gag reflex. He flashed to memories of Marty, puking useless air. "You sure this stuff is safe to drink?" he asked.

"How could it not be? The stuff sterilizes everything it hits. It's good for you, right, Ari? Tell him what Anatole says."

Anatole, Ari explained, was the source of the homemade vodka. A Jewish Muscovite who had emigrated to a Russian neighborhood near the yeshiva, he had hired Ari to tutor his sons in English. When he couldn't afford to pay in cash, Anatole compensated instead with bottles of vodka.

"He says he makes it just the way his grandfather showed him,"

Ari said. He picked up the unlabeled bottle and held it to the light. "His grandfather drank three shots every day of his life starting when he was fourteen. Anatole says the old man died with his fingers curled around a bottle"—now Ari poured a shot dramatically from six inches above the glass—"at the age of a hundred and seven."

Jacob couldn't help but do the math: three times a day, times three hundred sixty-five days a year, times ninetysomething years. He swallowed again against the rising swell of nausea. But it wasn't only the alcohol making him queasy.

What was he doing, sitting here on the scratchy carpet of his brother's room, chumming it up with Jonathan and his best Orthodox buddy? Could this be the same Jonathan who had written vitriolic tirades to their mother about not needing to honor your brother? Who had stood just two days ago at the Western Wall, wrapped in the superiority of his faith, as if Jacob didn't exist?

Monday, fleeing from the Wall, Jacob had vowed he wouldn't stand for this. He'd competed enough with Jonathan when they were kids, and he didn't need to prove anything now. He was not half of something. He was his own person. He had to be.

By the time he made it back to Etz Chaim, he'd decided to leave. His parents would be angry, but he had done what he had promised them, he'd tried. The thing he felt worst about was Nana Jenny. She had never given up the hope for a family, the simple proposition that everyone might get along, and she had no idea how deep the estrangements ran. Jacob wondered what lie he'd tell her to explain his returning early.

He had started to roll up his sleeping bag when Jonathan burst through the door. His yarmulke had been blown back, and dangled from a single bobby pin, flapping like a mutant ponytail.

"Oh," Jonathan said. "You're here."

Jacob tried not to show any recognition. For once, let Jonathan see how it felt to be ignored.

"I was davening," Jonathan blurted. "I closed my eyes a second and when I looked up you weren't there. What happened?"

What do you think happened? Jacob wanted to say. *How did you think I'd feel?* But his brother's genuine-seeming confusion threw him off.

"I had all these terrible scenarios," Jonathan said. "You were hurt or kidnapped or something." He steadied a hand on his panting chest. "Oh, thank Hashem. You're here."

Jacob pressed his fingers to his temples, as if he might find a Play button to push, to make him announce his decision. But Jonathan's concern had chipped away his resolve.

His brother knelt next to him. "Jake, are you all right? You look pale. Do you want some water?"

"No." The word came out too sharp. "I mean, thanks, no. I'm just a little overwhelmed."

"What do you mean?"

"I don't know," he fudged. "The whole scene at the Wall. There was just, like, a lot going on. I'm not used to it."

"Oh," Jonathan said, his eyebrows bunched in contemplation. Then, as if the answer to some riddle had just occurred to him, he repeated the word. "Oh! Hey, I totally understand. A lot of guys have the same reaction. You don't know how deep it'll hit until you're actually standing there."

"Yeah, I guess maybe that's it," Jacob said, even though that wasn't it at all.

Jonathan jumped to his feet. "I think we can catch the end of lunch," he said. "Come with? Kugel today. It's not bad."

Jacob was still shaky with adrenaline and with the maelstrom of emotions. Solid food would do him some good.

He rose and stood next to his brother. "Your yarmulke's all screwy," he said. He flipped the skullcap right side up again.

Jonathan grabbed the vodka bottle from Ari and set it aside. "Enough warmup shots," he declared.

He produced a dreidel from his pants pocket and spun it on the spiral notebook they were using as a makeshift playing board. The dreidel was cheap, mass-produced from blue plastic, the kind they used to hand out at Hebrew school.

"*Shin*," Ari announced when the dreidel toppled. "Good thing it doesn't count yet. Do you remember the letters, Yaakov?"

"I'm not sure," Jacob said, still jolted to be called by his Hebrew name.

Ari hunched close, cupping the dreidel in his palm. "This is *shin*," he instructed, then gave the top a quarter-turn. "This is *nun*. This is *gimel*. And this is *he*. Got it?"

"I think so."

"Well, you better. Because when things get a little blurry, there's not a heck of a lot of difference between a *gimel* and a *nun*. And your brother's pretty ruthless at Dreidel Drunk."

Jonathan cuffed him on the shoulder. "You're still just mad from two times ago. I won fair and square, and you know it."

So they did this regularly? Jacob was still reeling from the idea that Holy Jonathan would imbibe at all, let alone sit around the yeshiva late at night playing drinking games.

Jonathan placed the dreidel on the notebook. "It's basically the same as regular dreidel," he explained, "except there's obviously no pot you chip in to. You take turns spinning. If it comes up *nun*, nothing happens. If it comes up *gimel*, everybody else has to drink a shot. *He* means you get to choose who drinks. And *shin*, you have to drink two shots yourself."

"Two shots?" Jacob said. He could barely imagine smelling the vodka again without retching. "This must be a pretty quick game."

Ari winked. "You build up stamina after a while."

"All right," Jonathan said. "Spin to see who goes first?"

"Yaakov goes first," Ari said, handing him the dreidel. "The guest of honor."

Was he flirting, or did Jacob just wish he were? He accepted the toy nervously, still not sure this whole thing wasn't some bizarre setup, a vice cop's undercover come-on. But as long as he was in this deep, he decided to go for it. He shook the dreidel in the empty globe of his hands, then blew on his thumbs like shooting craps. The spin was perfect and seemed to last forever. When the plastic top finally collapsed, Jacob recognized the character for *he*.

"One of us drinks," Ari said. "You choose." His blue eyes beamed with the thrilled terror of a kid buckling himself onto a roller coaster.

Jacob hesitated to name Jonathan, fearful of reigniting the anger they had kept at bay the last two days. But he didn't know Ari well enough yet to make him drink. There was an intimacy implied in choosing someone first.

He nodded to Jonathan. "All yours."

Jonathan tossed back the liquor as if it were water, then nonchalantly licked his lips. He took his turn next, and his spin also came up *he*. "Allow me to return the favor," he said, pointing an elbow at Jacob in the universal male sign language for *drink*.

Jacob managed to pour the shot down his throat without really swallowing, so that he got the burn but not the noxious fumes. Still, his brain teetered with vertigo. He didn't know how much more of this he could take.

The rounds went fast until the bottle was two-thirds empty. Jacob's lips buzzed. The vodka began to smell like normal air.

He drifted in and out of attention, pondering the philosophical paradox of drinking games—how the whole point was to get drunk, and yet the drunkest ones were said to "lose." When he brought himself back to the game, Jonathan and Ari were at a stalemate, pointing their elbows like cowboys wielding loaded six-shooters. Jonathan's spin had left the dreidel perched between the notebook and the carpet. He claimed the dreidel had come up *he*, and that Ari should drink; Ari insisted it was *shin*, and therefore Jonathan was due two shots.

Ari appealed to Jacob with puppy-dog eyes. "Yaakov, tell him it's *shin*. Tell him he has to drink."

"You wouldn't betray a brother," Jonathan countered. "It's *he*, right? You know it's *he*."

Jacob had to think fast. He didn't know where it came from, but impulsively he imitated the Talmud-class rabbi. "You raise an interesting dilemma," he pronounced. "It might be *shin*, and it might be *he*. Who's to know but"—he caught himself before he said "God," which he had learned was frowned upon. He remembered the euphemism, the word that meant "the Name." "Who's to know," he said, "but Hashem?"

He panicked a second, thinking he'd gone too far. But Jonathan and Ari smiled. They had dropped their accusing elbows.

Jacob pushed further: "The Talmud says when in doubt, split evenly. So my decision is . . . Ari should drink half a shot . . . and Jonathan should drink one full shot . . . and each should give the other one-quarter of an ox."

"Bravo," Ari called, clapping a hand against his thigh. "Bravo. A wise judgment all around."

"You got it," Jonathan said. "You really did. Seligman would die if he heard you."

The thought of the rabbi sank Jacob with the uneasy feeling of being watched. "What would he say if he knew?" he asked, indicating the nearly drained vodka bottle.

"Seligman?" Jonathan laughed. "He's the one who helped get Anatole's family their immigration papers. For all we know, he's got a lifetime supply of this stuff at home."

"But I mean, is it, like, kosher?"

"Per-fect-ly," Ari said, enunciating each syllable with tipsy overcompensation. His pupils swam in the watery troughs of his eyes.

Jacob turned to his brother. "Then why'd we always have to have that Manischewitz crap?" His mouth puckered with the memory of the cough-syrupy wine. "I thought that was all Jews were allowed to drink."

"Wine and liquor are different," Jonathan explained. "In biblical times wine was the most common drink. The rabbis worried that if Jews drank with gentiles, they'd lose their inhibitions and have sex and bear non-Jewish children. So they decreed you can only drink certain wine."

"But it's so much easier to get drunk on hard liquor," Jacob said. "Why didn't the rabbis restrict that, too?"

Jonathan shrugged. "They didn't have hard liquor back then, I guess, or not so much."

"Well, they have it now," Jacob said. "It doesn't make any sense. Why haven't they changed the rules?"

Jonathan's voice knifed the air. "They just haven't."

"Hey, hey. Guys." Ari waved his hand between them like a referee separating boxers. "Relax. Don't look a gift vodka in the mouth." He held the the bottle's open end to his eye. Some of the liquid splashed out, wetting his cheek. "Oops," he said. "See what I mean?"

Jacob couldn't help laughing at Ari's innocent drunkenness. Jonathan laughed too, and confiscated the bottle. The anger evaporated from his face.

"Babes with toys," he said to Jacob.

"This can be dangerous," Jacob agreed with mock gravity.

It took Ari a moment to realize they were talking about him. "Hey, I'm only a year older than you," he said with drunken belligerence. "I mean younger. I'm not a babe."

Oh, but you are, Jacob almost said. He caught himself, remembering this wasn't just any old dorm room, where midnight innuendo could be passed off the next morning with a "Boy, was I drunk last night."

He looked at Jonathan, and without saying anything they communicated in the instinctive language of their childhood. They each grabbed one of Ari's elbows and hoisted him like an injured football player. Ari's body was leaden with inebriation, but between the two of them, they managed the load.

After they laid Ari in bed, Jacob expected the evening's strange intimacy to dissipate. Perhaps it was just a cheap trick of his psyche, a Hallmark yearning for conciliation. But back in Jonathan's room, just the two of them, the harmony pulsed even stronger.

"I had fun," he told his brother. "Thanks."

"Thank *you*," Jonathan said. "Against Ari, I need all the help I can get." He lolled his head over the bed's edge, sporting a vodka-soused grin. "Hey, you comfortable enough down there?"

"Sure, it's fine. Don't worry about it." The floor was hard, but Jonathan's concern alone made it more endurable.

"Remember," Jonathan said, "at the Cape house sometimes, how we used to sleep on the floor just so we could be closer?"

"You mean on sandpaper, don't you? That's what it felt like."

"Yeah, but it didn't matter. I used to think we should do everything together. *Everything.* You know: sleep, dress, eat." He croaked a froggy burp. "Did I ever tell you how much I couldn't stand kohlrabi?"

"What are you talking about?" Jacob said. "Kohlrabi was our favorite." Nana Jenny had served the vegetable with heavy cream sauce, an exotic German delicacy unheard of among their friends.

"That's just what I mean," Jonathan said. " '*Our* favorite.' I thought we were supposed to have identical tastes, so I pretended. But it's nasty! It's like eating soap."

Jacob was staggered—by Jonathan's admission, and equally by the fact of his brother's openness. "What else didn't you like?" he asked.

"Oh, I don't know, a million things. Mangos. All that stringy stuff that snags your teeth? But you loved them so much, I thought I just wasn't trying hard enough." Jonathan squirmed on the bed, retracting into a near-fetal position. "You know what really freaked me out, though? Remember in sixth grade, after those houses were robbed, and the police chief came to school?"

Of course Jacob remembered. Swashbuckling Chief Gamble had enthralled the all-school assembly. To win the kids' attention before his lecture on crime prevention, he unveiled handcuffs and let students arrest themselves. He spread ink pads on a table and asked who wanted to be fingerprinted. Jacob and Jonathan volunteered, ready to debunk theories of human uniqueness.

"I was just so sure our prints would be the same," Jonathan said. "How could they be different, you know? We were identical. So when Chief Gamble showed how you had that spirally thing on your ring finger, and I didn't, I just panicked. I spent the rest of the day bawling in the nurse's office."

"I remember you going to the nurse," Jacob said. "But I always thought it was just a stomach ache."

"No, it was the fingerprints. I wasn't prepared for us being, whatever, officially different. And then it just got worse in junior high, and high school, when you went off and did everything on your own."

"What?!" Jacob said. "*You* were the one who went off, with all your weird music and your druggie friends and crap."

Jonathan laughed a single weary laugh that made him sound old. "Jake, don't change history. I didn't do any of that until after you'd stopped hanging out with me. You moved into your separate bedroom, and started doing all that brainy stuff, the It's Academic team. I couldn't wait forever for you to come back."

The chronology confused Jacob. He'd always viewed Jonathan as the one who'd declared independence. Could he himself have been the instigator, cocooning himself in schoolwork to flee the first inklings of sexuality? Maybe his brother's crazy teenage dance, which Jacob had attributed to adolescent rebellion, was really the frenzy of an insect that's lost a wing.

Weakly, he said, "I thought you wanted your own room, too."

"Only because you did. I was too hurt to argue."

Jacob crumpled with shame. "I didn't know," he said.

"It's okay. It's ancient history." Jonathan rolled over heavily and faced the wall. "Let's just go to bed now, all right?"

"Okay, good night," Jacob said. "Jon? I'm really sorry."

"Good night," Jonathan mumbled into his pillow.

Jonathan sank quickly to slumber, but Jacob lay awake, his mind astir with memories, attuned to the dulcet metronome of his brother's snoring. He breathed in with Jonathan, breathed out, swallowed again the air his brother had just exhaled—and relaxed into the old, unmatchable comfort of their sleeping.

They'd shared a room until they were thirteen. Plenty of siblings slept together, Jacob knew, but he and Jonathan had seemed to sleep not only in adjoining beds but in each other's mind. It was something he couldn't explain and so had never told anyone, worried they would dismiss it as hocus-pocus. When he was eleven, Jacob had battled a recurrent nightmare. The dream found him balanced on a seesaw, the fulcrum of which was the peak of a towering skyscraper. If he stayed perfectly still, he was fine, but inevitably his back began to itch and itch. He restrained himself until the tickle was unbearable, and when he finally reached to scratch himself, the seesaw teetered and he fell—down, horrifyingly down, cannonballing to the black stretch of street. But every time he endured the dream, a split second before he would have slammed the pavement, he awoke in Jonathan's tightened arms. "I've got you," his brother reassured. "I've got you."

The fourth or fifth time it happened, Jacob asked his brother, "Was I screaming? Was I really loud?" And Jonathan told him, "No, you didn't make a sound."

"How did you know to catch me, then?" Jacob inquired.

Jonathan paused, only then seeming to consider the mystery. "It was in *my* dream," he finally said. "I dreamt that you were falling. When I woke up I was here in your bed, holding you."

Jacob never had the nightmare again.

Now he rolled onto his back. Waves of vodka sloshed against his stomach walls, but he didn't feel sick in the slightest. He was the perfect degree of drunk. The pleasant tipsiness made him think of something Jonathan had said that day at lunch. The ritual washing of hands had sparked an argument at their table. One student insisted they should hold their hands high above their heads, citing the line in the prayer, "Lift up holy hands." He demonstrated, waving his arms as if midway through a jumping jack. The others countered that the gesture was overkill; it was enough to hold your hands in front of you.

The argument droned on through the entire meal, ending with a decision to consult a certain rabbi.

"I don't get it," Jacob had whispered to Jonathan. "If you obsess about these details so much, how can you have time for anything important?"

"You've got it backwards," Jonathan said. "The details are there to *help* you think about important things. When you have to know the right way to wash your hands, it makes you think about how incredible your hands are, how lucky we are to have these amazing bodies. When you can eat only special foods, you think about what a blessing it is not to be hungry. There's a prayer to say after seeing a rainbow. There's even one for seeing an especially beautiful person. It's like tripping on acid. You get that heightened awareness of, you know, everything—of life."

The whir of alcohol in his head and limbs now made Jacob extend Jonathan's drug metaphor. When he'd first arrived at Etz Chaim three days ago, it had been like showing up sober at a party where everyone else is stoned—that same disconnection, the self-consciousness, the resentment. But eventually, in spite of yourself, you start to feel kind of giddy. You can't help but get a contact high.

The morning service was unexpectedly quiet. Students prayed in reverential silence or muttered hypnotically into their beards, with only occasional outbursts. Pages flipped at random intervals, a constant crinkling undercurrent.

Then miraculously, as if on command, the students all finished at the same moment. They shucked their tefillin and tallises and herded off, chattering, for breakfast. Only Jacob and Jonathan, who was completing some private prayer, remained in the *beit midrash*.

The room darkened eerily with the absence of bodies. It was a long, high-ceilinged hall, filled with tables and small lecterns. Clothbound volumes packed tall bookcases like rows of gritted teeth. The *beit midrash* was the center of Etz Chaim, the yeshiva's pulsing heart, serving variously as study hall, sanctuary, and hangout spot. Jacob likened it to his elementary school "cafetorium," which converted on any given day from lunch room to basketball court to theater.

Yesterday, he had observed the afternoon study session, when the *beit midrash* hummed with the contentious din of an auction barn. Pairs of students faced off across the long tables, arguing over sprawled texts, sometimes exploding up and jabbing emphatic fingers. Others paced the aisles or banged their fists on lecterns, expounding to no one in particular.

Jacob watched two students scrutinizing a shared volume, their foreheads pressed nearly together. Suddenly they cried out and leapt into a hug. They had solved some riddle, discovered a hidden meaning. They spun together in a clumsy two-man hora.

None of the other students seemed to notice. This was routine, a minor indulgence. But Jacob was riveted. He lifted a book to just below eye level so he could pretend to be reading while he stared. Eventually, the partners stopped spinning, and each man kissed the other on both cheeks. Even from a distance Jacob could sense the gesture's tenderness, the familiarity of a married couple.

The hug and kiss appeared completely innocent, but it was precisely the students' *non*-sexuality that telegraphed a pulse of arousal to Jacob's groin. He knew what sex with men felt like. But this brotherly embrace, this chaste dance of comrades, was the touch he had had once and lost.

"Am I that fascinating?"

Jonathan, who had been winding his tefillin straps into a neat ball, stopped in mid-rotation.

"Sorry," Jacob said. "Was I staring?"

"Like a zombie."

Jacob couldn't admit his daydream of the dancing students. "I was just thinking," he said, pointing to the tefillin, "how impressive it is."

"This?" Jonathan said. "Not when you do it every day."

"Well, I don't see how you learn all that stuff."

"Pretty soon you just get the hang of it." Then Jonathan snapped the fingers of his free hand. "Hey, why don't I show you? You can try." He began to unwind the package he'd been assembling.

Jacob stopped him. "No, Jon. I don't think so."

"Why not? I'll take you through it step by step."

"Right now?" Jacob stalled. He looked around the abandoned *beit midrash*. "Shouldn't we go for breakfast?"

"It'll wait. The food's usually cold anyway. Come on." Jonathan held out the tefillin.

"I don't know. I just don't think it would be right."

"Not right? It's the only thing that *is* right. It's an obligation."

"What I mean is, I don't believe in all the stuff it stands for. Wouldn't it be, like, blasphemous?"

"Jake, it's not like Christianity, where everything's all faith, faith, faith. One day you say you believe in something and then *ta-dah*, you're saved. With Judaism, it's what you *do* that's important. It's about action much more than belief."

"But you're still supposed to believe, right?"

"Of course you're supposed to. That's the ideal. But it's not essential. The rosh yeshiva always gives an example in his lectures: There are two guys, he says. One of them doesn't really believe in Hashem, but he figures there's a fifty-fifty chance, right? So as insurance, he goes through the motions, lives by all the commandments, keeps kosher and everything. Well, the second guy has total faith. But he's lazy, and he doesn't bother to observe the commandments. Which is the better Jew? The rosh yeshiva says it's no question. It's the first guy, the guy who acts observantly."

Jacob was stunned. Wasn't this admitting what their father always said, that Judaism was just a bunch of hollow laws? But if the head of the yeshiva would tell this parable, and if Jonathan would repeat it with such pride, there must be something more.

He thought of all the yeshiva students, all the observant Jews around the world, going through the identical motions every day like the connected legs of some enormous beast. Jacob had never been able to give himself fully to anything, to join without guarding a certain distance. He had thought for a while that gayness might be it, but the whole gay world seemed unbearably contrived at times—too new, too invented, too small. Like the inspirational quote book he had to publicize: Could he honestly say he believed in that?

Wouldn't it be wonderful to be truly immersed in something? To be so deep that you weren't always questioning? Conformity terrified Jacob, but also beckoned him. He remembered the old woman who had knelt at Ben-Gurion Airport, offering her lips to the steaming blacktop. She hadn't kissed an oil-stained patch of pavement, she had kissed Israel, an idea, a way of life.

Jacob wished he, too, could know the flavor of being *inside*. He wanted to taste belonging on his lips.

He thrust his hands toward his brother, wrists together, as if waiting to be handcuffed.

"Really?" Jonathan asked.

"Why not?" Jacob said. "Give it a try."

His brother's cheeks spread into a glossy smile. "Okay. First, get up. You have to be standing when you lay tefillin."

Jacob rose on jittery legs. Jonathan grabbed his left arm and stretched it as if adjusting a gooseneck lamp, seeming unsure just how to touch another person's flesh. "The hand tefillin goes first," he explained. "This box goes on your biceps so it will be closest to your heart."

He placed the leather, still warm from having been against his own skin, on Jacob's arm. "As you're tightening it you say the prayer. I'll say it, a couple words at a time, and then you say them after me. Okay? *Baruch atah adonai . . .*"

Jonathan waited for him to repeat the phrase, but Jacob couldn't. He found the procedure embarrassing in the same way as stripping in a doctor's office. "My Hebrew's pretty rusty," he said. "Why don't you just go ahead and say it?"

Jonathan's eyes glinted sharply for a moment, then dulled with acquiescence. "Sure," he said. "Sure, I guess that's fine."

He wrapped the leather band seven times around Jacob's forearm, then around his palm. Next he brought forth a separate loop, knotted in the back and decorated with a cube identical to the one already pressing Jacob's biceps. "The head tefillin," he said, lifting the bight onto Jacob's head. He arranged it so the box was in front, just at Jacob's widow's peak. "There," he said. "Fits perfectly." He mumbled another prayer.

The leather box on Jacob's scalp felt uncanny: weight but not weight, like when your arm has fallen asleep and moving it feels like someone else's body. He was amazed to think that just four days ago, he had been sitting on the airplane, making fun of the other passengers for donning these awkward leather horns. It had been easy enough to dismiss Michelinski and the other men as fanatics. But now he felt the box throbbing between his own eyes like a headache. Now he had to view them differently.

His assessment of Jonathan, too, needed revision. At the Western Wall, Jacob had seen his brother as usurping what should have been both of theirs. But if Jonathan was bent on hijacking Papa Isaac's legacy, why would he be trying to share this experience? Jacob felt suddenly ashamed for suspecting his brother's generosity. Perhaps *he* had been the stingy one all along. Not just in the last four days, but for their entire lives.

"Relax," Jonathan said.

"What?" Jacob wondered if his brother had read his thoughts.

"Your hand. Let go your fingers. I'm not done yet."

Jacob hadn't realized he had been straining so hard. He released his fist, and like a squeezed sponge swelling back to its natural shape, the fingers uncoiled.

Jonathan unwound the leather band from Jacob's palm. "Now this goes around the middle finger. Once here and twice here."

Jacob studied his brother's hands as they worked, his forearm hair which whorled in a twin pattern to his own—this arm he had wrestled to the dusty floor of Papa Isaac's study, now binding him at his own request. Jonathan chanted the next prayer, carrying the leather strap around Jacob's ring finger and then coiling the excess on his palm again. "*V'ayrastich li l'olam, v'ayrastich li b'tzedek . . .*"

Jacob enjoyed his brother's firm but gentle touch, the easy pressure of his fingers. It made him think of Yoni, the flight attendant, the soft brush of his hand on Jacob's thigh. He thought also of handling Marty near the end, rubbing moisturizer onto his friend's emaciated ribs. These were all the same caress, he thought, the same vulnerable laying of one man's fingers on another. Surely Jonathan could understand that. Surely he understood that his embrace now, tangled in leather, added to a single, larger embrace.

"The English," Jonathan said, "is kind of pretty: 'I will betroth you to myself forever; I will betroth you to myself in righteousness and in justice, in kindness and in mercy.' "

Jacob knew his brother was simply translating the prayer. But he heard the cadence as a personal vow directly from Jonathan. This was Jonathan's own apology, a sacred pledge of love. The leather he had looped around Jacob's finger was a ring, sanctifying the promise.

Jacob closed his eyes and silently composed his own version of the prayer: *I will betroth myself to you, too. We will be joined again, and share our secrets. We will accept each other with kind justice and love.*

When he opened his eyes, Jonathan was grinning widely. His dimples flickered in his cheeks and Jacob smiled too, knowing his own dimples would do the same.

"That's it," Jonathan said. "That's the mitzvah of tefillin."

"Then what?" Jacob asked. He was ready to learn more. He wanted to experience what Jonathan experienced, to see everything the way he saw it, from the inside.

"Then you take them off," Jonathan said. "Everything gets done in reverse."

Into a Mirror

Jacob had noticed the glow the previous summer, on cloudy nights when light hugged the ground. Blue and orange like a flaring gas flame, it made the marsh shimmer with shadows, birthing wispy figures between tall stalks of grass, then just as quickly stealing them away. He had surmised it was the drive-in movie theater, more than a mile by road but maybe closer as the crow flies. He had figured as much, but he lacked conclusive proof.

Now, lying next to Jonathan on their second night at Nana Jenny and Papa Isaac's cottage, he had a brainstorm.

"You asleep?" he asked the dark shape of his brother.

Seconds of silence. A throaty scraping of phlegm. Then Jonathan's croaking reply: "Not anymore."

"Good. Want to see a movie?"

"A movie? I don't know. I guess maybe if it rains tomorrow."

Jacob sat up and pulled on his shorts. "No, stupid. Now. We're going on the roof."

They visited Cape Cod every year for the three weeks before Labor Day, renting the same small house just a block from the place Papa Isaac bought when he retired as a rabbi. The Cape was a flexed arm extending out of the torso of Massachusetts, from the armpit at Falmouth all the way to the curled fist of Provincetown. When Jacob told anyone his family summered there, they inevitably asked which part; he had learned to hold up his left arm, mimicking the map, and point. They were in the triceps. Not very glamorous, but functional.

But that August, with Jacob a month shy of thirteen, his father was attending a geneticists' conference in Switzerland, the dates of which overlapped with their standard vacation. He had taken Jacob's mother with him. And so Jacob and Jonathan were staying a full week with their grandparents.

Nana Jenny and Papa Isaac's cottage was a gray-shingled box at the cul-de-sac of a silent lane. The ocean loomed past the backyard, just beyond a narrow swath of reeds and mud. On days when the wind blew in, the house filled with the smells of wet shellfish, rotting seaweed, all kinds of salty decay. The rich scent livened Jacob, sped his metabolism, as if the composted marsh air were fertilizer for his own growth. He could feel his muscles bulking, his body stretching into new and powerful shapes.

The goal was to get onto the garage. The roof of the main house was out of range, so high that even Papa Isaac, when he strained, could barely graze the gutter with his fingertips. But the garage roof was lower, connected to the main house by a short breezeway. If they could make it up here, the rest would be a cinch.

They built a ladder from the old picnic table and its two long benches. Dried by summers of exposure, the table had the disconcerting lightness of a balsa model, its wood parts warped in unruly twists. Balancing the benches on top of one another was as hard as stacking eggs. An inadvertent touch or a wrong look might disrupt the entire contraption.

Jacob hoisted one knee onto the top rung, but just as the second knee was about to make it up, his instincts made him lower the first again. He flailed that way awhile, like his mother riding her Exercycle, pedaling hard but not getting anywhere.

Finally he managed to secure both knees on the top bench. He rested a split second, then flexed to stand, but was swiftly flung off as if someone had pressed Eject.

When he had gathered himself and stood upright again, he whispered, "Makes you respect them, doesn't it?"

"Who?" Jonathan asked.

"Olga Korbut. Nadia Comaneci. The balance beam is, like, less than *half* as wide as these benches."

Jonathan groaned. "I can't believe you watch that gymnastics crap." He pushed Jacob out of his way and stepped onto the table. "Here," he demanded. "Hold it steady."

Jacob watched his brother climb up, place his palms on the edge of the roof, and propel himself into the air, all in one graceful motion. A sprinkle of gravel rained into Jacob's hair, settling like dandruff.

Jonathan squatted on the roof's edge. "Come on," he called. "It's great up here."

"How'd you do it?" Jacob asked, breathless with awe.

"Cake," Jonathan said. "Just don't think about it."

"I can't not think about it."

"Sure you can. Pretend it's easy, and it will be."

Jacob stepped onto the first bench and was surprised how much steadier it seemed. Then he positioned his knee on the top bench. He was trying not to think about it, the way Jonathan had instructed. He was trying to think instead of eagles and kites, things that soared in the air, trying to forget his body's mass.

The picnic bench tottered; crashed. Jacob's balls sucked into his stomach, and his stomach into his throat—the same plunging nausea as hitting turbulence in an airplane.

"I can't do it," he said. He heard his voice break. His legs quaked as if trapped on a sewing machine's seesawing pedal.

"Here," Jonathan said, extending a thin arm that shone strangely in the starlight. "Make it to the top again and then I'll pull you."

Jacob peeled a rust-colored chip of paint from the bottom bench. "I can't."

"I thought you wanted to check out the glow," Jonathan said.

"I do."

"Well then get up here."

Jacob reassembled the ladder, then tested the top bench. Wobbly as ever. But he knew it was possible. Jonathan had done it.

He stepped to the first level and, without stopping to catch his balance, kept going to the second. The roof's edge was only inches above his head. He reached—higher, higher, *there*. But just as his fingertips brushed the coarse shingles, the world collapsed under him. For a moment he weighed nothing, a marionette suspended in midair. Then he was nothing *but* weight; he fell backward and down.

Something clamped his wrists. A flash of burn and everything stopped. He dangled there, connected to the world only by Jonathan's clenched fingers. Their weight was perfectly balanced, as during the initial seconds of their arm-wrestling bouts, before one of them began the attack.

"Don't let go," Jacob whispered, unable to summon his full voice.

Jonathan didn't say anything, but rocked back on his heels, and Jacob was lifted, his stomach scraping the asphalt edge of shingles, until at last he hugged the cool roof.

The ivy-covered chimney provided ample handholds. They clambered from the breezeway to the main roof and then stepped—arms spanned like tightrope walkers', one foot on each side of the peak—to the TV antenna's rusty skeleton. They moved on tiptoes, in careful unison. Papa Isaac and Nana Jenny were an unsettling presence below, in the ponderous darkness of the house.

This visit was the first time Jacob had witnessed his grandparents in their daily existence, rather than for just a holiday dinner or special event. They were different people this way, people he didn't like as much. More than anything else, it was the silence.

Jacob had known hints of it before: Sometimes in the middle of a Shabbos dinner in Brookline, the phone would ring. Nobody would say anything, but the grown-ups all seemed to know the call was for Nana Jenny. When she returned to the table, she and Papa Isaac would not speak to each other for minutes.

But here, the silence was as permanent as the film of soot crusted blackly on the barbecue. Papa Isaac would sit for hours in his armchair, thick-rimmed reading glasses perched on his nose, making no sound besides the snap of prayer-book pages. Nana Jenny didn't talk either, except to herself. Sometimes, as she sat needlepointing a pillow cover, her lips would begin to move. She would tilt her head with a question, pause, then nod firmly with her own response.

Jacob was afraid to cough or chew food too loudly around his grandparents. They acted as though the house were an airtight box made of fragile glass. A disturbing noise might shatter the walls, and the air would escape, leaving everybody gasping.

But he wasn't in the house now. He was on top of it, on the roof, a different world.

The salt breeze swirled seductively, tickling its way into his nostrils. Reflected off the gray shingles, the starlight bestowed milky haloes on everything, making objects glow like the ghosts of bones in an X-ray. Jacob imagined he had special powers of vision, superhero eyes.

When he turned to face the marsh, he saw that his hunch had been correct. The drive-in screen was huge, even at this distance, a miracle of dancing light in the darkened sky. The entire shimmering rectangle was visible except for a trio of fuzzy blotches at the bottom, probably trees at the marsh's far edge.

"It's like at the movies," Jonathan said, "only bigger."

"Shh," Jacob whispered. "Can you hear?"

They held their breath in deference to the distant luminescence. There was only the rush of wind, the swish of marsh grass, the quiet roar of a seashell pressed against an ear.

"You can follow it anyway," Jonathan said. "She just told him not to go through that door, but he's not going to listen."

It was some horror thing from the year before, maybe one of the *Halloween* movies. Just as Jonathan had predicted, the male actor opened a door and entered a shadowy room.

"Now she'll follow him," Jacob said, excited by the game. "And the door will slam behind them and they'll be trapped!"

"Unh-unh. Too predictable. She'll wait for him outside, thinking it's safer, but when he comes out the bad guy will have gotten her."

They watched and waited. Jacob wanted to warn the woman, to tell her to follow her friend into the other room, but from this distance she was tragically unreachable. The director had inserted delay shots, panning around the room, close-ups of cobwebbed furniture. The quiet of the marsh was thunderous. Jacob invented music in his head to make the scene more familiar, more like what he expected at the movies. He conjured the menacing wail of violins, creepy black-key piano chords.

Suddenly the man on screen whipped around. Had he heard something? Had there been a scream? He ran out of the room and straight into the blood-soaked body of his female companion, a kitchen knife lodged in her back. Jacob recoiled and grabbed into the night. It was seconds before he realized that what he had clutched was not the antenna, not the roof, but his brother's hand. He was embarrassed until he felt the sweaty reciprocating squeeze. Jonathan had grabbed his hand, too.

They let go without looking at each other.

"Pretty real," Jonathan said.

Jacob shook imaginary blood from his hands. "*Too* real."

Jonathan concluded, "They should have stuck together."

After the gory murder scene came a long lull of exposition. It made no sense without the dialogue. Jacob grew bored. He found himself looking away from the screen for minutes at a time.

He and Jonathan sat at the very top of the roof, their elbows hooked over the peak. Jacob loved just lying there, soaking in the starry night. He blinked his eyes rapidly, creating strobe effects with the constellations. He imagined he was inside a giant whirling disco ball.

A small-engined plane buzzed overhead, lights flickering like a battalion of colored fireflies. Jacob knew the plane was on its way to the Hyannis airport, the one John F. Kennedy had used when he was president. Their father never failed to point out this fact, every time they circled the rotary in front of the airport's entrance. "You know JFK flew in here on weekends?" he would say. "They had to extend the runway so it could handle Air Force One."

"Yes," Jacob and Jonathan always answered dutifully, and then, as their father recited his favorite part of the inaugural address, they would mouth the words in unison: "Let the word go forth from this time and place, to friend and foe alike, that the torch has been passed to a new generation. . . ."

Jacob felt for the Kennedys. He knew it was a cliché—*everyone* felt for the Kennedys—but he was sure his connection with the family was special. He thought often of the brothers—Joe, Jack, Bobby, and Teddy—picturing them as portraits on a mahogany-paneled wall. One by one, the portraits shook and fell, the frames cracking on the floor, until only Teddy remained.

Jacob had always sympathized most with Teddy. Teddy, who should have been the pampered youngest, but ended up carrying the entire family's burden. Teddy, who had to watch his brothers, one after another, disappear into their dark, dusty graves. Jacob wondered sometimes what it would be like to lose Jonathan, to have to dress for his own brother's funeral. What would it be like to be a portrait hanging alone?

A surge of warm air washed up the roof's incline. Just as quickly, a cooler wave pushed in, repelling the warmth, the way pockets of different-temperature water torpedoed below the surf at Seagull Beach. Jacob shuddered, inched closer to Jonathan.

"Cold?" Jonathan asked. Without waiting for an answer, he scooted over, closing the gap still further. The short hairs on Jacob's calves stood at attention, dozens of tiny arms reaching out, stretching for Jonathan.

His brother lay quietly next to him. His head was tipped back against the sharp peak of the roof, his eyes closed. His nostrils flared wide with every breath as if he were trying to steal all the air for himself. Maybe it was the starlight, or the shifting glow from the drive-in screen, but Jacob was amazed by Jonathan's softness. It was the only way he could describe it—a softness like lamb's wool that compelled him toward it, made him want to bury his face in its plush caress.

Why couldn't things always be this way between them? It occurred to him that it was other people who messed up everything: their parents, Papa Isaac. If only they could be alone like this.

He had the urge to say something to Jonathan, something big. He thought of Teddy Kennedy, who could never, ever speak to his brothers again. Jacob should not take for granted what he still had. But the only sentences that came to mind were meaningless in their self-evidence: "It's just us," or "You're my brother." He felt the need to apologize for something, to touch Jonathan's arm and whisper, "I'm so sorry." But Jonathan might ask, "Sorry for what?" and he wouldn't know what to say.

Another plane flew overhead, this time heading away from Hyannis. Jacob pictured it swooping out past Seagull Beach and over the Atlantic, then continuing on and on to—where? Greenland? France? Some distant and exotic place. The buzzing of the plane's small engines tickled his neck, the same metallic shock of arousal as when Nick the barber clippered behind his ears. Jacob always squirmed at the electric razor's touch, twisting in the vinyl chair, and Nick threatened haircut disaster if he moved another inch. The clippers' vibrations, combined with the challenge of self-restraint, swelled Jacob's dick to a lump beneath the plastic apron.

It was like that now, hard and itchy in the cotton of his underwear. His heart was a jittering alarm clock. Bullets of hot blood shot through his neck. He shifted to hide the bulge in his shorts, but something inexplicable seized him; he shifted back, leaving it visible.

"You all tingly?" he asked Jonathan. He rubbed his palms briskly on his calves, creating a prickle of friction.

"My legs?" Jonathan asked.

Jacob nodded.

"Kind of," Jonathan said. "But you've got more hairs than I do." He pressed his right leg against Jacob's left.

Jacob thought he saw his brother's eyes glance at his crotch. He couldn't be sure. He trailed his fingers down the valley where their legs were joined. Jonathan's hand met his. Their fingers danced on each other's goosebumped skin.

And then Jacob was talking, forcing speech through the pounding gulley of his throat: "Some of the guys were joking. At camp? About being identical twins." It wasn't true, but Jacob couldn't admit that the thoughts he was about to confess were his own. "They wanted to know did we have identical everything. Like identical dicks."

He tried to say the last word softly, like a secret, but it crackled in the night air. He wished he could pull it back, swallow it, try again. There was a fluttering on his leg. He was too scared to look.

"What'd you tell them?" Jonathan asked.

"That how should I know. That we didn't sit around with our pants off all the time." Jacob was hoping to come off as blasé, the way other guys sounded when they talked about sex, but everything was coming out wrong.

"Have you?" Jonathan asked.

"What?"

"Wondered," Jonathan said. "You know. If they're the same?"

Jacob made a sound that he might be able to claim later had been a cough, not an affirmation.

"I don't care," Jonathan blurted. "I'd do it."

"You serious?" Jacob asked.

Jonathan's eyes flickered with the drive-in light, full of possibility. "Sure," he said. "Yeah. You want to?"

The wind had picked up, making the TV antenna hum like a

distant harmonica. A briny smell lifted from the marsh; lingered; passed. They leaned into each other, creating a sheltered canyon. Jacob imagined that they were more than twins, that they were the same person, the same brain, coexisting in two separate bodies.

They unbuttoned their shorts. Jacob's Sears briefs were grayer, more worn in spots than Jonathan's. He gripped the elastic band with his right hand so his brother wouldn't see how badly he was shaking.

Jonathan cupped his hand over his crotch, as if protecting a baby bird. "It's all hard," he said. He lifted his fingers an inch and pretended to peek.

"Me too," Jacob said.

"On three?"

"One . . . two . . . three."

Together, they lifted their hips and shimmied down the underwear. Jonathan's dick looked pretty much the same as his— four inches long, as big around as the Magic Markers their social studies teacher, Miss Pinter, used on the butcher-papered bulletin board. But Jonathan's had a freckle, a tiny beauty mark a pinkie's width from the hole. Jacob wondered why he didn't have one, too.

Jonathan's crotch was hairless, just a smattering of brown wisps in the smooth exposed V. Jacob knew each of the two dozen hairs in his own crotch by heart. But looking down now at his body, he could see none of them. The strange light obscured everything. Maybe Jonathan, too, had hair that didn't show.

They leaned closer until their shoulders bumped, balancing their bodies in a sturdy tepee. Every movement Jacob made was matched by Jonathan, as if they were connected by a pivot point. He thought of those dumb slapstick routines, when one character encounters another and thinks at first that he's looking into a mirror. He moves left, and the other guy moves left. He raises his hand; the other hand is raised. But then the other character thumbs his nose, and the illusion is shattered.

Jacob pushed his dick down so it poked straight at Jonathan. Jonathan did the same. Their dicks were parallel, an equals sign of flesh.

"They're the same length," Jacob said.

"Yeah, but yours is curved." Jonathan pointed with his chin.

Jacob had worried Jonathan would notice this. The deformity got worse every time he checked. "It's not that much," he said.

Jonathan giggled. "I bet it's from playing with yourself too much."

Jacob saw an opening to continue his fabrication. "The guys?" he began, swallowing hard. "They said we probably jerked each other off, because we'd know exactly what felt good."

Jonathan giggled again, harder this time, and the convulsions were contagious. They collapsed together laughing. Jacob's left arm was trapped between them, but he didn't mind. The tightness felt good, a hot security.

"Pretty dumb," Jonathan said. He wiggled closer.

"I know," Jacob said. "Really dumb."

Something brushed against his dick. It was an accident of motion. Neither of them pulled away.

"But they could be right," Jonathan said.

"They could," Jacob agreed.

He touched Jonathan first. His brother's dick was as hard as his, but warmer, the skin gummed with the tackiness of cheese that's been melted, then cooled again. Jacob tried to use the same amount of pressure that he used on himself, the same rapid motion with his wrist. But it was different because he couldn't feel the results. He didn't know what adjustments to make, or when.

When Jonathan curled a loose fist around him, Jacob flinched. His brother's fingers had the effect of a hypodermic prick, stinging the flesh and itching and throbbing numbly all at once. But the touch reached other places, too, deep below the skin. The sizzled lining of his stomach. His badly aching throat.

They continued silently. Jacob tugged on Jonathan; Jonathan tugged on him. Their arms were like jumper cables connecting car batteries, the current flowing from one body to the other, then back, the circuit complete.

Jacob had had his first ejaculation four months earlier. He'd been lying on the bathroom floor, his legs propped against the tiled wall, rubbing himself against his stomach. It wasn't until he was finished that he noticed the creamy fluid pooled in his belly-button. By now he was used to the feeling, the Morse code of muscles in his groin that signaled impending eruption.

Jonathan pulled two, three, four more times and the liquid pulsed deep inside Jacob's body. He was thinking of his brother's name, chanting it to himself: *Jon. Jon. Jon.* The softness of the o, an open mouth.

Jonathan jerked away. "Eew!" he shrieked, dropping Jacob's dick. "You got stuff on my T-shirt."

"Mmm?" Jacob was still in the trance of his orgasm. He looked down: two wet globs. "Oh," he said. "Sorry."

"It's disgusting! Get it off!"

"Shhh." Jacob pointed at the roof. "Their bedroom's right there."

Jonathan held the T-shirt away from his stomach as if it were soaked in acid.

"What's the big deal?" Jacob said. "It's what happens when you come."

Jonathan's jaw trembled. He looked like he was about to cry or throw up.

"Don't you come yet?" Jacob asked.

Jonathan kicked him. "Just get it off!"

A shiver ripped through Jacob's body. He felt suddenly exposed, lying there without his pants. Someone could see them. Anyone. Passengers in the planes to and from Hyannis could report them to the police.

He stood and tugged his underwear and shorts together over his hips. Jonathan was still splayed below him, still trying to keep the T-shirt from touching his skin.

"Get up," Jacob said. "We'll get caught."

Jonathan didn't move.

"Come on, get up!"

When there was still no response, Jacob turned away. "Fine," he said. "Stay. I don't care."

He strode across the roof, moving carelessly as if on flat ground. He hopped down onto the breezeway and made his way over to the garage. Loose gravel had lodged in his briefs. The grit scraped the tender skin of his crack, but he ignored it.

He caught himself at the edge of the garage roof, the height twisting his stomach. He'd forgotten that their picnic-table ladder had toppled.

Crouched along the roofline, the toes of his sneakers poking just over the edge, Jacob could feel the ground's magnet pull. The grass glistened, starlight glancing off just-formed dew. Somewhere over the ocean, a plane's engine faintly sputtered. He drew a breath and leapfrogged into the emptiness. The world crashed toward him in fast forward, then jammed to a halt. He had landed on his feet.

As he turned to walk to the main house, he heard a scratching from above. Jonathan stood at the roof's edge, kicking his sneakers at the shingles. He had stripped his T-shirt and wadded it into a ball, which he held at arm's length like a dead animal.

"How'm I supposed to get down?" he asked.

"You seemed to get up just fine," Jacob said.

Jonathan looked small from this perspective. Jacob could hold a fist in front of his face and block out his brother's entire figure.

"There were the benches before," Jonathan said. "I can't."

Jacob was going to say mean things, to hiss back Jonathan's own advice—"Just don't think about it"—but decided it wasn't worth the effort. He turned the garage corner and headed for the house, the wet grass spitting on his ankles.

A Curve at High Speed

"Hold on," Jacob's mother said. "Let me get your father."

Through the receiver Jacob heard the familiar click of plastic on Formica, rapid footsteps growing dimmer, then the expensive whir of an international connection. He stood at the pay phone outside the *beit midrash*, from which the evening prayer service rippled in occasional crescendos, like a radio station tuning in and out of frequency. For the first three days, the nasal melodies had annoyed him, but now they were almost comforting in their predictable dissonance. Without thinking, he began rocking on the balls of his feet, the way Jonathan did when he was davening.

"Hey, Jake! Qué pasa?" His father had picked up the extension in the den. He always acted his friendliest on the phone, when the distance between them was fixed and insurmountable.

"I'm all right," Jacob said, keeping his voice low so it wouldn't carry to the study hall. "It's weird to hear you. You know, the outside. What's been happening in the real world?"

"You don't want to know," his mother said, returning to the kitchen phone. "What a mess. Bush vetoed the Family Leave Act, and Clinton can't get him to debate."

"Now Perot says he's in the race again," his father added. "Can you imagine? Ross Perot as president?"

"Wow," Jacob said. "Maybe I should defect."

"Don't even joke," his father said.

"And you guys? You're okay?"

"Sure," his mother answered. "You know us."

Jacob felt crippled by the small talk, more alone now than before he'd placed the call. His parents wanted so much to hold the family together, but sometimes he wondered if there was anything there to hold.

"Well, what else?" he said. "I sent you a postcard. You probably won't even get it until I'm home."

"That's all right," his mother said. "It's the thought."

He had mailed three postcards that morning. After the perfunctory note to his parents ("Thanks for making this possible. Details when I'm back"), he'd tackled the requisite one for Nana Jenny. The card he'd picked for her showed the Dome of the Rock, glinting gold in a radiant sunset: the classic view of Jerusalem. Normally with postcards, Jacob's difficulty was limiting himself. He would shrink his handwriting to magnifying-glass proportions, squeezing in the address as an afterthought. But this time he was at a loss for what to say. For minutes he stared at the blank card, stumped. Finally, he boxed off the entire right side and wrote Nana Jenny's address in embarrassingly big block letters. In the tiny space remaining on the left half, beneath the printed caption, he wrote: "Even nicer here than the picture. Too hot, though. Thinking of you. Love, Jacob."

The stamp's bitter glue was the taste of his depression as he prepared to send the card, realizing he could have written the same generic message without bothering to fly to Israel. Since he'd come out of the closet, and since his father had forbidden him from telling Nana Jenny, their relationship had been reduced to this: a struggling string of clichés.

In an attempt to cheer himself, he'd penned a third card, to Chantelle—veteran of her own family skirmishes, who'd left her father's house at fourteen and never looked back. She got the one with a short-haired woman in military fatigues, a machine gun nestled between her breasts. "Soldier goddesses," he wrote. "You'd love it here. Me? Don't know. Possibly losing my mind. You'll be the first to judge, I'm sure."

"So, Mata Hari." His father's voice rose to the familiar caustic tone. "What's the report? How's the Holy One, praised be He?"

Jacob glanced over his shoulder, as if worried someone might overhear his father's sarcasm. Usually, he joined in. They had any number of mocking names for Jonathan: the Holy One; H.H., for His Holiness; Freddy Frum. But now, standing in the yeshiva, Jacob didn't like the teasing. He felt the same constricting burn in his throat as when his freshman roommates had told their idiotic fag jokes and he'd blithely laughed along.

"Jon is fine," he said. "He's good."

"You two haven't killed each other yet?"

"It was tense at first," Jacob admitted. "But we really seem to be getting along."

"Can you convince him?" his mother asked. "Is he coming home?"

"Mom, this isn't some extended vacation he's on. This is where he lives now."

"He lives *here*," she insisted. "He just needs to get away from that place so he can think straight again."

"Jake," his father cut in. "Your mother and I are counting on you. Now, seriously, have you talked to him at all about leaving? Even for a short trip?"

"Actually," he said, "we've discussed my staying longer. It's kind of interesting here. I sat in on a couple of the study sessions. If you can believe it, this morning Jon even helped me put on tefillin. He wants me to stay for Rosh Hashanah."

"What do you mean, stay?" his mother asked. "You can't. I mean, the ticket, among other things."

"I checked with El Al. It's only thirty bucks or something to change the reservation."

"You are *not* staying for Rosh Hashanah," his father said.

"Why not?"

"Because one son in the Holy Roller society is bad enough."

"Dad, come on. It's not like I'm being brainwashed."

His father spat into the receiver. "That's what Jon said two years ago, and he's still there. I call that brainwashed."

"Gene! That's enough!" His mother might have been berating a disobedient dog. "You know I don't like Jonathan being there any more than you do. But you will not talk about our son that way."

The phone line rustled with electricity, static stuttering its angry breath. Jacob imagined the scene: his mother in the kitchen, probably standing, her elbows jabbed onto the countertop; his father in the den, tipped back in his leather chair. Jacob knew that when they hung up they would remain in their respective spots, like wrestlers poised across the ring, until bedtime; then they would crawl together under the covers, peck each other on the lips, and nod off as if nothing had happened.

"Jake," his father said, more mildly now. "Can't you see? He's trying to convert you."

"He can't exactly convert me, Dad. If you hadn't noticed, I'm kind of Jewish already." Jacob meant it as a joke, but no one laughed. "He's just being nice, that's all. He's excited for me to see his life."

"You think he'd be acting so nice if he didn't want something from you?"

"It's not like that," Jacob said. "It's not like there's any pressure."

"You said he had you in tefillin!"

"Well, I asked. Sort of. I mean, I wanted to try."

"Sure, that's how they do it. They make you feel like it's your decision, it's what *you* want. Before you know it, they've roped you in."

Jacob heard a roaring squall, like a flock of pigeons bursting into the air. At first he thought it was something on the line, a tsunami deep in the Atlantic disrupting their intercontinental link. When a whoop of human voices erupted above the thunderous pounding, he realized the sound came from inside the *beit midrash*.

"Hold on," he said, "I can't hear. Something's happening."

His mother shouted through the phone, but the commotion blocked out her voice. Jacob closed his eyes to concentrate. He crushed the receiver against the side of his head and stuck a finger deep in his other ear. The noise was still too distracting.

"It's no use," he said. "I'm going to hang up. I'll call again if I change my plans."

He opened his eyes just as the first wave of students danced past. A twisting snake of men spilled from the study hall's door, arms around one another's shoulders. They undulated rambunctiously down the corridor, cheering "Mazel tov!" and "Soon by you!" Others shouted nonsense sounds, pure animal joy.

Jacob backed up against the wall and made himself as skinny as possible. He imagined himself an unsuspecting tourist caught in Pamplona at the running of the bulls.

A hand pinched his shoulder and he was yanked into the rushing line. The only way to keep from being trampled was to go with it. He wedged himself between two guys and wrapped his arms around their shoulders. He moved his feet as quickly as possible, watching the sets of shoes nearest his and attempting to match their pattern.

A voice breathed hotly in his ear. "Don't look so scared. Relax. Enjoy it."

Jacob turned and saw Ari's burnished cheeks, the impish smile that squeezed lines around his light blue eyes.

"What is this?" Jacob asked. "What's going on?"

"Celebration. Shmuel just announced he got engaged."

"You do this every time someone gets engaged?"

"Sure, why not? It's one of life's greatest blessings."

The hallway arrived at a T, and the heaving line of men was compelled to turn the corner. Like passengers in a car taking a curve at high speed, they accordioned in a melee of flesh. Ari's underarm steamed on Jacob's neck. He could smell Ari's scent, fresh and nutty like just-turned earth.

They daisy-chained their way to a large classroom, where pastry-laden trays adorned a long buffet. There were stacks of plastic cups and a cluster of unlabeled bottles that Jacob recognized as Anatole's homemade vodka.

Ari poured him a shot and was about to say something when another of the students called out in Hebrew and pulled him away. Ari shrugged apologetically and disappeared into the crowded room.

Jacob stood alone amidst the commotion. Toasts were made: "L'chaim!" "The groom-to-be!" The plastic cups were filled and filled again. The students broke into circles and spun in barely controlled tornadoes of clothing and limbs and hair. Jacob spotted the guy who must be Shmuel, being lifted onto some other students' shoulders, head tossed back in laughter.

He finally found Jonathan in a corner, chatting with Rabbi Seligman. His brother noticed him, waved him over. "Here. Jake. We were just talking about you."

The rabbi must have seen the nervous surprise on Jacob's face. "Good things," he assured. "Only good things."

"We were saying how excellent it is you're seeing this,"

Jonathan said. He spread his arms to encompass the whole scene. "So you can see we're not all grind and study. We take care of one another. It's a real family."

Jacob considered pointing out that this wasn't Jonathan's real family. His real family was the one on which Jacob had just hung up. Instead, he nodded and said, "I never would have guessed."

"I told the rabbi you were hoping to stay for Rosh Hashanah," Jonathan said, "but that you might need a little more persuading."

Rabbi Seligman grinned as if auditioning for a toothpaste commercial. "We'd love to share the New Year with you. It's an important time for family to be together."

The pleasant tang of alcohol in Jacob's throat turned rancid with doubt. Could his father be right? Were they conning him, trying to suck him in? He didn't want to believe Jonathan could be doing it. Maybe it was just Rabbi Seligman. There was something Jacob had never trusted about rabbis, that too-gentle voice they cultivated, as falsely soothing as sleeping pills.

"How about it?" the rabbi asked. "We'd be more than happy to put you up."

The motion of so many people in the room dizzied Jacob like carsickness. Body odor curdled the air. The vodka had stormed its way through his kidneys and was now an insistent urge. "I'm sorry," he said. "Would you excuse me a minute?"

He pushed past the rabbi, out of the room.

The bathroom was blessedly calm. Thick concrete walls muffled the party's din, and along with it, Jacob's confusion. He positioned himself at the urinal and closed his eyes.

When his bladder was too full like this, he often experienced a panicky shortness of breath, as though his chest were a bathtub, and the urine, water swelling toward the overflow. Pissing came as wonderful relief: the drain unplugged, restoring space for his lungs to expand again.

He pushed out the last few drops, shook himself off, and breathed in to fill his chest's reclaimed cavity. When he opened his eyes, he was greeted by the mirror image of Ari's grin.

They stood fixed on each other's reflections. Ari was disheveled from dancing, a shock of dirty blond hair toppled over his brow. The arms of his white shirt erupted in pink sweaty patches like hives.

Ari's look was devious and innocent all at once, his eyes glassy in the fluorescent glow. He must have been drunk again on Anatole's vodka. Jacob broke the stare, not wanting to be accused of anything. Only then did he remember to zip his fly.

He turned for the door, but Ari lunged in the same direction, blocking his path.

"Sorry," Jacob said. "Here. I'll get out of your way."

"That's not why I followed you," Ari said.

Jacob laughed. "You're drunk again."

"I'm not. I only had two shots."

The space that had just been emptied in Jacob's abdomen filled again, this time with a hot muscle-swell of arousal. He remembered something Jonathan had mentioned, a blessing to recite upon witnessing a beautiful person. He wished now that he knew the Hebrew words.

Ari stepped closer, pushing a leg between Jacob's two. Jacob placed his hands on Ari's skinny waist, locking onto the hipbones. They were in slow-dance position.

Jacob had been doing his best at the yeshiva to keep his attraction cordoned behind imaginary police lines. This had been his end of the bargain. But now, freed by Ari's approach, desire surged. His head felt like a let-go balloon, looping through the air on the jet stream of its own energy.

The first kiss was brief, a brushing of lips. They pulled back, looked at each other, then dove in again to share breath and spit. Ari's sweat dripped onto Jacob's face and clothes. Jacob licked the salt from Ari's neck. Ari shivered and fell closer against him.

He reached to Ari's head. He had been wanting to touch Ari's hair since the moment they met, this hair that was straight and blond and got him teased for looking like a goy. Jacob rubbed the shaved hairline at the back of Ari's neck and dug in with the five-furrowed plow of his hand. But when he hit the yarmulke he stopped short.

"We can't do this," he said.

"What do you mean? We can't *not* do this."

"Not here, at least. What about—"

Ari pressed a soft, hot finger to Jacob's lips. He moved his mouth close and whispered, "Follow me."

They hustled down the corridor, in the opposite direction from the party. With each stride, the sounds of celebration—bottles clinking, the frantic stomping of shoes—began to fade. A wordless klezmer melody floated on the air: *ay ya yay yay yay, ay ya yay yay.* Jacob thought he could hear Jonathan's voice above the others, punching out the syllables with drunken confidence.

Ari stopped in the doorway. He touched the silver mezuzah nailed to the frame, then brought his fingertips to his mouth. Jacob kissed the mezuzah after him, remembering the gift he had promised Nana Jenny. He would buy it tomorrow, before stores closed for Shabbos.

He hadn't really looked at the room the night he and Jonathan had carried Ari to bed. It was the same drab arrangement as Jonathan's: the industrial carpet, the bureau built into one wall, the dripping sink. But Ari's bunk was draped with a brilliant log-cabin quilt. The neatly stitched strips of purple and blue cloth were a private stash of color amidst the yeshiva's abundant gray.

Jacob wanted to comment on the quilt, but he wasn't sure if he was still supposed to keep quiet. As if in answer, Ari shut the door and mashed his mouth onto Jacob's. Ari's tongue wrestled his, pinning the wet muscle to the side.

Jacob placed his hands on Ari's neck, and he could feel Ari's pulse thrumming there like the tick in an electric fence. It had only been a month or two since he'd had sex, but feeling Ari's tender artery—this live beat beneath strictly forbidden skin—Jacob felt as though he had never held another man.

He tackled Ari to the bed and pinned him down, grasping his wrists in one hand and trapping them above his head. He leaned as if to kiss Ari, but bit his lip instead, hard enough to make him flinch. Then he moved down to the neck, chewed at the quivering heartbeat in his carotid. Lower still, his chest. Jacob gnawed the shirt, the cloth supple and tangy with sweat. Only now did he notice the second layer beneath the white button-down: a slightly yellowed, coarser material. It was Ari's *arba kanfos*, the four-cornered Orthodox undergarment.

Jacob's mind blanked with obsession. He had to get his hands on this hidden tallis, this secret religious underwear.

He released Ari's wrists. "Take off your clothes," he ordered. "Everything but the tallis."

Ari complied, his fingers fumbling with buttons. While he worked on the shirt, Jacob pried off Ari's shoes, wondering if there was a proper Jewish way for their removal as for their tying: right, then left; left, then right. He stripped Ari's black cotton socks, revealing calves as hairless and pale as baby skin.

Ari unsnapped his slacks and Jacob tugged them roughly off, taking the white briefs with them. Ari's erection caught in the fabric and he arched his back until it sprang free. The dick was slender but long, a shade darker than his other skin, as if it had been exposed to the sun while the rest of his body was covered.

"Come on," Ari said, offering his hips into empty air.

Jacob let him writhe. He studied the sweat-stained *arba kanfos*, which resembled a poncho, a plain square of fabric with a hole cut for the head. He ran his fingers along the cloth's edge. On each corner hung a tassel of knotted string—the tzitzis.

Jacob lifted a corner of the fabric and whipped the string, lashing Ari's abdomen. Ari jerked away, but Jacob struck again on the other side. He used the tzitzis as a mini-cat-o'-nine-tails, pinking the skin in stripes.

"I want you inside me," Ari breathed. "Will you? Yaakov?"

Jacob's Jewish name rushed his brain like poppers, speeding sensation, slapping every nerve awake.

"Please. I've thought about this for so long."

"I know," Jacob said, "I know. I have too." As the words left him, Jacob recognized their absurdity. He and Ari had met only four days ago; they were still strangers to one another.

But lifting the corner of the *arba kanfos*, then whipping once more with the ritual fringe, Jacob understood it wasn't just the immediate attraction that impelled them together. True, he had known Ari less than a week; but for months, maybe years, he had wanted to have who Ari was. If he couldn't feel within himself the fervor of certainty, perhaps by entering someone who did—someone like his brother—he would touch that heat.

"Will you?" Ari pleaded.

Jacob watched him beg, his hips grinding like a motor stuck in gear. Ari, too, must be desperate for what he couldn't have.

"Yaakov. Will you?"

"I can't," Jacob said.

"Come on. Please. I want you to."

"I do, too. But I don't have a rubber."

"We don't need that."

"Yes we do."

Ari looked in Jacob's eyes, *inside* his eyes. "Can't you feel it? This is sacred. How could anything bad come out of it?"

Jacob twisted the tzitzis around his fingers, struggling with the competing impulses. He'd never done anything even remotely unsafe. But this was different. Ari's words felt true. There was also the convincing safety of logistics: Ari had been locked in the yeshiva, a world away from sickness and death.

There was a hand on his face, softly rubbing. "I promise," Ari whispered. "It will be beautiful." His eyes caught the quilt's multicolored hues and sparkled like tiny kaleidoscopes.

"I know," Jacob whispered back. "I know it will."

He was still wearing all his clothes. He undid his pants and pulled them down just far enough to maneuver between Ari's legs. He covered his finger with spit and pushed it in to the second knuckle. Ari was already moist, the inside of his hole slick and soft as a mouth. Jacob spat again, into his palm, and lubed himself. He nudged forward on the bed; he aimed.

He was amazed how truly different it was without a rubber. He could feel Ari seizing him from the inside, the hot texture of hidden membranes. Ari lifted his legs and Jacob caught them, wrapped them around his neck. He pushed gently at first, letting Ari adjust, then gradually added force to his thrusts. He lost track of which parts belonged to whom.

Ari tugged at his own erection, now even darker, the tip purple-brown with blood. His hand was a blur of motion, two pumps for every jab of Jacob's hips. He was naked except for the *arba kanfos*, its tzitzis shimmering like a belly dancer's tassels.

"Say my name," Jacob commanded.

"Yaakov," Ari said, just a breath.

"Again."

"Come on, Yaakov. Keep doing it."

Jacob pushed as deep as he could, driving into the unbearable heat of Ari's insides. And finally, his muscles somehow loose and clenched tight all at once, he released his own warmth.

Below him, Ari had stopped breathing. He was still pumping with his hand but he didn't make a sound. Then he inhaled sharply once and expelled the air with a groan. Semen burst out in reckless gobs, splattering his stomach, liquid-soapy white on the yellowed cloth of the *arba kanfos*.

The sight triggered an instinct, a hungry animal drive. Careful to stay inside of Ari, Jacob bent down and lapped at the fabric. He tongued the puddles, one after another. He swished Ari's salty freshness in his mouth. He swallowed.

And collapsing onto Ari's chest, he wondered if there was some Hebrew blessing, some prayer for the imbibing of this precious fluid. *Baruch atah adonai,* he began silently, but he had no idea how to finish.

They both jolted at the rapid knocking. Jacob's fading erection squirted out, leaving a gooey print on Ari's quilt. They tried to cover themselves, but neither could move fast enough.

Jonathan stood in the doorway, his mouth wrung in anger. His head was turned askew, as if he couldn't bear to look at them straight on. As if he would be contaminated by the sight.

"Yoni, please," Ari managed to say. "We did nothing forbidden. It depends on interpretation." But Jonathan ignored his study partner. He seemed to see only Jacob.

"This is what you came here to do?" he said. His voice was calmer than it might have been, but everyone in the hallway would still hear. "I thought you were understanding. I thought you were learning the way back."

Jacob held up his hands, trying to think of things to say—defending himself, or maybe accepting the blame to protect Ari—but he was stripped of his vocabulary.

Hatred crackled from Jonathan like electricity. "Get your things," he shouted, pointing to the door. "Get your things and get the fuck out of here."

Condemned

They gathered in Brookline for a Chanukah dinner in December 1980. Over coffee, the adults discussed politics. Reagan's impending inauguration was bemoaned. El Salvador was mentioned briefly and then dismissed. By tacit agreement they avoided the more contentious subject of Israel.

Soon the conversation turned to the topic that for a year had been inescapable: the hostage crisis in Iran. Was there an end in sight? How much longer could the hostages last? Jacob's father spoke of the bungled helicopter rescue. His mother assessed the chances for a negotiated settlement. Their tones were hushed, defeated, hopeless.

Suddenly Papa Isaac's face brightened. "Enough with speculation," he declared. "Let the boys determine exactly what happens to a man condemned."

"Isaac, please," Nana Jenny objected, as though she had recognized the first line of an off-color joke.

"What? It's a good lesson. It's perfectly apropos."

"Not tonight," she begged. "Not on a holiday."

But Papa Isaac had already stretched forward, anchoring one heavy hand on Jacob's shoulder, another on Jonathan's.

"A man waits in jail," he began. "Let's say an Iranian jail, just like the hostages now. And this man is condemned to death. For what is he condemned? For anything; you can imagine the reason. The guards tell him the execution will take place sometime in the next ten days. They refuse to tell him when, only that it will be a day when he does not expect it."

Papa Isaac tipped back in his chair, the blood vessels in his cheeks purple with excitement. Jacob had never seen someone so pleased about a pending execution.

"So," Papa Isaac said. "Can either of you tell me? When does this man get killed?"

Before Jacob or his brother could respond, Nana Jenny tried one more protest. "It's not right," she said. "There are people over there, people who could really die."

"Shush, Jenny." Papa Isaac waved his hand in her direction as if dispelling a foul odor.

She stood and began clearing dishes. Jacob's mother rose, too, and joined her. Only the men and boys remained at the table.

"Now," Papa Isaac said. "Now tell me the man's fate."

Silence fogged the room with its hazy thickness. Jacob tried to dissect the puzzle in logical terms, the way they were learning in math. If x, then y. He searched for the syllogism.

But he kept getting distracted by the pictures screening movielike across his mind. He conjured the face of the condemned man, hollow cheeks tarnished with a week's growth of beard. He saw the grimy cotton blindfold, and then a tear slipping out beneath it, washing a streak of clean skin on the haggard jaw.

The screen blinked, a jumpy reel change, and now Jacob's view was from inside the blindfold. He saw the darkness, the lack of seeing. He felt the cinch of cloth on his skull. Now he could smell the jail cell, too, the metallic dampness of concrete and rusting pipes.

"Jacob?" Papa Isaac said. "What do you think? This condemned man, when does he die?"

Jacob brought himself back to this room, this table, the lingering holiday scents of roast chicken and candle wax. He saw the dare of his grandfather's flickering eyebrows.

"Um," he said, "I guess I'd say the first day. Yeah. They'd kill him right away. Because if they've told him he might have up to ten days, who'd expect them to do it so soon?"

He spoke the last words as a question, his inflection rising in search of approval, then plummeting when he noticed Papa Isaac's tight-lipped, condescending smile.

"Jonathan?" Papa Isaac said. "Your try."

"I think Jake's on the right track," his brother began. "It's gotta be something about either the first day or the last, 'cause the days in the middle are really all the same, aren't they? So I'd say . . . it's the tenth day. It's definitely the tenth day."

"No, wait," Jacob said. Like vapor condensing into crystal droplets, the correct answer materialized. "It can't be that. Definitely not. Because if they leave it until the very last day, then he would know for sure they were about to do it. He would be expecting it."

Papa Isaac lowered his chin in a single nod of endorsement.

"And once he's figured out it can't be the tenth day," Jacob continued, "then it can't be the ninth day, either. Right. It can't be the ninth day, because then *that* becomes the last day, and so he'd be expecting that, too. Same thing with the eighth day, and the seventh, and so on."

The logic pulled in on itself like two halves of a zipper coupling, just the way his math teacher said it should. The links notched tighter and tighter until the conclusion was unmistakable: "Yes! That's it. He can't be killed after all."

Jacob beamed. He was proud for having solved the puzzle before Jonathan. But greater than any satisfaction from winning the game was the jolting, omnipotent realization that his cleverness had saved a condemned man. His thinking, his own sharp young brain, had prevented a man from death.

They had been living under the cloud of the hostage crisis for so many months, the whole country pressed down by the seemingly inevitable deathwatch. But now Jacob saw an out was possible. If only the Iranians could be taught the paradox of the condemned man, if only they gave Jacob the chance to explain, he could save all those innocent Americans trapped at the embassy. He had that power. He could be a rescuer.

Papa Isaac smiled, his cracked lips gleaming. "Very good, Jacob. You are sure this is the answer?"

"Yes," Jacob said, triumph brassing his voice. "They can't kill him at all. They can't!"

Papa Isaac patted him on the shoulder. "Such confidence I like," he said. A gurgle of laughter brought phlegm into his mouth, and he spat coarsely into his handkerchief. "Yes. You think exactly as any condemned man would. Trying to find some easy way out of a bad situation."

He cleared his throat again, but this time it was the sound of a saw grinding through a knot of wood. He stared, first at Jacob, then at Jonathan, his eyes deep holes stealing light from the room.

"Don't you see?" he snarled. "If this man follows your clever logic, if he concludes so smartly that he cannot in fact be killed at all, then he *can* be killed on *any one* of the days. As soon as he stops expecting death, his captors can kill him as they wish."

The true answer slapped Jacob like an icy hand. How absurd to have pretended that real men's lives could hinge on the trick of a brain teaser! How could he have let himself believe the fantasy?

As Papa Isaac scraped his chair away from the table to signal dinner's end, Jacob's vision lit again with the face of the condemned man: now ghastly and bloodless, his waxen lips warped in a final, unanswered plea.

Lineage

Jacob's expulsion had been nightmarish. Less than half an hour after his brief bliss with Ari, his clothes were stuffed into his backpack and he was speeding in a taxi to the airport. Jonathan refused to let him shower or even make a phone call. He wouldn't look Jacob in the eye.

But on the flight home—soaring high above the Mediterranean and then the darker, blue-black Atlantic—Jacob was less angry or embarrassed than relieved. He comforted himself with the thought of sleeping on his own bed, instead of Jonathan's prickly carpet; speaking without constant self-censorship; returning to work, where his knowledge carried value.

Maybe, he decided, this was for the best. He and Jonathan had long teetered on the edge of complete estrangement, their antagonism surging at periodic intervals but never quite surmounting the sea wall of brotherhood. Now the wall was breached beyond repair. Now each would be free to forsake the other.

He wondered how to tell his parents, then decided not even to let them or Nana Jenny know he was home yet. Jonathan wouldn't say anything, either—nothing real ever got said in their family—so Jacob would simply call when he was supposed to have returned, and chat about the usual trivia. Life would go on. His life.

But by this, his third day back, cooped in a dank basement office in Chinatown, Jacob was incapacitated with a suffocating despondency. Compared to the yeshiva's intensity, his Boston routines seemed pathetic, inconsequential. Small qualms he'd had before the trip now grew into looming doubts. He was certain he didn't want Jonathan's life, but what did he want for his own?

In a better mood, he might have appreciated the irony that this dark closet of a room was the meeting space for the Coming Out Day Planning Committee. There were no windows and no ventilation. What little air inhabited the room tasted fuzzy, as if the individual particles of oxygen were encrusted with mold.

In his absence, Jacob had been elected committee co-chair, along with Chantelle. With two years' experience, they were uncontested veterans, grizzled and battle-worn compared to the supposed "activists" who came and went as fast as litters in a rabbit hutch.

Marty had recruited Jacob to publicize the event in 1990, flattering him by calling his media savvy invaluable. As it turned out—at least that first year, when the story was fresh—selling the media on the occasion's importance wasn't nearly so difficult as convincing the gay community. Jacob honed his skills of persuasion to rope in a bevy of volunteers. Sure, he told them, Coming Out Day was a bit contrived, but so was Mother's Day—a shameless marketing ploy of the Hallmark company. Did that mean millions of mothers didn't actually have their spirits lifted on the second Sunday in May?

This year, though, Jacob had trouble believing his own pitch. Maybe it was Marty's absence, the fresh memory of his matchstick corpse tainting the prospect of a feel-good event. But apparently, Jacob wasn't the only one with misgivings. The torrent of media interest he'd hoped to incite remained a trickle. Volunteer recruitment flagged. Despite their résumé-quality name, the Planning Committee was about as impressive as its office space. This afternoon it comprised just three of them: Jacob, Chantelle, and some woman he hardly knew named Amber.

Chantelle was on the phone, arguing with a *Boston Herald* editor. "No, you're right," she said. She planted a fist on the wide handle of her hip. "There's no new angle since last year. But there's no new angle on Halloween either, is there? And I just bet you're still going to cover that."

She had cut her hair again while Jacob was gone, in a crisp Carl

Lewis flattop. A lightning bolt of gray jagged from her left temple into the black.

"Uh-huh. . . . Uh-huh." Chantelle rolled her eyes. Her face, normally root-beer brown, flushed like the glowing rocks around a campfire.

Jacob loved how fierce she could act when she chose to, so different from the bookish editor he once thought her. When they'd first met, through work, their friendship was based on long lunches in the North End, discussing James Baldwin and Toni Morrison. They went to screenings of old Italian films at the Brattle Theater. Jacob called her his mental friend, meaning not crazy but intellectual, a complement to Marty's brash carnality.

The first time he'd seen her rowdy side was at a Red Sox–Yankees game. (None of Jacob's gay male friends would go with him.) They sat behind the Yankees' on-deck circle, and Chantelle mercilessly harassed the players. "You cracker wuss!" she shouted at Wade Boggs. "You couldn't hit your own ass with a frying pan!" Jacob laughed so hard he spilled his beer.

But that was nothing compared to the show Chantelle put on when Pat Buchanan campaigned outside Faneuil Hall. Somehow she fought her way to the front of the crowd, and when Buchanan started speaking, she pelted the podium with mud-filled balloons. "Pigs like mud!" she screamed. "You're a pig! You're a pig!"

Jacob liked that he was never sure which mode Chantelle would be in: private and thoughtful or on the attack. The *Herald* editor was getting a heavy dose of the latter.

"Uh-huh. Yeah, sure. Fine." She slammed down the phone. "That fucking idiot. 'This topic is not of wide enough interest.' It's his asshole that isn't wide enough."

"Screw him," Amber said. "He doesn't know what he's missing."

Amber was a sculptor from Somerville, and a little too something for Jacob's taste. Too granola? Too pseudo-punk? Or maybe, beneath the radical façade, too much like a JV cheerleader.

"Well, apparently," Jacob said, "he's not missing much. Where the hell is everybody?"

"Steve and Kurt had another meeting," Amber said. "Something at AIDS Action. Melissa's in New York. I've got no idea about anyone else." She flipped her dyed-black hair out of her face with a disconcerting metallic clang. She was in full regalia today: four copper bracelets hooping each wrist, earrings hooked through her double-pierced lobes like fishing lures.

"It's fine," Chantelle said, coming back to her calmer self. "It's better with just three of us anyway. Maybe for once we'll accomplish something."

She moved to the easel at the front of the room, wielding a squeaky Magic Marker. "Okay," she said. "Throw out some names. Let's get as many as we can to start."

"Thoreau," Amber offered.

"Good," Chantelle said. She wrote the name in thick fuchsia letters. "All those journal entries about the beautiful boys swimming in Walden Pond. Who else?"

"How about Gertrude Stein?"

"Was she from here?"

Amber shrugged, her bracelets chiming discordant music. "She didn't grow up here, but she went to Radcliffe."

Again, Chantelle flourished the marker: "Up she goes."

The plan was to construct a large backdrop for the rally stage. Under the heading "Massachusetts' Own," they would assemble a collage of famous queers from the state's history, overlaid with tag lines like "Pilgrim Pansies" and "Bay State Bulldykes." The concept had seemed perfect when Jacob hatched it three weeks ago. It was the kind of in-your-face appropriation Marty had always championed. But now the strategy felt hollow and puerile, a joke to which he already knew the punch line.

Chantelle and Amber continued brainstorming, but their enthusiasm rolled off him like rain from a waxed car roof. He tuned them out, doodling on a scrap of paper. His pen squiggled of its own accord. A dot extended into a curving line. A wave. More curves, longer: a snake. He remembered the dance of men through the yeshiva's hall. The sweaty twisting, the shouts, the excitement—it had all been so vibrant, so uncontrived. He flashed to the day in the *beit midrash*, to the students leaping up in their dizzy embrace.

Chantelle stared at him, one eye squinted, like a jeweler searching a stone for flaws. "Jake," she said, "you can't think of anybody?"

"Um," he said. "Let me see. I don't know."

"Come on," Amber encouraged. "This can really work, but it has to be, like, a whole barrage of names."

"Okay, okay. I'll think. Give me a minute."

But Jacob still couldn't ignite his concentration. He drifted off again, adding to his doodles, keeping vague watch as the easel filled without his help: Ralph Waldo Emerson. Sarah Orne Jewett. Elizabeth Bishop. Horatio Alger.

What kind of role models were these? Elizabeth Bishop? An alcoholic poet who even in death was closeted. Jacob knew because the Common Press had published an anthology of lesbian poetry, and Bishop's estate had refused permission to reprint her work. Horatio Alger? He had been run out of the state for having sex with preadolescent altar boys.

Jacob found this desperate scouring of history for forebears thoroughly debasing. He'd felt a similar humiliation as a kid, reading through the book Papa Isaac had given him and Jonathan as an afikoman present, *The Jew in American Sports*. Was Jacob supposed to feel some special affiliation with Hank Greenberg, just because the baseball star refused to play on Yom Kippur? Or with Benny Leonard, "the Greatest Jewish Boxer in History"? Jacob couldn't stand boxing.

But at least Greenberg and Leonard and the other athletes were Jewish. Nobody doubted that. What was degrading about scrounging around for gay "ancestors" like Bishop and Alger was that the very trait supposed to make them kin more often than not was open to argument. Was he or wasn't he? Did she or didn't she? It made Jacob wonder if perhaps no lineage at all was preferable.

The sharp rustle of pages brought him back to the meeting. Amber was flipping through a notebook she'd pulled from her bag. "Okay," she said. "Here's a good one. Kahlil Gibran. You know. The guy who wrote *The Prophet?*"

"Was he gay?" Chantelle asked.

"Well, it's, like, impossible to prove. But he's got to have been. He had this mentor who was a total homo. Some photographer." She thumbed through her notes.

The air in the office was even more stale than before. Jacob imagined he could see Amber wasting it with her pointless breath, molecule by molecule, suffocating him.

"It's here somewhere," she said, still flipping pages. "I know I wrote it down."

Jacob couldn't take it anymore. "God!" he yelled. "Who the fuck really cares?"

Amber's face froze. "What do you mean?"

"I mean this is bullshit. What good is it going to do arguing whether a hundred years ago, some stupid writer sucked someone else's dick? What the fuck does it matter?"

Chantelle held her hands out as if to restrain them. "Hey, cool down. Let's not get upset about it."

"No," Jacob said. "That's the problem. We *should* be getting upset, but instead we're dicking around with this dumb party game of Who's a Homo. What about those people in Oregon who just got firebombed for being gay—do you think they care about Kahlil Gibran?"

Jacob lashed out with his hand for emphasis and smashed inadvertently into Amber's wrist. Her notebook skidded off the table, plummeting to the grimy floor.

Chantelle grabbed Jacob's arm, cutting off the circulation. "Jake! I can't believe you just hit her."

"I'm sorry," he said. "I didn't mean to." He reached down to retrieve the notebook, but Amber got to it first.

"Asshole!" she shouted, rubbing her wrist. "You're the one who came up with 'gays from history' in the first place. So don't fucking yell at me."

"I'm sorry," he said again, but Amber was already up and at the door, her bag slung over her shoulder.

"If you *ever* touch me again," she said. She spun on her heels and stormed from the room.

Chantelle glared at Jacob. She capped her Magic Marker, the plastic snapping into place like a knuckle cracked.

They crossed Tremont and entered the Common, heading up the hill toward the State House to scout logistics for the rally. The footpath was sprinkled with the first fallen leaves, singed and curling at the edges like the pieces of paper he and Jonathan once charred to simulate ancient treasure maps. Above them, still clinging to branches, heartier leaves blushed the loamy shades of pumpkin and apple skins.

Jacob felt better just to be outside, away from the stifling office. The air crackled with the sudden coolness of evaporated alcohol, still a relief after Israel's stinging heat. He imagined that if he breathed deeply enough he could smell Canada.

Chantelle didn't seem to share his sense of improvement. She plowed along the crowded walkway, dodging tourists, refusing to look at him.

"Chantelle," he pleaded. "Chantelle. Come on."

She didn't even blink. She increased her stride.

Jacob almost tripped over a baby stroller pushed by a young couple in matching blue sweat suits. "I told her I was sorry," he said. "It was a total accident."

Stiff and unreachable as a soldier, Chantelle marched ahead. Her heavy thighs shuddered a warning with every step.

"Come on," he tried again. "This is crazy. She was just getting on my nerves, that's all. I know you don't like her any more than I do."

Chantelle stopped short. Jacob almost knocked into her, but she pushed him away. "What did they do to you over there?" she said. "They must have done something."

"What? I told you, I didn't—"

"I'm not talking about Amber. I'm talking about everything since you got back from Israel. This is even worse than after Germany. Did you have some screwed-up sex thing again this time?"

"I'm just frazzled," he said. "I don't know. Culture shock."

"It's your brother," she said.

"It's not. Well, yeah, of course it is. Partly." What could he tell her about Jonathan? That they were not speaking now, yet he felt as though he understood his brother more than ever? That he should hate Jonathan for what had happened, and pity his blinkered existence, and that he did—but that he also admired and envied him? "We had a fight," he said. "It's not that big a deal."

"Uh-huh," Chantelle said. She began walking briskly away again.

The same bullshit detector that made Chantelle the best editor at work made her a tough audience for any kind of dissemblance. Jacob could practically see her blue-penciling in the margins of every conversation: *argument weak here; I'm not convinced; clarify.*

Maybe he should try her. Maybe he should spill out his claustrophobic tangle of emotions about what had happened in Israel, and let her put her editorial skills to work. He would have no problem telling Chantelle about the infomercial host of a rabbi and the ludicrous Talmudic convolutions. He could tell her about Papa Isaac's tallis bag and the disaster at the Western Wall. He could even confess to being caught with Ari. What Jacob didn't think he could explain—what he hadn't been able to explain yet to himself—was how in the yeshiva, with every thought and action restricted, he had still somehow enjoyed a freedom missing here at home. How Ari had not been just sex, but had promised to connect him—for once—with something beyond the physical. How if he hadn't been kicked out, he might have extended his stay.

"Listen," Chantelle said when he caught up again. "I don't deal with secrets, okay? I had plenty of that from my father when I was growing up."

"Nothing's secret," Jacob said. "It's just . . ." He had never felt so totally unmoored. He couldn't even grab hold of words.

"That's fine," Chantelle said, wiping her hands together as if getting rid of dirt. They had reached the top of the hill, just below the State House. "If you don't want to talk about it, fine. But then let's just not talk about anything."

She pushed onto Beacon Street, angling the wrong direction, away from the capitol. Jacob tried to get in front of her and block her path, but she elbowed him aside. She jogged through traffic across the street.

"Don't do this," he called. "Please, Chantelle." He couldn't bear to have another person cut him off. "Chantelle. Hon. Give me a chance."

But she was already too far away.

Jacob waited for a gap in the cars and then slowly crossed, tracing Chantelle's path. He scuffed along the sidewalk, watching her fade into the shadows of the row houses, wanting to be angry but instead envying her ability to stick by her convictions.

Soon Chantelle was just a moving silhouette, but Jacob still had no trouble recognizing her: the butch swagger; the tight haircut on top of the bulky frame. The whole world could see exactly who she was.

Stumbling now down the slope of Beacon Street, Jacob was overcome by the same dizzy sense of inadequacy that had unhinged him at the Western Wall. Chantelle had her unmistakable flattop. Jonathan had his tallis, his beard. Why didn't *he* have anything?

He slumped against the entryway to the nearest town house. Breathing was a strain again, as if the air pressure of the world were far greater than that inside his lungs. He hunkered against the door, ignoring the quizzical stares of people walking past. Who did *they* think he was? Maybe just a bum, a homeless crazy.

It was when he stood, pulling himself up by the polished knocker, that he noticed the tiny box in the doorframe. The length and width of his pinkie, tarnished silver gemmed with a single watchful eye of turquoise, the mezuzah blazed like a proclamation of his guilt.

He leaned until his forehead bumped the door, a captured animal discovering the dimensions of its cage. He had promised Nana Jenny. This one thing she had asked of him—to bring back a gift from her Holy Land, a small piece of silver to bless the threshold of her home—and Jacob had failed her utterly.

Of course he felt trapped. Of course he could barely breathe. He was the co-chair of the Coming Out Day committee, and he wasn't even out to his grandmother.

It was still a shock every time Jacob saw her. When he thought of Nana Jenny, the image was still the grandmother of his childhood: orchestrating flawless holiday dinners, bending nimbly to sweep crumbs from the floor. This ancient woman shuffling to the car seemed only a distant relative.

Her spine had stayed straight, but she had shrunk from what had never been a very impressive height. Now she barely came up to his shoulders. Eighty-seven years of wrinkles had deepened and joined until the sides of her face folded like purse flaps toward her mouth. Violet capillaries spidered her nose's length.

What had remained unchanged were her eyes. The blue circles were specked with random silver sparks, tiny mars that looked to be tricks of light but never went away. She stared through the flecked lenses as though they were the windows of a snowbound farmhouse: There's a storm raging, they seemed to say, but I'm still standing here in the dark, watching, waiting until the blizzard stops and quiet comes again.

Nana Jenny reached up to Jacob with her delicate, bony fingers. "This face," she said, brushing his cheek with the cool back of her hand. "It makes me so happy to see this face."

Jacob bent to kiss her, enjoying the dry tickle of her old-lady fuzz. "It's good to see you, too," he said. "You look pretty. That's quite a hat."

"What, this?" Her hand fluttered up to tinker with the angle of the brim. A size too big, the slate-gray fedora threatened to swallow her. "It's too flashy? I should get a different one?" She turned back toward the building's entrance.

"No," Jacob assured her, coaxing her to the car. "No, it's fine. It's positively beautiful."

It was true, he thought, lending an elbow as she sank to the seat. The hat was beautiful, and so was she. Who else in the world was more willing to do anything—change a hat, offer a compliment, whatever it would take—to make other people happy?

In many ways Jacob dreaded their times together now: the halting half-answers, the conversations that skirted the edges of his life as if it were a jungle pit lined with spikes. But even with all that remained unstated, it took only the mild lilt of her accented voice to ease him into a primordial security.

When he had called yesterday to wish her a belated happy new year, Nana Jenny had said she couldn't talk long because the taxi was about to come. She never stayed on the phone more than a few seconds, as if the technology were somehow dangerous; but such a specific excuse was unusual. "Where are you going?" he asked, assuming she would say the hair stylist or the kosher grocery. When she answered, "To see your grandfather," he almost dropped the phone. He remembered Jonathan saying she had sounded fuzzy a week or two ago. Could this be the onset of Alzheimer's?

Then she clarified, "To the cemetery," explaining that she always visited Papa Isaac's grave at this time of year, during the Days of Repentance between Rosh Hashanah and Yom Kippur.

"A taxi?" he found himself protesting. "All the way to West Roxbury? Don't be crazy."

"Yes," she said. "Why not? It's what I always do."

Jacob hadn't been to the cemetery in ten years. But now he was insisting that Nana Jenny wait a day so he could bring her. He would take the afternoon off, borrow a friend's car. There was no need for her to pay a stranger.

"Here," she said. "Turn here."

Jacob followed his grandmother's pointed finger and swung the car past the maintenance building, onto the narrow lane. The granite graves stretched on either side in seemingly endless rows, the names engraved large enough to be read from the road: Rosenblatt. Yaronsky. Aronoff. Silverstein.

Nana Jenny stared out the window, her forehead almost touching glass. She mouthed the names silently as they passed, as though attempting to summon the dead back to life, or perhaps trying to remember if she had known them.

The Baker Street Cemetery was actually a patchwork of smaller, adjoining graveyards. At each section's entrance was a gate and a sign noting the affiliation of the bodies buried within. The custom tailors' union had their own plot, as did the Independent Workmen's Circle. Other sections were marked with the names of towns in Poland and Russia. People who had lived as neighbors in the old country, before the war, had chosen to be buried side by side here in America.

Jacob studied the wrought-iron signs, envying the confidence of identity they proclaimed. What assurance—to know after half a century, across an expanse of ocean, where and with whom you belonged for eternity. Where would *he* choose to be buried? Not in Chevy Chase, even though he'd spent his childhood there. Maybe on the Cape, near the ocean? Here, next to Papa Isaac?

Nana Jenny instructed him to pull over in front of the Immigrant Mutual Aid Society plot. He helped her from the car, her weight almost nothing even as she leaned fully on him. She straightened her dress and checked the slant of her hat, then with a curt nod began down the narrow sidewalk into the expanse of graves.

Jacob followed, eyes cast down, suddenly shaky with the memory of the first time he made this walk. It was November. Oak leaves, shriveled to brittle curls, snapped like firecrackers beneath his feet. A swirling wind whiplashed the men's jacket tails and set yarmulkes flapping against their bobby pins, threatening to lift off and scatter like startled birds.

After the groundskeepers lowered the pine box into the hole, Rabbi Dinnerstein offered a shovel. "Who will begin?" he asked.

Jacob and Jonathan approached. They both claimed the shovel, grasping the handle the way baseball captains stack fists to see who's the home team.

Jonathan tugged, and Jacob, already dizzy with grief, lost his balance. He dropped the shovel, lurched, slipped perilously close to the hole. A spray of dirt machine-gunned onto the casket.

"Here," the rabbi said, grabbing Jacob's hand and wrapping it back around the handle. "Both of you, now. Together."

Stiffly then, like some four-armed horror-movie creature, they plunged the spade into the honey-colored dirt. Together they lifted the load, moved it over the gape, and let go. Soil dropped into the grave, onto the coffin, onto Papa Isaac.

The sound was sickening—a cold, inanimate clap unlike any human noise. It was a sound that warned of the end of sound. A muffled bomb. A lock clacking shut.

How could Jacob have known that it wouldn't be the close of anything? That his and Jonathan's struggle would only grow more contentious?

He hardly recognized the plot. When they had erected Papa Isaac's headstone, it had been one of perhaps nine or ten in the entire area, jutting isolated like a freak of geology. Now other people's polished markers crowded his plain gray stone: BELOVED FATHER; DEAR MOTHER; IN HONOR AND MEMORY. The dates of death on most of the monuments were only months apart, noting a wave of burials in the past two years. It was as if all at once this group of survivors had decided they had proven their point, and now it was time to go.

Nana Jenny bent unsteadily to the neatly mowed ground and scooped a whitish pebble into her palm. Jacob kept close watch, waiting to see if she needed help, but she managed to rise and right herself. She balanced the pebble on top of Papa Isaac's headstone, her lips moving in some private prayer.

He found his own small rock and placed it beside his grandmother's. When she shifted to the side, he saw how the headstone's right half had been left blank, awaiting the inscription of her own name. Nana Jenny gazed into the burnished granite as if into a mirror. How unsettling it must be, he thought, to stand on your own grave.

Then he recalled the day with Marty at the AIDS Quilt, a year ago. Marty could still walk fine at that point; his weight was only ten pounds below normal, and the neuropathy hadn't started yet. But he knew he was getting close. He knew it was a matter of months, not years. Marty knelt in the very center of the Quilt, surrounded by the varicolored reminders of his impending death. He touched the fabric of a stranger's marker, next to which his own memorial might eventually be laid, and asked Jacob to make him a panel. "I want people to see," he said. "I want them to remember."

Without hesitating, Jacob had given Marty his word. He had pledged to sew the panel and add it to the growing sprawl of cloth. He had promised never to let anyone forget.

Now, standing with Nana Jenny on the sod that would someday engulf her, a guilty chill ripped through Jacob's chest. When she joined Papa Isaac and the others, would he come and leave pebbles on her grave? Why hadn't he made the same promise to her?

Nana Jenny motioned for him to come closer to the headstone. Jacob approached and draped his arm around her shoulders. She felt preciously frail in his embrace, like the robins' eggs he used to find in the woods behind his parents' house, their beauty so easily destroyed by a casual touch.

"Do you remember your Papa?" she asked.

"Of course," he said. "Of course I do."

"What do you think of when you remember him?"

Jacob had to filter the first images that swamped his mind: Papa Isaac's stern face; the command to wrestle. "I think of his voice," he said, remembering how just one word from his grandfather's throat, the mere mention of his name, could make his insides crinkle with pride or shame. "I think of his beard. I don't know, a million things."

"He loved you," Nana Jenny said abruptly, as if she had changed her mind and didn't want to hear his memories; as if this statement were the only knowledge of his grandfather he needed to retain. "He loved you very much."

"I loved him, too," Jacob said.

Nana Jenny patted the headstone. "You and Jonathan," she said. "He loved both of you."

Jacob loosened his grip on her shoulders, afraid he might crush her if the anger entered his muscles. Was even his own grandmother unable to think of him simply as Jacob, as a person separate from "both of you"?

"You are fighting, now, yes?" Nana Jenny said. "You and Jonathan?"

"No," he answered in a panic. "No. Who told you that?"

"I don't need to be told. Some things I know."

Her words hung menacingly between them, prongs of a hook that might snag Jacob with its barbs. What other facts had she guessed?

"We're not fighting, exactly," he hedged.

"What, then? Why haven't you said anything about your trip to Israel?"

"I was going to. I just didn't know if you wanted to hear about it when we were—you know, not today." The lie burned like vomit in Jacob's mouth.

"So, you get along fine?" she said.

"It's a little hard, that's all. You know. Since Jon became observant, we don't have so much in common."

Nana Jenny pulled roughly away. "Not so much in common? Is *this* not so much?" She pointed to Papa Isaac's grave, her finger jabbing the glossy stone. "The same grandfather? The same family?"

From the headstone, the two pebbles glared their judging eyes.

"He loved both of you," she said. "He would not want you to be fighting."

"Well, what *would* he want?" Jacob said. "I mean, he would be happy that Jon is Orthodox, right?" He didn't voice the obvious implication: that his grandfather would be equally displeased with Jacob's lack of faith.

"If being *frum* makes Jonathan happy, Papa would be happy. Yes, of course. He hoped for observance in his family. But never to stand between people. He saw that already too many times."

Nana Jenny shook her head the way people react to news of a distant catastrophe, a plane crash or flood on the other side of the globe.

"Your Papa would never tell," she said. "He didn't think it was right for a grandson to learn of his grandfather's mistakes. But maybe now you should. Maybe after all this time."

She sighed, exhaling more air than Jacob would have thought

could fit in her shrunken lungs. She scuffed her feet on the carpet of grass. "When Papa was young," she said, "your age—no, a few years younger—he got full of new ideas. There were many Jews who were changing. Your Papa was not alone. And like the others, he became for a time unobservant. He stopped laying tefillin. He ate *treyf*. He forgot the yarmulke.

"Papa's father, your great-grandfather, was rabbi of the largest congregation in Berlin. You already know this, I think, yes? So you can imagine the difficulty it caused. His father would not have it. He would not have his own son flouting the command-ments, making a disgrace. He forbid your Papa from the house. He threw out any letters Papa tried to send. He declared Papa was not his son.

"Papa had never wanted to leave his family. That was not his intention. He just did not like the restrictions. He thought, in the way young people think they know things, that he could not live his life that way. And so he was cut off from his home."

Nana Jenny illustrated with her hands, slicing across one palm with the imaginary knife of the other. In his mind, Jacob saw a dif-ferent gesture. He saw Jonathan's angry arm ordering him from Ari's room.

"What happened?" he asked. "What did they do?"

"They continued like this. Papa's father refused every contact. And when Papa's mother, your great-grandmother, got sick, still he was not allowed to come home. She died before he ever saw her again."

"My God, that's horrible."

"It was only when he came for her funeral," Nana Jenny said, "when he sat shivah for her and promised his father that he would follow the commandments again, that he was allowed into the house. After this, he was observant, always."

The story was like a drug, distorting at first, but hinting within the distortion at unprecedented clarity. Did it mean that Papa Isaac understood doubt, understood being pulled between two opposite poles? Or was this a parable about youthful indiscretion?

"How could he go back?" Jacob asked. "Just like that? After what his father did?"

"His mother had died," Nana Jenny said. "He saw what could happen. He knew it was the right thing."

"But could he just apologize and go back to the way things were? After his father had treated him like that?"

Nana Jenny stiffened. She stared the way blind people do, as if their eyes are mirrors and they see only the reflection of what exists inside their skulls.

"How could his father do that?" Jacob persisted.

His grandmother shuddered now, pulling her arms into herself. Her body seemed to get smaller next to him, tightening, trying to disappear. "That was your Papa's father," she said. "But your own Papa was a good man. He was a religious man."

"I still don't understand," Jacob said. "I mean, if he had so many doubts then, how could he ever become a rabbi?"

"I'm chilled," Nana Jenny said.

Jacob slipped his arms out of his jacket. He didn't need it anyway; he was sweltering with the new knowledge of his grandfather. "Here," he offered. "Take this."

"No," Nana Jenny said. "I want to go."

Jacob held the jacket uselessly between them. "All right, I guess. If you're ready."

Something had closed in her. Some door had whipped shut while he wasn't looking, and now Jacob yearned to be let back inside.

Nana Jenny stepped to the headstone one last time. She bent down and rubbed the smooth surface of the marker's unengraved half, then moved her fingers over and traced the letters of Papa Isaac's name.

"I'm coming, Isaac," she whispered.

Jacob reached for her. "Don't say that, Nana. Don't say a thing like that."

"It's all right," she said. "It isn't bad."

She raised herself and turned toward the gate. Jacob saw her lips move again, silently repeating her promise to Papa Isaac.

Creamed

It was August, at Papa Isaac and Nana Jenny's cottage on Cape Cod. One of Papa Isaac's old associates from the Rabbinical Assembly, Rabbi Epstein, was on his post-retirement tour of the country and dropped in for a night, parking his Winnebago on the sandy edge of the lawn.

Jacob couldn't remember his grandparents ever entertaining a guest before. He hadn't considered the fact that they might have friends. To mark the occasion, Nana Jenny treated them to one of her succulent brisket dinners. She baked fresh rye bread, grated a beet-and-carrot salad in honor of the visitor.

Rabbi Epstein was loud in the house. He told bad jokes: "Two Catholics walk into a bar . . . which is surprising, 'cause you'd think the second guy would have stopped when he saw the first one smack his head!" Even Papa Isaac laughed.

Jacob was amused by Rabbi Epstein's goofiness. The rabbi's hair was blue-black, clearly dyed, and Jacob liked that, too. Along with the pinkish Hawaiian shirt he wore, it showed he wasn't about to give up on life. Jacob imagined what it would be like to have Rabbi Epstein as his grandfather.

After dinner, Rabbi Epstein proposed that he provide the coffee. It was the least he could do, he said, to repay their hospitality. Nana Jenny said don't be crazy; she had a percolator right here in the kitchen. But the rabbi insisted. He wanted the chance to show off his Winnebago's amenities. Wasn't it amazing? A two-burner stove *inside* your vehicle?

As he set out for the RV, Rabbi Epstein turned and asked who wanted black and who wanted creamed.

A brittle silence gripped the room. The air froze into impossible-to-swallow crystals. It had been barely thirty minutes since they'd ingested Nana Jenny's brisket, nowhere near the six hours you were supposed to wait after meat for dairy products.

Papa Isaac stared at Rabbi Epstein as if searching for signs of dementia. "Arnold," he said, "surely you are mistaken."

Rabbi Epstein remained cheerfully oblivious. "I can't imagine what you mean," he said.

"To suggest creamed coffee so soon after meat. This is not right."

"Feh!" Rabbi Epstein swatted the air between them as if batting away a swarm of gnats. "That's nonsense. You're living in the Old World." Then he thrust a triumphant finger in the air like a starter's gun. "It's a new day! Change with the times!"

Papa Isaac lurched forward, and just when Jacob thought he might punch the visitor, his grandfather doubled over in laughter. Rabbi Epstein joined in; Nana Jenny and his parents, too. The old people wheezed and wiped their eyes.

Jacob stared at the table, wondering what could be so hilarious about creamed coffee.

Rabbi Epstein returned from the Winnebago with a tray of five steaming styrofoam cups. He sat down and, sipping his light brown liquid, told the story:

"It was, I don't know, fifteen years ago? Twenty? Picture your grandfather with more hair. And me with natural black. Ha! It's true. I didn't always have to do *this* to it.

"We were at an Assembly meeting in Manhattan, all the rabbis from the East Coast. Lunch was corned beef and cold latkes. And who happens to sit at our table but Rabbi Sachar. He was—what, Isaac?—a hundred and twenty years old? More! He had taught the teachers of our teachers. Everyone was terrified of him.

"So, the meal ends and Isaac, your grandfather, offers to get coffee before we recite the *birkat ha-mazon*. We all say we want some, Rabbi Sachar included. But Isaac doesn't do what I just did. No, he doesn't ask, he just comes back with everyone's coffee already creamed.

"Well, I tell you, Rabbi Sachar's face was white as milk. Whiter. He says, 'What is this abomination?'

" 'Not so fast,' says Isaac. 'Never judge a book.' And he pulls out, from I don't know where, maybe his sleeve, like some kind of magician, a bottle filled with white powder.

" 'What?' shouts Rabbi Sachar. '*Powdered* milk you think is any more kosher?'

" 'No milk at all,' Isaac says. 'It's Coffee-mate. Completely artificial.'

"Well, this was new. None of us had seen this before.

"Rabbi Sachar insisted on inspecting the bottle. He scrutinized the label, then dipped his pinkie into the powder. Finally—and you can believe me his hand was shaking—he sipped a little bit from his cup.

" 'Wonderful, no?' says your grandfather.

"Rabbi Sachar found teeth he didn't know he had. That's how wide his smile was. 'Tastes like milk,' he says. 'No. Better. Like cream. What we used to have, in Russia when I was a boy.'

"And then he stands up, this man who could barely stand anymore, that's how old he was, and he makes a toast. 'To a new day. And to Coffee-mate. Change with the times!' "

Rabbi Epstein placed a hairy, affectionate hand on Jacob's head and squeezed as if palming a basketball. With the other hand he tilted his styrofoam cup and slurped the dregs.

"So now you know our little joke," he said. "After that, your grandfather was a walking commercial for the stuff. Any Jewish-looking person he passed on the street got treated to a testimonial on the benefits of nondairy creamer." The rabbi laughed, two frivolous, easy cackles. "And why not? It changed our lives. It really did."

In the morning, Rabbi Epstein's Winnebago was gone, but Jacob was sure he still smelled the burnt-wood trace of coffee in the air. He could still feel the pressure of fingertips on his skull.

This was the same summer Jacob's mother had been put in charge of salads. For years, she had begged Nana Jenny to let her help more with family dinners, to make some contribution beyond the occasional kitchen backup duty. She had not yet given up the campaign to convince her in-laws that she had been a good choice for their only son. With hesitant generosity, Nana Jenny delegated the minor responsibility of salad making.

Jacob's mother undertook the task with utter seriousness. Each afternoon she disappeared to the Stop & Shop, then returned home and in the secrecy of her kitchen concocted a spectacular vegetable fiesta. First she garnered praise for her mix of lettuces—butternut, red leaf, romaine—exotic and luxurious compared with Nana Jenny's perennially drab iceberg. Subsequent nights, she added miniature ears of corn, baby carrots. After that, sweet peas, and sunflower seeds roasted in tamari.

It became almost a game. What could she think of next? How could she possibly top herself? Even Papa Isaac, who normally ate with distracted indifference, as if food were merely a necessary annoyance, complimented her marvelous inventions. The flattery only fueled her quest for more creative elements.

Then one night, a week or so after Rabbi Epstein's visit, it seemed Jacob's mother had run out of ideas. She made her salad as always in the afternoon, but the usual hum of excitement was absent from the house. At dinnertime, when they walked the short block to Jacob's grandparents', she plodded mournfully. The salad bowl was shrouded like a miniature coffin with layers of paper towel. She set it on the credenza, saying she was too embarrassed by its plainness to display it on the table.

"Sarah, Sarah," Papa Isaac consoled her. "I've never known you to make anything but a wonderful salad."

"It's no good," she said, her face drooping. "I don't know what happened. This time I just didn't have it in me."

"Nonsense. I'm sure it's wonderful. Here, I can't wait to have some."

Papa Isaac grabbed the bowl, removed the paper towels, and without even looking heaped a large serving onto his plate. He stabbed a forkful and stuffed it into his mouth. Suddenly his face knotted with disgust.

"What is this?" he said, trying not to chew.

Jacob's mother shrugged enigmatically.

Papa Isaac's eyes splayed with confusion and rage. The edge of his forehead flushed red. "Sarah," he demanded, "what have you done?"

"Okay, I confess," she said. "I found something after all. Fooled you, didn't I? Rabbi Epstein's story made me think of it." She reached under her chair and hoisted the jar like a trophy, playing it just the way Rabbi Epstein had described in the Coffee-mate anecdote. "Don't worry," she said, "it's not real bacon bits. They're Bac-Os. Not a shred of pork."

Her disclaimer didn't calm Papa Isaac. He spat out his mouthful of salad. Green juice poxed the tablecloth.

"How dare you?" he shouted when his mouth was clear.

Jacob's mother thought he simply hadn't understood. "It's completely kosher, Papa. Look." She held the jar for him to take, pointing to the label's circled U, the symbol that the product was approved by the Orthodox Union.

Papa Isaac smacked the jar away, and it clattered to the floor. Red-brown flakes spilled like flecks of dried blood.

"I don't need to look," Papa Isaac announced. "Real bacon or fake, it doesn't matter. We do not eat it."

"But you drink Coffee-mate after meat," Jacob's mother said. "What's the difference?"

"The difference is that it's different."

"How? Explain to me how?" She was laughing, but only, Jacob was certain, so she wouldn't cry.

Papa Isaac rattled a deep breath. Then he spoke with strained patience. "Milk is kosher. We wait after meat to drink it, but that is a separate law for separate reasons. Bacon comes from the pig. It is *treyf*. We do not eat it and we should not want to."

"But it's not—" his mother tried again.

"Enough," Papa Isaac yelled. "Not in my house."

A Fist Against His Heart

Jacob dreamed of Seagull Beach on Cape Cod. It was a perfect day, the ocean winking its tiny white waves, the sun gently massaging his back. His parents and Jonathan were off somewhere, swimming or playing Wiffle Ball. He was alone on a large towel in the sand.

Suddenly the sky turned, a swooping shadow of clouds fusing with the bland expanse of beach until everything was the suffocating gray of smoke. Jacob blinked once, twice, his pupils hunting light, but the world continued to darken. Flakes as big as thumbnails clotted the atmosphere. At first he thought it was snow. But the flakes were sooty and snagged in his throat. The not-snow cascaded thicker, the air heating until it burned like car exhaust.

And then the flakes burst into flame. They flared into embers that stuck where they landed, searing pink and purple splotches on his skin. Jacob rolled in the sand, trying to douse the pain, but the cinders clung hot to his flesh.

An avalanche of laughter rumbled above him and he gazed into the smothering sky. Papa Isaac's face hovered high in the clouds, his white beard like the glinting blade of a knife piercing the darkness. An orange light blazed near his mouth.

A scratching suck of wind. More smoke. And then, amid another onslaught of gravelly laughter, an unseen finger tapped the cigar's glowing end. The sky filled again with fire.

*   *   *

He awoke feverish, his heart racing, buried by a crushing heaviness. He ripped the blankets off, but the air itself weighed too much, insulting his chest like a dentist's leaden bib.

With the blankets gone, Jacob shivered uncontrollably. Sweat greased his skin, as if he'd been bathed in Vaseline. A dark ghost of his head had soaked into the pillowcase. The simplest movements punished him, glass shards of pain deep inside his limbs grating with every dreaded shift.

At first the dream lingered only as an indistinct memory: of inescapability, of heat raining down. There was guilt, he sensed. There was fear. But he could not attribute the emotions.

Then he noticed the smell of his body, of his drenched sheets, his own tremulous panic. It wasn't his normal sweat, the fresh pungency of a good workout, but a bitter, almost fermented odor. He recognized it as the smell that had infested Marty's bedroom during the worst weeks of his fevers, when he would foul three or four T-shirts in a night.

And now the dream's details charged from their ambush: Papa Isaac's face, his judging laugh; the livid assault of lesions. Jacob gauged his own fever, the real heat consuming his body, and everything connected.

He could barely reach the night table to find the telephone. He misdialed the hotline number twice. The buttons swam in his vision like minnows darting from a fisherman's net.

"Can you tell me about seroconversion fever?" he asked when a volunteer picked up on the other end.

"I'll do my best to help you," the voice said. It was a man's voice. Slightly too upbeat. "Was there a particular incident?"

"Yes," Jacob said. He remembered Ari below him, the slippery swelter; the mineral tang of semen on his tongue.

"Do you know about the testing window?" the volunteer asked. "HIV antibodies don't appear for up to six months. Was the incident in question recent?"

"I just want to know about seroconversion fever," Jacob said. "I thought there was some new data. Wasn't there just a study?"

"There's really no sense even thinking about it for six months. You'll just worry and worry, and there's nothing you can do. But I can tell you that some people have a reaction upon seroconversion. It can range from a small, almost invisible rash, to a large rash with symptoms of mild flu. Other people get the flu symptoms with no rash."

Jacob checked his body. There was a hot red patch on his hip, big around as a pancake. He touched the skin in horror, his fingerprint leaving a white bull's-eye. He'd never had a rash there before. Then he realized it was only a sleep spot, where his hipbone had irritated the flesh from lying on one side too long.

But his fever was undeniable. It must have been at least 102. The achy heaviness, the shivers, the sweats.

"When would symptoms show?" he asked.

"Whenever actual seroconversion takes place. Usually within three months of exposure. But it can take as long as six."

Jacob counted back to the night with Ari. "Ever heard of it happening in, like, twelve or thirteen days? I mean, if you were exposed, couldn't it convert right away?"

"I don't think so. I think you've probably just got a little bug, a regular change-of-the-seasons flu. Do you want to talk about the incident? Maybe I can reassure you that the chances of infection were pretty slim."

Technically, Jacob knew, his risk hadn't been that great. He had been the insertive partner, not receptive. He had swallowed a few drops of come, but digestive acids were thought to kill the virus. But how could he explain the other factors? The dream? The convergence of all his transgressions?

"Listen," the volunteer said. "Want my advice? Mark six months on your calendar and schedule a test. Until then, forget about it."

Jacob slammed down the phone. What kind of counselor told you just to forget the problem you called about?

He eased himself to the center of the bed, his muscles still shredded by untouchable pain. How could this be happening to him? *Him?* He had always been the cautious one.

He flipped his pillow to the dry side. Nestling his head into the soft mass of feathers, he tried not to believe in irrevocability. If something was really important, you would get a second chance, wouldn't you? A chance to learn from your mistakes?

He concentrated on stillness, on keeping his body in a perfect plane with the mattress. He breathed, then forgot he was breathing, and finally fell back to sleep.

                          *   *   *

He woke again almost ten hours later, hungry and imprecisely sore. Light drizzled through the windows. The clock said 12:45 P.M.

He stood slowly and shuffled to his desk. The fever had abated, but he felt as though his brain were functioning through a thick swathing of gauze. Residual sweat soured the air. He scanned the desk calendar to orient himself. It was Wednesday; he should have been at work hours ago. A single appointment was scrawled in the day's box: *Coming Out Day meeting, 5:30.* Today, he remembered, they would assemble the backdrop for the rally stage, gluing blowups of "Massachusetts' Own" onto the large nylon banner.

Then he saw the small black letters beneath the numerals of the date. Not his own writing, but the calendar company's printed notation. Today was Yom Kippur.

Air rushed into his tender chest. The unexpected swell was painful but laden also with hope, with the promise of sufficient breath. Maybe there *was* another chance.

He phoned work and told the receptionist he was sick. He asked to be transferred to Chantelle, but she was on another line, so he left a message on her voice mail: "I can't make the meeting today. If Amber shows, tell her it's nothing about her. Or you. I'll explain everything later. I know this'll sound totally crazy, but I have to go repent."

The synagogue's air was stale as an airplane cabin. Jacob half expected his ears to pop.

Nana Jenny sat in the spot he remembered from years ago with Papa Isaac, four rows from the front, in the left side along the aisle. She wore a round hat, navy blue to match her pinstriped dress suit. Her head was bent studiously over a black prayer book that looked like it might crush her legs with its weight.

"Room for me?" he whispered.

"Yes, of course," she said politely, before looking up and recognizing him. "Jacob? What are you doing here?"

"I decided at the last minute," he said.

Flustered, Nana Jenny forgot the prayer book as she stood to let him into the pew. The book toppled from her thighs and hit the floor, creasing pages at crazy angles. Jacob picked it up and dusted the cover with the side of his palm.

"Kiss it," she commanded. "When it drops you must kiss it."

The cloth volume tasted like straw. Grit stuck to his lips. He remembered Jonathan kissing his tallis at the Western Wall, and how he himself had stood bare-shouldered, a cone of cardboard on his head, a pitifully obvious impostor.

He handed back the prayer book and sat on the hard wood next to his grandmother. "I hope this is okay," he said.

Nana Jenny was still trying to unbend the prayer book's folded pages. "I'm sure it will flatten out," she said.

"No, I meant coming. Should I stay?"

Her quavering hand told him to keep his voice down. "It's all right," she said. "I'll make an extra contribution."

Yarmulked men milled at the sides of the sanctuary, greeting one another with exaggerated holiday handshakes. Children, fighting boredom, hide-and-go-seeked between the men's legs. On the pulpit, a cantor droned nasally. He kept losing himself in the prayer's monotony and bumping his lips against the microphone, assailing the congregation with grenade-like explosions.

Jacob noticed another large man sitting on the bimah, smiling at him. It was Rabbi Dinnerstein, the one who had led the funeral service for Papa Isaac, still here after all these years. In his all-white holiday robe, the rabbi looked like a child dressed for Halloween. His hair was thinner now, fully gray. He had lost some weight, making the skin sag from his face like a wet plastic bag.

Others smiled at Jacob, too. Ladies in veiled hats and old men with dried-peach ears. *You're doing the right thing*, they implied with their parched grins and creaky nods. *Here with your grandmother. Such a good boy.*

Jacob wished he could be so sure.

He thought of Jonathan's parable: the nonbeliever who follows the ritual laws only as an insurance policy, and the one who believes, but shirks observance. The first man is the better Jew, Jonathan had said. Action is more important than belief. Well, wasn't Jacob here? Wasn't he acting?

He battled a pounding on the left side of his forehead, like a clenched knuckle rapping his skull. He'd neglected to stop for food on the way over, and now was nauseous with hunger, his stomach writhing to escape its own undiluted juices. Last night's sweating had left him dangerously dehydrated. His tongue choked him with its cottony mass.

It wasn't until the words had almost fled his mouth that he caught himself. He was about to excuse himself and get a bite to eat in Coolidge Corner. He was going to ask Nana Jenny, "Can I get you anything? A bagel?"

Then he reminded himself that this was Yom Kippur; he was *supposed* to be famished and miserable.

Jacob did not believe in divine intervention. He would not entertain the notion that his accidental fasting proved some sort of miracle. But if, by luck or coincidence, he'd made it this far, shouldn't he now keep going? Wasn't it awfully cheap insurance?

Jacob realized this was just the type of revelation converts always described: You are dead to the world, a stony-faced nonbeliever. Then one day you find yourself in an unfamiliar place, dizzy and uncomfortable, starved for something you can't quite name. In a flash, the path becomes clear.

The disorientation and discomfort accurately described his condition. He was certainly hungry, nothing if not hungry. He had every symptom except the transcendental clarity.

"Please rise," Rabbi Dinnerstein called from the pulpit. "And again we recite together the confessional."

Jacob offered Nana Jenny an elbow, but she declined, pulling herself up on the pew in front of her. He stood, too, flipping for the right page in a prayer book. It took him a moment to realize he had it backwards; it was supposed to go from right to left.

The rabbi began a sluggish descending chant like a child's complaint, and the congregation chorused along. *A-sham-nu. Ba-gad-nu.* Without being told, everyone balled their right hands into fists and, with the enunciation of each phrase, beat their chests.

Jacob's muscles were still sore from last night's fever. It killed him to hold the heavy prayer book with only his left hand. But he didn't want to do anything that would bring disrespect to Nana Jenny. And so, self-consciously, in time with the other congregants, he brought his own fist against his heart.

"We have trespassed," he read in the translation of the litany. He hit himself again, a dull rippling ache. "We have dealt treacherously, we have robbed, we have spoken slander, we have acted perversely, and we have wrought wickedness."

Next to him, Nana Jenny beat on her delicate, birdlike frame. She had never robbed. She had wrought no wickedness. If anyone in the world was blameless, it was she. Jacob wanted to tell her to stop hitting herself, but he knew she would never listen. And if she was standing there pounding her own heart, how could he not do the same?

So he beat himself again and again, the flesh throbbing under his shirt. He imagined a bruise blooming like spilled wine.

The second part of the confessional began. Jacob scanned the long tally of infractions:

"For the sin we have committed before Thee under compulsion or of our own will . . . For the sin we have committed before Thee by unchastity . . . And for the sin we have committed before Thee by unclean lips . . ."

This was crazy, he thought at first, this list of vague sins. It seemed a cheap carnival gimmick, like the fortuneteller who peers into a crystal ball and speaks in such broad terms that everything seems to apply. But as he read more of the litany, Jacob began to recognize the violations as his own.

"For the sin we have committed before Thee openly or secretly. For the sin we have committed before Thee knowingly and deceitfully . . ."

He considered his lies to Nana Jenny, the evasions.

"For the sin we have committed before Thee by breach of trust . . ."

He had broken his word to her, forgotten the promise of the mezuzah. Jonathan's trust, too, he had betrayed. Jacob struck again the muscle below his clavicle.

"For the sin we have committed before Thee by ensnaring our neighbor . . . For the sin we have committed before Thee by association with impurity."

That was when the sweat started again. Jacob clutched with the memory of Ari and of last night's dream, rolling in the sand but unable to escape the fire. There were things he should not have touched, should not have swallowed.

He glanced up to the bimah, and he could have sworn Rabbi Dinnerstein winked at him, as if to say, *Good thing you came. And not a second too soon.*

"And for the sin we have committed before Thee by stretching forth the neck in pride . . ."

Jacob's collar was too tight, his tie vising the top button against his Adam's apple like an accusing finger.

"For all these, O God of forgiveness, forgive us, pardon us, grant us atonement."

Jacob slammed his chest with the hammer of his hand. Don't let me be sick, he pled silently. He wasn't sure whom or what he was asking, but he repeated the petition anyway. I will do something. I will change. Just please don't let me be sick.

He lowered his fist again.

Jacob's stomach wasn't even growling anymore. Like a tumor, it lurked mutely inside him, a shrunken, malignant pit below his lungs. He didn't know how much longer he could last.

Rabbi Dinnerstein stood on the pulpit, his white robe darkened in patches by sweat. He wiped his pasty forehead with a crumpled handkerchief and leaned to the microphone.

"The concluding service of Yom Kippur, Neilah, means literally 'the closing of the gates.'" The rabbi spread his arms wide, then brought his hands together to simulate two shutting doors. "The heavenly gates are closing for the year. God is on one side, and we are on the other. It is up to us, through our atonement, to meet Him at the threshold and be welcomed inside. As we say during this final segment of the liturgy, 'Thou dost put forth Thy hand to transgressors, and Thy right hand is stretched out to receive the penitent.'"

Rabbi Dinnerstein paused and looked out over his tired, hungry congregation. He scanned the entire sanctuary, then trained his gaze front and center. Jacob's eyes darted down.

"Don't reject the hand," the rabbi beseeched. "Take God's hand. Embrace it and all its strength." He paused again, and in the silence, Jacob pictured Papa Isaac's cigar-stained, arthritic fingers. He thought of his grandfather's atonement, his return to his father's house.

When Rabbi Dinnerstein spoke again, he employed a less dramatic tone. "It is traditional to stand for the entirety of this last portion of the service. I encourage you to do so, but if you feel weak, don't push yourself. And now we begin Neilah."

They rose. Like a newborn colt trying for the first time to rise, Nana Jenny faltered, her legs buckling. Jacob caught her and held her a breathless instant.

"You don't have to do this," he said. His own legs were brittle as candy canes. He imagined they could snap any second, crumble into a chalky mess on the floor. But he had to stand. He had made a bargain.

Most congregants chose to stay seated for the duration. They slumped in their pews, fanning themselves and checking their watches. Some of the older ones craned their necks, taking note of who endured this ultimate test. Jacob felt their scrutiny sweep over him like a passing shadow, and he welcomed their approving stares, because it was not him they were really admiring, but Nana Jenny. Eighty-seven years old, and after a full day of fasting and prayer she was still on her feet. After everything she had been through.

Jacob held his grandmother closer. Without her, it occurred to him, he was nothing. Literally. She had created the father who created him.

He thought then of Jonathan, the only other person who could make that claim. Jonathan was so sure of himself, certain he was honoring his grandparents' heritage. But where did his observance put him? Israel, halfway across the world; breaking the fast with strangers. His piety, like Papa Isaac's youthful *lack* of piety, had cut him off from his own family. Jacob was the one who stood by his grandmother, now in this last hour of hunger. It was he who had caught her when she stumbled.

Rabbi Dinnerstein, his fatigued frame listing like a neglected barn, asked those not standing to rise again now. The cantor joined him, removing his shofar from a wine-colored velvet covering. The ram's horn was two feet long, curled in an elegant question mark.

The rabbi stepped to the middle of the bimah. In full voice, without the microphone, he began the Shema. Even Jacob knew this most basic Hebrew prayer, the profession of faith in one God. The phrase itself stirred him not at all. But hearing Nana Jenny's wisp of a voice beside him, he decided that action sometimes did supersede belief. He did not have to believe in the words, only in the rightness of saying them; of being here, next to his grand-mother. He joined in the somber collective cadence.

Rabbi Dinnerstein sang another line, three times over, and the congregation chanted along with him, their voices strengthening with each repetition.

"*Adonai hu ha-Elohim,*" the rabbi intoned. The Lord, He is God.

Again the sanctuary was a single voice: "*Adonai hu ha-Elohim.*"

The synagogue's air thickened with fervency. But as the rabbi and congregation chanted the sentence again, and again, and again—six times—a cramp gripped Jacob's hungry body. This should not be all, he realized. More than hollow recitations were needed to fulfill his bargain.

He opened his lips as the prayer was repeated a seventh and final time: "*Adonai hu ha-Elohim.*" But now his mouth was dry. He could barely find the courage to push out any sound. When at last he released the whisper from his throat, the words crackled like kindling set on fire.

The blast caught him by surprise. He had assumed there would be some ceremonial benediction, but without warning the syna-gogue rang with the shofar's raw animal wail. The cantor puffed with purpling face and improbably stretched cheeks. He blew into the horn longer than Jacob would have thought possible, sustain-ing the awesome note, which wavered in a pleading vibrato, prying the gates open for just that much longer, *just that much*, delaying judgment with the force of its moan.

Jacob clung to Nana Jenny, his jaw weakened by the urge to cry. He closed his eyes and listened, not wanting the shofar's sound to end, but needing it to, needing to hear the last urgent gust twist up in its unanswerable inquisition, then finally stop so he could breathe again.

Below them the Common was a crazy quilt of colors. The tree-tops were lacquered by the last angles of sun, their reds and oranges overdone as a drag queen's makeup. It had been one of those perfect October days, the sky so bright that even shadows seemed to gain three dimensions. The darkening air swirled with the faintly burnt smell of ozone and fallen leaves.

Jacob, enjoying the strop of the brisk wind on his face, admired their staging area on the State House steps. Six feet high and more than twice as long, spattered with sprays of pink Day-Glo paint, the backdrop yapped in the breeze like an attention-demanding child. As if tickled to be in on the joke, Gertrude Stein, Thoreau, and the others smiled through the stenciled letters of PANSIES and DYKES.

Yes, the stunt was over-the-top, maybe even a bit silly. But against the view of the gold-domed capitol, the banner would clinch a perfect photo op. So far, though, Jacob had noticed only one *Globe* reporter and a two-person field crew for WBZ News. Tonight was the first Bush/Clinton/Perot debate. *That* was the story of the day, the frenzied editors all told him when he placed the last round of follow-up calls.

Chantelle, emceeing, finished an announcement about tomorrow's Columbus Day protest march. Then Amber approached the mike to provide an update about the antigay initiatives in Oregon and Colorado. Cloaked in a kaleidoscopic Mexican serape, she too could have been too much. But today her outrageousness seemed appropriate. Jacob made a mental note to compliment her later.

Listening to Amber's speech, he was struck by the convergence of so many momentous happenings: the initiative campaigns, the presidential debate, the Columbus quincentenary. This weekend also marked the AIDS Quilt display in Washington, the memorial's first complete exhibit in years. It was the kind of uncanny coincidence fundamentalists would cite as evidence of impending Armageddon.

Jacob couldn't help feeling a bit millennial, too. In the four days since Yom Kippur, he had been tagged by an unshakable on-the-verge feeling, the sensation of having lit fireworks that don't immediately explode. You jump away, crouching, waiting for the flash of launch, but all you hear is a foreboding hiss. Is it the fuse, still burning, about to ignite the mortar after all? If you check, will the round blow in your face?

A warm presence beside him blocked the evening breeze. "Well," Chantelle said, "we made it. I never think we're actually going to, but we do."

Jacob motioned to the banner and the huddled crowd. "If you build it," he said, "they will come."

She gave him half a hug around the waist. "Marty would have loved this. I'm really glad we did it again."

"Me too," he said. "Me too." Returning her hug, Jacob could smell the faint apricot of Chantelle's body lotion, the bubble-gum scent of the gel glistening in her hair. Since they'd patched things up a week ago, he had been cataloguing these details, refusing to take anything for granted.

"How about next year? I swear I won't freak out this time."

"If you *swear*," Chantelle said.

"Don't worry. I never want to endure your wrath again." Jacob reached up and affectionately brushed her flattop, the clippered curls stiff as Astroturf.

"How're you doing about your brother?" she asked. "Feeling better?"

"I'm not sure I'd say better. Clearer, I guess. He's over there, I'm here—I have to take care of *my* business."

"Sounds good to me." Then she snickered. "Of course, I still think sending him a gift subscription to *Playguy* wouldn't be a bad idea."

Jacob spanked her on the butt. "You are beyond incorrigible."

An electric voice splintered over the loudspeakers: ". . . back to the co-chair of the Coming Out Day committee, Chantelle Peterson."

"Oops," Chantelle said, "got to run." She pecked Jacob on the cheek and scurried off.

He stayed in place, feeling still the relentless funneling of events, like sand crowding the pinhole of an hourglass. If you build it, he had told her, they will come. But he didn't know *what* would come. What entropic scatter waited beyond the opening?

Chantelle introduced the next speaker, a staffer from the governor's office. The man was just-past-handsome in the manner of a TV sportscaster, a rainbow flag ribbon pinned to his blue lapel. "From colonial days onward," he boomed in a South Boston accent, "when she provided a home for religious refugees, Massachusetts has been a bastion of tolerance. . . ."

Jacob paid only half-attention to the speech, applauding when the crowd cued him with its whoops. It wasn't the politician's carefully imprecise words that mattered; his mere presence signified tremendous progress. The first year Jacob had helped with

Coming Out Day, the governor's office didn't even return phone messages. This time, they called ahead to request a slot.

The turnout this year was bigger, too: sixty, maybe seventy, plus the occasional curious passerby. Jacob recognized two men from AIDS Action and the red-haired woman from the Lavender Alliance, but most of the faces were welcomely unfamiliar. A group of students from Harvard hoisted a crimson banner. Contingents from MIT and BU gathered nearby, jostling in poorly masked flirtation. In their fraternity sweatshirts and turned-around baseball caps, they looked as though they had taken a wrong turn on their way to a tailgate party.

Then Jacob zeroed in on a figure who didn't belong amid the student swarm. Instead of a baseball cap, she wore a sheer silk scarf, out from which poked dove-colored curls. She was shorter by half a foot than the surrounding collegians. The governor's representative swelled to another peak in his speech, and the woman cheered, pumping her fist in the air. A towering boy in a Harvard Swim Team jacket bent to put an arm around her shoulders. Then Jacob saw her sign: PROUD OF MY PROUDLY GAY SON.

Yes! he wanted to shout—the same galvanic urge he often had to hurrah a movie hero's escape from danger. *Yes! We win!* But immediately he amended his enthusiasm. *They* win. This was not *his* family.

Jacob stung with an equal mix of anger and guilt. But he couldn't think of himself now; he had to think of the event—and you could hardly ask for better footage. He buried his burning ambivalence and searched for the TV news crew. He looked to the corner where they had set up, but the newsmen were no longer there. Maybe they had circled behind the microphone to get the speakers' view. He glanced up, but they weren't there either.

Finally he found them at the very bottom of the steps. The reporter, tall even without the extra plume of moussed silver hair, coiled a microphone cord as he strode toward their van. The technician followed, camera dangling at his side like a briefcase.

Jacob ran down the steps after them. He was not going to let them get away. Not the only station that had bothered to show.

"Hey!" he called when he was close enough. "Hey, wait. Where are you guys going?"

The reporter looked over his shoulder, but didn't slow his pace. "Back to the station. We got everything we need."

"But you have to see this pair. Mother and son." Jacob turned and pointed, but now he'd lost the older woman in the crowd. "Anyway, the main speeches haven't started. You've got to at least film those."

Now the reporter stopped and turned, his face tight with irritation. "Listen, you should be glad they sent us at all. There's no real story here."

"What," Jacob said, "it doesn't count as news because it's gay?"

"Whoa, whoa. Don't get all worked up. Sure it's news—there's just no human interest. It's Coming Out Day; the story would be someone coming out. You know, someone who wouldn't normally show up at a rally. What you've got here is just preaching to the converted. That's not particularly compelling footage."

Jacob spoke without even thinking. "What about me?"

"You're not getting my point," the reporter said. "I'm talking about people who aren't already out of the closet."

"I know," Jacob said. His groin tickled the way it did when he stood too near the edge of a tall drop-off. His pulse bit the inside of his throat. "Turn on the camera," he said.

The reporter looked at his watch. "We've got two more gigs tonight and it all has to be edited by ten. Honestly, we've got to get out of here."

Jacob's ears sizzled with a blistering hiss, and he knew the fuse that had been burning for the last four days—for the last four years—was almost expended. "Just interview me," he pleaded. "It'll only take a minute."

The reporter checked his watch again, adjusted the band on his wrist. Then he looked over to the technician. The other man shrugged *why not?* and heaved the camera onto his shoulder.

"All right, fine," the reporter said. "Let's make this quick. Get the rally in the background." Then he turned to Jacob, extending a microphone's fuzzy head. "Okay. You owe me one. Let's start with your name."

Suddenly, as he faced the dark unblinking eye of the camera lens, Jacob's brain spun in neutral. For some reason he was trying to remember who the WBZ news anchors were. He knew he knew them, but the names floated annoyingly just out of reach, like mosquitoes buzzing in a darkened tent.

"What's your name?" the reporter repeated.

"My name," Jacob said. He remembered Nana Jenny tracing the letters on Papa Isaac's headstone. He saw the embroidered word on Jonathan's yarmulke. "My name is Jacob Rosenbaum."

"And why did you come here today?"

"I came here today because, um, I think it's important? You know, for gay people to do that. To say our names. Because it shows that we all come from families."

Jacob forgot the reporter. He forgot where he was. All he knew were the words spilling out.

"Four days ago," he said, "I was with my grandmother for Yom Kippur services. I'm not really religious. I mean, I hadn't been to synagogue in ages. It felt good, though, being with her, everyone looking over and smiling, knowing we were family. Except it was fake, because they weren't seeing the real me—or all of me. Not even my grandmother, because she doesn't know I'm gay."

"Your grandmother doesn't know you're gay?" the reporter asked, his interest perking. "Why haven't you told her?"

"My family . . . my father doesn't want me to. He says it would hurt her too much. That she's been through too much already."

"What has she been through?"

"It's true," Jacob said. "She and my grandfather came from Germany. They got out just in time. But her brother was killed in a concentration camp. A lot of other friends and relatives, too.

"So till now I've gone along. But standing there? In the synagogue? I started to think: This isn't what she survived for. This isn't why she lived, to be lied to by her own grandson. Her whole life's about standing up for who you are."

The reporter nodded. His eyes sparkled in the fading light. "And that's why," he said, "you're here this evening at the National Coming Out Day rally."

"That's why I'm here. And that's why I want to say"—Jacob paused and looked up, directly into the camera; he bit the inside of his cheek to force the words out—"that's why I have to say to you, Nana, that I'm gay. It's who I am. It's who I'm proud to be."

Jacob didn't know he was finished. He had planned to go on, to extend the Holocaust metaphor and make an appeal for others to join him in coming out. But the sudden clapping jarred him. He stopped. A crowd had gathered around the TV camera: the Harvard swimmer and his mother; a dozen strangers. Their applause whipped the air like a helicopter's rotor, a discomfiting frenzy of sound. Jacob's first instinct was to duck, to protect himself. But he sucked a deep breath and let the sound embrace him, let it wrap his body like a man's thick tender arms.

PART II

April 1993

April Fool

Jacob's office was a greenhouse. Sunlight sliced through the closed window, mercury streaks ricocheting wall to wall as if frantic for escape. The room was perfumed with the thrilling sweetness of freshly heated air, like the custardy smell of cotton towels removed from a spinning dryer.

The calendar claimed it had been spring a week and a half, but until today, the first of April, the atmosphere had swirled with a cool, mocking undercurrent of impermanence, as if winter might attack again any instant. Until today, just now, gulping lungfuls of this deliriously confected air, Jacob had not allowed himself to believe. But *this* was unadulterated warmth.

His first shove at the window was unsuccessful; the frame stuck with months of disuse. He tapped around the perimeter the way a doctor thumps a patient's chest. The glass coughed in response, short worried rattles against the painted wood. He pushed up again, bracing his palm heels against the frame's lip, and the window opened.

There was a moment of immaculate stillness, like the clean hole left by a diver before his splash disrupts the pool. The world paused, everything in balance. Jacob had been swamped these past weeks with work, trying to capitalize on the media frenzy building for the March on Washington at month's end. A million people were expected, the largest gay gathering in history. There were hundreds of press kits to assemble. Bookstores to call.

Authors to prep for public appearances. But in this pristine calm, Jacob was sure he would get it all done on time.

Then the first gust pushed in.

Manuscripts scattered like blown leaves. A stack of press releases shrank as quickly as a blackjack dealer's deck, papers slipping from the pile in twos and threes. *Hit me,* Jacob imagined a greedy gambler demanding as the pages rushed away. *Hit me again.*

He slammed the window shut. And as the mess of papers fluttered to the floor, he did hit himself, a punishing fist against his open palm: How could he forget the paperweights?

Jacob was famous for his collection. Paperweights were his standard birthday gift; friends always returned from travels bearing souvenirs to add to the accumulation. But the treasured objects had hibernated since October in the unused bottom drawer of his desk. In that brief span, those six months of closed windows, his consciousness of them had vanished.

Jacob worried sometimes that he suffered a bizarre form of arrested development, a failure to graduate from the object permanence phase. Take away the immediate stimulus and, like a dog who thinks of hunger only when the empty food dish is in view, he had trouble conceiving of a thing's continued existence.

The shock of changing seasons was the most banal example. But there was also an emotional forgetfulness, which was more willed and more problematic. Jacob consigned unpleasant feelings to an out-of-the-way stash; and without an immediate reason, he never opened that mental drawer.

And so, after last fall's crisis subsided, Jacob rarely thought of Jonathan or the disaster of their parting. There were occasional prompts. In January, watching Clinton's inauguration on the lunchroom TV at work, Jacob remembered the inaugural parade in 1977, when his father had brought him and Jonathan downtown. They'd taken turns on their father's shoulders, and it had been Jacob, hoisted to the giant's-eye view, who spotted Jimmy Carter walking down Pennsylvania Avenue.

"Did I ever tell you we were at Carter's parade?" he asked Chantelle, watching with him. "It was amazing. We were like five feet away from him."

"Who's we?" Chantelle asked.

"Oh—my father," he said, excising Jonathan from the memory. "My father and me."

Two weeks later, scrolling through his computer Rolodex to make a list of valentines to send, Jacob flashed onto Jonathan's address. He paused a moment, then clicked the mouse and made it disappear.

Other than these minor nagging intrusions, Jacob considered himself effectively brotherless. Seeming to intuit the irremediable estrangement, even their parents never mentioned Jonathan. For the first time Jacob was able to conduct a life of "I" instead of "we."

Nor had he thought much of Ari, or of the possibility of infection that on Yom Kippur had sent him into panic. The objective reasons for worry remained: He had ingested another man's semen; he had fucked with no protection. But the intensity of his anxiety, the visceral terror, had faded along with October's colored foliage.

Even two weeks ago, when he called the Fenway Health Center to schedule a test for this afternoon, he hadn't been especially nervous. The test was just a concession to the gods of superstition. Six months had passed; this was his end of the bargain.

But now, in the sudden warmth, Jacob battled a creeping sense of doom. No matter how well you succeeded in forgetting, the seasons did always change. Was everything equally inevitable?

He pulled open the desk drawer and removed the paperweights, a motley museum of his life. There was his first and favorite, the JFK half-dollar suspended in a cube of polyurethane, purchased with lawnmowing money one summer in Hyannis Port. Then a toy glass of solid black "beer" from England. The rest were mostly mementos from friends' holidays—small plastic bubbles that, when shaken, brought snow to unlikely locales like Hollywood, Key West, the Alamo.

He found the two most recent acquisitions: the heavy enamel pink triangle Marty had given him last June; and the globe of sky-blue glass with the word *Shalom* etched on the surface, a birthday gift from Nana Jenny.

Jacob sank to his knees and began gathering the jumble of papers, filing them into neat stacks of all the work he had to do. He would moor them now carefully with the paperweights, these accumulated trinkets of his past, restoring some semblance of order before he reopened the window.

Chantelle burst in without knocking, a clanging high-speed train.

"Sure, come on in," Jacob called to another, imaginary Chantelle who stood patiently at the door, awaiting permission.

"Well," she said, stretching the word like a rubber band that might snap back against flesh.

"Well what?" Jacob said. "What's up? How was San Francisco?"

"Don't 'How was San Francisco?' me. Don't play innocent."

"I'm afraid I have to," he said, "because I am."

Chantelle made a sucking sound with her teeth. "There isn't something you want to tell me?"

"I don't think so."

"Great. Luis you can tell. Luis who you don't even know. But not me?"

"Oh, that?" Jacob chuckled. It was true; he barely knew Luis, the new design manager. But the story had slipped out at the coffee machine Monday morning. He'd had to tell *somebody*.

"Chantelle," he said, "believe me, if you'd been here you would have been the first to know. How was I supposed to tell you when you've been on the West Coast all week?"

She uncrossed her arms and sat down with an exaggerated, sullen huff. "Ever hear of the phone? You could have found out what hotel I was in."

Jacob geared up to defend himself, but then realized she had a point. After last fall's blowup about the trip to Israel, he had promised not to keep anything from her.

"I'm sorry," he said. "You're right. You are absolutely right."

Now Chantelle's grim demeanor cracked. Air sputtered through her lips, the sound of a kid blowing bubbles in a glass of milk.

"What?" Jacob said. "What's so funny?"

Chantelle wiped her eyes. "You. I love it when you're contrite. Did you really think I was serious?" She lifted a plastic New Orleans street scene and shook it, blanketing the tiny Streetcar Named Desire with artificial snow. "I see the tchotchke collection has reappeared," she said.

Jacob snorted, still angry at her manipulation. "Don't think you can get on my good side just by talking Jew talk," he said.

"Hey, sure. Shoot me down for trying to respect your heritage. See if I care." Chantelle curled her shoulders in a shrug of detached confidence. She joggled the souvenir again.

Jacob couldn't stand it when she pretended not to need him. He tossed a rubber eraser playfully in her direction. "So, you want to hear it," he said, "or are you just going to inflict perpetual blizzard on those poor citizens of New Orleans?"

Chantelle smiled and set down the paperweight. "You're really gonna tell? This is so exciting. Should I be sitting down?"

Jacob winked and reminded her that she was.

He rarely went clubbing, even when Marty had been around to make it fun. Since Israel, he hadn't ventured out once. But something had inspired him. Some spring itch. Some need to be reminded that this other world did exist.

Bobby's was the club of choice on Saturdays because it was eighteen-and-over, which meant the college boys could all get in legally. And for some reason—maybe its location, virtually underneath the expressway—the place also seemed to attract the working-class kids from north of Boston, from towns with butch names like Saugus and Revere.

Jacob approached the door with hand on wallet, ready to show ID, but the bouncer didn't even ask. He seized Jacob's wrist and brusquely snapped on the yellow plastic bracelet that designated him old enough to order alcohol. Jacob imagined it a biologist's tag, used to track some lumbering endangered species.

He bought a Rolling Rock and climbed the stairs to the narrow balcony. The walkway was packed shoulder-to-shoulder with lean and hungry men blatantly scoping the dancers below. It made him think of those fish tanks in Chinese restaurants, where you could pick which sea bass or lobster you wanted to see minutes later on your plate: No, not that one. *That* one.

Jacob claimed a spot among the dejected and vulturous, and gloomily swigged his beer. If he could recognize that other guys, too, were in his position—pathetically alone, hoping for any stranger's slight smile of acknowledgment—why was he always so sure *he* was the most desperate? But he *was* different from the other men. Even if they stood with him now on the fringes, their exclusion was only temporary. They were enjoying brief pit stops from the frenzied sexual race, refueling, tightening their tires.

He, on the other hand, had never even learned to drive. He felt as though he had missed some crucial orientation. Where had he been the day everyone was taught what kind of jeans to buy; how to tuck in their T-shirts properly, or when not to; the way to dance with their arms in the air without looking like Richard Simmons leading an aerobics class?

Jacob knew none of these things. He was congenitally, terminally unhip. And he understood that being so clueless at twenty-four was far worse a crime than simply being too old. The legitimately older men who showed up at a place like Bobby's—lurching on the dance floor to a different decade's beat—were largely forgiven their unseemly style. But Jacob had no excuse.

There were four of them: two with dark hair, a redhead, and a blond. All four had stripped their T-shirts and hooked them into the waists of their acid-washed jeans, exposing hairless torsos that gleamed in the pulsing strobe. They danced as a single creature—chest against back against chest against back—a writhing octopus of tender flesh.

But the redhead stood out. At first Jacob thought the familiarity a trick of his media-saturated mind; the kid looked like the rising class of models, boys who three years ago might have been dismissed as twiggy and gawking, but now were prized for their waifishness. Then he recognized the resemblance to Marty. It wasn't in specific features; the kid's size and coloring weren't even close. But there was something in his carriage, the same loosely angled elbows that created space for himself without pushing others away.

The redhead and his three friends continued their collective dance. There was kissing; there was grinding of hips. Occasionally hands disappeared from view and Jacob heard high-pitched laughter. They were drunk, but not on alcohol, on youth and pure energy.

Fantasies whirled: The four were suitemates in a freshman dorm at Northeastern, all queer by some stroke of serendipity. Or they were childhood buddies from Methuen, Boy Scouts from the same troop who had just realized they had *this* in common, too.

Why was he so attracted to boys this young? The armchair analysts would say he wanted them because he really wanted to *be* them. And yes, Jacob did want to be that young again. But he wanted to be a boy precisely so he could fall in love with other boys, with no awkward age difference, no accusations of cradle robbing.

Watching the four friends, Jacob was caught in a vortex of admiration and regret. How could he not be thrilled to see them, so uninhibited, reveling in the intoxication of queerness? This was the payoff for all the Coming Out Day rallies, the marches, the letters to the editor. But the sight also filled his mouth with the gritty taste of jealousy. He was not so much older than they were—really just four or five years—but still there was this unbridgeable gulf. He felt as though he had helped to build a house and then was barred from living inside.

He drained the last, foamy mouthful of beer, the liquid bitter as it trickled down his throat. It wasn't healthy to torture himself, ogling these aloof Adonises. He should go home to his porn magazines; at least those boys stared back.

Balancing the empty bottle on the balcony railing, he peered over for a final glimpse. It was then that he felt the eyes. Amid the sea of bobbing heads, one face was upturned. The redhead's.

The boy's unblinking stare so startled him that Jacob forgot his shyness. He kept looking; leaked a goofy, unpracticed smile.

The boy's face was sharp even in the smoke-filled room: the ski-jump nose, the high cheekbones, the peach pit of muscle at the corner of his jaw. Then the jaw moved. The kid was mouthing something. Jacob missed it the first time; he squinted for a better view.

When he understood the words, their complete and utter meanness, his chest felt like a tin can being crushed.

"Go blow," the guy had said.

Jacob pushed along the crowded balcony, kicking empties from his path. He stepped on people's heels without apology. How could he have believed this perfect boy might have wanted him?

At the bottom of the stairs, the boy was waiting. Jacob stopped, thought to retreat, but remembered there was only this single exit.

"Don't you like me?" the boy said.

Jacob felt the edge of sarcasm like a cold blade on his neck.

"If you don't like me, then why were you staring?"

"I wasn't—" Jacob's voice broke unattractively. "Of course I like you. You're cute, okay? Do I have to say it?"

"Then why are you running away?" The redhead reached out and touched Jacob's chest, just beneath the heart. "I don't get it. As soon as I said 'Don't go,' you bolted."

When Jacob explained the misunderstanding, the laugh they shared turned into a hug and then a long, tickling kiss. He would have sworn the boy's tongue touched the inside of his Adam's apple. Only when the coat-check guy and the doorman began to applaud did they pull apart.

His name was Danny. He lived with his mother in Wilmington, halfway to the New Hampshire border. He was even more perfect up close.

They decided to dance. Danny was as wild as he had been with his friends. He flung himself at Jacob, pressing his chest until the outside of Jacob's shirt was stained with sweat. He twirled on tip-toes, his sneakers squealing. And somehow his movement became Jacob's movement, until Jacob's own legs were churning, his arms flailing in the air. He hadn't done this in so long.

Danny squatted to the floor like a Russian peasant dancing, and nudged his face into Jacob's crotch. Jacob looked around, expecting somebody to stop them. But they were invisible in the crushing crowd. Danny bit the waistband of Jacob's pants. He yanked like a terrier on a rag, made playful growling sounds.

When he stood back up, Danny slipped his hands into Jacob's jeans. Jacob felt the shocking heat of another person's skin on his own. He felt the squeeze of fingers that, instead of constricting him, made him swell larger. He imagined he might swell forever and float away.

It wasn't just that Danny was so beautiful. It wasn't even that this flawless boy had chosen him, not the other way around. There was simply a shimmering perfection to the moment, a throbbing eureka sense that dwarfed any explanation. Jacob felt a tug toward completion, as palpable as the pull of an unseen fish on a line, a hidden reward that you know will soon break the surface and sparkle in the brilliant sun.

There was still an hour until closing, but already they wanted to be alone. Danny said goodbye to his friends and pulled his T-shirt over his damp torso. He and Jacob walked out, past the smirking bouncer, into the chilled night air.

They paused, balancing on the curb's edge, still breathing heavily from the dancing and the rush of attraction. Jacob studied Danny in the street lamp's light. His wan complexion, now flushed to the thin pink of pulled bubble gum, induced a warm, almost maternal feeling. Jacob wanted to cook healthy food for Danny, to buy him vitamins. He wanted to make sure he dressed warmly enough.

Danny widened his green eyes, daring Jacob to make the next move. Jacob looked down, intimidated, and staring at his own hands, noticed the yellow bracelet still fastened around his wrist. The plastic stuck to his sweaty skin.

"Well," he said, "I guess it doesn't matter anymore that I'm over twenty-one." He ripped the band with a sharp jerk and tossed it into a nearby trash can.

Danny hiccuped a laugh. He pulled a wallet from his back pocket and slid out a driver's license. "Well," he said, wetting his thumb and rubbing it on the lamination. "I guess I don't have to pretend anymore I'm eighteen."

Jacob couldn't think of anything to do except kiss Danny, a reward for his audacity. He reached for Danny's hand and they walked together bravely to hail a taxi home.

"Seventeen, Chantelle. The kid is *seventeen*." Jacob drumrolled his knuckles on the desk. "It was my total fantasy. He's a senior in high school!"

Chantelle rattled the New Orleans paperweight like a maraca. She kept shaking it, not stopping to let the fake snow settle.

"God," Jacob said, "he's so perfect. This little Irish boy. You should see how smooth his chest is."

Chantelle glared at him. "You're out of control."

"I know," he laughed, "a dirty old man before I even hit twenty-five. Just give me an overcoat and a bag of candy."

Now Chantelle dropped the paperweight. The plastic cracked against the desk. "I'm not kidding," she said. "I think it's sick."

Her words stung like a sucker punch.

"It's not that big a difference," Jacob said. "Seven years."

"Sure, and seven years on the other side of him is a ten-year-old." Chantelle's eyes narrowed to sallow slits. "Aside from the fact that it's probably illegal, I just think it's screwed up to have sex with someone who isn't even through with puberty."

Jacob sank in his chair. How had they avoided this argument until now? Was it only because this was the first time he'd fulfilled his attraction?

Now he recalled Chantelle storming from a meeting once, when another editor had presented a manuscript on "reclaiming the Greek boy-love tradition." He considered the fact that she never spoke in detail about her father, or why she ran away from him.

"It's not like I'm molesting him," he said. "I mean, Danny was in the club. If he's mature enough to find his way to Bobby's, don't you think he can decide if he wants to have sex?"

Chantelle set her jaw. She brushed the side of her head, where the lightning bolt of gray slashed through the tight black curls.

"Anyway," Jacob said, "it's not about sex. I mean, the sex was great, I'm not denying it. But there's something else. It's like, I don't know, an older brother/younger brother kind of thing."

"Oh, great," Chantelle said. "That's just what you need. Don't you have enough problems with your *real* brother?"

"Fuck you. That's not fair. You know what I mean. Here's this kid—in high school—and he's already over all that idiotic self-hating shit. I mean, I was only a couple of years older when I came out, but somehow it's totally different. He didn't go to some gay students' association, or some coming-out support group. He's just *out there*. It's who he is.

"He told me he wants to go down to the March on Washington. Can you believe that? I grew up a mile outside of D.C., and when I was seventeen I hadn't even heard of a gay rights march. It's perfect, because I was dreading the thought of going alone. I mean, bringing down Marty's panel and everything. And since you have to be at your sister's wedding."

Chantelle stared off through the window, her only movement the flaring of her nostrils with each measured breath.

Jacob picked up the pink triangle paperweight from a stack of memos. He knocked it like a gavel against his desk.

"Maybe I'm crazy," he said, "but I thought there was a *tiny* chance you'd be happy for me. You know I haven't gone out in ages, and I've barely ever managed to have a second date, let alone a boyfriend. Well, somebody finally liked me! I was hoping maybe you'd want to meet him."

Jacob replaced the paperweight. "But . . . I guess . . ."

Chantelle turned to him. "Jake, you know I want you to be happy."

He curled his lip dubiously.

"Honey, you know I do. And I would go with you to D.C. if it was anything except Sherry's wedding. I would give anything to be there." She took Jacob's hand, rubbing it with her lotioned fingers. "I'm sorry for coming down so hard, all right? This stuff just freaks me out. It's about me, not you."

Jacob was mollified. "Danny really is cute," he said. "Ultra-cute. Marty would have adored him."

"I'm sure he would have."

"Actually, he kind of reminds me of Marty. You know that way he could make you feel better just because he was there? Just the way he stood with his shoulders back and smiled? I swear Danny has that, too. People are going to be all over him in Washington."

"Well, can I ask?" Chantelle said. "I mean, what's up with Marty's panel? It's less than four weeks away."

Having missed the Quilt display in October, Jacob had vowed to finish Marty's memorial for the next showing, at the march. But here it was, April, and they hadn't started.

"I never should have asked his parents," he said.

"What? I thought they were supposed to be pretty cool."

"Chantelle, these people! I went there last week, okay? Mr. Bergman's really nice. Asks me what I think we should do. So I give my spiel about how it should be things from Marty's life, things that represent him. He and Mrs. Bergman love it. I'm Einstein or something for having such a good idea. They ask me what specifically I have in mind.

"I was good. I didn't even mention the cock ring, or the nipple clamps. I suggested things like his ACTUP T-shirt, photos of him with his first boyfriend, that pink boa he always wore on Halloween. Things that were *him*, right? Well, Mr. and Mrs. Bergman are just staring at each other. Finally Mr. Bergman says, 'I don't know, Jacob. It all seems a little, well, private. Do you understand what I'm saying?'

"Yeah, sure. I know that code. What do they think? I mean, their son is going to be in the AIDS Fucking Memorial Quilt, and he did not have hemophilia, and he did not shoot drugs. I hate to tell them, but people are going to guess he was a homosexual."

Chantelle shook her head. "Have these people heard of therapy?"

"Anyway, I ended up just leaving. If they want to make their own panel, fine. There's nothing that says a person can't have more than one. But I wasn't in the mood to hear any more of that crap. It started to weird me out about my own test and stuff."

Chantelle bit her lip. "Oh, shit, I totally forgot. Have you made the appointment yet?"

Jacob glanced at the small clock on the corner of his desk. "Yup," he said. "In just about an hour they'll be taking my blood."

"No way. Today?"

"Yeah, I figured it was perfect. April Fools' and all."

"Oh my God. It is, isn't it?"

"Uh-huh. One of life's little ironies."

Chantelle leaned back in her chair. "Well," she said, "I guess it is appropriate. You know how people say God sent AIDS as a punishment? Bullshit. I think God—if there is such a thing—sent it as a total prank. When you were a kid, did you ever feed your dog peanut butter, just to watch him go nutso licking the roof of his mouth? *That's* AIDS. I think God gets off on seeing how crazy we get trying to deal with this shit."

Jacob flailed his tongue, imitating a frustrated dog. He barked pathetic whimpers, grotesquely rolled his eyes.

"Don't do that," Chantelle howled. "That's horrible."

"It was *your* analogy," he said, adding a final epileptic waggle of his tongue. "Anyway, I'm trying not to get too worked up about it. At this point there's nothing I can do."

He got up and began gathering papers into his backpack. "I better get going," he said. "I want to stop off at my apartment first before I go over to the Fenway."

He stabbed numbers into his phone, forwarding calls to the receptionist. He hauled the window shut.

Chantelle approached. She cupped a warm, silky hand around his neck. "Are you gonna be okay? You want me to go with you?"

"No, thanks. It's really all right. I just have to go through with this."

Chantelle pecked him on the cheek. "You'll be fine," she whispered. "I know you will."

"The good thing," Jacob said, "is I decided that I deserve a treat for doing this. You know, like the lollipop after you see the doctor? So Danny and I are meeting for dinner."

"You're actually seeing this boy again? It *is* serious."

"I told you," he said, flipping off the light. "I think this is really something. I'm not sure what. But something."

Jacob grabbed his mail—a bill from Boston Edison, a coupon Val-U Pak, the latest *Advocate*—and climbed the three flights of stairs. The hallway smelled sweetly burned, like chili powder. The yuppies in 4-A must have moved on to Mexican, he thought. He'd already endured a month of curry odor, and before that, the lemony sting of Thai cuisine.

He undid both locks and stepped into his own more familiar dirty laundry/dusty books scent. The studio was nothing to be proud of. One wall was dominated by the hulking swaybacked couch he had found on the sidewalk last spring, so much stuffing leaked from its pillows that the plaid covering sagged like an old woman's skin. Clichéd art prints were thumbtacked to the walls: van Gogh flowers, a bluish Matisse. The newest addition was the touch that maybe saved the place. It was a doctored poster of Bill Clinton and Al Gore, naked, pretzeled in a tantalizing almost-sixty-nine. Jacob had stolen it from the dumpster of a nearby dance club in January, after their Inaugural Ball. For some reason, having the leaders of the free world hanging on his wall, engaged in a carnal act, made the place start to feel like home.

He had moved to Park Drive a year ago, after eighteen dreary months in Somerville. It was more money and less space than any other place he'd lived, but he liked being closer to the heart of things. He gained comfort from the constant background noise: the hum of traffic on Boylston Street and, in summer, the cheering crowds and molasses-voiced announcer at Fenway Park.

The real selling point was the wide bay window overlooking the Fens. The window's limpid light polished Jacob's meager furnishings until they shone almost like legitimate possessions. It also provided a great view of the men who streamed in and out of the park each evening. Not that Jacob ever had the guts to cruise the infamous reedy labyrinth. But he sat at the window and watched, fancying himself a fortuneteller supervising a crystal ball. He would sight a man headed into the park and concentrate all his energy: *Let him find it,* he would beseech some cosmic force. *Let him find whatever it is he seeks.*

Walking into the apartment, Jacob always faced a moment of dry-throated nervousness—the same anxiety he imagined gymnasts must experience after their routines—as he waited for the answering machine's fickle eye to judge his life. Five winks today: one of his all-time highs. He jabbed the Playback button.

"This is Miller Management, calling to remind you that the exterminator is scheduled to spray tomorrow. If you do not want him to enter your apartment, please leave a note to that effect on your door. Thank you."

A nasal, robotic voice noted the time of the call—8:57 A.M.—and the machine broadcast its admonishing beep. So much for his stellar social life.

The next message was one of those infuriating hang-up calls: three seconds of silence followed by a nasty click. Now he was zero-for-two.

The machine beeped again.

"Hi, it's me. It's Danny."

Ah, the voice. Danny still had that wonderfully vague teenage tone, each word uttered with a tinge of uncertainty, as if he knew his adult voice was out there, somewhere, but he hadn't quite discovered it.

"I've just got a sec before third period, but I wanted to double-check about tonight. Six o'clock at Tower? I'll be right in the lobby. Okay, cool. See you then."

Jacob enjoyed a ticklish warmth, similar to arousal but more mellow, located somewhere higher, maybe his chest. How long had it been since someone had sounded this excited to see him?

"10:03 a.m," droned the machine. Another electronic bleat, and then a strained, unfamiliar man's voice spoke at him.

"I'm trying to reach Jacob Rosenbaum. I'm very sorry to leave a message, but we need to get in touch with you."

Jacob turned up the volume control.

"I tried earlier and didn't have any luck. This is Dr. David Sandler at Beth Israel Hospital. We found your name in your grandmother's address book. When you get this message, please page me as soon as possible at 555-4232, or if you can, come directly to the hospital. Thank you."

Four. Or was it five? How many hours ahead was London?

This was the first thought that came, and it filled Jacob's mind like concrete. His parents were in London, at a conference, his father delivering some research paper. Jacob needed to figure the time difference. Maybe he had an old atlas somewhere.

Then he remembered that he didn't even know their hotel. How could he possibly get in touch with them?

The end-of-message announcement croaked that the doctor had called at 11:17. Nana Jenny had been there almost all day.

Jacob dashed into the bedroom, driven by the conviction that something vital was there, but then he couldn't think of what it was. He turned around. He checked the window's lock. He had no idea what he was doing.

Then he saw the nightstand's photograph of him and Jonathan as kids on the giant dinosaur. Israel was seven hours ahead. He had the yeshiva's number. He knew Jonathan would be there.

Jacob approached the phone but didn't lift it. It had been six months since they'd spoken. He couldn't.

He returned to the front hall and removed a windbreaker from the closet. As he reached the door he heard the end of the fifth and final message. It was the recording that came on when a caller hung up too soon, and the machine malfunctioned: "If you would like to place a call, please hang up and try again. If you need help, hang up and then dial the operator."

Help, he thought. Yes, I need help.

The operator's voice cut off abruptly and the machine blared with the industrial tone of an alarm.

Jacob hadn't been to a hospital since Marty. He'd forgotten the defeated look that shadowed everyone in such a place. Even the parking attendants appeared weary and grim.

He thought he was fine until he passed a bouquet of irises awaiting delivery to a patient's bedside. Their overripe breath gagged him with the memory of Marty's room: a glut of cheery floral arrangements mocking his imminent death, their scent too weak to mask the stench of his rotting guts.

Breath quavery, he approached the front desk. The gray-haired receptionist told him to try floor eight. She pointed a wattled arm in the direction of the elevator.

As the small cage lurched up on its cables, Jacob paced. What would Nana Jenny look like? What if there had been a disfiguring accident? Trying not to think about it, he read the brass plaque above the grid of numbered bubbles: *This elevator the gift of S. Robert Stone and children in honor of Clare S. Stone.*

He thought: This is what happens when people die. They become names—etched into plaques and headstones, sewn onto sprawling quilts. What was the alternative? To hold a person only in your memory, where she would fade like the inscription on an heirloom photograph, labeling some relative no one could recognize?

Jacob fought the image of Nana Jenny as a name trapped in cold brass letters. "Not yet," he whispered. "Please, not yet."

At first he thought the man was just another orderly. Then he read the nametag. Dr. Sandler looked far too young to be a doctor. His blond hair lolled in an unkempt mop. It was unclear how much of his jaw, if any, he had to shave.

"You got the message," the doctor said. His thin lips were the same pale color as the surrounding skin, so that his mouth fell into his face, an unexpected hole. "We tried a few of the numbers in your grandmother's address book, but we just got machines everywhere."

"My parents are out of the country," Jacob explained.

"So you're the next of kin for now."

The inevitability in Dr. Sandler's tone startled Jacob. He wanted some choice in the matter, the way airplane passengers are allowed to switch out of an emergency exit row if they're not prepared for the responsibility. "I guess," he said. "I mean, until my parents can come."

"Then it would be helpful," the doctor said, "if you gave us some more complete information. Are you in school?"

"No," Jacob said. "I work. Downtown near Government Center."

"Oh." Dr. Sandler looked perplexed. "Your grandmother didn't seem to have a work number for you."

Jacob flinched. Of course she didn't have a number. He still hadn't told her anything beyond the most veiled facts: a publishing company, sub-rights and publicity. He still hadn't told her anything about his life.

After Coming Out Day, he had expected everything to change. Dozens of people called him, praising his bravery. But from Nana Jenny, nothing. Maybe she had missed the TV coverage, he told himself. The interview had aired on the eleven o'clock news, and maybe by then she was already in bed. Or maybe she tuned in to a channel other than WBZ. But wouldn't one of her friends have seen?

The lack of response was unbearable, and so, like the cold war with Jonathan, Jacob stashed it away, willing himself to ignore it. He, too, said not a thing.

Now he choked on the consequences of his inaction. "How is she?" he blurted. "You haven't even said what happened."

Dr. Sandler shifted his knobby shoulders, on which his white coat drooped apologetically. "I'm sorry. I know it's hard walking into the middle of things. Your grandmother . . . this morning your grandmother suffered a stroke."

Jacob winced against the word, against the horrifying image it brought to mind. He remembered his junior-high baseball coach, encouraging a well-hit line drive: "Really stroke this one. Stroke it hard. Smash it to bits."

"Where did it happen?" he asked. "How did she get here?"

"Apparently it happened in a market. She was very fortunate that someone saw her losing her balance and caught her before she could hit the floor. They called the ambulance right away."

"But she's okay now?" Jacob said. "A stroke happens quickly, right? It's over in just, like, a second?"

Dr. Sandler brushed a loose strand of hair from his forehead. "Listen, I'm not going to give you false hopes. This was a massive stroke. We can't know yet what her prospects are. The only thing to do right now is wait."

Jacob shuddered. He had heard these words before. It was what Marty's doctor had said after his last bout of seizures. Marty had died two days later.

Dr. Sandler placed a hand on Jacob's shoulder, urging him down the hall. "Why don't you go see her?" he said. "She's still not responsive, but she's stable now."

*   *   *

It wasn't the machinery: the oxygen tubes stuffed in her nose, the IV pole hovering like a gallows, all the complicated sterility that mobbed the room. Jacob had seen enough of these things during Marty's vigil. He had expected this.

What stopped him in the doorway was the simple sight of Nana Jenny on her back. It hadn't occurred to him until this moment that he had never seen his grandmother in bed. Even the time he stayed with her on Cape Cod, she had always woken before he did, was well into her day's routine when he emerged for breakfast.

Jacob couldn't believe how small she was. Her legs were pressed together, her arms locked against her sides, as if she worried about hogging too much room. Her weight was so negligible that her body didn't even bend an impression into the mattress. Her tiny mouth, usually cinched in its anxious knot, was slack; her lips parted as if she had been on the verge of saying something, then thought better of it.

Jacob forced himself to walk to her. She had been alone all day, touched only by the cold hands of strangers. He wanted to lend his body heat to the air around her. He wanted her to know he had come.

He knelt to put his face at her level. The oxygen tubes hissed. His own breath was deafening in his skull.

He reached two fingers to his grandmother's cheek. He had always been fascinated by the dark brown mole on her jawline, by the three hairs that sprouted from it like an insect's outsized antennae. As a boy, five years old, he had pointed and asked, "Why do you have this?" He had meant only for Nana Jenny to explain the physical phenomenon, the curious growth absent from his own face, but her answer was philosophical. "It's to remind me," she said, "that I must always reconcile with my blemishes."

Jacob fingered the mole, embarrassed to be touching her when she was so defenseless. The bump of skin was damp and rubbery, the hairs stiff as wire. He wondered if the growth had nerve endings, if Nana Jenny could feel pain or tenderness.

He stroked the mole again, but she remained deep in her hollow of unconsciousness. Jacob moved his hand away, brushed his fingers on the thin hospital sheet. He had never fathomed why people would talk to a comatose body. What was the point of a confession that couldn't be heard? But now he understood the impulse. He wanted the chance to reconcile with his blemishes.

"You should know . . ." he began.

But when the words hit air they crystallized with a sudden and different clarity, like photographic paper exposed to light. Jacob repeated the line in his head. *You* should know. You *should* know. *You should have known.*

A spasm tore through his arm, an ugly urge to do violence. He thought of digging his fingernails into Nana Jenny's wrinkled face, gouging out the mole, drawing blood. He wanted to do something to make her feel his presence, to feel him as a person with desires and fears and beauty marks of his own. Wake up, he wanted to shout. Wake up. This is *me.*

The anger retreated as quickly as it had come, condensing into a hard pit in Jacob's core. And then he knew, in the absolute way you can know things in the shape of the organs within your chest, that this would not be how it ended. Nana Jenny would not die without at least one more chance.

He relaxed his limbs, slowed his breathing to normal. There was business to be done, he reminded himself. Papers to sign, insurance forms. His parents still had to be tracked down.

But he let himself linger. He would be ashamed to admit it, but he liked being the only one with Nana Jenny, the first on the scene. It felt important to sit here, just the two of them, breathing. Just two people connected by blood and love and frustration, performing the basic act of staying alive.

Jacob perceived the woman's presence before he heard her, sensed it as a shift in the air pressure of the room. He felt himself come under a shadow that had nothing to do with light or lack of it, but with gravity and breath and emotion.

"I came as quickly as I could," the woman said.

Jacob stood as if to protect himself. She must have been in her sixties, but everything about her seemed younger, the kind of woman you would see carrying a placard at a protest march and think: Good for you. Her short silver hair leapt from her scalp in energetic spikes. Hoops of metal dangled from her ears, glinting in the room's fluorescence. She was probably Jacob's height, but stood so much straighter that she gained two or three inches.

The woman set down a large shoulder bag. "The message said they couldn't reach any of you on the East Coast. They were just getting answering machines. I got on the first nonstop."

She took a single step closer. Jacob could see her eyes clearly now, penetrating blue scarred with white imperfections.

"How is she? Is she all right?" The woman started to move forward again.

Jacob reached for Nana Jenny's bed. "Who are you?" he asked, gripping the guardrail.

"Ingrid," she said. She touched her cheek as if to prove she was real. "I'm your Aunt Ingrid."

Once Those Are Gone

Jacob never planned an entire collection. It began, as most obsessions, with just one that caught his eye, a single possibility so compelling that it taught him how much more to want.

It was a Saturday, early in the summer before he turned thirteen. His mother went shopping at the Bethesda Farm Women's Market and asked him to accompany her. The building bustled with activity. Voices bargained, calling out prices and weights. The caramelized aroma of homemade berry pies mingled with the savor of smoked meat.

Jacob followed from booth to booth as his mother tested the plumpness of tomatoes, scrutinized free-range eggs. At first it was fun compared to the sterile supermarket where they usually shopped. But after a while each stall blurred into the next. The vendors were too aggressive; the noise got to him. He told his mother he wanted to browse in the flea market out front.

Most of the stuff was junk. Water-stained paperback romances spilled from cardboard boxes. A battered mannequin was festooned with costume jewelry: diamond earrings like strings of rock candy, a necklace bulging with pearls the size of grapes. At one table, a wizened man sold Washington Redskins glasses for two bucks each, even though you could get them free at the Exxon station across the street every time you purchased five gallons of gas.

Jacob roamed until he reached the last stall. Nobody seemed in charge, just an empty director's chair behind the listing card table.

The stuff here was mostly trash, too, delaminating jigsaw puzzles and plastic cups with spiderwebby cracks. But a ratty cigar box drew his attention. There was something about the mustached man on its cover, the blue-gray curls of smoke that wreathed his head. Jacob looked around guiltily, as though he were about to read someone else's mail. Then he opened the box.

Judging by the subjects' clothes and the smoky fading colors, the photographs were at least fifty years old. Some of them must have been a hundred. The one on top showed a girl of six or seven astride a wooden rocking horse. The girl and horse were blurry against the sharper background of stately bookshelves. But within the unfocused oval of her face, the smile was unmistakable.

Another shot depicted three women in Adirondack chairs on the shore of a waveless lake, grimly staring at the camera. Below that: a photo of two men on a giant redwood stump, axes tipped on their shoulders as casually as baseball bats.

But the snapshot that sucked the air from Jacob's chest was the one of a dark-haired boy standing alone. The boy was young—he couldn't have been more than a year older than Jacob—but he wore a neatly creased three-piece suit. A bowler tilted optimistically on his head. In each hand, he held a bulging suitcase.

The boy's expression was one of restrained eagerness. He gazed into the camera, but his eyes were focused somewhere beyond. Jacob wanted to know where the boy was going, who he would become once he got there. He wanted to know why nobody had bothered to keep this photograph.

He had heard people discuss what they would rescue if their houses ever caught on fire. "Take the photos," they all agreed. "Everything else you can replace. But once those are gone . . ." His friends' houses were filled with antique pictures. Stern matriarchs holding blanket-swaddled babies. Great-uncles in military uniforms, their pants billowing from high-laced boots.

But at the Rosenbaums', there was nothing to save in an emergency. No cracking sepia snapshots, no family albums. Jacob's mother might have had photos of her parents, the grandparents who died before he was born. But he wouldn't have recognized these people if he saw them, and so the desire did not occur. It was his father's side that he knew just enough about to crave more.

Beyond Papa Isaac and Nana Jenny, what was there? Where did he come from? The house's blank walls offered no clues.

"You like that one?"

A heavy, gray-haired woman, her face as puffy and white as Wonder Bread, plopped herself in the director's chair. She winked at Jacob. Or maybe it was a tic.

"Yes," he said, quickly replacing the photograph in the box.

"Me too," she said. "You get the feeling, I don't know, that he's not quite sure if whatever's about to happen is really about to happen. Like, is this really his life?"

Jacob glanced again at the photo, trying to agree, but he detected something more confident in the angle of the boy's chin. And in how the suitcases, though they must have weighed a ton, didn't seem to strain his arms.

"What do you think?" the woman asked. "What's the story?"

"I think he's ready." Jacob's voice came out breathless, sharp with certainty. "I think he's excited. You know, about leaving. But maybe he's trying not to look *too* excited, so his parents, or whoever's taking the picture, so they won't be hurt."

The woman smiled and let out a knowing hiss of air. "I guess you can understand a guy like that?"

"I guess," Jacob said.

She leaned back, the canvas chair squeaking against its wooden frame. "Well, better take it, then."

Jacob perked with an impulse buyer's adrenaline thrill. Yes, he thought. This could be mine. But the feeling caved in on itself. He stared at the ground. "I don't have any money."

The woman nodded, jiggling the pallid skin below her jaw. "The important thing," she said, "with these old pictures? Is for somebody to remember them. To remember the people that maybe other people have forgot. If you promise to do that, you can have it."

Just then Jacob's mother called from the market's door. "Use some help with the bags, honey. It's at least two trips."

"Okay," Jacob yelled, but he didn't turn. He bent to the table, almost close enough to kiss the fat woman. "I promise," he whispered. "I will."

She took his hand, stroked it as a fortuneteller might. Then she placed the photograph face-up in his palm and closed his fingers around the edges of the ancient print.

*   *   *

That night, Jacob propped the photo on the table by his bed and told himself the story of the suitcase boy.

His name was Adam, Jacob decided. Cousin Adam from Germany. He was the oldest boy and the smartest, and so his parents had used all their savings to book him passage to New York. There was good-paying work there, they had heard, even for a boy so young. All the way across the ocean for a new start, and when he had established himself he would send for the rest of them.

But Cousin Adam would meet a friend on the ship, another boy, three years older, blond and tall. This boy's parents were sending him to New York, too—or so they thought—but he was going to California instead. You could make a fortune, he told Cousin Adam. Gold and silver and cattle. And so Adam, too, would forget about New York. He would travel west with his new friend. They would get rich and build houses next to each other on the side of a steeply sloping hill. They'd get married and raise their families together, nine kids for each, enough for two baseball teams.

Maybe the houses were still standing, Jacob imagined. Maybe the families were still living there. Somewhere out in California he had relatives, a whole branch of his family that didn't even know he existed.

People always talked about family trees. The word for "tree" was even right in Jacob's own name: Rosen*baum*. He had learned what the German meant in fifth grade, when they sang "O Tannenbaum" for the holiday pageant, and Mrs. Marshall pointed out the similarity. But when Jacob tried once to draw the branches of the Rosenbaums, starting at the edge of a large sheet of construction paper, the diagram ended up stunted and bare as a Charlie Brown Christmas tree. He decided then that it was the *rosen* part, not the *baum*, that applied to his family. Their genealogy was like the rosebush Nana Jenny had planted in the Cape house's sandy backyard: scrawny and thin, twice as many thorns as blossoms.

Jacob touched the face of the boy in the picture, then brought his finger to his lips. He turned out the light. And as he slipped into sleep, he thought of his promise to the flea-market woman. I will remember you, he murmured to the photograph, now barely visible in the darkened room. I will never forget.

*   *   *

The next Saturday Jacob returned to the Farm Women's Market. This time he brought his allowance money. He paid the woman three dollars and fifty cents for two more photos: one he hadn't seen the week before, a snapshot of a matron knitting in a sun-drenched garden; the second, the picture of the girl on the rocking horse.

At home that night, he wrote on the back of the first print: "Great Aunt Ruth making baby blanket for Cousin Adam." And on the reverse of the second: "Adam's youngest girl, Cecily, sixth birthday present." He placed the new photos on the nightstand, next to the picture of Adam and the suitcases.

Jacob made a list of other flea markets. He scoured the classifieds and the Safeway bulletin board for notices of estate liquidations. He read yard-sale announcements taped to telephone poles. On weekends he made his mother drive him around the back roads of Montgomery County, stopping the car whenever they passed a sign advertising ANTIQUES AND COLLECTIBLES.

Almost immediately, the collection outgrew his nightstand. When it consumed Jacob's desk as well, he had to start doing his homework on the dining-room table. For a while he displayed the photographs in plastic frames. Then he bought an album with a red velvet cover and reverently filled every page.

He identified the back of each snapshot with a name and brief description. Sometimes he estimated a date. In a separate spiral notebook he charted their relationships: the marriages, the births, all the convoluted twists of a sprawling bloodline.

Jacob's father complained about the dining-room mess. Why couldn't Jacob still do his homework in his bedroom the way Jonathan did? He fumed about the unhealthiness of a boy spending so much time in a fantasy world. He threatened to curtail Jacob's allowance.

"At least they're not centerfolds," his mother defended. "They're historical. He's learning a lot."

"Tell you the truth," his father said, "I kind of wish they *were* centerfolds. Wouldn't that be a bit more natural?"

His parents didn't realize how well sound traveled through the heating vents, transmitting their conversations in the den like soft radio music up to Jacob's bedroom. He sat paging through his album, listening to the argument, wondering how they could comprehend so little about him. Even his mother had no idea what the photographs really meant.

The only one who understood was Nana Jenny. She and Papa Isaac visited Chevy Chase that September for his and Jonathan's bar mitzvahs. The night after the celebration, the last before they would return to Brookline, his grandmother knocked on Jacob's door. Already in bed, he told her it was okay. She padded into the room and, without saying anything, found the velvet-covered album on the desk. She turned the pages, bringing certain snapshots close to her face. Then she came and sat softly on the bed.

"Your father told me about your collection," she said. "It's even larger than I imagined."

Jacob wondered what his father had said. Had he dispatched her here to convince him there was something wrong with his hobby? "I found them all myself," he said. "I paid for them with my own allowance."

"Yes," she said. "I know." She removed a small envelope from her jacket pocket and laid it next to Jacob's pillow. "I thought maybe I could help. A little bar mitzvah gift."

Jacob was confused. His grandparents had already given him and Jonathan their presents: a set of tefillin and a $1,000 Israel bond for each.

"It's just something I found," Nana Jenny said. Her hand lingered on the envelope; Jacob thought he saw a tremor in her fingers. "You don't have to tell your parents. Or Papa Isaac."

She let go and her hand drifted to her left temple. As if trying to recall the answer to an old riddle, she tapped four quick times. Then she left before Jacob could thank her.

Inside the envelope was a single black-and-white photograph. One corner was dog-eared, almost ripped off. A yellow stain covered the bottom third like the dampness of a receded tide on sand. The picture showed a woman kneeling next to a young girl, maybe four or five, who wore a frilly lace dress and a large bow in her hair. The woman was beautiful in the manner of a silent-movie actress, the line of her nose sharp, her eyebrows and lips precise as if painted on, although it was clear she wasn't wearing any makeup. The woman was more glamorous than anyone Jacob could have known, yet there was something familiar about her. A nervous pinch in the smile, a slight squinting of the eyes.

A story began to form about who the woman and her daughter were. The girl's name was something old-fashioned, Gertrude or Rebecca. She was about to go off to kindergarten for the first time. Jacob knew just where in the album they belonged.

He flipped the picture over to write his description, but there was already an identification. In a flowing script across the photo's upper edge, the ink faded to an almost translucent purple, were the words *mit Ingrid, 1932.*

Connection

In the confusion of rushing to Beth Israel, it hadn't occurred to Jacob that he'd stood Danny up. He was aware of missing his HIV appointment, but only when he returned home and saw the answering machine's frantic blinks did he remember the dinner date.

It was past ten o'clock, but he called anyway. Danny picked up on the second ring. His eager, pliable voice immediately balmed Jacob's weariness.

"I'm so glad you're there," he said. "It's me, Jacob."

No response. Air on the line. TV jingle in the background.

"Danny?" he said. "Are you there?"

The phone slammed with a train-wreck crunch.

"Wait!" Jacob shouted at the receiver, as if the mechanism itself had rejected him. He wished he could plunge his arm into the phone cord, reach up through its winding helix to Wilmington and retrieve his friend.

He hit Redial. There was the jarringly cheery sequence of beeps, then the phone's pulsing trill. Again. Again. Jacob counted the rings: nine, ten, eleven.

Suddenly Danny's voice broke through. "My mom's trying to sleep, all right? Will you quit?"

"Danny, wait," Jacob blurted. "Hold on."

"I don't want to hear it, okay? Goodbye."

"No, please! Danny. Listen."

Jacob braced for another hang-up, but it didn't come. He heard breathing on the line.

"I'm sorry," he said. "I should have tried to call or something. But I can explain, okay? Nana Jenny, my grandmother. I had to go to the hospital. She had a stroke."

Jacob waited. Did he expect an apology? Not an apology, just an acknowledgment. The comfort of another person knowing what he'd been through.

Ten seconds passed. "Danny?" he said. "Did you hear me?"

The line clicked and cut off. Jacob felt himself cut off, too. How could he redeem himself if other people wouldn't hear him? Nana Jenny, deaf in her coma. Jonathan bunkered in Israel. Now this.

Then it made sense that he should lose not just one thing, but everything. Why should he expect otherwise when there was so much he had done wrong?

At five minutes past eleven his buzzer rang. When he opened the door, Danny stood there breathless, T-shirt untucked. His face was different from Jacob's memory, the ruddy confidence replaced with a bruised uncertainty.

"What are you doing here?" Jacob said.

Danny didn't speak. He asked with raised eyebrows if he could come in.

Jacob stepped back and let him enter, but he maintained a wary distance. "You hung up," he said.

"I'm sorry. I couldn't explain on the phone."

"Well, I hope you can now. I think I deserve an explanation."

"I know," Danny said. "I'm just—"

His voice cracked. Jacob heard his youngness, his fragility.

Danny sat on Jacob's futon. "You know how the first night we were together? I told you I live with just my mom?"

How could Jacob forget? They had lain together on this very bed, sharing skin and the promise of so much more. Jacob had thought: This time is different; this is real.

"Well, I didn't really tell you everything." Danny pulled a pillow to his lap and stroked it like a kitten. "I don't normally talk about it. But I can trust you, right?"

Jacob shrugged as if to say, You'll have to take your chances.

"Well, four or five years ago? Five, I guess. I was twelve. We had basketball practice, county league, at night. Afterwards, my dad always picked me up and we'd go for McDonald's.

"So this one night? Practice ends, and I go out front with the other guys. It's freezing, and my hair is like icicles, you know, 'cause of the sweat? You could actually make it make this clicking sound if you shook your head. Anyways, one by one, everyone else's parents show. It's just me and Pete Sculley left. Pete's a total jerk-off, so we didn't even talk. And when Pete's dad comes, he asks me if I need a lift, but I say no thanks, my dad'll be there any minute. He's probably just working late.

"And so I'm waiting there. It's nine-thirty. Ten. Quarter past. I'm starting to really freak. I don't even have a dime to make a phone call. My head's so cold it's killing me.

"Finally Mrs. Taylor, our neighbor, pulls up in her van. She's crying so bad she can barely talk. 'It's your dad,' she says, and I'm like, '*What's* my dad?' And then she just says it: 'He's had a heart attack.'

"I get in, and her heater's on high, so my hair's dripping everywhere. I remember that part because I kept saying, 'I'm sorry. I'm getting everything all wet. I'm really sorry.' By the time we got to the hospital it was too late. I mean, there I am, standing there, waiting and waiting for him to pick me up, and all the time he was already dead."

Jacob sank onto the futon, next to Danny, and cuddled his shoulder. "Oh, God. I left you standing there, too."

"No. It's not your fault, obviously. You had to be with your grandmother. I just still . . . sometimes it still freaks me out."

Jacob pulled Danny to his chest, wrapped his arms around the skinny frame. "It's okay," he whispered into Danny's neck. "It's okay. Don't worry. It's okay."

Nudging into the soft red wisps of Danny's hair, Jacob could smell his sweat, his shirt's dirty collar, like the scent of flannel sheets after sex. He didn't mean to get aroused at a time like this, but he couldn't contain his attraction. It was all one thing: this tenderness, this touching, this security.

They kissed. Jacob covered Danny's mouth entirely with his own. He wanted to breathe for Danny, to take control of his functions. If he could have pumped Danny's heart, he would.

Later, when they had pulled apart, Danny asked, "What about your grandmother? Is she all right?"

And Jacob told him: about her fall in the market, her aloneness, about Ingrid. He told Danny everything, and in the telling it was both much worse and more endurable.

At midnight, he asked if Danny would stay with him.

"I'd love to," he said, "but I can't. I promised my mom I'd be home."

As they kissed goodbye at the door, Jacob thought: Yes, keep your promises while you can.

In the hospital, everything exuded an odd aura of normalcy. Crises erupted, but no one flinched, as if the man in the next room was supposed to have a heart attack at just that certain instant, and the woman down the hall was on schedule when she started vomiting blood. Jacob was aware of the cycles of life thrust into fast forward. A baby was born in one room, and somewhere else, perhaps just a floor or two below, someone died. Incisions were stitched up; new ones were scalpeled open. Health and sickness passed each other in the glistening corridors.

And yet, amid the constant churning, the stasis was unbearable. Nurses changed shifts, but they all looked and talked alike. The IV dripped relentlessly. Time wound its Möbius strip.

Nana Jenny lay exactly as Jacob had first seen her yesterday. Her skin had drained to an unnatural white-bluish tint like Tupperware. Her thin hair was mussed, exposing patches of scalp; she would have been mortified without her hair net. Worst of all was how relaxed she looked, released at last from worrying. The doctor explained it was probably paralysis of the facial muscles, but Jacob knew he saw something more. He wondered—then hated himself for wondering—if Nana Jenny would be better off never regaining her faculties, and with them the agony of consciousness.

When he returned from the nurses' kitchen, Ingrid was sitting in the chair by Nana Jenny's bed, turned to the wall. Jacob couldn't see her face, but he was certain from the way she hunkered into herself that she was sobbing. He stopped short, a wave of coffee sloshing over each styrofoam cup, and started to tiptoe back out. Then Ingrid shifted, and Jacob saw the spiraled phone cord trailing from the bedside stand.

"Let me ask you this," she said, her voice corrosive. "How many papers have you delivered at conferences?"

She paused, shaking her head at the response. She was definitely not crying.

"Mm-hm. And how many mothers have you had?"

Jacob had only been gone long enough to walk down the hall and pour the coffee. Had Ingrid waited for the moment, then phoned his father as soon as he left the room?

"No, Eugene," she said, spitting the syllables like a playground bully's taunt. Jacob bristled. Nobody called his father by his full name except Nana Jenny—and, years ago, Papa Isaac.

"No, I'm just saying that since she is in fact your only mother, I would think you'd want to see her as soon as possible."

A dry bitterness scratched the back of Jacob's throat, the chalky gag of a half-swallowed aspirin. He wanted to steal the phone from Ingrid and tell her not to talk to his father that way. But he couldn't. He'd said the same things himself that morning when he'd finally reached his parents in London.

Jacob hadn't expected his father to cry when he got the news. He hadn't expected an outpouring of emotion. But he had thought his father would at least rise to the occasion of an emergency. Instead, he heard the usual stony disengagement.

His father explained that he was supposed to present his paper Saturday afternoon, after which he and Jacob's mother and a group of other scientists would see a play in the West End. They were scheduled to return Sunday to Washington, then fly to Boston on Monday for the seder. He would see if they could switch flights, he said, and fly directly to Boston. But he was adamant about sticking to Sunday as the return date.

"Jesus, Dad," Jacob had said. "She's your mother."

"Jake, I'm just being practical. Did the doctor say she's stable?"

"Yes," Jacob conceded.

"Did you already tell me there's nothing to do but wait?"

"Yes."

"Then what's the point of getting there twenty-four hours earlier? I've traveled a long way to give this paper."

Jacob couldn't say anything. He pictured the black ocean looming between them.

*   *   *

Jacob wished Ingrid would at least keep her voice down. He had taken to whispering in the room, padding around as he would in a nursery so as not to wake the baby. It made no sense, since he wanted more than anything for Nana Jenny to wake up. But it felt wrong to talk about her in the third person, as if she weren't right there in front of them. What if somehow through her coma she could hear? What if she could hear her own daughter—Jacob had to remind himself periodically who Ingrid was—arguing with her son, just to convince him to visit?

But as much as he wished Ingrid would quiet, Jacob couldn't help admiring her toughness. He liked how she threshed her hands as she debated into the phone, jerked her head in a sturdy *no*—the body language so much a part of her communication that she maintained the display even though his father could not see. Her unself-conscious insistence reminded him of Chantelle.

He still couldn't get used to the idea that this silver-haired woman, in her faded jeans and purple blouse, this stranger yelling at his father, was his relative.

Jacob had learned he had an aunt when he was fourteen, from the last paragraph of Papa Isaac's *Boston Globe* obituary: "Rabbi Rosenbaum is survived by a son, Eugene Rosenbaum of Chevy Chase, Maryland, and his wife, Sarah; by a daughter, Ingrid Rosenbaum-Schiller of Berkeley, California; and by two grandchildren, Jacob and Jonathan Rosenbaum, also of Chevy Chase."

Jacob had reacted with immediate hostility. Who was this person, and why had no one told him about her? Why was her name listed in front of his?

But when he read the name again—*Ingrid*—he remembered the photograph Nana Jenny had given him. He realized that now he had another clue, another shard from which to reconstruct the shattered artifact that was his family. He clipped the obituary and carried it in his wallet like a check to cash.

The promise of a new relative never materialized. Ingrid did not attend the funeral or visit during the shivah. She did not come for Passover to fill Papa Isaac's empty chair. Jacob asked about her, but his father shrugged the questions away. "She was older," he said. "She left when I was a kid." Jacob pressed him again a week later, and his father hinted at hostilities. "She and Papa Isaac disagreed on things. When one person refuses to talk to another, it's not possible to stay in touch." The next day, when Jacob asked for Ingrid's address, his father closed the discussion for good: "Don't try to create something that just isn't there."

This mysterious gift of an aunt remained little more than a line of newsprint, crumpled and fraying in Jacob's wallet.

"Your father wants to talk to you."

Ingrid extended the receiver the way a road-crew boss might hold out a shovel: *Here, take this, get to work.* Jacob traded one cup of coffee for the phone, set the other on the nightstand.

"Dad?" he said.

"Hey, Jake. Just wanted to see how you're holding up."

There was an echo on the long-distance line. His father sounded as though he were imitating the announcer at Fenway Park: "Ladies and gentlemen gentlemen, boys and girls girls, here are today's today's, starting lineups lineups."

"You sound weird," Jacob said. "Everything's repeated."

"I know. It's on this end, too. I was getting a big double dose of your Aunt Ingrid."

"Uh-huh," Jacob said, hoping Ingrid couldn't hear his father's echoing laughter. She had only moved a foot away, and stood over him like a schoolteacher trying to prevent cheating.

"How is it with her?" his father asked.

"Um. Okay, I guess."

"You can't really talk? Is she right there?"

"Yeah."

With the burden of candidness on his father, the conversation stalled. Jacob listened to the blank hiss of the connection, wondering if silence could have an echo.

"Huh," his father said. It came across as *huh huh,* an idiotic chuckle. "I guess I always figured it would take something like this for you to meet her."

"Oh, so you had thought about this?" Jacob said.

"Well, you know. It was bound to happen sometime."

"Great. I'm so glad one of us had prepared. Maybe when you bring yourself to show up here, you can tell me what other little experiments you've been waiting to observe."

"Yeah, um, hold on," his father said. "Here, I think your mother wants to talk."

A thump boomed on the line, a hand over the receiver. Jacob recognized the muffled inflections of argument. Finally, his mother's voice emerged.

"Honey. Hi. How are you doing?"

"I'm all right, I guess," Jacob said.

"This must be so hard for you. It's something nobody should have to go through, ever, let alone somebody your age."

I've been through this already, he wanted to say. *With Marty. Why doesn't that ever count?* But she had only meant to be comforting.

"I don't want to do anything wrong," he said. "I can't make these decisions alone." He looked up to see if Ingrid had understood his meaning: that he *was* alone, that she didn't qualify. His aunt stared at the floor.

"Don't worry," his mother said. "We'll be there just as soon as we can. Cross my heart." Her voice changed then, slowing, stretching thin. "Jake, honey. I spoke with Jonathan."

Jacob swallowed hard. He had prepared for this. "When's he coming in? If Ingrid stays here I can meet him at the airport."

"He isn't," his mother said.

"What?"

"He says he can't until after Passover. He has to be somewhere kosher and everything. He's staying at the yeshiva."

Jacob clamped the phone with the vise of his chin. "What is with this fucking family? Does anybody understand what a stroke is? Nana Jenny could . . . I mean, this could be it. Why is everyone treating it like it's just something they'll try to fit into their schedule?"

"Nobody's treating it that way, Jacob. It's just hard when something happens so unexpectedly."

"I'm sorry, Mom, that's bullshit. What kind of religion would tell you to stay away from your grandmother if she was sick?"

"It makes me angry, too. You know it does." His mother sounded exhausted, on the verge of tears. "I tried to tell Jon some things are more important. I said we'd work out a way for him to observe the holiday in Boston. But he's so closed now. I just couldn't get through."

The phone's cold plastic buzzed the cartilage of Jacob's ear. Numbness slunk like dope into his muscles.

"Jake?" his mother said when he didn't speak. His name repeated ominously, bouncing between continents. "Jacob? What happened in Israel?"

"Why? Did Jon say something? What did he say?"

"He didn't say anything. But I know something must have. I know it has something to do with this."

Jacob remembered Jonathan blocking the doorway of Ari's room, his face so taut it looked as though the skin would split over his cheekbones. That fragile, anemic skin. The same unpleasant hue of Nana Jenny's skin now.

"I don't want to talk about it," he said.

"If you don't want to say anything to me, fine. But I think you should talk to Jonathan."

"If he would come here, maybe. But apparently he's too holy to visit his own grandmother."

"Honey, please."

"What? I said I would pick him up at the airport. I'm willing to try. But he's got to at least make some effort, too."

"Just please call him," she said. "Please. For me."

Neither of them spoke. Jacob listened to the crackle of nurses on the intercom. He could feel his pulse against the collar of his shirt. The receiver stuck like taffy in his sweaty hands.

After a while he heard his father faintly in the background, noting how expensive the call would be.

"I guess I should go," his mother said.

"Fine," Jacob said. "Then go. Goodbye."

"We'll see you Sunday evening. Okay? Please think about it."

Jacob dumped the phone in its cradle, staring at the marriage of the plastic parts. He didn't want to turn and face Nana Jenny's cadaverous mass. Or Ingrid. Loneliness smothered him.

His aunt cleared her throat. "Want to talk about it?"

Jacob chugged the remaining lukewarm coffee like a shot of whiskey. A rancid aftertaste burped into his mouth. "No. I think I've had enough for now."

His impulse was still to keep things from Ingrid, to resist divulging even the most mundane details: the time of his parents' arrival, the name of Nana Jenny's building manager. She already knew so much that he didn't.

"I think I just need to get out of here," he said. "You know, clear my head." He reached for his windbreaker.

Ingrid grabbed her own jacket. "I was just thinking the same thing. Do you know nice places to walk?"

"Walk? Um, sure. There's a path along the Riverway. And the Harvard Med School quad is kind of nice, around the corner."

He didn't mention the Fens, the obvious place, where he was going.

"I trust your judgment," she said. "I'll just follow along."

There was a clog where Jacob's vocal cords should have been. He couldn't make himself say that he didn't want her to come. By the time he regained his voice, the elevator had dropped them together to street level.

Nothing was in bloom yet, not even the willows with their wisps of neon green. But the air simmered with a muddy, thawing smell. Yesterday's warmth had provoked movement, fermentation, the release of long-dormant seeds. Jacob imagined he could hear blades of grass pushing bravely up through the soil.

He and Ingrid walked without speaking. Their shoes scuffed the pavement in asynchronous cycles, like two just-off clocks ticking beside each other. Every dozen yards their strides matched in brief unison; then one set of footsteps slipped away again.

They crossed the street into the park. The usual group of boys jostled on the basketball courts, intent on after-school pickup games. One team had their shirts off, and their chests gleamed in the shallow sun, brown and black like polished leather.

Jacob often sat in the bleachers, pretending attention to the boys' basketball prowess, but actually admiring their teenage perfection. Now their lithe, unconscious beauty, their minnowlike darting on the court, reminded him of Danny and his story of being abandoned after practice. Danny—the one thing in his life that was going well, the only person he wanted right now to be with.

The kid with the ball swatted at a short boy with a shaved head. "The fuck off my wrists," he shouted.

"I didn't touch that shit," the bald boy countered.

"The fuck you didn't! That's a fucking foul."

"Shit, you can't take the heat, go back to your mama's kitchen." With a quick jab, the bald boy stole the ball.

Jacob grinned at the kid's mangled aphorism. He saw the amusement on Ingrid's face as well. Maybe this would break the ice. He had been hunting for tidbits of possible conversation the way he might scavenge a campsite for kindling.

"Talk about can't stand the heat," he said. "I am so glad to be out of that hospital."

"Seriously," Ingrid agreed. "Just to get away from that smell, if nothing else. What *is* that?"

"I don't know. It's like they sterilize the air or something. Like you're breathing fake plastic molecules instead of oxygen."

Ingrid made a sour face. "Whatever it is, it makes me feel dirty in comparison. As though I haven't washed in days."

"And all that background noise," Jacob said. "I can't believe they keep the intercoms on all the time. How the hell is anyone supposed to rest?"

They had slipped easily into the small talk of sickness. When Marty was hospitalized, Jacob had learned an entire vocabulary for these circumstances. The tiniest details—an overcooked meal, a certain nurse's haircut—provided fodder for hours of discussion.

"And that phone ringing all the time," Ingrid added.

"Tell me about it." Jacob had fielded a dozen·calls: Nana Jenny's neighbors, well-wishers from the synagogue. "How did people manage to be sick before the telephone?"

"At least Mother doesn't have to answer the calls herself. Can you imagine? Her having to actually talk on the phone?"

Jacob offered a smile of recognition. This was the first sign that the woman he knew as Nana Jenny, and the woman Ingrid knew as her mother, were in fact the same. As long as he could remember, his grandmother hadn't allowed a phone conversation to last beyond a minute. She would pick up the receiver, her voice tinged with panic, as if the ring had startled her from sleep. Jacob would identify himself, and almost without pause Nana Jenny invariably said, "Nice to hear you. Thank you for calling. Good-bye."

"Not much of a phone person, is she?" he said.

Ingrid shook her head. "Like pulling teeth."

"It must be hard. I mean, she's been around telephones for what, three-quarters of her life? You'd think she'd have gotten used to them. But if you don't have something when you're a little kid, maybe you never really do."

Ingrid pulled her jacket close around her shoulders. "They had telephones when she was a girl," she said.

"Do you think so? I don't know. I thought it was like a luxury back then. Just for really rich people."

Ingrid gazed upward, distracted, and Jacob followed her eyes. Clouds scalloped the sky in crazy wisps like uncombed hair. Higher, a contrail jagged, an incision in pale blue flesh.

Finally, Ingrid spoke into the blueness. "It wasn't that," she said. "It was after that."

"After what?"

Now she looked directly at him. "In Berlin. People believed the Gestapo could listen in on you through the phone wires, even when you weren't talking on it. We used to keep a big feather pillow over the phone."

Jacob reeled with the strangeness of the image. He pictured families clustered in well-furnished living rooms, afraid to speak or move, waiting for a muffled ring.

"After we came over," Ingrid added, "we convinced Mother she didn't need the pillow anymore. That things were different in America. But she still never trusted telephones."

Jacob cringed with shame, as if he had just told a cancer joke only to discover that the person whom he'd told it to was dying. The Berlin living room materialized again, now with a young Ingrid in the picture: the angelic face from his album's cracking snapshot. He began to connect that Ingrid, that little girl in antique clothes, with the white-haired woman walking next to him. She had been there. She knew things.

Slipping again to silence, they walked on, skirting the obsidian mirror of the small pond. They passed the rose garden, which would not grant roses for another three months, the bushes still craggy and bare as skeletons.

Soon they approached the granite mass of the war memorial. From behind, it looked like any banal piece of public sculpture, perhaps the stage of an amphitheater where oom-pah bands would play in summer.

"What's this?" Ingrid asked.

"It's nice," Jacob said, jumping at the chance to show her something he knew. "Here. Let's go around this way."

Jacob passed the memorial almost every day, but he'd never paid much attention. Now he examined the monument with a tour guide's keen eye. The main structure was a gray stone crescent, maybe ten feet tall and twenty feet along the arc. Across the top, black words read: IN MEMORY OF THE MEN AND WOMEN OF BOSTON WHO LOST THEIR LIVES IN WORLD WAR II. Below the dedication were two dozen bronze plaques displaying alphabetical lists of names.

The focus point around which the granite curved was a tall sculpture of some kind of goddess. Jacob could tell the winged figure was supposed to be a woman, but the face could have been a man's, or even a boy's. She held a huge sword and something else, maybe an olive branch.

"Pretty, huh?" he said.

Ingrid nodded slightly.

"It's a lot more tasteful than most memorials. No big guns or anything. I'm kind of amazed they restrained themselves."

He inspected the pockmarked metal at the sculpture's base, worn in places to the dusty green of bread mold. He rubbed the surface, wondering how long it would take for the alloy to corrode entirely. When he looked up again, Ingrid was gone. He glanced to the stone arc, but she wasn't there either.

He took two steps and found her on the opposite side of the statue. She languished against the solid folds of the goddess's flowing robe, her eyes closed as if against pain.

"Are you all right?" he asked.

Ingrid opened her eyes, and Jacob saw that they were damp. His aunt emitted a hiss like a bicycle tire deflating, then wheezed a deep breath, her shoulders heaving. "I'm sorry," she said. "I guess I'm really drained."

"It's been a long day," Jacob said. "Plus jet lag. It catches up with you."

"Yes, maybe. Maybe that's it."

They stood wordlessly together. Jacob found himself pulling deep swells of air to compensate for Ingrid's strained puffing. A breeze had picked up, clicking in the leafless trees. The chatter of the basketball courts was a distant, haunting soundtrack.

"I think I need to go," Ingrid said.

"Sure," Jacob said. "Want to head back to the hospital?"

"No. Not there. My hotel."

"I actually live right here," he offered, pointing to his building. "It's literally like a hundred yards. Come up and I'll call a cab."

It was only unlocking the second bolt that Jacob realized she would see everything. Not just the clutter of his secondhand existence, but the queer books and magazines, the porno-graphic Clinton and Gore. Had he hidden the bottle of Aqua Lube from a week ago with Danny, or was it still in plain view beside the bed?

He froze, gripping the doorknob. "It's kind of, um," he began to warn, but he couldn't conjure an appropriate word.

"Don't worry," Ingrid said. "I'm sure I've seen worse."

Jacob decided the only course was to be matter-of-fact. He pushed the door open and led her to the main room. "Why don't you sit here," he said, clearing a sprawl of magazines from the couch. Thankfully, the copies of *Torso* were buried in the pile. "Can I get you some water or something?"

"Water would be nice," she said.

Jacob walked past her to the kitchen and found two glasses. He scrutinized them for smudges and dust, nervous as before a date. "Fizzy or normal?" he called.

"Normal for me, please."

He ran the tap until both glasses brimmed, then brought them to the living room. "Thanks," Ingrid said, taking her drink. She had sunk into the foundered couch, directly beneath the naked president. Jacob went to the windows and tugged up the blinds, hoping the view might provide a distraction. But the infusion of light only threw the poster into more blatant relief.

Ingrid crossed her legs, fighting to stay upright in the too-soft cushions. She glanced around, looking but not looking, the way people in a doctor's waiting room try to divine everyone's afflic-tion without appearing to stare. Her gaze landed on the end table by Jacob's futon.

"Your mother's family?" she asked, pointing to the photo of the young boy with the suitcases.

Jacob had retired his collection years ago, stashing the album in a box at his closet's bottom. But he had framed Cousin Adam and displayed the picture in his miniature shrine, alongside the photo of him and Jonathan, and the shot of Marty at Herring Cove Beach.

"No," he said. "He isn't anybody. I mean, he's not related."

"Nice picture, though. Great expression on his face."

"Thanks. I've always really liked that one."

Jacob was grateful Ingrid had chosen to comment on this photo rather than the more provocative image above her. As he gauged his appreciation, he felt guilty for not displaying his snapshot of her, an actual relative; for burying it in his pile of junk.

"Should I call the cab?" he asked, wanting to do something to make up for his neglect.

"Actually," she said, "do you mind if I stay a bit? It feels good now just to sit and rest." She patted the couch, fomenting dust spirals that spun in the shafts of light.

"Of course," Jacob said. "As long as you want."

"I'm sorry about before," Ingrid said.

"About what?"

"I'm usually fine with that stuff. You know, the memorial."

"Oh . . . oh, God, it didn't even occur to me."

Ingrid fanned her hand vigorously, as if erasing an invisible blackboard. "No, please," she said. "There's no reason it should."

Of course it should have. He should have considered what Ingrid would have gone through—a little girl, the fear.

"It must be so hard," he said. The words came out stupid, too open-ended. "I mean, seeing Nana Jenny. It must bring back a lot."

Ingrid rocked herself from the couch's trough and stood. "There's so much I haven't thought of," she said. "Haven't let myself." She shuffled across the room as if lost. The gap between them was so vast, Jacob thought. They were like the first and last players in a child's game of Telephone, a chain of intermediaries having garbled the original message beyond recognition.

Ingrid drifted to the table by Jacob's futon and examined the photos up close. She ran her fingers over the picture of Adam, then the one of Jacob and Jonathan.

"I want to tell you . . ." she began, but seemed to lose herself again. She examined her finger, dusty from the photo frames, as if checking for blood. She wiped a gray streak absently on her jeans.

When she spoke again, her voice was more measured. "I want to tell you so many things. But I'm sure we'll have plenty of time."

Jacob realized this was a perfect opening. He could say, "I have things I need to tell you, too." But the words jammed in his throat.

He didn't even know what to call her. Aunt Ingrid? Just Ingrid? How did he address this woman?

He hadn't noticed her moving back near the couch.

"I have a grad student who would kill for this," she said. She tapped an admiring finger on Clinton and Gore.

Jacob had to suppress the urge to throw himself in front of her like a bodyguard, to protect her from the luridness.

"Yeah," she said, "Rick's a sweetheart. One of my best students. And he's just obsessed with Al Gore." She traced the outline of Gore's glistening figure—actually the body of some porn star on whom the vice-president's head was superimposed.

All Jacob could manage to say was, "Al Gore?"

Ingrid laughed. "I know. Can you believe it? Rick thinks Gore is the sexiest man alive."

"Well, your friend is crazy," he said. "Everyone knows Bill is the cuter one."

"Yes, well, taste is so unaccountable. The lesbians in my class are all nuts for Hillary. I tell them to quit wishful thinking and stick to a known quantity, like Donna Shalala."

"Or at least Janet Reno," Jacob said. "Don't you love that army-helmet haircut?" He giggled, and Ingrid's machine-gun chuckle rattled in to join him. His hand found her shoulder. They were touching, laughing together.

When he caught his breath, Jacob turned to her with a sheepish shrug. "I guess you figured out I'm gay?" He imagined the word as something tangible: a shining bubble lofted between them.

Ingrid rolled her eyes at the poster. "Kind of hard to miss."

"I guess so," Jacob said. "I'm not used to having visitors."

Ingrid pointed to Jacob's nightstand, to the photo she had skipped over earlier, the one of Marty. "I didn't want to ask before," she said. "Your boyfriend?"

"No. Just a close friend. He died last year."

"I'm sorry," Ingrid said. "That's always hard." Then she tried a smile. "Do you have a boyfriend?"

Jacob's mouth automatically began the "no"; it was the only answer he'd ever given to this question. But now there was Danny. Did he qualify? Jacob didn't want to jinx anything, or to have to explain Danny's age. "Um, not exactly," he said.

She looked at him then, kindly but with a serious cast to her eyes. "It must be difficult with your brother."

"You know about Jonathan?"

"Mother told me about the yeshiva, how he's even more strict now than she is. I guess a certain kind of, well, fervor seems to run in the family."

"Then do you know if Nana Jenny . . . ? Does she know about me?"

Ingrid smiled sadly, a brief twisting at the corners of her mouth. "I'm sorry. I don't know."

"She could tell something was up with me and Jon," Jacob said. "She definitely sensed that. She tried to get me to talk about it once, but I couldn't. I hated it, upsetting her."

"When was the last time you talked with him?"

"God, forever. Six months? We didn't exactly part on the best terms."

"And that's why he isn't coming?"

"He told my mother it's because of Passover. That he needs everything super kosher, et cetera. But I know I'm part of it, too. I'm sure I am. When I was in Israel, I kind of hooked up with this other yeshiva student, and Jon walked in on us. He said he never wants to see me again."

Ingrid finished her glass of water. She tilted the glass to her lips longer than it took to suck down the remaining liquid, as if drinking air, or maybe her own thoughts. When she snapped back, there was a new tightness in her face.

"I don't want to lay a whole trip on you," she said, balancing the empty glass on the couch's arm. "We don't know each other well enough. But can I just say one thing?"

"Sure, of course," Jacob said. "Go ahead."

"Don't close any possibilities. Not yet. You're too young for that." Her eyes flashed to the poster above the couch. "That doesn't mean you should be someone you're not. But don't assume it means you have to lose other people, either. No one's ever going to give you another brother."

When they heard the honk, Jacob walked Ingrid downstairs and helped her into the cab. She lifted her hand in a tired wave from the backseat, and as the taxi pulled away, Jacob saw his own raised hand, reflected in the rear window, shrink to the size of a child's, then disappear.

He turned to head inside, but kept spinning until he'd circled a full revolution. He couldn't bear the empty apartment. He stood disoriented in the middle of the road.

The air, cooler now than when they had walked from the hospital, raised bumps on his triceps and his neck. The wispy clouds had migrated together, weaving into a dense mat of gray above the treetops.

A loud blare stippled more gooseflesh into his back. The driver of a yellow Porsche pounded his fist on the steering wheel, shouting angry words that fogged the windshield. Jacob stood in the way, a stunned animal.

The horn screamed again and Jacob woke to the danger. He jumped onto the grass median, then kept moving across Park Drive, toward the Fens, returning to the place they'd been.

Caressed by strokes of the last, caramel sunlight, the memorial appeared almost fake: not granite, but cardboard painted to resemble granite. The monument's base and the surrounding walkways were engulfed in shadow. They radiated a seductive coolness like the breeze near a swollen river.

He approached the bronze goddess and ran his hands along her giant foot. The rendering was impressively human. Jacob searched for a plaque identifying the figure, but found only the names of the sculptor and the company that had executed the casting. He wished he knew more about the classics, those soap-opera epics of gods falling in and out of love, siring children and banishing them.

He moved to the gray stone with its lists and lists of names. Starting at the left, he skimmed the terrible roster. There were hundreds of them, maybe thousands, alphabetical in raised bronze letters. The arrangement's democratic simplicity reminded him of the Vietnam Veterans Memorial in Washington. Jacob had seen the memorial the week it opened, when he was in high school. There weren't many regular tourists yet; most visitors were veterans themselves, or people who had lost loved ones in the war. A bald man, maybe forty, stopped him at the deep center of the haunting blackness. The man pinched him by the shoulder, and when Jacob turned, the man had lifted his pant leg. Where the left foot should have been hung a doughy, puckered stump.

"All-state two years in a row," the man said. "Record for longest field goal in a high school championship. My good foot." He thrust the stump at Jacob. "My good foot."

Recalling the crippled veteran, Jacob now thought also of Ingrid, of the complicated grief in her silences. Fifty years had passed, and still she could be transported back to Germany by a slab of granite, by an innocent ring of the telephone. How could you ever truly know another person's loss?

He continued scanning, and when he reached the end of the list, he shuddered. The names stopped. Just like that, in the middle of one plaque. Below the abrupt cessation was an expanse of empty metal, smooth and innocent as skin. To the right, a final plaque had been left blank.

Jacob was horrified. How could the engravers have made such a serious miscalculation? He reached for the vacant plaque as if in apology. But as he traced the chilled metal surface, the memorial's true meaning pricked him like pins and needles in a limb coming awake. He could not know what the Vietnam vet had been through, or Ingrid, or the men and women honored here. Nobody ever could. And that, precisely, was the point. The list was left imcomplete because that was the nature of grief. This final plaque declared with its unblemished readiness that the remembering could never be finished.

Jacob read the last names again, this time out loud, pronouncing the syllables like an invocation to bring these strangers briefly back to life.

Zitoli, Frank A.

Zmuszien, Edward J.

Zwiercan, Alexander.

He stopped. There was one more name, but it was wrong. It should not have been there, far from its proper place in the alphabetical sequence.

Kelly, Stanton H.

Jacob repeated it, so different from the preceding, ethnic-sounding surnames. *Kelly, Stanton H.* A revision. A late discovery. Names got added, he told himself. It could never be finished.

Infinity of Angles

It had been less than two years, but already the trip to Germany had lodged in the myth-space of Jacob's mind, as though it were history, a parable, not his own recent adventure. In the way of most memories, it was at once etched with diamond clarity and blurred like a view of the world through tears.

The Common Press was feeling flush in the fall of '91. The Mellon grant had come through, and the mystery novel Chantelle had acquired on a whim proved a surprise bestseller. This year they could afford to send someone to the Frankfurt Book Fair.

The trip turned out to be too full of business to allow much pleasure. Jacob worked the noisy exhibit hall, pitching the mystery at booth after booth in hopes of clinching translation deals. In the evenings, after meetings with distributors, he was too exhausted to do anything but sleep in the hotel's stiff bed.

But the last night, knowing he'd never forgive himself otherwise, Jacob mustered the energy to go out. He studied the listings in his *Spartacus Guide*, ruling out half a dozen clubs with names like Blue Angels and Construction 5 as American wannabes. Finally, he picked one by its German name and its unglamorous address, in a small alley off the Alte Gasse.

Bierstube Funzel was a dingy corridor of a room, with a bar along one wall and orange vinyl booths along the other. The place didn't resemble a nightclub so much as a railroad-car diner.

Jacob half expected to smell the smoky perfume of sizzling bacon.

He ordered a draft—pushing a wad of marks to the bartender and trusting he'd receive correct change—then claimed a seat in an empty booth. At the room's far end was a tiny dance floor, ten feet wide and five deep, mottled with weakly colored lights. Nobody danced. Jacob almost spat up his beer when he heard the song whimpering through the toaster-sized speakers: *Boogie oogie boogie woogie dancin' shoes, keep me dancin' all night. Boogie oogie boogie woogie dancin' shoes, make me queen of the night.*

The oddest thing was that the walls were covered with a sheer reflective material—something between tin foil and aluminized mylar—so from his seat Jacob enjoyed a multitude of views of every spot in the bar. It was like sitting in the barber's chair when he held the mirror behind your head, and you saw yourself from an infinity of angles.

Unsettled by the voyeuristic decor, Jacob lowered his eyes to the wheaty froth of his beer.

"Yes, it is strange."

The hot force of the words accosted Jacob's neck. He looked up to find a man crouched beside him, shockingly close. He wore a black mesh T-shirt tucked into pristine, pressed white jeans.

"It is strange," the man repeated in a light German accent, "but think of the advantages for cruising. Normally, you see somebody across the crowd, you think he is good-looking, you approach. But when you see him from the front, you discover he is hideous. Here, this is eliminated. For example, I knew before I walked over that you were handsome from every side."

Too startled to acknowledge the compliment, Jacob merely motioned for the man to sit. He was baffled and somewhat ashamed that everyone in Frankfurt spoke to him immediately in English. He had dressed in what he thought was the Euro uniform—black shoes, jeans, button-down shirt—and had even slicked some gel into his hair, but still they were able to pick him out.

The stranger stared. His squat face followed the outline of a battleship's hull, jawbones angling sharply to the keel of his chin. His straw-blond hair flopped in symmetrical crests from a neat center part. The cut reminded Jacob of the men in his antique photographs, painfully sincere as they posed for the slow camera.

"I haven't introduced myself," the man said. "My name is Hannes."

Jacob shook his hand, bony but firm. "I'm Jacob."

"Jacob. Beautiful name. In German we would say 'Ya-cob.' "

"Actually," Jacob said, "I *am* kind of German. My grandparents."

Hannes scanned Jacob's face the way a grocery shopper might scrutinize produce. "Jewish?" he asked.

"I was raised Jewish," Jacob qualified.

"Yes. Yes, I could tell."

"You could tell? I don't know, that sounds a little scary."

"Oh no. Please. Don't mistake me." Hannes encircled Jacob's wrist with gentle fingertips. "I love Jews. Judaism. In fact, that's what I study at university. American Jewish literature."

"Seriously?"

"Yes, yes. Saul Bellow, Philip Roth. Singer. Malamud. Potok. I read them all. It's going to be my dissertation."

"Wow," Jacob said. "You're more Jewish than me. I saw the movie of *The Chosen.* Does that count?"

Hannes tightened his grip on Jacob's wrist. Below the table, he wedged his knee between Jacob's two. "You have to *read* Potok. He is very subtle."

In America, Hannes's brazenness would be too much, a wrecking ball of a come-on. But here Jacob accepted it. "How did you get into all of this?" he asked, placing his own hand on top of Hannes's, constructing a stack of flesh on the beer-sticky table.

"It's the most dynamic strain of American writing, don't you think? So many issues. I just finished Wiesel's *Night* again, maybe the fifth time. It never stops fascinating. The whole question of how to believe in God after Auschwitz."

Jacob chuckled. "It's never been that big a dilemma for me. I mean, I don't think God was too convincing *before* Auschwitz."

Hannes's pale lips opened a divot in his face. "No, you can't be serious. Please tell me you are joking."

"Oh, sorry. Are you religious or something?"

"No, but you should be," Hannes said, squeezing Jacob's arm with frightening force on the *you.* "You are part of such a beautiful tradition. Don't you feel lucky to be Jewish?"

Jacob shrugged. "I guess the grass is always greener."

Hannes's eyebrows collapsed into an adorable curving V, like a child's crayon rendition of a bird, all wings. "I do not know what this means," he said.

"The grass is greener? You've never heard that? I'm surprised. Your English is really good. It means, um, that things never look as good from the inside as they do from the outside."

Hannes seemed to swish the idiom around his mouth as though it were expensive wine. Then he moved his face next to Jacob's, so close that the tiny hairs on Jacob's earlobes stood on end. He whispered, "I would like you to see me from the inside."

The words tickled like mild electricity, a thrilling, almost painful sting on Jacob's skin. He opened his mouth to laugh, but the sound was muffled by Hannes's tongue. He choked for a second, then thrust back with his own tongue, testing the sharpness of Hannes's rear teeth.

A moment later he froze, certain he was being watched. He retreated his tongue partway and looked up: Three more of himself mimed the gesture in the reflective wall paneling. He was kissing this broad stranger, and kissing him, and kissing him again.

Jacob gazed into the foily reflections, expecting the sudden clarity of revelation. But the paneling was dull and dented in spots. He saw only a blurry, generic figure staring back.

Hannes's apartment was on the fifth floor of a concrete block building. Climbing the steep stairs, Jacob felt a tackiness of sweat between his shirt collar and his neck, like the gummy lip of glue on an envelope. He could smell the yeasty warmth of his own underarms. He hadn't tried this in far too long.

The place was tiny. A single bed was pushed into the corner, its frame rusted as a summer-camp cot. An overturned cardboard box bowed with the weight of library books. Everything wore the sallow dinginess of the lone light bulb that dangled from the ceiling, a tiny upside-down skull casting more shadow than light.

"This is it," Hannes said, crouching to avoid knocking his head on the hanging bulb.

The long climb had squeezed Jacob's bladder; the need to pee radioed from his abdomen in urgent waves. "Is there a bathroom?" he asked.

"Over here." Hannes ushered him inside and flipped the light, then backed out and closed the door.

Jacob drained himself with a forceful stream, and as his chest regained room for air, space freed also in his mind to consider the best approach. He wanted to connect this time, to achieve more than a rote physical release. How could he take the encounter to a deeper level?

When he came out of the bathroom, Hannes was standing naked at the foot of the bed, holding five strands of thin black rope.

"Tie me," he demanded.

Jacob's stomach lurched with fear and excitement. Okay, he thought. Fair enough. Maybe Hannes was the one with a plan.

Hannes's body was as spare as his apartment. The satin skin of his chest was interrupted only by a tiny heart of hair between the gum-colored nipples. A whorled stub of bellybutton jutted from his flat stomach, as if he were so skinny that there was no room for this extra piece of flesh.

"Tie me," he said again. He tossed the ropes.

Jacob caught the strands in one fist. With the other hand he began unbuttoning his shirt to catch up with Hannes's nakedness.

"No," Hannes said. "Tie me first."

He lay on the bed, his arms and legs flung to the corners of the frame. Now Jacob allowed himself to examine Hannes's dick. The shaft appeared smooth, devoid of the usual veins, as if made of plastic. A snorkel of foreskin hung compliantly from the tip.

Hannes's chest heaved in the studied, serious breaths of a weightlifter preparing to lift the bar. Jacob hovered over him, fumbling with the ropes. The positioning was awkward. There wasn't room to stand.

"Here," Hannes instructed. "On top."

Jacob climbed on the sunken mattress. His shoes were still on. He worried about hurting Hannes, about soiling the sheets. He looped one black strand through the bedframe's rusty pipes, then wound the rope around Hannes's wrist. When he pulled the knot, his balance slipped. He lunged, catching his entire weight with one desperate knee. The knee thudded directly on Hannes's sternum.

Hannes gasped in a convulsing reflex. Jacob tried to right himself, to alleviate the crushing load. But looking down, he saw the pain had torqued a dreamy smile onto Hannes's face.

The smile injected a roller-coaster thrill into the walls of Jacob's gut. He shifted his full weight back onto Hannes, rolling his knee pestle-like in the hollow of his ribs. He hadn't known this drive since he and Jonathan were kids and staged brawls in the leaf-strewn backyard—this desire to see how much he could get away with.

He fixed the first knot, then tied the other wrist, not consciously inflicting pain, but not caring if he did. He bound both ankles, then found the fifth rope and zeroed in on the crotch.

By now Hannes was fully hard. His balls rose and fell with his excited breath, shifting beneath the pink wrinkled scrotum like some elusive undersea creature. Jacob wound the rope twice around the entire package, then a third time, jerking the strand upward the way a cowboy snugs his lasso's noose.

"Tight enough?" he asked.

Hannes's response was high-voiced and shivery, as if his throat were the thing being squeezed. "Tighter."

"Like this?" Jacob yanked once more and secured a final knot. Now the veins showed in the skin of Hannes's dick, a blue-red reticulation as intricate as an autumn leaf's underside.

Jacob's own dick surged as well, levering his underwear's elastic band. He stood and stripped his shirt.

He climbed back onto the bed and knelt between Hannes's legs. Bending, he licked Hannes's chest with tiny paintbrush strokes. He lapped around the swatch of hair, then up to the neck, over the chin's peak to the mouth.

Hannes jerked his head away. "No," he said. "No kissing."

The injunction startled Jacob. It was confusing to be in control but not. He snaked down Hannes's body, grazing the skin with his incisors. He sucked a nipple into his mouth and nibbled gingerly. Hannes arched his back, pushing the flesh further between Jacob's teeth. The nipple was tough but stretchy; it was like chewing a rubber band.

Hannes's breath quickened. "Go on," he said. "Go ahead."

Jacob moved to the other nipple, but Hannes shook his head. "No. Not that. Aren't you going to hit?"

Jacob had never hit anybody. He had play-spanked a guy once, but nothing for real. Now he took an experimental swipe at Hannes's chest. The sound was flat as a fake movie slap.

"Don't hold back," Hannes coached. "I want you to hurt."

Jacob recalled Hannes's zombie smile when he had kneed him in the chest, and he wanted that power again. He wanted to punch the expression back onto Hannes's face. His hand cut the air in a blurry arc. This time the apartment echoed with a fleshy thud.

Jacob slapped again, lower this time, on Hannes's stomach. The clean *pop* thrilled his ears. He whipped down another time. A pink impression of his hand stained the skin. It was intoxicating: the clap of flesh, Hannes's gasping twitch, the dangerous burn on his palm.

Then he grabbed the shaft. He'd only had sex with one uncut guy before, and that just a fumble in the dark. He had never had the chance for close study. There wasn't much play left, because of the binding rope, but Jacob tugged the clam's foot of skin until the dick seemed to consume itself, a turtle retracting into its shell.

"*Ja*," Hannes moaned. "*Ja*. That's good."

Jacob pinched, digging his fingernails in the silky skin.

"Hit me," Hannes said, lifting his hips. "Hit me there."

Jacob was paralyzed. Some instinctive empathy would not permit his arms to move.

"Come on," Hannes said. "Do it." His voice was now a breathy rasp. "I know you've thought of it. You must be full of hate. After all the things we did to you."

Now Jacob flinched with understanding. And suddenly he did want to hit Hannes. He wanted to knock these crazy thoughts back inside him, far away, out of reach.

His hand flashed down, smacking the tight globe of flesh. Hannes spasmed against the blow, but Jacob did it again. He allowed himself to forget the damage he could do.

A bead of liquid leaked from the German's cock. Jacob could tell he was close. "The dresser," Hannes said. "Top drawer."

Jacob leapt from the bed, breathing hard. It was the same place he kept condoms in his own apartment. The drawer was filled with underwear and neatly balled socks. He rifled through, searching for the familiar shiny foil packages. Then, probing in the corner, his fingers bumped something hard and cold. He appraised its perilous weight as he pulled it out. The knife was locked in its open position, the four-inch blade exposed like naked flesh.

"Here," Hannes called. "Bring it here." His voice was distant and strangely liquid.

Jacob followed the command. His brain felt swollen, pressing his skull the way it did in an airplane descending too rapidly.

Now Hannes was crying, heaving wet gulps of air. "Please. Take revenge. Use the knife."

Jacob's fist clenched the burnished handle. Ripples of nausea pulsed from a sour spot at his stomach's bottom.

The German writhed in his restraints. His erection had lost some of its stiffness. The loosening foreskin bunched around the head like kissed lips.

"Cut it," Hannes said. "Like yours. Make me like you."

Jacob was not his body, not his legs or his arms. He bent over Hannes, pointing the knife in front of him the way he would aim a flashlight to penetrate darkness.

Then he sliced. A single swiping motion.

He cut the right wrist free so Hannes would be able to untie the other. He dropped the knife, kicked it far under the bed. Then he grabbed his shirt and ran for the door.

The Way Back

After another day at Nana Jenny's bedside, Jacob was swamped by the utter exhaustion that comes from doing nothing. His feet were giant anchors, burdening his legs; if he fell into a pool he'd sink and drown. But the sight of Danny offered the prospect of buoyancy. Danny stood outside the hospital's overlit entrance, hands shoved in the back pockets of his baggy jeans, whistling into the evening air.

Jacob came up from behind and plopped his chin on Danny's shoulder. "Hey," he said. "Am I glad to see you."

Danny turned and took the weight of Jacob's head in his hands. Their kiss drew stares from two doctors in aqua scrubs.

"Here," Danny said, handing Jacob a skinny carton of something. His florid cheeks looked like a child's watercolor of *happy*. "Sorry it's store-bought. I never learned how to make it."

Jacob studied the label. "Eggnog in April?"

"It's what my gran always makes when you're sick, or when something bad has happened. When I was at her place today, I remembered. I thought, you know, since it's *your* grandmother."

"Thanks," Jacob said. "I guess."

He pried open the bird's mouth of cardboard; swigged. The eggnog was yolky and oversweetened, with a chemical nutmeggy bite. But the smooth liquid salved his raw throat.

"Well?" Danny asked.

"I never would've thought," Jacob said. "But it's perfect. Thanks." He gulped another mouthful, then gave Danny a milky kiss.

They headed down Brookline Avenue toward Jacob's apartment. They had a couple of hours to kill before meeting Chantelle. Jacob walked close to Danny, but not too close to ruin the view. He was still in the stage where what he wanted most was just to watch, to study Danny, reveling in the novelty.

Danny moved with an appealing leggy bounce, each stride stretching just beyond a casual step. The elastic gait gave the impression he was constantly on the verge of a trot. But after Thursday night's confessional, Jacob could see the vulnerability coexisting with the self-assurance. He thought of Danny as like a butterfly: the finesse of its splashy flitting dependent on a paper-thinness that leaves it prey to being crushed.

"So," he said, the eggnog's creamy aftertaste still coating his tongue, "you had a good visit with your grandmother?"

"Gran's the best," Danny said. "One of these Saturdays you'll have to come meet her."

"That would be okay? I mean, does she know?"

"Oh, yeah, Gran's cool. Jim and Karl—the guys she rents her third floor to?—she's known about them forever. She used to send me up to hang out with them, you know, like babysitters. I guess watching them was kind of what clued me in about myself. Hey, that reminds me." Danny poked a kidding elbow at Jacob's ribs. "I didn't know you were such a big TV star."

"Huh?" Jacob said.

"Don't play modest with me."

"No, really. I don't know what you're talking about."

"Well, I popped up to see Jim and Karl today, 'cause I hadn't seen them in like a month? So I was saying what's been going on, meeting you and all. And Karl goes, 'Oh, you mean the guy who came out on TV? He's cute!' He told me all about that speech you made."

Jacob groaned. "Oh God, how embarrassing."

"I just think it's funny," Danny said. "I never pictured myself going out with, like, the gay-positive poster boy."

"Hardly. Most of the time I'm a total failure at being gay."

"Well, if what I've seen is failure"—Danny cupped a hand on Jacob's crotch—"I can't wait to be around for your success."

Jacob swatted him away. "I appreciate the vote of confidence. But in this relationship, kiddo, *you're* the poster boy." He pinched Danny's cheek, leaving a pink butterfly of fingerprints.

Chantelle had prescribed a medicinal night out. The club around the corner from Jacob's apartment was experimenting with Saturday theme parties, and tonight was New Wave Nostalgia. "Come on," she'd said. "It'll be great. It'll be just like high school."

"High school was bad enough the first time," Jacob said. "I don't see why we need to relive it now."

But he knew this would be his last chance to relax. His parents would arrive tomorrow; Jonathan wouldn't, and Jacob was sure they were blaming him. He needed something to steer his mind away.

Though he lived just around the block, Jacob had been inside the club only half a dozen times. From what he remembered, it wasn't especially different tonight. The same epileptic lighting. The same choking disco smoke. Three gel-haired boys, decked out in tight T-shirts and flaring jeans, pushed by in a puppylike flurry of energy. They looked far too young to have made it past the doorman, let alone to be nostalgic for anything.

When Chantelle had said tonight was New Wave Nostalgia, Jacob was too embarrassed to admit he didn't know what that really meant. In high school, terrified of asserting any individual taste that might betray his difference, he'd found it easiest to ignore culture altogether. Like a kid who nods off on a long car ride and wakes in an unfamiliar destination, he felt as though he had slept through his adolescence.

Danny pointed to the bar. "Is that her?"

Jacob followed the finger to Chantelle, her dark skin glossed by the flashing lights to the caramelized sheen of a candied apple. "Yeah," he said. "Good call."

"Well, from your description, it was kind of obvious."

At the packed bar, people gave Chantelle a wide berth. Her leather jacket's collar winged up. Her flattop was impeccable.

They pushed across until Jacob was close enough to flag her attention. "Ms. Peterson," he called. "Delivery for Ms. Peterson."

"Hey," she said, smudging a wet kiss on his lips. "I was just about to come knocking. I thought you'd bagged out on me."

"He wanted to," Danny said, "but I wouldn't let him."

"Chantelle," Jacob said, "this is the famed Danny. Danny, Chantelle."

"I've certainly heard plenty about you," she said. "Jacob claims you make him happy, thankless task though that may be."

"It's a tough job," Danny said, "but someone's got to do it." Then, turning to Jacob, as if Chantelle weren't there, he said, "I don't know, her bark doesn't seem so bad."

"Excuse me?" Chantelle said, butting between them.

Danny flashed a toothy grin. "Oh. See, Jake said not to be put off, that you might be, like, kind of cold at first? But that it's just a cover, that your bark is much worse than your bite."

Chantelle huffed. "What else did he say?"

"Um, well, that you wouldn't like me, but I'd win you over."

"Bullshit!" Jacob said. "I didn't say anything remotely like that."

Danny shrugged, all sweetness and light. "Okay, you're right. I just figured it out on my own."

Chantelle shook her head, speechless, but Jacob saw the smile she was restraining. Most people never found Chantelle's soft side, but Danny had cracked her in a minute.

The generic blast that had been rocking the club shifted to a more melodic synthetic warble. It sounded as though someone were tossing the speakers into the air, Dopplering the tune's notes.

"Hey," Danny said. "Even I know this. 'Whip It,' right?"

"Not bad," Chantelle said. "When this album came out you were what, six years old?"

"Yeah, but I mean, duh. This is, like, famous."

Jacob stared at the floor; he'd never heard the song.

"Come on," Danny said. "Let's dance!"

He hooked Jacob's elbow and started dragging. Jacob resisted with all his weight, a dog fighting the leash.

"You came all the way here," Danny said.

"Forget it," Jacob said. "I don't want to."

"Please. Just this one song."

Jacob's arm was a tug-of-war rope. "I said no."

For an instant, disappointment wilted Danny's face, but the usual smile quickly reappeared. "Fine," he said. "I bet Chantelle will dance."

He took her arm and dove again for the dance floor. Caught off guard, Chantelle couldn't counteract the momentum. She stumbled along, looking over her shoulder apologetically.

Jacob, ashamed to stand alone in the middle of the crowd, fought his way to the room's edge and pressed his back against the wall. Why had he agreed to this ridiculousness?

Among the thrashing clubkids were older individuals here for the theme night. One thirtysomething guy jerked with mechanical precision. He wore a jacket two sizes too big and a silver necktie as skinny as a Popsicle. A crew-cut woman loped to the beat in a yellow jumpsuit. Jacob wondered how she could see anything through her robotic wraparound sunglasses.

If he hadn't understood the classification earlier, Jacob now recognized New Wave as what Jacquie Radatz must have been. Jacquie tooled around their high school in a powder-blue Volare, the back stuffed with amplifiers, guitars, and the kids in her band, the Canisters. Membership in the Canisters didn't depend on musical talent—as far as Jacob recalled, they never actually performed—but rather on some inexplicable coolness quotient in which he was sorely lacking. They had haircuts you couldn't get at Nick's barbershop; sported secondhand clothes that on Jacob would have seemed joke Halloween costumes, but on them zinged ultra-hip. At lunch, they chain-smoked on the gym steps. Some of the guys wore makeup.

Jacob's disdain for Jacquie's groupies was rivaled only by his desire to be like them. He didn't want to play their music or style his hair or wear eye shadow; what made him jealous was their assured alienation. He, too, had always wanted to express his difference. But his fear of ridicule was too great. And so he envied the Canisters' concerted deviance; envied it and despised it and made sure to keep away.

Standing now in the strobe-lit club, his stomach pulsing with the spacey music, Jacob sank with the same trapped resentment of watching Jacquie Radatz speed by in her Volare. As a teenager, he had thought coming out would parole him from his solitary confinement; once he was honest about his sexuality, he would assume his place in a community of kindred souls. But here he was, even now, on the fringes. An outcast among the outcasts.

He gazed across to Chantelle and Danny. Chantelle appeared to have been suckered in by Danny's charm, just as he'd prophesied, smiling the kind of warped, uncontrollable grin induced by laughing gas. They spun in a crazy version of a 1940s swing dance, holding each other by both hands and crashing together, then away, then close again. Why couldn't he fit in like them?

The music shifted to a new track, and the entire dance floor shimmered like a school of fish changing direction. Jacob lost sight of his friends. He craned his neck, trying to relocate them, but the writhing sea of dancers obscured his view.

Before he knew what was happening he was yanked forward, feet performing a panicked hopscotch to keep from tripping.

"Wait!" he called. "Wait, what's going on?"

"We're getting you off your ass," Danny yelled above the pumping noise.

"Just do it," Chantelle added. "Don't put up a fight."

Jacob tried to wrench free, but he wasn't strong enough for the two of them. They towed him into the heart of the worming throng.

He stood rigid, a sick pinching in his stomach. "Guys," he said, "you know I don't do this."

Danny and Chantelle pretended not to hear him. They resumed their giddy twisting.

"Really!" he shouted. "This is way uncool."

Still no recognition.

"All right," he said. "I'm leaving."

He turned to storm a path of escape, but Danny clutched his shoulder. "Jake. Wait. What're you doing?"

"Danny, you know I can't dance. I don't know this music."

"You danced with me at Bobby's," he said.

"That was different."

"How?"

"God, I don't know. Why do I have to justify myself?"

"Because," Danny said. "Because I don't understand. I think you really want to, but for some stupid reason you won't."

Jacob kicked at the floor. "Is it stupid not to want people to laugh at me? I'm not all hip and trendy, okay? I never was."

Danny put his face next to Jacob's, his breath a tickling spritz in Jacob's ear. "Don't you know I don't care? I don't care if you stand there with your hands in your pants. I just want to be with you."

"But why?" Jacob said. "Why would you want to be with me?"

"Because you're beautiful. You're incredible. I like you."

The words jimmied the clamp of Jacob's resistance. "You really do?"

Danny uttered something between a laugh and a sob. "God," he said, "of course I do. What do you think we're doing here?"

His pupils, dilated in the club's dimness, looked big enough to climb inside. The knot in Jacob's stomach threaded loose.

"Okay," he said.

"Okay what?"

"Okay, I'll stay with you. I'll try."

Danny grinned. He mouthed "Thank you" and went back to dancing.

Jacob poised on the balls of his feet, as though waiting to duck into a double-dutching jump rope. He lifted one foot and then the other. He bumbled; chased the beat.

When he finally found the groove and looked around, he noticed that nobody had witnessed his clumsy entry. Nobody was watching him. Even Chantelle and Danny were lost in their own motion, a liquid blur of limbs.

Jacob smiled at the spectacle, and at the fact that he was part of it. Danny's words still tickled his ear, a hot, vaporous pledge of acceptance. The music took hold of his limbs. He floated on the sound and the movement of the roiling crowd. He tried his own version of Danny's loose-limbed shuffle, bumping hips with him and Chantelle, feeling their sweat mingle on his skin.

And as the song thumped toward its conclusion, they formed a misshapen triangle, arms locked around each other's shoulders. Jacob leaned into Danny on one side, Chantelle on the other, and the centrifugal force glued their whirling forms. They twirled so fast Jacob almost couldn't breathe. Then he closed his eyes, realizing that even if he tried, he couldn't possibly break free. They were holding him. There was no way he could fall.

At four o'clock the next day, Jacob called British Air, hoping the agent would apologize in a smooth royal accent and confess that his parents' flight was delayed. Instead, the woman informed him that headwinds were lighter than expected; the plane would arrive twenty minutes early.

He took the Green Line to Government Center, then switched to the Blue. Like a moored boat rocking in waves, the train quivered as it hurtled down the track. Jacob's head knocked the glass window in synch with the triple-timing wheels.

He stared at the map above the door, reading the station names like found poetry: Wood Island, Orient Heights, Suffolk Downs. On a previous trip to the airport, a Japanese tourist once tapped him on the shoulder. "Wonderland?" he asked. "What is Wonderland?"

Jacob knew the man was only inquiring about the Blue Line's final stop, but he couldn't help hearing the question's existential overtones. Jacob himself had often fantasized about riding all the way to this optimistically named station, ascending the escalator and emerging into some perfect universe.

He hadn't had the heart to tell the Japanese man that Wonderland was nothing but a dog track.

"Airport," the intercom croaked. "Doors opening on the right." The train screeched to a halt and Jacob stepped off.

He hadn't been to Logan since September, when he snuck back incognito from Israel. Unshaven, unshowered, in the same wrinkled clothes he'd worn with Ari, he felt then the refugee's humiliation. Other passengers shunned him at the passport check and baggage claim. He was an exile, an untouchable.

Standing in the terminal now brought back his bitterness. How dare Jonathan have put him through that, when all Jacob ever wanted was acceptance? And the unfairest part of all was that if Jonathan—who'd embraced exile—finally agreed to come home, he would be deferred to, coddled, accommodated. Why was there so much more power in *not* wanting to be wanted?

His mother emerged from customs bleary-eyed and blinking, as if stepping into unexpected sunlight. Jacob hadn't seen her since Thanksgiving. She looked older: a dulling of the chestnut hair, a flagging of the skin below her jaw. A new pair of quotation marks had wrinkled around her eyes, and for an instant Jacob saw her not as who she was, not his own mother, but just some haggard-looking woman in an airport.

"Mom!" he called, frightened by his trick of vision. "Mom. Over here."

She stumbled, her right arm dragged by the unruly weight of a suitcase-on-a-leash. Jacob's father had bought her the luggage in the early eighties, when the innovation was all the rage, and she continued to use the gift loyally despite its flawed design. As if conscious of its metaphorical gimmick, the suitcase jerked and stalled like a disobedient dog.

Finally she reached him, and from up close, she was again his mother. They collapsed into a tight hug. Jacob burrowed his fingers into her back.

"Jake, honey?" she said. "What is it? What's wrong?"

Jacob was still thinking of his own arrival here six months ago, how terribly alone he'd felt. But now his mother's strong arms were around him.

"Are you all right?" she asked, pulling away.

"I'm fine," he managed. "You know, considering. How about you? You look exhausted."

"It's been a *long* trip. Eight days with your father and those scientists."

His father's absence hadn't struck Jacob until now. "Where is Dad?" he asked, looking around.

His mother shrugged as if it hadn't occurred to her, either, to miss him. Then, softly: "Oh. Over there."

Jacob's father lumbered through the doorway, tilting left to counterbalance the overstuffed garment bag that sank his right arm. His left hand hefted a leather briefcase, dwarfed in comparison. He was a cartoon of Justice with her scales awry.

"Jacob," his father called. "Here." He thrust the bulging bag into Jacob's hand, keeping the briefcase for himself. "Let's get out of the flow."

Heaving the bag, Jacob's arm felt as though it might rip from its socket like an overcooked chicken leg. He wondered how his father had managed on his own in Heathrow. Then it occurred to him that he hadn't; he would have paid someone.

They regrouped by the windows. Jacob dropped the garment bag and wriggled his arm to loosen the muscles. His father set down his briefcase. Just as Jacob moved forward to initiate a hug, his father extended a stiff hand for shaking. They collided, caught in a tangled dance of trying to retrieve their respective gestures.

"Well," his father said when he extricated himself, as if by uttering this single word he fulfilled his conversational obligation. He scratched at his bald spot. Jacob noticed that the bare patch had grown since their last meeting to the size of a small yarmulke.

Jacob was overwhelmed by his father's imperfections. But instead of the dangerous rage he had anticipated, he felt a surprising relief. After so many years, there was a soothing familiarity to their estrangement.

He had been holding in so much these last four days. Ingrid had supported him, Chantelle and Danny, too; but none of them knew him, *all* of him. Now, facing his parents, Jacob was unhinged by the depth of their connection. These were the people who had birthed him, who had fed him when he could not feed himself. They had witnessed every stage of his growth.

In the security of their presence, Jacob's anxiety breached forth. Grief clogged his throat like mucus.

"Hey, I almost forgot." Jacob's father socked him on the shoulder. The punch was playful, but the unexpected force almost knocked him over. "I brought you a present."

Jacob wavered on his unsteady legs. "A present?"

"From London," his father said, reaching for his briefcase. "You're gonna love this. It's the perfect thing."

Jacob's mother pulled Jacob to her, wrapping her arms around. "Gene, honey," she told his father. "Not now."

"It's right here. It'll just take a second." He unlatched the leather case.

Indistinct tears gathered in Jacob's eyes, then began to leak in a confusion of wetness. His mother wiped his cheek with her thumb. "Gene," she said, "this is really not the time."

"I carried it all the way over here, Sarah. I want to see him open it."

"Gene!"

"It's okay," Jacob interjected. "It's fine." If his father wanted to give him something, why not let him? It wasn't very often that he tried.

A blue ribbon bound the small cardboard box. Jacob attempted to untie it, but the knot only drew tighter. He stretched the sheer material until its shape distorted, then slipped the whole ribbon, still tied, from the package.

"It's for your collection," his father said.

Jacob lifted the lid and removed the paperweight. It was a miniature replica of a pint glass of Guinness, filled with solid black material that resembled tar.

"Thanks, Dad," he said, replacing the trinket. "Thanks a lot. It's really nice."

He didn't mention that his father had given him this exact paperweight three years ago, after his last London trip.

The taxi idled at the hotel while his parents dropped their bags, then ferried the three of them to Nana Jenny's.

"Ingrid's supposed to meet us at six," Jacob said as they climbed the stairs. "We've got about twenty-five minutes."

"Can't wait," his father said.

Jacob's mother swatted the backs of his legs. "Gene. Stop. Let's at least start things off on the right foot." She craned her neck around the stairwell. "Did they repaint in here? Something's different."

"I don't think so," Jacob said, but something was. It was the smell. The old people who used to occupy every unit—cooking latkes and brisket with their heady scents—had been usurped by younger tenants who no doubt favored low-fat, odorless meals.

At the door, Jacob fumbled with the keys. He turned them left as usual, but the knob refused to budge. Then from nowhere a loud click split the air. The knob twisted in his hands as if possessed.

Ingrid greeted him with a smile.

"God, you scared me," Jacob said. "How'd you get in?"

"Keys," she said, as if it should have been obvious. She wore a green T-shirt and faded jeans. A grimy rag draped her shoulder.

How would she have keys? Every time Jacob thought he was figuring out Ingrid's story, new information surfaced that didn't quite fit. She had been invisible for his entire life, but now, in an almost creepy way, it seemed she was everywhere.

Jacob wondered about his obligations. Was he supposed to introduce Ingrid? Had she and his mother ever met?

"Eugene," Ingrid said, taking charge. Jacob's father shook her hand with a butler's cold formality, just the way Papa Isaac used to greet him.

Ingrid reached next for Jacob's mother. "Sarah," she said.

"Good to see you, Ingrid."

Jacob still couldn't tell if they had met before, or if they just knew each other's names.

"Come on in," Ingrid said. "Sit down. You must be exhausted."

They gravitated instinctively to the dining room table. China plates and bowls glittered immaculate, sparkling silverware—all the special-for-Passover things. An open jar of polish, pink as cotton candy, filled the room with its bitter smell.

Ingrid dipped her rag into the jar and picked up the large Elijah cup. "I thought I'd get some of the things ready," she said, buffing the gracefully curved silver. "You wouldn't believe how much tarnish builds up."

"You've done a marvelous job," Jacob's mother said.

Ingrid worked the rag with fluid concentration, and everyone focused on the project, silent as strangers in a subway car. Here they were, together at last: the family. But like a poor counterfeit, the image was off-kilter. Ingrid sat in Jonathan's seat.

"There's potato salad in the kitchen," she said. "Some chicken, too. Did you eat on the plane?"

"We're fine," Jacob's father answered for all of them.

"Well, help yourself later if you want."

Quiet again settled over them. Jacob's father turned a soup-spoon in his stubby fingers as if it were a compass needle that would point to their destination. When he set it down, his fingerprints smudged the freshly polished metal.

Jacob looked at his father, then Ingrid—brother and sister together before him for the first time. Ingrid was taller, her hair a lighter gray. She looked more elegant in her ratty T-shirt and jeans than his father ever could in his pressed slacks and Oxford shirt. But her chin had the same arrowhead pointiness. Between their eyebrows slashed identical wrinkles.

"We appreciate your flying out," his father said. His tone suggested the implication: Now that *he* had arrived, there was no need for her to stay.

"There wasn't any question," Ingrid said.

"I mean, for Jacob's sake. This was a lot for him to handle."

"Well, he's more mature than some fifty-year-olds I know."

Jacob hated that they spoke about him as if he weren't right there, tugging him back and forth for their own purposes. He imagined them as children, arguing over a doll's pretend needs: "He wants to be fed." "No! He wants his diaper changed."

Jacob's mother broke the stalemate. "So, Ingrid. How long will you be able to stay east?"

"It depends on Mother," Ingrid said. "And what the doctor says. At least a week, I'm sure."

"That's all right with the university?"

Ingrid nodded. "I'm not teaching classes this term, just advising grad students. They'll be glad for the break."

"And David?"

"Oh, he can take care of himself. Believe me, he's had plenty of practice."

At first Jacob thought they were referring to a son of Ingrid's. A cousin, someone his own age. Then Jacob's mother said, "I guess men are more liberated in northern California," and he understood that David was Ingrid's husband.

Jacob prickled with betrayal. How did his mother know these things? He felt like the victim in some initiatory hazing, ignorant of the rites to which everyone else was privy.

"Look at me," Jacob's mother said, starting to rise. "Letting you do all this work. How can I help?"

"No, no." Ingrid waved her off. "It's just this and the seder plate left. I'll do that tomorrow."

Jacob's mother was caught half-standing, crouched ridiculously above her chair. "Are you sure?"

"Of course. You just got here. Don't worry about anything."

Jacob's mother rose the rest of the way. She crossed to the wall, straightened a perfectly horizontal picture frame. "Well," she said, "if everything here is under control, maybe we ought to head over to the hospital. Don't you think so? Gene?"

Jacob's father looked up vacantly. He had retreated into himself the way he used to when Papa Isaac commanded this table. Jacob had come to think of his father's zombie-like isolation as a physical place, a remote island with limited access.

"Oh, you can't leave yet," Ingrid said, replacing the shiny Elijah cup on the table. "It's just sundown. Don't you want to stay for *bedikat chametz*?"

"What?" Jacob's mother asked.

Ingrid wiped her hands on the dirty rag, then balled it and

tossed it aside. "Searching for the *chametz*, the leaven, to make the house clean for Pesach. I know Mother would want us to."

Jacob hadn't recognized the name, but he had dim memories of the ceremony: stalking through darkened rooms to collect crumbs of bread. He had done it here once, with Papa Isaac.

"I don't think so," Jacob's father said.

Ingrid frowned. "Of course she would. She always did it."

"That's not what I mean. I don't think we want to stay."

"But don't you—"

"No!"

Silence shadowed the room, a collective cessation of breath. Everyone stared at their laps.

Gingerly, as if easing into a too-hot bath, Jacob's mother found her voice. "How long does this take?" she asked. "We don't want to miss visiting hours."

"Fifteen, twenty minutes?" Ingrid said. "Besides, the nurses will let you in all night. You're family."

Jacob's mother looked then at his father, asking with her eyes for a compromise, but he refused her gaze.

"This is crazy," he said. "We came here to see my mother, not to clean her apartment. Let's go." He stood, his thighs knocking the table. Stacks of china clattered, threatening to crack.

Ingrid saved the teetering Elijah cup before it fell onto the bone-white soup bowls. "Eugene, wait. Don't you think Mother—"

"No. I think my mother is in a coma, and she has no way of knowing if her apartment is kosher for Passover."

Jacob's mother twisted her hands. "Please. Gene. You don't have to talk that way."

"What? What way? I haven't said *anything*. I didn't object that she's been rooting around in my mother's apartment when no one else was here. I even agreed to do the seder tomorrow night. But this . . ." He wheeled around to Ingrid. "Since when did you of all people get so concerned with being observant?"

"It's not for me," Ingrid said. "It's for Mother."

Jacob's father scoffed. "Come on. Sarah. Jacob. We can call a cab from the street."

He strode to the door. Jacob's mother hesitated a moment, then followed.

"Jacob, come on," his father called.

Jacob was still sitting at the table. He looked around at all the empty chairs. "I think I'm going to stay," he said.

"What?"

Jacob cleared his throat. "I'm staying here and helping Ingrid. I think Nana Jenny would want us to."

He didn't look up to see his father's reaction. He heard the door slam into its frame.

First, Ingrid explained, they had to scatter crumbs throughout the apartment; that way there would be something to remove during the ceremony. How quintessentially Jewish, Jacob thought: create an obstacle for the sole purpose of overcoming it. The rest of the world operated on the principle that if it ain't broke, don't fix it. Jews followed a twisted, obverse logic: Break it so you have an excuse to fix it; the experience is bound to improve you.

In the kitchen, Ingrid found half a stale challah and an end of pumpernickel. She handed Jacob the darker hunk and they crumbled the bread as if to feed pigeons, gathering the marble-sized bits in a plastic bowl.

When they had enough, they each scooped a handful and began dropping token chunks. Ingrid spread four or five on the Formica countertop. Jacob tossed a smattering below the breakfast table. They moved on to the dining room, sullying the windowsill, the rug along the breakfront's base. Like mushrooms after rain, brown crusts sprouted everywhere.

The living room was next, then the hallway, then Nana Jenny's bedroom. Sneaking into his grandmother's secret spaces, Jacob felt like a spy. He had to remind himself this was not a violation. After all, he was doing it for her.

Finally, Papa Isaac's study. It had been a decade since Jacob had been inside; Nana Jenny had kept the door resolutely shut. His heart raced now at the prospect of entering the site of so many memories, this actual room that corresponded with the dream room in his brain. He thought of Jonathan's sweaty grip, the pinning victories.

Ingrid paused, too, at the door. She shook the plastic bowl, the last bits of bread rattling like a snake's tail. Then she turned and walked back to the kitchen.

Jacob slackened with disappointment and relief. He touched the doorknob. Not this time. Not yet.

*   *   *

Ingrid abandoned the bowl of crumbs and now produced a medium-sized grocery bag. "Okay," she said. "I think this is everything. Here's the Haggadah. And a candle and a book of matches. And I found the feather I think Mother uses." She pulled out a long gray feather like the ones Jacob used to scavenge on Seagull Beach. "I couldn't find a wooden spoon," she added, "but we can just collect the crumbs in this bag."

Ingrid's knowledge of the procedure perplexed him. Jacob had assumed that her falling out with Papa Isaac had been precipitated by a rejection of Judaism. His father's crack about her belated concern for observance seemed confirmation.

"Do you do this kind of stuff at home?" he asked.

"What, make a mess all over my house? I don't have to. My husband takes care of that."

"No. Jewish stuff. Do you keep kosher and everything?"

"Please. Nothing so drastic."

"Well, you seem pretty much like an expert."

Ingrid smiled. "I guess I have my own mix-and-match version of things." She picked up the feather and stroked it against the grain, then the right way, smoothing the soft gray hairs. "Like this," she said, "*bedikat chametz*. It's one of my favorite ceremonies. But you have to separate out all the nasty stuff."

"What's nasty?" Jacob asked. "I thought it was just getting rid of bread."

"Yes, but everything always has another level." She opened the Haggadah and read aloud: "Our Sages regarded leaven as a symbol of *yetzer hara*—the evil inclination. By removing leaven from our homes, we stress the importance of liberating ourselves from the corrupting influences that make men subservient to their passions and evil desires."

Ingrid shrugged I-told-you-so. "Yuck. What a horrible way to look at life. So I use my own interpretations. For me, it's about making your home special, free of its 'daily bread,' so you can think about what freedom really means."

"That's nice," Jacob said. "That makes a lot of sense."

But secretly he liked the idea of sweeping away corrupting passions as easily as crumbs of bread. If only he could decide what corrupted and what purified. Hannes, in Frankfurt, had meant to absolve himself through passion, but Jacob had ended up feeling tainted. What about Ari—had he liberated Jacob or condemned him? And Danny, his latest attraction? Jacob was subservient not to passion, but to uncertainty.

Ingrid snapped the Haggadah shut with the crack of a judge's gavel. "Ready?" she said. "Turn out the lights."

They stood in the dim dining room. The shapes of walls and furniture merged into an undulating muslin haze. In the absence of light, Jacob's other senses heightened. Cars passing below the window beckoned in a static hum like an empty seashell's plaintive murmur. He could locate Ingrid's heat next to him, the effect of her flesh on the air. He smelled her, too, a vegetable earthiness cut with the tang of residual silver polish. He felt suddenly that he knew Ingrid—the essence of her—in the deep way blind people must know things.

"The candle," she whispered, a wraith of a voice.

Jacob struck a match and touched it to the wick. The flame flared, confusing his pupils with its brightness, then settled to a mellow glow. A softened Ingrid took shape next to him, her face a swath of color against the darkness.

They padded through the rooms in reverse: Nana Jenny's bedroom, the hallway, the living room. At each pile of crumbs, Jacob held the candle close to the ground until Ingrid found every bit of bread.

"It's like Hansel and Gretel," Jacob said, "following their trail out of the forest."

"Except the birds stole their bread crumbs," Ingrid pointed out. "They couldn't find the way back."

The living room's walls shimmered magically, pulsing as if alive with breath. The hushed whisk of Ingrid's feather and the paper bag's busy rustle were the only sounds. Jacob breathed as little as possible, not wanting to disrupt the drama.

In the dining room, crouching with Ingrid beside the tall breakfront, he noticed a dull pain in his fingers. Wax had streamed over the candle's lip and molded onto his hand. He thought to switch hands and wipe off the scalding residue, but memory kept the candle firmly in his grip. He was shocked back to the time he and Jonathan had searched for *chametz* with Papa Isaac. They had both helped, taking turns with the candle. And at one point, when Jonathan handed him the burning taper, the wax spilled over, singeing his knuckles. Jacob kept silent, refusing to complain, refusing to seem less capable. In the darkness, no one saw his tears.

How unlikely, he thought, that it would come again to this—to him stooping in this musty apartment, enduring the pain of a burning candle. But now he chose to endure. Papa Isaac was gone. Jonathan, too. It was he who was here. He and Ingrid. The two of them.

Jacob felt himself settling, his internal scales tipping to a new balance point. He had heard of strangers trapped in elevators, who emerge hours later bonded as lifelong friends. He could understand that now, the almost surreal but utterly honest closeness two people could achieve in the right circumstance. It was the same way, too, he felt already with Danny.

"I'm really glad we did this," he told Ingrid. They were back in the kitchen, collecting the last pieces of bread.

"Me too," she said. "I didn't want to be alone."

"Think we found it all?"

Ingrid peered into the sack. "I think we did." Then, as if speaking to someone else, someone inside herself, or someone very far away, she said it again: "Yes, I think we did."

She opened the blood-colored Haggadah and handed it to Jacob. "But we still have to say the nullification."

Jacob pried the stiff book open with his thumb and pinkie, and by shifting candlelight, recited the words: "May all leaven in my possession which I have not seen or removed, be regarded as nonexistent and considered as mere dust of the earth."

It seemed at first another classic Jewish trick. You scatter crumbs and ceremonially remove them, and only then, after you've gone through the motions, do the authorities reveal this easier incantatory sleight of hand.

But as he considered the prayer, Jacob appreciated its wishful thinking. The words invoked a world in which intent was as potent as action, in which the thought really was what counted. *We proclaim the leaven nonexistent, and so it does not exist!* How wonderful if things could be that easy.

He read down to the last paragraph, where the completion of

the ceremony was outlined. Tomorrow morning, according to the prescription, they were supposed to light the paper bag on fire. And as the bits of stale bread flamed, they should recite a longer version of the declaration: "May all leaven in my possession, whether I have seen it or not, or whether I have removed it or not, be regarded as nonexistent and considered as mere dust of the earth."

Yes, he thought. Yes, let it be so. A few simple words, and let another year's corrupting passions burn to char.

Burning

He smelled smoke from a block away. Just a faint trace at first, a dusty cayenne tang garnishing the pollinated air. How predictable, he thought. A barbecue, maybe a phalanx of barbecues. It might as well have been a scratch-and-sniff card labeled *suburb*.

At home for the summer after his freshman year at Amherst, Jacob wasn't adjusting well to being a commuter. The job wasn't bad—research for an English professor at Georgetown. And the ride back to Chevy Chase was a straight shot, the bus dropping him five minutes' walk from his parents' house. What he couldn't stomach was the ritual of return: the pack of power-tied men filing androidlike into the neighborhood, peeling one by one up flagstone walks to their respective waiting families. Jacob had watched his father enact this routine for years. But to be complicit now himself in the mindless march left him each evening feeling sullied, as if the diesel clouds of bus exhaust had oozed into his skin.

As he started up the small hill of his street, the smell intensified—more chemical now, the plasticky smolder of things not meant to burn. Jacob's stomach palsied with a premonition: This was no harmless barbecue; his house was burning down.

He jogged over the crest, blood sluicing through his heart. What if his mother had left a burner on? What if something had shorted in the circuitry?

When he saw the familiar yellow door, the soothing protrusion of the kitchen's bay window, relief splashed him with its cool comfort. Everything was still intact. He strode down the narrow side path to the backyard, breath returning in happy, fitful gulps. He found his father hovered over the Weber grill's black enameled half-shell, and smiled at his own foolish worry: a harmless barbecue after all.

"I'm home," he called.

His father, intent on the coals, must not have heard, but Jacob forgave his distraction. These days they were giving each other the benefit of the doubt.

When Jacob returned home two weeks earlier, he'd been nervous: Was he now a guest? A tenant? Still a son? His father, uncharacteristically, seemed to grasp the need for adjustment. "You're not a kid anymore," he said at the first night's dinner. "You've lived away now, and I'm sure you have your own ideas about how things should be. That's fine. Your mother and I will only ask what we ask of anybody else. Common courtesy. Decency. Respect." Generic-sounding as it was, Jacob appreciated his father's gesture. He was willing to give the new regime a try.

His father still stared into the grill's gaping bowl. The licking flames reflected an orange tan on his face.

"Hey, Dad," Jacob said. "What's up?" He noticed a pile of envelopes sprawled on a deck chair. "Cool. My mail finally came?"

He had forwarded his mail for the summer break, but to his great annoyance, nothing had been delivered so far. Now it looked as though the two-weeks backlog had arrived all at once. He grabbed a fistful of envelopes and flipped through. A couple of postcards. A credit card bill.

"What's on tonight?" he asked. "Shish kebab?"

He peered over his father's shoulder. The ash-coated bowl swirled with flames, but there wasn't the usual blushing mound of charcoal, no grease-dripping chunks of meat. What Jacob saw instead through the heat-wrinkled air was a magazine, its pages blistered leprously. Below that, a stack of newsprint smoked. Blackened shards of paper, raddled like old lace, rose and fell on the fire's buoyancy.

The magazine was almost obliterated, but Jacob still recognized the formatting. He made out a running footer at the bottom of a shriveled page: *The Advocate.* In the remnants of the newspaper below, a masthead: *Gay Community News.*

"Dad!" he yelled. "What the fuck are you doing?" He stabbed into the flames, but his reflexes saved him. His knuckle hairs curled with burn.

His father remained absorbed in the fire. He looked as though he were studying something, scrutinizing a dropped piece of china for a hairline crack.

"What are you," Jacob said, "some kind of Nazi?"

He wanted to hurt his father, to shove his hand into the hot ash until it sizzled. But quickly the rage turned against himself: This was not how things were supposed to happen.

He had planned to wait another week or two, until life settled back to routine. Then he would take his parents to dinner on his new MasterCard. And as he treated them to a good meal, he would tell them about joining the gay students' group. About the relief of finally being honest.

Now he had lost his chance. Now it would always be a dirty secret they'd exposed.

His father still hadn't said a word. He fished a fallen branch from the ground and poked it into the fire. He stirred methodically, churning unburned scraps to the top. Jacob noticed a rising fragment that was not newsprint or magazine paper, but the thicker material of a mailing envelope, and he clenched with a deeper anxiety. *The Advocate* and *GCN* were both sent in plain wrappers. His father could not have discovered them unless he had snooped, opening envelopes. He must have had reason to suspect.

Jacob spun around and dashed to the house. He entered the dark basement, found the stairs with blind memory, and pulled himself up by the banister. Just as he reached the top, his mother walked through the front door, her arms loaded with brown grocery bags.

"Hi, honey," she chimed. "How's my son the commuter?"

Jacob stared. He knew this woman, his own mother, but suddenly he doubted his recognition. "Mom?" he said. The word sounded ludicrous, a nonsense syllable.

"Jake, honey," she said. "What's wrong?"

"Mom, we have to talk."

She set the grocery bags on the floor as gently as if they were toddlers. "All right. Do you want to talk now?"

"In a minute," he said. "First I have to do something."

In his room, Jacob went straight to the closet and pulled down the ratty backpack. The magazines were stuffed between a chemistry book and handouts from freshman comp: two more *GCNs*, his tattered copies of *Playguy* and *Honcho*. His bottle of lube nested in its sock at the pack's bottom.

A nib of relief pricked the shell of his apprehension: His father didn't know so much after all.

He zipped shut the backpack and returned it to the shelf. But stuffing it behind his old baseball gear, he paused. Why should there be any more secrets? If this was what his father wanted, why not provide it? He didn't need magazines to tell him who he was.

The fire had petered out, but his father lingered at the barbecue. The sooty stick drooped wretchedly from his hand.

Jacob opened his bag and extended it. "There's more where that came from," he said. He nodded to the scorched magazines.

His father stared into the cinders, his face doughy and expressionless. After a minute he still hadn't raised his eyes.

"Here," Jacob said, dumping the pile at his father's feet. SODOMY CASE TO SUPREME COURT, proclaimed a banner headline. A *Honcho* splayed to its glossy centerfold. "Take these, too," he said. "Go ahead. Burn it all."

Though He Tarry

The tablecloth was stained with memory. Brown splotches like liver spots on an old woman's hand marked the places he and Jonathan had sat as kids—testaments to sloppy soup spooning, upset cups of wine. The empty setting at the table's head was foxed with smaller blemishes. Jacob pictured Papa Isaac dunking sugar cubes into his artificially whitened coffee, oblivious to the liquid plumes he sent geysering over the rim. But considering they had used this tablecloth for every holiday in the past two decades, the linen was remarkably clean. Jacob thought of all the stains that were no longer visible, the ones Nana Jenny must have bleached away.

The seder plate was the table's nucleus, with its five symbolic foods in their appointed indentations: the mud-colored *haroset*, the gnarled horseradish root, the parsley, the roasted egg, and the lamb shank (which, since the Star Market had been sold out, was actually a baked chicken leg). At the corners of an invisible rectangle sat four identical china settings, each surrounded by a Kiddush cup and a bowl of toothpick-speared radishes in salt water. Glass saucers, like outsized contact lenses, overflowed with individual scoops of *haroset*.

Jacob had been jolted when he saw the table arranged exactly as Nana Jenny always laid it out. He wondered how Ingrid had pulled it off, considering she hadn't attended a Rosenbaum seder in at least twenty-five years. Perhaps it was something encoded, passed in the genes from mother to daughter.

Still, the table jarred with his internal image. Normally, memory rendered past objects larger than they ever were: You return to your elementary school and discover that the water fountain, a looming challenge at nine, now nudges mid-thigh; the front yard that seemed bigger than a football field is revealed as a postage-stamp lot. But the seder table was affected in reverse. In Jacob's memory it was always too small, every inch claimed by a bottle of wine, a salad plate, a candlestick. He remembered Nana Jenny having to walk around during the meal, serving from trays of food that couldn't fit on the overcrowded surface. Now, the oval seemed disconcertingly spacious. No enlarging leaves had been added. All the requisite ritual objects were still in place. And yet so much was missing.

Jacob's father flipped a Haggadah page and cracked the spine to keep his place. He was clearly not thrilled about being here, but so far he hadn't fussed. Jacob's mother must have reprimanded him after their tense departure last night. Now he wore the politely amused expression of a jock taken to the opera—skeptical, but too fearful of the consequences to misbehave.

"Well, Jake," he said, grinning. "Looks like you're the lucky winner tonight."

Jacob grinned back. His mother and Ingrid smiled, too. They were all on best behavior, because it was unclear who were guests and who were hosts.

"Winner?" Jacob asked. "What do you mean?"

"Well, with this crowd of fogies, I don't think we need to get out the birth certificates!"

Jacob flipped in his own book then and saw the familiar, dreaded Four Questions. "Oh, God," he said. "You're not serious?"

His father was smug. "I don't see how you can have a seder without the Four Questions."

In their large-type Hebrew letters—printed bigger than any other part of the book, in order that the youngest child be able to read with ease—the questions composed a declaration of his captivity. Once again, he was punished for his willingness to abide the family, while Jonathan, in his hiding, got off scot-free. But as angry as Jacob was at the injustice, more than anything else, he found he missed his brother. Things weren't the same without someone to argue with.

He propped his Haggadah defeatedly on the table's edge. He cleared his throat, prepared for humiliation.

"Wait," Ingrid said. She raised her left hand to ear level like a student flagging the teacher's attention. "I don't think just Jacob should do it."

"You're kidding me," his father said. "We *do* have to get the birth certificates?" His chuckle was too forced to be genuine.

"That business is for when there are little kids," Ingrid said. "We're all adults here. We should share. One question each."

A chair squealed against someone's shifting weight. The candle flames flickered with anxious breath. Jacob wanted to tell his aunt to forget it; she didn't know their history.

His father flashed a smile, but behind his tightened lips the gritted teeth shone. "I don't know what you do in Berkeley," he said, pronouncing *Berkeley* like the name of a trashy amusement park. "But out here we've realized life is not always fair."

"It's not about fairness," Ingrid shot back. "It's about participation." She poured a glass of seltzer and the water hissed with bubbles. "Sarah," she said, "what do you think?"

Jacob's mother folded and refolded her napkin in an origami of nervous tension. "Well," she hedged. "I'm not sure I should really vote. I mean, even if you three want to split it, I can't read Hebrew."

"So you do it in English," Ingrid said. "No problem."

"No problem?" Jacob's father brushed nonexistent crumbs from the tablecloth. "It was no problem before you stuck your nose in. I had to do this when I was a kid. Now it's Jacob's turn. If he wants to get off the hook, maybe it's time *he* had a kid."

It was a cheap shot, but it hit Jacob like clenched knuckles. He gulped from his Kiddush cup.

"Fine," Ingrid said. She pounded her palms flat on the table. "Then it's just the two of us. That all right with you, Jacob?"

Jacob looked at his aunt, then over to his father. This must be the way his mother had always felt, tugged by her competing allegiances. He glanced at her, too, and she narrowed her left eye—not quite a wink, but enough to signal support.

"Yeah," he told Ingrid. "Thanks, I could use the help."

At Ingrid's nod, they began the chant. The verses were imbedded in the folds of Jacob's brain. He could almost hear the cranial curves creak and groan, loosening after the long hibernation. But spurred by Ingrid's voice, the words found their way. "*Ma nish-tanah, ha-layla ha-zeh* . . ." Why is this night different from all other nights?

Ingrid's singing voice was deep, with an old woman's throatiness. Jacob could imagine her crooning folk songs in a German beer hall. But there was a softness beneath the rough surface, a soothing, lullaby quality.

Together they rode the roller-coaster tune. Jacob stumbled on two or three Hebrew phrases, but the tether of Ingrid's voice caught and held him. He thought of Danny, whirling with him on the dance floor. This was the same floating, the same security.

Her coup complete, Ingrid piloted them through the ritual's serpentine twists with the confidence of a jungle guide.

"Page twenty-one," she announced. "The ten plagues. Everyone ready?"

"Hold on," Jacob's father said, reaching for the squat bottle of Manischewitz. They weren't supposed to have drunk yet from the second cup of wine, but he had been sipping compulsively. By now he needed to cheat, topping off the wine so he would be able to reach the level with his dipping finger.

Another time, Jacob might have been annoyed by his father's indiscretion, but tonight he was grateful for the postponement. As a kid, he had loved this symbolic reenactment. You dunked your pinkie into the Kiddush cup, once for each of the nasty plagues. He and Jonathan competed to see who dripped all ten drops the fastest.

But what amusement could there be now, even in metaphorical plagues?

He had called the Fenway that morning to explain his missed test and to schedule a new appointment. The receptionist told him they had a cancellation that afternoon. Did he want to come in?

Jacob panicked. Last week the test had seemed a formality: a quick needle jab, a vial of blood, a confirmation. He could laugh it off as the perfect April Fools' joke. But now the whole thing felt jinxed. The fact that he had missed his original appointment loomed like a dangerous portent, all the more foreboding because what had made him miss it was Nana Jenny's stroke, the trickery of her own complicated blood.

Dry-mouthed, he promised the receptionist he would show at four-thirty sharp.

The test was routine. A technician stabbed the inside of his elbow before he had time to flinch. The blood emerged much darker than he anticipated, almost black instead of red. Its rush into the vial disturbed him. Was it that eager to flee his body?

The technician thumbed a bar-coded label onto the test tube and plopped it into a rack of others awaiting analysis. Later, she would examine it. She would, or someone else. They would culture the sample in a Petri dish or whatever high-tech equivalent. Everything would be meticulously tracked.

The clinical precision should have reassured him. In two weeks' time he would know for sure. But Jacob's fear wasn't about knowing. It was about *not* knowing. About the things you didn't even know you didn't know.

His mother pushed up her sleeve, wincing as if she'd swallowed sour milk. "This is so morbid," she said. "Can we get it over with?"

"Okay," Ingrid said, her hand poised above her Kiddush cup. "Start your engines."

They declaimed the plagues in unison, dipping their fingers with the name of each affliction. *Dam. Tz'fardea. Kinnim.* Blood. Frogs. Vermin . . .

Jacob could barely bring himself to follow along. What if the splashing wine really *were* blood?

. . . Wild Beasts. Cattle Disease. Boils . . .

Three more drops on the plate.

Now everything was a reference to AIDS. Jacob thought of the animal diseases that attacked people with HIV: MAI was bird tuberculosis; toxomplasmosis you could get from cats. The Haggadah illustration for "boils" showed two miserable, lesion-covered figures, with a third sprawled dead in the background. He envisioned Marty in the picture. Then himself.

. . . Hail. Locusts. Darkness. Smiting of the First-born.

The tenth plague had always been Jacob's respite, a secret reassurance from above. If God went after the first-born, then Jacob had no reason to fear. Jonathan had been first; he was safe by sixteen minutes.

But as he dunked his finger a final time, the childhood magic eluded him. Why did he think Jonathan would protect him? No one could protect him but himself. He stared at his plate, splattered with ten purple drops like sarcomas on deathly white skin.

They sang "Dayyenu," then sipped from the second cup. They recited motzi over the salted matzah. Jacob tried not to think of the HIV test, or Jonathan, or anything. Like a passenger on a speeding train, he rode the ritual's motions, his mind as limply susceptible as a body shuttled through space.

His parents seemed equally resistless. His mother sat in her own quietude, face blank, as if watching a foreign film without the benefit of subtitles. His father, still sulking from the Four Questions, settled also into a harmless passivity.

The other night, Danny had asked Jacob to describe his parents, but Jacob had not been able to. He failed even at describing their physical features. He had no objective view.

"Let me come to the seder, then," Danny suggested. "I want to see where you come from."

"Don't you think it's early?" Jacob asked. "I've barely known you a week."

"Just bring me as a guest. They wouldn't have to know."

"Oh, sure. A faggy little Christian kid who's just dying to sit through a night of Hebrew and bad wine. They wouldn't think that was weird at all. Besides, I wouldn't be able to keep my hands off of you."

Now, though, part of Jacob wished he *had* brought Danny. He would like to see how his father, who had enough trouble dealing with Jacob's theoretical sexuality, would react to a flesh-and-blood boyfriend. But a larger part was glad to keep things separate. Jacob had always said his parents should know his "real" life; but now that he was finally having one, there were things he didn't want them to know.

Ingrid continued to charge ahead, her leadership unchallenged. But when it came time for the bitter herbs, Jacob's father perked. Something had energized him. Maybe it was the wine.

Ingrid had bought a jar of beet-juice-sweetened horseradish, the commercial kind you could find in the supermarket. It was one of the few things she had done differently from Nana Jenny. She spooned a dollop onto her plate and passed it to Jacob, who took some and passed it to his mother. When she in turn tried to hand it to Jacob's father, he smirked and refused the jar.

"Give me the real stuff," he said, indicating the brown root on the seder plate.

"I thought the shredded kind would be easier," Ingrid said.

"It's not supposed to be easy. It's supposed to be painful. That's the whole point."

Nobody handed his father the root, so he reached for it himself. He palmed the gnarl and carved it with a silver knife the way an old-timer would whittle a block of wood.

"Anybody else?" he offered.

"The red stuff's fine for me," Jacob's mother said. "I'm not a glutton for punishment." She collected a tiny bite of the carmine pulp on her spoon and cut it with some cinnamony *haroset*.

"I'll take one," Ingrid said, holding out her hand.

"Me too, I guess," Jacob said.

His father doled out two shards of yellow-white flesh.

After the blessing, Jacob nibbled half an inch from his allotment. It was not tough and stringy as usual, but moist and crisp as a carrot. This wouldn't be so bad, he told himself.

Ingrid and Jacob's father each bit significant chunks of the root. Like the hinged mouths of nutcracker dolls, their matching pointed jaws pumped mechanically. Watching them—brother and sister, together after so many years apart—Jacob thought again of Jonathan, of their own reunion last September. They had been separated only two years, yet Jacob had not been certain he would recognize his brother. What if it had been twenty years instead of two? Forty? At what point did someone, even a sibling, cease to be a part of you?

Then it hit him. A burning somehow not in his mouth but already behind and above it, a searing rush that scalded his sinuses. He tried to swallow, but it was as though a drug in the horseradish numbed his reflexes, slowing the signals from brain to jaw.

The toxic fumes swirled in his skull, pressed on his eyeballs from inside. Tears began to seep. He was afraid to wipe them off because his fingers, too, might be contaminated with the sting.

When he managed to gulp down the bitterness and found the

napkin to dry his vision, he saw that his father and Ingrid were both still chewing. They blinked against the tears that dripped down their own cheeks, stealing occasional glances at each other. They chewed and blinked and glanced, prolonging the agony, neither one willing to swallow first.

Throughout dinner, they continued to face off like embattled litigants across a courtroom. Jacob passed trays of food between them, a reluctant conduit, feeling each time he helped one that he betrayed the other.

Ingrid served apricot chicken and brisket, cucumber salad tossed in vinegar. Jacob's mother complimented the meat's tenderness, but Ingrid shrugged off the praise, deprecating her cooking as merely passable. Then they fell back to their dogged chewing. The steady scrape of silverware was the sound of an animal scratching to be uncaged.

When the china had been cleared and coffee poured, they opened the Haggadahs again. "Let's get this finished," Jacob's father said. He licked his index finger and skimmed for the right page. Impatience and too much wine flushed his brow.

He got there before the rest of them. "Oh," he said; Jacob couldn't tell if it was pleasant surprise or disappointment.

A second later, Jacob found the page. Then Ingrid and his mother came upon it, too. A collective paralysis gripped the table. No one had remembered the Afikoman.

When Jacob was younger, the Afikoman game had been the highlight of the holiday. Since the after-dinner portion of the ceremony could not proceed without this specially designated matzah, he and Jonathan would hide it from Papa Isaac, then demand a gift as ransom for its return.

Their cue to steal the Afikoman was when Papa Isaac set down his coffee and announced, "Now I will retire for a few minutes." "Retire" was code for smoking a cigar in his study, the only place Nana Jenny would abide the habit. They would wait for the click of the study door, then filch the Afikoman with conspiratorial grins.

The yearly matzah heist was one of the rare times he and Jonathan cooperated. Sometimes they would have planned the crime days in advance, diagramming their grandparents' apartment from memory. Other times it was a last-minute decision. Inside the M (for matzah) volume of the *Encyclopedia Judaica* was one of their proudest brainstorms. Hiding the special cracker in the box of other, anonymous matzahs had been their all-time triumph.

When Papa Isaac returned after ten or fifteen minutes, ready to resume the seder, and noticed the missing object, he would sink into a frightening gravity. Countenance stern, bushy eyebrows twitching, he asked first, politely, for the Afikoman. Jacob and Jonathan offered only their practiced, stoic shrugs, and so their grandfather began his search. He lifted couch pillows and peered underneath, peeled back the corners of rugs. But Jacob and Jonathan were too good. Each and every year, they claimed their gifts before surrendering the matzah.

Just once, the last Passover before he died, did Papa Isaac come close to beating them. He had emerged from his study much sooner than expected, and in a panic, Jonathan shoved the Afikoman into a pile of magazines atop the television. It was a miserable hiding place, the first spot anyone would look.

Papa Isaac made his rounds, voicing the usual distress. What would he do if he couldn't find the Afikoman? Did anybody know where it was? Suddenly he was at the television, and Jacob's heart sagged into his stomach. Papa Isaac checked under the TV, behind it, then started shuffling through the periodicals.

After what seemed an hour, he slowly pivoted. By some miracle, his hands were empty. He checked the couch one last time, then acknowledged defeat by producing two gift-wrapped packages. For a second Jacob wondered if he himself had been fooled. Had he forgotten the true hiding place? But when he and Jonathan ran to the TV, there the matzah was, exactly where they had left it.

He didn't admit to himself until months later what he must have known all along: that in this one delimited arena, Papa Isaac had chosen to let them win.

"This is terrible," Jacob's mother said. "I don't have a present. I didn't even think." She peered around the dining room, as if hoping to find something she could pass off as a gift.

"Come on, Mom," Jacob said. "You just got back from London.

Besides, that's only for kids." But he secretly wished that despite their lapse, there was some way to maintain the tradition. He shifted in his chair, debating whether he should grab the matzah now and stash it someplace. Even if he hid the Afikoman, though, who would search for it? His father? Ingrid? It made no sense without a grandparent.

"We can at least do the circles," Ingrid proposed. "Shouldn't we at least do that?"

Jacob's father groaned. "After that meal? I don't think I could even swallow it."

"Gene," his mother said. "It's just matzah. It doesn't take up any room."

"Yes!" Jacob said, handing Ingrid the middle matzah. "Yes. The circles. We have to."

His aunt snapped the Afikoman into four squares and passed out the pieces like tickets. The table fell quiet but for the wet clack of tongues and teeth.

The goal was to bite the matzah into as close to a perfect circle as possible. Jacob presumed there was some theological justification: the circle representing spiritual wholeness, or the yearly ritual cycle. But the Rosenbaums adhered to the tradition strictly as a means of pitting each family member against the next, one more opportunity to be ranked.

"Oh! I'd forgotten how hard this is." Ingrid slumped in her chair. "How can you possibly . . . ?"

"Visualization," Jacob's father said between nibbles on the edge of his round. Having resigned himself to the activity, now he twittered with competitive energy. "You have to be able to see the end product you're shooting for. Isn't that right, Jake?"

Jacob didn't know which of his father's incarnations he liked less: the defeated sulker or the too-chummy pal. "We all know what a circle looks like, Dad," he said. "I don't think that's really the hard part."

"But you can't see just any circle. You have to see *yours*."

"Well," Ingrid said, "I'm not sure I can see anything, but . . ." She sighed and resumed her chewing. Instead of taking front-teeth rabbit bites like everyone else, she gnawed recklessly from the side of her mouth. Jacob was startled when he recognized the technique. Papa Isaac, too, had always chomped from the side, where he retained a row of real teeth. He still never managed much of a circle, but since he was the competition's judge, no one could disparage his clumsy entries.

The unorthodox style seemed to work for Ingrid. Jacob could see a coherent circle taking shape, rough in spots, but evenly proportioned. She was clearly going to be the one to beat.

"Damn," his father said. He tossed his matzah onto the table. A piece had cracked off along one of the perforations, rendering his supposed circle the shape of a flat tire.

Jacob's mother clucked her tongue. "I always tell you, Gene, the trick is knowing when to stop. You too, Jake. Pretty soon you won't have anything."

"I know," he admitted. His own piece, a four-inch square when he began, was down to the size of a silver dollar. "It's starting to look like one of Nana Jenny's."

"No, not even close," his mother said. "Hers weren't *half* that size."

Jacob laughed. "Remember how she always hid her piece when she was working on it? Like a hand of cards?" He mimicked the gesture, concealing his matzah behind a fan of fingers.

"Yes!" Ingrid said. "Yes, that's her exactly. As long as I can remember, she did that, and made them so tiny. This morning, when I burned last year's, I knew right away which was hers."

Jacob blanched at the thought of his grandmother's circle gone to ash. He knew this was part of the tradition: Nana Jenny saved the rounds, then incinerated them at the next Passover along with the newly collected *chametz*. But he hadn't considered that her circle from last year might be her final one.

It was foolish, he knew, to mourn a half-chewed piece of matzah. But the absence felt bigger. It was lost evidence.

Jacob felt the walls of memory hemming in, isolating him. He could say to Ingrid or his mother, "Do you remember?" and they could answer "Yes," but in the absence of evidence, how could they know if their memories coincided? It was like comparing colors: Who was to say your blue was not another person's green?

"Should we call time?" Jacob's mother asked.

"I'm out anyway," his father said. He flicked his flattened circle across the tablecloth.

"I guess I'm done, too," Ingrid said.

Jacob shrugged, resisting one last bite.

His mother collected the entries. Hers had the smoothest circumference, but bulged in a distinct egg shape. Ingrid's, which had appeared so promising, was missing a large crescent where a bite had strayed too far.

It looked like Jacob's was winner by default. But when his mother held it up for judging, the tiny circle cracked in half.

"I'm just not sure we've got a winner this year," she said. "Are we allowed to do that? To say nobody wins?"

"Forget it," Jacob's father said. "Let's just get this done." He opened his Haggadah.

Jacob's mother stacked the four rounds into a teetering pile. "Well, what should I do with them, then?"

"Here," Jacob said, reaching for the crackers. "I'll keep them for next year. I mean, shouldn't I? Shouldn't someone?"

They moved on, chanting the blessing after the meal and drinking the third cup of wine, but finishing seemed almost pointless now. Everyone was stuck in the melancholy of the failed Afikoman competition. Jacob imagined them as a high school basketball team gathered for a twenty-fifth-reunion game: all the intensity and talent gone, nothing left but nostalgia.

He could hardly bear the irony that the ritual's next segment was the welcoming of Elijah. Elijah, champion of the oppressed, bringing hope and relief to the downtrodden. The rescuer, the miracle worker. When the prophet arrived on earth, the Haggadah informed them, he would resolve all religious disputes. He would "turn the hearts of parents to their children, and the hearts of children to their parents."

It was as if the Haggadah's authors had anticipated that the Rosenbaums would need this—would need *something* to lift them from the mire of their own decomposing history. But what a flimsy hook on which to hang their hopes. Elijah was nothing more than a folk legend, the closest thing Jews had to a Santa Claus.

As a kid, of course, Jacob had believed the magic. When he and Jonathan raced to the apartment's door to let in the visiting prophet, he was certain Elijah really came. You couldn't see him, Jacob always reasoned, because he had to visit every Jewish home around the world, and to do so had to fly at lightning speed. But if you looked closely at the level of wine in his chalice, you could see it had dropped a millimeter, proof of a prophetic sip—at least Jacob always wanted to think he could.

His father poured Manischewitz into the tall Elijah cup, assessed the amount, then splashed another dose. "Better make it a double," he said. "It's been a long night for the little guy."

Jacob groaned at his father's attempted humor.

"You ever think," his father continued, "about how much wine he has to drink? A sip in every house? I feel like an enabler. Maybe we should send Elijah to AA."

"Jake," his mother said. "Quick, open the door, before your father scares Elijah off with his so-called jokes."

Jacob got up, feeling silly for his complicity in the superstition. Why was everything in Judaism so embarrassingly literal? He swung the door wide on its hinges.

"Not so much," his mother called over her shoulder. "We don't want to bother the neighbors."

"What?" his father said with Henny Youngman inflections. "You think such a great man can fit through a tiny crack?"

"Of course he can," she said, chuckling. "He's a prophet."

"Poor Elijah! Alcoholic and now anorexic, too."

"Enough!" Ingrid shouted. "Really, that's enough."

"Oh, relax a little," Jacob's father said. "It doesn't have to be doom and gloom *all* the time."

"I just think we could take this a little more seriously. If nothing else, I think we owe it to Mother."

Jacob's father thrust his hands at Ingrid, palms up, as if to say, *Here take it. It's all yours.* "Fine. If you don't think this is depressing enough, feel free to remind us at every chance."

Still at the door, Jacob said, "Am I supposed to stand here forever, or what? I could have let in an army by now."

They all stared at him as if at an apparition. Ingrid glanced quickly at his father, then back at Jacob, her blue eyes sure as steel. "Just another minute," she said. "Until after we sing."

Jacob expected his father to object, or at least to make some snide comment, but he remained silent.

The wrinkles between Ingrid's eyebrows deepened, and in a low voice she said, "*Baruch ha-bah.* Blessed be he who comes." Then she began "Eliyahu Ha-navi." The bleak, plodding melody seemed more a dirge than a hymn of welcoming.

When the song finished, Jacob closed the door and returned to his cushioned chair. They had made it; the heavy stuff was over. Now they would cruise through the concluding prayers, sing two or three songs, and be done.

Ingrid's voice jarred like an emergency bulletin: "Let us now pause," she said in fervid syllables, "to recall the bitter catastrophe which so recently has befallen our people in Europe."

"What?" Jacob's father interrupted.

"It's the responsive reading," Ingrid said. She tapped her Haggadah. "Forty-five. The next page after Elijah."

His father's eyes narrowed. "I don't think we do that part."

It was true. Papa Isaac and Nana Jenny had always skipped ahead at this point.

"Well, *I* do it," Ingrid said. "We're supposed to consider how the Exodus relates to us, in this day and age. What does it really mean to be brought forth from bondage?"

His father mocked a smile. "Thank you, Maimonides. But don't you think this is taking long enough without adding things?"

"It's not adding. It's right here." Ingrid clasped the Haggadah like a passport.

Jacob pressed his fingers to his temples. "Dad," he said, "do you have to object to everything? In the time you spend arguing, we could have finished by now."

"He's right, Gene," his mother said. "How long can it take? Let's just do the reading and we're almost through."

His father's mouth tensed, prepared to hiss the sharp *s* of "Sarah," or perhaps some harsher word. Then he went void. Jacob could see the pupils retract into the dull color of his irises. He imagined his father pushing off in his tiny boat, rowing out to his private mental island. In Jacob's vision the island was shrinking steadily, its banks eroding into the pounding sea. Soon there would barely be room for a man to stand.

Ingrid resumed the call-and-response with a steady cadence: "When in the past our brothers were massacred in ruthless pogroms, the poet Bialik, in his 'City of Slaughter,' cried out against the bloody savagery."

Jacob and his mother answered in the stiff inflections of people reading from an unfamiliar text: "Today we mourn, not for one 'city of slaughter,' but for many such cities where six million of our people have been brutally destroyed."

"The cruelties of Pharaoh," Ingrid said somberly, "Haman, Nebuchadnezzar, and Titus, cannot be compared to the diabolical devices fashioned by modern tyrants in their design to exterminate a whole people."

"No generation," they replied, "has known a catastrophe so vast and tragic!"

"The blood of the innocent who perished in the gas chambers of Auschwitz, Bergen-Belsen, Buchenwald, Dachau, Majdanek, Treblinka, and Theresienstadt, cries out to God and man."

The names of the camps shocked Jacob like curse words. Like shouting *motherfucker* in synagogue or at a funeral. His grandparents' careful silences, rent apart.

He and his mother read together: "How can we ever forget the burning of synagogues and houses of study, the destruction of the holy books and scrolls of the Torah, the sadistic torment and murder of our scholars, sages, and teachers?"

"They tortured the flesh of our brothers," Ingrid responded, "but they could not crush their spirit, their faith, nor their love of Torah."

"The parchment of the Torah was burnt, but the letters were indestructible."

Jacob was reading from the printed text, but the words felt as though they rose from the hot pocket of his heart. He stared at the candle in the table's center, thinking how something that burned *could* remain indestructible. He pictured Ingrid, burning last year's matzah circles. His father at the Weber grill; the shards of magazine.

His aunt continued: "In the Warsaw ghetto, Jews valiantly defied the overwhelming forces of the inhuman tyrant. These martyrs lifted up their voices in a hymn reaffirming their faith in the coming of the Messiah, when justice and peace shall finally be established for all men."

Jacob did not believe in professions of faith. In elementary school, he had even refused the Pledge of Allegiance. But now he parted his lips. Now he preached the printed affirmation, caring not so much about the creed's meaning as about the fact of pronouncing the syllables with his mother and his aunt, about the three of them speaking with one voice.

"I believe with a perfect faith," they chanted, "in the coming of the Messiah; and though he tarry, nonetheless do I believe he will come."

It was then that Jacob noticed the Elijah cup, awash in candleglow. More light emanated from the polished silver than could be accounted for by mere reflection. The four inset gems below the cup's rim were unblinking alien eyes, and he prickled with the sensation of being watched. It was like standing in the bright cone of a spotlight, knowing that every detail of his face could be seen by the audience, but blinded himself by the glare. A childhood sense of awe and mystery buzzed his bones. He wanted to look into Elijah's chalice. He wanted to peer in and check the level of the wine. But he was too terrified of what he might find.

The fourth cups of wine were poured. Jacob's mother and Ingrid took tiny, symbolic tastes; his father sipped absently. But Jacob drained his cup. He downed it all in memory of those he had just read about, who had perished in the camps and the ghettos, keeping their faith against the greatest odds.

This was the way to remember, he thought. Not with vengeance, as Hannes misbelieved; not with more destruction.

Jacob drank, too, for Ingrid. He drank because she could have been among the ones lost. But she had been saved. She and Papa Isaac and Nana Jenny. She had been saved and now had arrived in his life, and he drank in thankfulness, watching her speckled blue eyes glimmer with what could have been joy, or fatigue, or the beginning of tears.

The wine's sick-sweet aftertaste threatened to gag him, but he accepted the discomfort as necessary. There should always, he thought, be a reminder.

Ingrid raised her Kiddush cup and toasted: *"L'shana ha-ba'ah b'yerushalayim."*

"Next year in Jerusalem," his mother echoed.

Jacob said it, too. "Next year in Jerusalem."

Ingrid grasped the wine bottle and lifted it to fill their fifth cup—the optional cup, which had been added to the ancient ritual only this half-century, in gratitude for the creation of the State of Israel.

She spilled splashes into Jacob's cup and his mother's. Then she reached across to top off his father's cup.

His father had been lost for minutes, his eyes glazed reptilian. "No," he said softly now, as if waking from a dream. But Ingrid had tilted the bottle. Wine leapt in a purple arch.

"No!" This time it was a shout, and his father knocked the bottle. The wine jagged like a lightning bolt to the tablecloth, landing on a blemish from years ago.

"Gene," his mother said. "Honey, what are you doing? You can't do things like that." She sprang from her chair and blotted the puddle with her napkin.

The muscle of his father's jaw bulged in a bullet shape. "*I* can't do things like that? *I* can't? I'm just trying to hang on to some kind of normalcy. Why don't you say anything to *her?*"

Ingrid had set down the bottle, but still gripped it as if she needed to keep her balance. Rivulets of wine leaked down the glass, dyeing her fingertips. "Eugene," she said. "I don't understand. What did I do?"

Jacob's father drummed his fingers on the table's edge, slowly at first, then building to a frenzied rumble. "You're really something," he said. "You know? You waltz in here after not showing your face for however many years and boom!, you think you can just up and run the show. Well, I've got news for you. We've got our own family, and we've got our own way of doing things. Maybe I don't want to give thanks for the State of Israel. Maybe the State of Israel is the fucking place that stole my son."

There it was. After hovering unseen all night, Jonathan had materialized at last like some kind of reverse Elijah.

"That's not fair, Gene," Jacob's mother said. "You know we're all as upset as you are. We all wish Jonathan were here, but he's not. That's not Ingrid's fault."

She fussed futilely with the linen's bleeding stain, smothering the spot with seltzer, blotting it, dousing more. "Just let her pour you another cup," she pleaded, abandoning the wet purpled heap of napkin in front of his father. "It's symbolic. It's just something that you do."

"It is not something I will do. I will not pray for next year in Jerusalem. They could fucking bomb Jerusalem for all I care."

"My God," Jacob said. "How could you say a thing like that?"

"Jacob, don't," Ingrid told him. "We don't have to do this. It's really not that big a deal."

"It *is* a big deal. It is. I don't think he understands."

Jacob had never thought he would defend Israel. But the responsive reading rang in his head. He thought of all the people who had been saved by Israel, and all those who might have been. He thought of the men he had seen at the Western Wall, men like Papa Isaac. His mind shifted then to the other wall, the War Memorial across from his own apartment, the last blank plaque bolted to the granite arc.

"How can you be so fucking ungrateful?" he said. "If one thing had been different, *one little thing*, Papa Isaac and Nana Jenny might not have made it, and you wouldn't ever have been born. So fine, they did make it. And they happened to go to America instead of Israel. But Israel was that one little thing that made a difference for a lot of people."

His father's face had puffed with anger. His shirt collar dug like a noose into his neck. "Great," he said, "thanks for the history lesson. Now can you tell me why it's so important to save people who have no need to be saved? Who in fact would be much better off if they just stayed where they belong?"

"What *I* want to know," Jacob said, "is why it screws you up so much that Jonathan wants to be religious. Is it because *you* couldn't do it? Is it because he's doing what Papa Isaac wanted *you* to do?"

Jacob's mother stepped back from the table. "I won't listen to this," she said. "This isn't helping anything."

"But I want to know, Mom," Jacob said. "I want to know why it's such a terrible crime. I mean, I don't agree with Jonathan or what he believes in. But at least he believes in *something*, which is more than I can say for some people."

His father took aim with a stiff finger. "Just look at yourself, Jacob. Of all people to be defending this. Just take a good look at yourself. They don't want you in Israel. Your brother doesn't want you. They hate everything about you."

"Gene! Stop it. Just stop." Jacob's mother covered her ears with her forearms. It looked as though she were trying to unscrew her head, to twist it like a bottle cap from her neck.

Ingrid refereed across the table. "Please don't do this, Eugene. Don't be like Father."

"What the hell do *you* know about our father? You didn't see him for thirty years. You didn't even come to his funeral."

"I knew him before you were born," she said. "I know plenty of things you don't." Ingrid thrust both hands at him. It could have been an attack; she could have been throwing something. But the move turned tender, as if she were reaching to caress his cheeks. "Don't you realize? Don't you know how lucky you are? To have two healthy sons?"

Jacob's father grabbed the wine-soaked napkin and wrung it with enough force to tear the cloth. "Sure. That's what everyone said when they were born. Twins! Every father's dream, what a blessing! Well, I wonder what they'd say now. I'd be happy enough with just one *normal* son."

"Get out!"

Jacob surprised himself with the force of his own voice. He rose and walked to the door and thrust it open.

His father stared. "What do you mean, get out?"

"I mean get the fuck out of here. Go to your hotel. Back to Washington. I don't care."

"Please," Ingrid said. "Jacob, sit down. We'll sing. We'll finish the seder."

"I don't want to finish. I want him to leave."

But now Jacob's father was up, too. "You will not order me around," he said. "This is *my* mother's apartment. You have no business telling me what to do."

"Well, you have no business telling anybody anything. You're just as shitty a son as you are a father."

Ingrid called again, helplessly, from the table. "Can't we all just please sit down?"

But Jacob and his father held their ground.

"All right," his mother said, "that's it." She pushed back from the table and stepped between them. "Jacob, move away from the door. Gene, come on. Let's go."

"Sarah! I'm his father. Are you going to let him speak to me like that?"

"No, I'm not. And I'm not going to let you, either. That's why we're going. Now. Come on." She seized his elbow and marched him to the door. "We'll talk tomorrow," she said to Jacob. "Call me in the morning."

When he reached the threshold, Jacob's father looked at his hands. Only then did he seem to realize that his left fist still clenched the napkin; he had squeezed the cloth like a pistol this entire time. He cast it to the ground and walked away.

Jacob closed his eyes and tried to calm himself with measured breaths. His parents' footsteps echoed in the stairwell, then dwindled to faint thuds, then silence. He looked up at last and saw Ingrid, standing at the door. She had lifted the soggy napkin and clutched it to her mouth. The livid stained cloth gagged her sobs.

Resemblance

Later, when they were alone, when neither had said anything for some time, Ingrid disappeared into the bedroom. She returned with the photograph, hugging it to her chest, the image turned inward, sheltered. She gnawed her lower lip as if to sever invisible sutures binding her mouth.

Finally, she gave the photograph to Jacob. She let him scan it for a few seconds. Then she spoke:

He was sixteen when this was taken. Sixteen or maybe fifteen. The last picture I have. No, you don't recognize him. Even your father doesn't know, so how could you? But see the dimples in his cheeks? Deep almost like scars, the same as mine. People could always tell we were siblings. I think you and Jonathan inherited them, too.

That's right, I had a brother. Josef.

My parents—your Nana and Papa—had a son before they had your father. You would have had an uncle. Or maybe you still do. I'd like to believe that.

It's confusing, I know. Nobody has told you these things. But I'm telling you now so the mistakes won't be repeated. I don't want to see it happen again.

Josef was four years older. Mother had him when she was only nineteen, and Father was twenty-two, almost as soon as they were married. This was just after Father became observant again, after his mother died. He was always trying to make up for that, I think, for his years of eating *treyf* and not going to synagogue. For not seeing his mother when she was sick. His whole life, he was making up for that; but the first few years, studying to become a rabbi, must have been especially intense. So Josef got caught in that. Father raised him to be the perfect Jewish boy.

Of course, I don't know this. How could I, since I wasn't born yet, or just barely? But they used to tell me Josef was chanting Torah portions when he was only four years old. Reading Talmud by six or seven. A father's dream come true.

He was a dream for me, too. The kind of boy a younger sister could fall in love with. You can see it a little in the photo. Here— the soft chin, those lips almost like a girl's. And you can't tell in black-and-white, but those eyes, the color of sea water at the edge of a sandbar.

But see, I'm already turning him into a myth, something untouchable. It's hard not to when somebody has been lost to you for so long. Lost but still with you every day.

So I'll say it: He was not perfect. Beautiful, yes. But not perfect. Is anybody? Still, he was a wonderful brother. He meant everything to me.

How can I ever tell you?

This may sound crazy, but when I think of Josef I always think of the flute. We had a neighborhood orchestra, and Josef was first in his section. His flute was silver, but secondhand and tarnished, the metal pocked from the previous owner's sweat. But somehow that ugliness made the sound even sweeter. It was the kind of flute with open holes. And do you know the sound a good player can make with the open holes, if he covers only part of the opening, then slides his finger slowly over? That moan, that out-of-breath begging to land on the proper note?

Josef was so good at that, at getting all the shades. He was never afraid of starting slightly off and then finding his way to the center of the sound. And eventually, he always did find his way. He was always on the way to somewhere, looking ahead, finding the next destination. He was always two feet in the air and just about to land.

*   *   *

I could tell you so many things. The sound of his voice. His ripple of a laugh. But it's the last story, of course, that you need first. The story of why you don't know any of this.

It was the fall of '41. In September, we had to start wearing the yellow star, and emigration was blocked. Then, at the end of October, Berlin was declared *Judenrein*, clean of Jews. Soon after, the deportations would begin.

Father's friends the Schmitts had a house all the way below Munich, not too far from the Swiss border. We thought if we stayed there, we might eventually be able to cross and get protection. So we packed what we could carry and we left. I don't even remember it as especially emotional. It was just the thing we had to do.

The Schmitts were good people, non-Jews: Fritz and Elise and their three children. Fritz was a banker. He and Father had met at university. Fritz risked so much for us. Elise, too. They risked so much, and still they couldn't save us all.

It wasn't probably what you're thinking, like Anne Frank. It was not quite that bad yet. Yes, we lived in the attic, without much for furniture. We couldn't go to school or to synagogue or anywhere. But we had our own school. Josef taught me philosophy and languages. He was seventeen and already he knew French and Italian and some English. He wasn't the best teacher, because he couldn't understand why I didn't learn as fast as he wanted. But he tried to be patient, and we had lots of fun together. Mother learned with us. She seemed to have Josef's same knack for languages—or I suppose she was the one who gave it to him. She would read to us from books of poetry, making us close our eyes and listen to the sounds. I knew some of Shakespeare's sonnets by heart in English before I had any idea what the words meant.

There was a kind of security to Fritz and Elise's attic. All the heat in the house rose up and gathered there under the rafters. It was sleepy, every day a dream. I can still smell it. Just thinking about it almost makes me need to sneeze.

It's strange. We had left our home and all our friends. We were hiding for our lives. Anything could happen. But I have to tell you that I remember most of it so fondly. We were together. We were together and we had time to get to know each other, to really get to know each other. How many families have that chance?

Not Father, perhaps. He was so preoccupied, worrying enough for all of us. But Josef and Mother and me.

Father spent much of the time writing letters—to people in America, England, Palestine, any connections he had to try and get us out. He even wrote to Martin Buber once, and Buber said he would try to help. But of course nothing came of it.

Father would leave the house sometimes, and we would have no idea where he had gone. Maybe he had some job, to pay back the Schmitts for letting us stay there. He wouldn't say. Everything had to be so quiet. We would wait and wait, and just when it seemed he might never return, he would walk up the stairs, his hat crumpled in his hand, and get into bed without taking dinner.

Did I say the Schmitts had children? We never really got to know the two girls, because Elise kept them close to her all the time. But the boy, the oldest one. Erich was fifteen—exactly halfway between me and Josef.

Erich looked just the way the Nazi youths were supposed to. He had that perfectly straight golden hair, and straight white teeth, and cheekbones that jumped out of his face. His eyes were blue as a uniform. But it was only his looks. Erich never shouted like the other German boys. His voice was a whisper, the voice you would use with a puppy. His hands were big and bony, but they were soft when he touched your shoulder. I remember him once swatting at a fly. He was quick, so he got it on the first try, but he didn't kill it. He caught it in his hands and cupped it, then carried it downstairs so he could let it out a window. I think maybe I was in love with him. Almost as much as with Josef.

The Schmitts were supposed to pretend that we weren't living in their attic, but sometimes Erich would sneak up. We would play cards, or talk about what was happening outside. He would bring us newspapers—a week or two old, but we didn't care.

Sometimes he joined us in our school. He was good at memorizing the poetry. He and Josef would have contests, alternating lines of a poem and seeing how far they could get before one of them messed up a word. It's hard to imagine, maybe, with something so small as poetry, but for us, in the attic, it was like the Olympics. It was all the excitement we needed. At least it seemed that way for a while.

Josef started getting restless. I can't remember any specific thing. But he wanted to spend less and less time studying, less time talking. He kept to himself, writing in a notebook he hid under his pillow.

I asked him only twice: Has something happened? Did I do something wrong? And he said no. Both times, no. But he was different. His eyes. You couldn't be sure anymore what he was looking at.

He started leaving the attic. Only when Father was gone, of course. Mother would argue with him, would try to get him to stay, but Josef didn't listen. He put on his heavy coat and crept down the stairs without ever waving goodbye.

I assumed it was something political, resistance work or plotting an escape. Whatever it was, I knew it was good. Josef always had the right instincts. But still, I worried for him. I worried and I missed him. We had less time for philosophy, less time for poetry. Without Josef with us in the attic, it was too easy to think of all the bad things that were happening. It was too easy to remember why we were there.

And once Josef started spending more time away, Erich came up less and less frequently. I had thought he was a friend of both of ours, that Josef and I shared him equally. But now it was clear he had cared more for Josef all along. If it was just me left there in the attic, he was not so interested in visiting.

I got lonely. There had been three of us, but now I was the only one. Yes, Mother was still there. But she was holding so much inside herself, there was nothing left for me.

It was the middle of the afternoon. Father was gone, Josef too. Mother napped in her small bed below the roof.

Suddenly a crash. The door at the bottom of the stairs burst open. Mother woke, trying not to scream because we were supposed to stay quiet. But the quiet was already broken.

Josef came stumbling up the stairs. He didn't have his coat. His shirt hung mostly off, the buttons undone, as though it had been ripped. His cheeks were streaked red. He had been crying, or maybe someone had slapped him.

Mother was shaking. "Are they coming?" she asked. "Oh God, they're coming. Where's Isaac? Why isn't he here?"

But Father *was* there. He was right behind Josef, pounding up the stairs. He gripped his hat in his hands, squeezing it so tight it seemed as though his knuckles might rip the skin.

"Isaac," Mother said, "what's happening? What should we do?"

Father walked to her, put his arms around her shoulders. He beckoned me close, too, and crushed me against his side.

"It's all right," he said. "It's all right. We're safe. We'll be fine as soon as this stranger goes." His voice rose on the last words and he clasped my shoulders even harder. "Get out," he shouted to Josef. "I don't want to see you."

Josef scrambled for his clothes, throwing them into a small suitcase. His hands trembled. He had trouble grabbing things.

Mother pulled away. "What are you saying? I don't understand."

"He is not our son," Father said. "He is a sickness. He never existed."

"Don't be crazy. Of course he's our son. Josef, stop. What happened? What are you doing?"

But Josef couldn't stop. He was still gathering the few things he had left. A woolen vest. A pair of denim pants.

Mother fell to her knees. She turned back to Father, pleading. "Whatever it was," she said, "it couldn't be so bad."

Father didn't say anything. He wouldn't look at her. He watched Josef like a prison guard.

"Don't send him away," Mother begged. "Think, Isaac. Think what you are doing."

The last thing Josef took was his notebook. He shoved it into the suitcase and backed toward the stairs. His face was covered in mucus and tears. He stood there, moaning a little, the kind of sound an animal makes. His body leaned. I think he wanted to come forward, to touch Mother, and me, to say goodbye.

Father raised a fist. "Get out!" he shouted.

Josef stepped back and seemed to crumple down the stairs. I saw only his head for a second, then nothing.

I ran to my bed and under the blankets, wishing I could disappear. I was crying, but mostly because of the shouting and because of Mother's crying. I don't think I really understood. I was only thirteen. Under the hot tent of my covers I kept thinking: Where will he sleep? Where will he spend the night? Aside from the Schmitts, we didn't know anyone.

When my crying calmed I heard Father. He was trying to talk softly, but he never really could. He told Mother he would speak of it this once, and never again.

He had come home earlier than expected, he said, discouraged because his contact in Switzerland hadn't cabled. On his way up he decided to use the Schmitts' bathroom on the second floor, a luxury we rarely permitted ourselves, instead of the bucket in the corner of our attic.

He walked into the bathroom and there was Josef. Josef was in the bathtub, Father said, but there was no water. No bath had been drawn. Josef lay in the empty tub, and lying there with him was Erich. Neither of them was wearing any clothes.

The shock of it made me forget my desire to be invisible. I peeked my head from the covers and watched Father tell the rest.

He couldn't bring himself to say what exactly they were doing. He started to make a gesture with his hands, but even that was too much. Father said he had asked Josef, "Why? Why are you doing this?" And Josef had responded, "Because, Father. Because we love each other."

I understood then that all this time Josef had not been leaving the house. He had only been going downstairs, to Erich, to their secret.

Mother was still shuddering. She pulled at her hair and at her cheeks, as if she wanted to rip off any feature that made her recognizable. I wanted to do the same thing. I didn't see how I could live anymore, how any of us could, as the people we had been before. I wanted to go back. I wanted everything to go back.

Mother said something to Father. I couldn't hear what it was. But then I saw his hand. It came up slowly, almost too slowly to believe, as if he never worried for a second that he might miss. And when it reached her face the sound was like a plate crashing on the floor. It was the only time I ever saw him hit her.

That night at supper, Father declared Josef dead.

He made us tear our clothes. He made us sit shivah the whole seven days. He enforced all the rules of mourning.

Twice a day we were supposed to say Kaddish. But I only moved my mouth, pretending. I whispered nonsense words. I said the wrong things. My brother was *not* dead. At least I prayed he wasn't yet.

I violated other parts of the shivah, too. Father had covered the one mirror we had in the attic, but when he wasn't looking I would pull the cloth away and stare at my reflection. I would pretend the face gazing back was not my own, but Josef's. I smiled at him, and he smiled in return. He would be fine, he assured me. Everything would be fine. But even then I knew it was a fantasy.

Two weeks later, the deportations began. All the Jews in town received orders to pack their bags. We knew there would be searches. It was our last chance.

Fritz had a friend who owned a truck. We said goodbye to Elise and the girls, to everybody but Erich, who I think was maybe locked in his room. We made a secret compartment inside a load of lumber, just big enough for three people and three suitcases. There were no questions at the border. It looked like any normal delivery. We made it to Zurich. A month later, America.

For a time I tried to speak of him. I would imagine what he would think of our new surroundings. "Josef would hate the houses here," I would say. "The walls are too thin. Too much noise." I believed that by saying his name, I could keep him alive.

Father never raised his hand against me, as he had against Mother. He never punished me for mentioning Josef. He simply would not respond. When I said Josef's name, Father would ignore me for a day or two, maybe three. Then finally he would start again as if nothing had happened.

Eventually, I gave up. I kept Josef to myself. What else was I supposed to do?

I cried, of course. I wrote him letters that I never sent—there was no place I could send them to. I started a notebook of my own, like the one Josef had kept under his pillow, and filled it with stories about how he had escaped. Sometimes Erich was also in the stories. Sometimes it was only Josef.

Your father was born less than a year after we arrived. He was everything new, all of the hope and the joy of surviving. They named him Eugene. Their American son.

How could I not resent him? How could I not?

But I tried my best to be a good sister. I tried not to blame Eugene for things he hadn't done.

I was old enough to help Mother now, and she needed a great deal. Some days—the days she got out of bed—she would start crying in the middle of doing something, cooking soup or washing dishes, and not be able to stop for ten, twenty minutes. She still pulled at her cheeks. I got used to the fingerprints, the red streaks on her skin where she had clawed.

I ended up feeding Eugene. I changed his diapers. I practiced English in front of him so he would get used to the sound of other voices. And I tried to love him. I tried.

Father had his position at the synagogue. He was busy learning the way things were different here. He was out almost every night, visiting each family in the congregation—their shepherd, their spiritual father.

In the little time he was home, he put everything into Eugene. He was not going to squander another son. You could see it in his eyes, the way he stared at Eugene, searching for defects. You could see it in the way he held him, squeezing too hard for a child. He couldn't understand why Eugene cried. He didn't see that his grip could hurt so badly.

As soon as Eugene was old enough, Father tutored him in English and in Hebrew. English was what we spoke all the time now. If I used a German word to ask for something, Mother and Father would pretend they hadn't heard. I had to go away and learn the English word, then come back and ask again.

And so Eugene grew up knowing nothing of German, but he was smart. Father pushed him so hard, always testing him, demanding more. Nothing was good enough for Father now. He would not be fooled again.

My English got better, too. I graduated high school. Mother still needed me, so in the fall I went to community college, part-time.

But it was harder and harder to be at home. Eugene was four now, a healthy boy, and people would tell me, "You're lucky to have such a brother. Things will be good for you here in America."

And I would die inside, this pain, like someone twisting knuckles in my heart. *I had a brother already*, I wanted to say. *Josef is my brother.*

Then Passover 1948. Eugene had just turned five. Father taught him to ask the Four Questions, and from now on Eugene would be the one, instead of me. Father turned the Exodus story into a kind of quiz: "What was the name of the sea Moses parted?" "Why was the matzah baked flat?"

Eugene made almost no mistakes. He was sharp for a five-year-old. But there was still so much he didn't understand.

When we counted the ten plagues, Eugene began to cry. Mother said it was too late for a little boy. She suggested he be put to bed. But Father insisted he remain.

"What is it?" Father asked. "Why are you crying?"

Eugene sniffled nonsense sounds. I gave him a glass of juice, and the swallowing seemed to calm him.

Finally he stopped crying long enough to speak. "Would it have hurt me?" he asked. He pointed a stubby finger at the Haggadah page. "Would I have been smited?"

"No," Father laughed. "No, no, no. That's not at all what it means. How could you ever think such a silly thing?"

"But you told me," Eugene said. "I'm a first-born."

Father put his hand on Eugene's shoulder. "It was the *Egyptian* sons who were killed, not the Jews. God would have protected you. He would have sheltered you. That's why we give thanks. But besides that, you are protected, because you are not the first-born of the family. Ingrid came before you. You are only the first *son*. The first-born son."

Eugene still seemed confused, but mostly satisfied. He sat quietly for the rest of the seder. And I, too, just sat there. I sat with them at the table, with Mother and Father and Eugene, but in my mind I had already left.

Sometimes it is a little thing. A thing that by itself, perhaps, you could tolerate. You could dismiss it, or forgive and move on. But if it comes after so much else, after so many years of other little things building and building, then it bears the weight of everything combined. Father telling Eugene he was the first-born son was like that. Just a few words, really, a sentence. But for me the words were explosions. They gouged wounds that could never be sewn shut.

I don't remember how long it took me. Two weeks? Three? Not a month. I had enough for a one-way bus ticket and I went to California, as far as I could get.

*   *   *

Berkeley was cheap after I established residency. It was a new world, new people. No one punished me for telling the truth.

I still went home sometimes. Once a year at first, for the High Holidays, then once every few. Mother sent me money for the tickets. I wanted to see her. I didn't want to lose everything.

But I couldn't bear Father's face. I couldn't go to synagogue and listen to his sermons, everything sounding like lies.

Father would not look at me, either. I guess for him I was another failure, the second of three chances wasted. He was almost fifty. He was tired. What energy he had left he wanted to invest in Eugene, in the future. He had calculated the odds and decided I would never pay off.

I stopped coming home. I never saw him again.

Do I sound angry? Of course I am.

You're probably angry, too. About what happened, about never being told. You might even be mad at me. It's understandable.

But what I want to tell you is that anger is not the end. You need to be angry, yes. But if you stop there, then you have failed.

Just because someone is terribly wrong doesn't mean that *you* also can't do wrong. My father was not a father. I am certain of that. He forfeited his claim to the title. But now I think maybe I was not a daughter, either. And now I truly wish I would have been.

Jacob propped the picture of Josef on the table beside his futon. He leaned it between the snapshot of him and Jonathan on the dinosaur, and the one of Cousin Adam.

He lay down on the bed, his head where his feet should be and his feet perched on the pillows, in order that he could see the photograph if he wanted to. For now, though, he didn't look. Something told him it could be dangerous, like staring at the sun during an eclipse.

A cool intruding breeze tapped the windows. The sparse traffic on Park Drive whispered by as if on tiptoes. The apartment echoed with ghost-town noise.

Jacob's skull still buzzed with the story Ingrid had told him, the way his head would continue to ring on the rare nights he went dancing, hours after escaping the club's throbbing bass. The beat was relentless: *an uncle, an uncle.*

An aching malaise inched through his body—like the beginnings of a hangover, although he knew it wasn't from the Manischewitz. He was thinking of another time he felt similarly disoriented, the first night he had slept in this apartment. He had known he would love the new space, the high ceilings and wooden floors. He was certain that moving was the right decision. Still, that first night, in the exhaustion of having boxed up and transferred his belongings, he found himself longing for the ratty security of the Somerville apartment, the dump that only hours ago had repelled him so thoroughly.

Now, in the same paradoxical way, while he burned to know more about his newly discovered relative, Jacob also wished he could return to his ignorance.

Wasn't this the legacy he had wanted all along? A forebear? A family photograph he didn't need to invent?

But the reality was more complicated, precisely because Josef was real. Jacob was constricted by the facts and by Ingrid's imperfect memory. Instead of being afflicted with general ignorance about his family, he would be haunted by specific questions. Was Josef really gay? Had he been caught and sent to the camps? Could he have found Erich again?

Jacob turned finally and gazed at the photograph. Ingrid had said Josef was fifteen or sixteen in the picture, but the eyes looked older. His uncle stared at the camera as if into the future, as if seeing everything that would happen to all of them.

Jacob studied Josef's face, wanting so badly to see himself in the image. How many times had he fantasized about this, the discovery of a long-lost connection? The similarities would be uncanny, a goosebumpy resemblance.

There *were* similarities. The dimples, for a start. Ingrid was right, they were standard-issue Rosenbaum. And though it was hard to judge without full color, the hair, too, seemed the same—his own just-before-black shade of brown.

Jacob grabbed the photograph and headed for the bathroom. He would hold the picture up to the medicine chest mirror, next to his face, and make a more accurate comparison. Like a scientist cracking the genetic code, he would look for the crucial repetition, the indisputable proof of a link.

Three steps down the hall he stopped himself. The photograph gathered a strange weighty thickness in his fingers, sticking with the glue of sweat. If there was truly a resemblance, he realized, if Josef did indeed look like him, then he must look equally like Jonathan.

PART III

April 1993

Attachment

In the *Guide to Jewish Religious Practice* he borrowed from Nana Jenny's, Jacob learned that in Israel, Passover was seven days, not eight. The seventh day, according to tradition, was when the children of Israel had escaped through the Red Sea, leaving Pharaoh's army to drown in their wake. The ministering angels wanted to sing songs of praise, but God rebuked them for their heartlessness. "My creatures sink into the sea, and you want to sing?"

Early Monday afternoon, when it was still Passover in Boston but the holiday had ended in Jerusalem, Jacob phoned the yeshiva. He asked whoever picked up the phone for "Yoni Rosenbaum," proud of himself for remembering to use the Hebrew name. A sharp crack was the receiver being dropped on a desk. Then the fading squeak of footsteps; then static.

After a minute the squeak crescendoed in reverse.

"Hello?" The voice was flat and businesslike, as though someone had happened across the phone off its hook and was checking to see if the connection was still live.

"Yes," Jacob said, "I was trying to find Yoni Rosenbaum?"

"Yes, hello."

"Were you able to find him?"

"Jacob," the voice said. "It's me."

"Oh, Jon. Hey. You didn't sound like you."

It was not an accent so much as a stiffness in diction.

Jonathan enunciated the overcautious syllables of a non-native speaker, each word measured as though translated from another language.

"I only have a minute before evening study," Jonathan said. "Why are you calling?"

"Mom says you're coming now that Passover's done?"

"Yes. Thursday. She knows the flight."

"Good," Jacob said. "Very good." He found himself simplifying his own language, the way he would talk to a foreigner. "I just wanted to say, um, I'm glad you're coming. If there's stuff I can do to make it easier—"

"It won't be easy," Jonathan cut in. "But some things we have to do anyway."

"I know," Jacob said. "I mean, I think that's what all of us are doing. Listen, I understand that you have . . . that there are certain things you require. Keeping kosher and all that."

"That's not your concern."

"I know, but I thought it could be hard to arrange from over there, so I made some calls. I talked to someone at that Orthodox synagogue in Cleveland Circle—Aish Ha-Torah? They've got a hospitality committee. The woman said they're more than happy to find a family who'll take you in for Shabbos dinner, or even to stay a few days or a week."

Jacob waited for a response. Was Jonathan caught off guard by his conciliation?

"If you want," he continued, "I can give you the number. Or I can call them again myself. They're perfectly friendly."

Another pause. Then a storm across the wires: "What is this?"

"What's what?" Jacob said.

Jonathan's old voice, the natural voice, cracked through. "Just what are you trying to do?"

"I'm telling you what I found out. I'm trying to help."

"Well, I didn't ask for your help."

Jacob's throat tightened, blocking sound. How did you respond when you held out your hand and the other person slapped it back into your face? What would Ingrid do?

When Jonathan spoke again, his voice had recovered its affectation. "The class is starting," he said. "I need to go."

Jacob held his end of the phone, listening to the deadness when

Jonathan hung up. Was this it? Would they lapse now back to silence?

A click. Then the dial tone's angry warning.

Danny, sitting Indian-style amid the fabric scraps on Jacob's couch, flapped the butterfly wings of his knees. "A *million* fags," he said. "I can't even, like, imagine."

"I was at the march in '87," Chantelle said, squinting into a needle's eye. She poked thread through the tiny hole; doubled it back on itself. "I think we had half a million then. Of course, according to the Park Police there were forty-seven of us."

"Well, I don't care about the politics," Danny said, "as long as there are really that many good-looking guys."

Chantelle question-marked one eyebrow. "I hate to break this to you, hon, but it's not going to be *all* guys, and they're not *all* going to be good-looking."

"Oh, you know what I mean. I'll be psyched no matter how many people show. And of course I'm not going to have my eyes on anybody but my date. Right, Jake?"

Jacob vaguely registered his name. He traced his index finger around a blue corduroy M, cut from the thigh of an old pair of Marty's pants. The appliqué balanced atop the A, R, T, and Y, all snipped from castaway clothing. He'd counted on seeing Marty's panel added to the Quilt. And now this new incentive for the trip to Washington: a vision of marching down Pennsylvania Avenue hand in hand with Danny through the cheering throng. But maybe none of it would come true.

"Jake?" Danny asked again.

"Sorry," he said. "What? I'm listening."

Danny slid onto the floor beside Jacob and nuzzled into his neck. "I was just saying how much fun we're going to have in D.C."

"Yeah," Jacob said. "It should, um, be great."

"Mmm," Chantelle said. "That was convincing."

Danny plucked proprietarily at a tuft of Jacob's arm hair. "What's the deal?" he said. "You don't want to go?"

"No, I do. Of course I do. It's just . . . I think I might need to stay here with my grandmother."

"What about your brother?" Danny asked. "Isn't he flying in tomorrow?"

Jacob recalled Jonathan's voice, the brittle formality, telling him things wouldn't be easy. "He'll be here. I'm just not sure I trust him. He's not the most responsible."

Chantelle balanced the needle in her mouth like a cigarette. "I hear you," she said through clenched teeth. "You know what pisses me off? Gay people are supposed to be so anti family values, but you *know* we're the ones holding things together. Look at us. I can't even go to the march, since no one has spoken to my supposed father in ten years, and *I* have to give my sister away at her wedding. And now you might not go either, because you have to take care of your grandmother. Without gay people, there wouldn't be any families left to *have* fucking values."

Jacob didn't say anything. Chantelle was right, of course. But he was too ashamed to admit that his consideration of staying was not entirely selfless. Since the conversation with his brother two days ago, he had been consumed by the thought that if he went away to Washington, and Nana Jenny died, Jonathan would be at her bedside, not him.

Danny scissored rhythmically, trimming squares of colored fabric into the numerals for Marty's birth date. "What do you think are the chances?" he asked. "I mean, isn't your grandmother pretty stable now?"

"She could stay like this awhile," Jacob said. "The doctor said it's not unusual with a stroke for someone to have been in this stage for two weeks. It could be that much again, or longer."

"Two weeks?" Chantelle said. "Is that all it's been?"

"I know. Doesn't it seem like forever? But it's not even. She had the stroke April first. It'll be two weeks tomorrow."

"Then how are you going to decide?" Danny asked. "I mean, if nothing changes?"

"I'm not sure," Jacob said. "I'm just not sure."

They had met with Dr. Sandler the day after the seder, just before Jacob's father flew back to Washington alone. His father wasn't speaking to Jacob, or to Ingrid. He stood by the wall, pretending to read the framed diplomas. Jacob kept seeing him as the little boy in Ingrid's story, terrified of being smited, and he felt more pity than anger. His father didn't even know he'd had a brother.

"This is always a hard conversation," Dr. Sandler said. His pale lips contracted like inchworms when he spoke.

"It would just help," Ingrid said, "to have some idea of the possible scenarios. I'm here from California. They live in Washington. There's a grandson in Israel. It's difficult to plan."

Dr. Sandler frowned. "It's frustrating for us, too. It really is. But it's impossible to say what will happen in a case like this. She could remain in her current condition for a time, never waking up, and then die of, say, pneumonia. That would not be uncommon. Or, she might show improvement."

The doctor shrugged as though speculating about a mystery novel's resolution. "After this long in a coma," he continued, "the one thing of which we can be pretty certain is that even if Mrs. Rosenbaum regains consciousness, there will be significant impairment. She's not going to be able to take care of herself."

Jacob heard Ingrid swallow next to him, an embarrassing, wet-sounding gulp. His mother twisted in her chair.

"I know it's not easy to hear," Dr. Sandler said. "But you may want to look into nursing facilities."

No one said anything as they left the office. Dr. Sandler had merely voiced what they knew, but had been unwilling to admit: Things would never be the same.

"Is this good?" Chantelle asked. She suspended Marty's third-grade report card inches above the panel, as though it were a helicopter waiting for landing clearance.

"Down a little," Jacob instructed. "There. That's fine."

Chantelle pressed the report card, laminated in protective plastic, onto the cloth. They all paused to admire the addition.

"I still can't believe that's real," Danny said.

"I know," Jacob said. "It's pretty great, isn't it?"

He had found the evaluation in Marty's scrapbook. The grades column showed consistent A's, with O's for "outstanding" in the nonacademic categories of music and attendance. But it wasn't the grades that were so remarkable. In the space left for comments, a Miss Eberly had written in flowery script: "Marty is an expressive boy who makes friends easily. Though his demands for attention can be tiring, his flamboyant sense of humor and generous affection add a great deal to the classroom. A joy to have."

A *joy to have.* Even then, Jacob thought, they knew. If Marty had composed a personal ad fifteen years later, he wouldn't have had to change a word.

He reached behind him for another laminated memento. In the snapshot, Marty knelt within a sea of multicolored cloth, back straight, hands clasped as if praying. The picture had been taken at a Quilt display in 1991. When it appeared in the next day's *Boston Globe*, Marty had liked it so much he tracked down the photographer for the negative.

Jacob lay the picture on the cloth and ironed it with the balls of his palms. He spread the hidden layer of glue to the edges, taking extra care to tack the corners. The instruction sheet sent by the Names Project office had stressed the importance of proper attachment. Any glue used should be heavy-duty enough to sustain extremes of weather. The end product must be easily foldable. Most important, the guidelines specified, in order for each panel to fit into the display, the cloth had to be a three-foot-by-six-foot rectangle: the size of a grave.

Jacob had balked at the imagery. Wasn't the Quilt itself morbid enough? But as he worked now with the spread of fabric, seeing how it was indeed large enough to conceal a body, he appreciated the symbolism. Marty didn't have an actual grave; he had been cremated according to his instructions, his ashes scattered in Provincetown. But tangibility was important. This rectangle of cloth would cover the bottomless grave of memory—the same infinite space Josef occupied.

Jacob couldn't get the photo to sit right. "Does that look centered to you?" he asked.

Chantelle closed one eye. "Looks okay from here."

"I don't know," he said. "I think it's a little low."

He peeled off the picture and daubed more milky adhesive on its backing. He pressed it into place, a centimeter higher, but still it looked off. "Is that any better?"

"I told you," Chantelle said, "it's fine." Then she chuckled. "You know, it makes this kind of like a meta-panel. Maybe somebody will take a picture of this and put it in theirs. Then it'd be really cool: a quilt within a quilt within a quilt."

"It was one of Marty's favorites," Jacob said defensively.

"Honey, I know. Relax. I'm only teasing."

Danny looked up from sewing a Silence=Death patch onto the panel's corner. "I think the picture's the coolest part," he said. "I mean, it really gives you a sense of Marty. Not that I ever got to meet him or anything, but that's what I'm saying. It works for, like, people who didn't know him. I kind of wish we'd done something like that for my dad."

Was it possible to mourn someone you never even knew? Jacob had been wrestling with the question since Ingrid's revelation. In a way, grieving for his uncle seemed presumptuous; he hadn't lost Josef the way she had. But still he felt this hungry absence—somehow more disorienting than his feelings for Papa Isaac, or even Marty. Papa Isaac, he had buried with his own hands. He'd watched Marty deteriorate by inches. But Josef wasn't someone he'd lost; he was someone he'd never had the chance to hold.

Perhaps because there was so little to grasp onto, Jacob hadn't told anyone. He had slipped Josef's photo into his dresser drawer, deciding to keep his uncle to himself awhile, to cherish him like a rabbit's foot tucked in his pocket. Uncle Josef: his private guardian angel.

Danny ticked a finger on Jacob's knee. "You okay?" he asked. "Are you remembering Marty?"

"Yeah," Jacob said, deciding it was not a lie: He was *remembering*; that was the important thing.

Danny replaced his finger with an entire hand, and rubbed Jacob's thigh. "Well, you should be proud. The quilt's beautiful."

"I don't know," Jacob said. "I just wish I could be sure we're doing what he would have wanted."

"Marty trusted you, didn't he?"

"Yeah, but—"

"Jake, if he hadn't trusted you, he wouldn't have asked you to be in charge. You know, when my dad died, Father Tom said we should have an open casket. And Mom was freaking about should we do it? Would Dad have wanted that? She didn't know what to do. Then Gran told her not think about what Dad would have wanted, but what he would have wanted for *us*."

Danny pinched Jacob's thigh, including him in the "us."

"We're the ones who are here," he said. "We're still alive."

He resumed his confident stitching, sewing this memorial for a man he never met. He seemed older than seventeen, his eyes too full of knowledge, like Josef's in the old photograph.

When the patch was secured, Danny looped the thread against itself. He tied a double knot, then bent to the panel as though he would kiss the cloth.

"There," he said, biting off the end of string. "That's on for good. That baby isn't going anywhere."

Jacob's mother had rented a car. It took her all of a day after his father left to decide.

"I'm an adult," she told Jacob. "Adults rent cars. Right?"

"Of course, Mom. You don't have to justify it."

His father didn't believe in renting cars, argued against the extravagance. But he was back in Washington; Jacob's mother would be here another week. There was no reason on earth for her not to. She chose a silver Honda, the model she had wanted to buy last year when Jacob's father insisted on the Oldsmobile.

Sitting now behind the sleek dash, maneuvering the tight curves of Storrow Drive, she looked blissfully in control. Jacob imagined her a teenager, accorded the keys for the very first time, driving herself to the high school sock hop.

Evening had already stolen much of the light. As the darkness thickened, the city's reflection emerged in the Charles River like a photograph developing in its chemical bath. T-shirted yuppies Rollerbladed along the Esplanade, some in pairs, others in the company only of their antennae-like headphones. The car whooshed past the tag team of billboards advertising a condominium development: IF YOU LIVED HERE . . . YOU'D BE HOME NOW.

Jacob had ceded the front to Ingrid, who sat half-turned to his mother. He had been nervous at first when both women planned to stay in Boston, devising ways for them to avoid contact during the week's overlap. But despite his interference, they sought each other out. They apologized for the seder, then settled into a surprising compatibility. They had even started lunching together, just the two of them, when Jacob was at work.

The Honda's engine groaned as they ascended the steep

expressway on-ramp. Ingrid rubbed her hands together in a pantomime of anticipation. "Excited?" she asked.

"And a little nervous," Jacob's mother said.

Jacob leaned between the headrests, not wanting to miss any conversation.

"How long has it been?" Ingrid asked.

"Oh, God. A year? Just more than a year. Jake, was it last March when Dad and I flew to Jerusalem?"

Jacob nodded. His own trip to Israel had been less than seven months ago, but it felt as though three lifetimes had passed.

Ingrid reached across and cupped a hand over Jacob's mother's, the way a driving instructor might assist a student's steering. "Everything's going to be fine," she said.

"I hope so. I really do. Maybe I shouldn't admit this. Especially in front of you, Jake. But the thing with kids? With having them grow up? You never really know for sure. It's like you're a sculptor, and you work twenty years perfecting your masterpiece. You chip away a little here, a little there, until you think it's finished. You want to donate it to a museum or something. But it doesn't happen that way. All this careful work you've put in, and still everything gets changed. You wonder why the heck you spent so much time in the first place trying to get it right."

She changed lanes, not bothering to check the traffic. The car was a bubble of silence.

"Gee, thanks, Mom," Jacob said.

"See? I knew I shouldn't have said anything."

"No, no. I'm glad. It's good to know you found parenting such a rewarding experience. That you think of us as, you know, some defective hunks of clay. I'm flattered, really."

His mother glanced into the mirror. "Honey, I'm sorry. Are you honestly mad?"

Jacob couldn't maintain the charade. He poked the meat of her shoulder. "Mom, please. Can you lighten up a little? With Dad gone I thought you'd get back your sense of humor."

"Don't make fun of me," she moaned. "Not tonight, okay?"

They ducked into the Callahan Tunnel. A pulsing fluorescence haloed everything with unnerving clarity. The ceiling—curved and shiny like the underbelly of a mammoth fish—coruscated with the reflections of rushing taillights. Jacob imagined he was peering into the choppy fathoms under which the tunnel burrowed.

It was not a conscious decision to stop breathing. He became aware of his body's lack only now, with the first stabbing cramp in his abdomen.

When he and Jonathan were kids, they had cleaved steadfast to superstition: You had to hold your breath all the way through the tunnel, or some horrible fate would befall you and your family. All tunnels required this precaution, but the Callahan was the greatest challenge. Even in good traffic, the roadway's length required tremendous stamina.

Like so much else, they made it a competition. Any strategy was considered fair. Jonathan would tickle Jacob under the ribs, trying to force him to laugh and take a breath. Jacob would retaliate, pinching his brother's knees.

Once, stalled in a rush-hour jam, Jacob had forfeited willingly. Cars crawled. The tunnel's exit would not arrive for minutes. Not satisfied with victory by default, Jonathan determined to hold out until the end. He bit his cheek, punched his own thigh to distract himself from his suffocation.

Finally, tears welling in his eyes, he gave in and sucked lungfuls of air.

"There's no way," Jacob told him. "We're not even moving a mile an hour."

Still gasping, Jonathan shook his head. "I could have made it," he said. "Maybe I could."

It didn't dawn on Jacob until years later that their competition made no sense; that if they truly believed the superstition, they should have cooperated for mutual victory. After all, the punishment was visited on your entire family. If either one lost, both would end up suffering.

Jacob had never seen so many Jews in Logan Airport. The international arrivals area swarmed with men in yarmulkes and dark fedoras. Children clung to their mothers' stockinged calves. It was as if the members of some Brookline synagogue had descended en masse to create an auxiliary outpost: Congregation Terminal E.

They all looked so happy, Jacob thought, and why shouldn't they? Any moment they would be reunited with loved ones returning from what to them truly was the Holy Land. He, on the other hand, didn't even know if Jonathan would speak to him.

Ingrid's flight was scheduled to leave in less than an hour. She had walked to the terminal's far end to check her suitcases at the Northwest counter. Now she reappeared with just her canvas carry-on and her purse.

"Late?" she asked, looking for one of the television screens that displayed flight information.

Jacob's mother shook her head. "They say the flight's already here. It's just taking forever through customs."

His mother brought her pinkie to her mouth's corner and bit down. She had been doing this incessantly since they arrived, nibbling her cuticles raw and dabbing spots of blood into a wadded Kleenex. Her other hand gripped an empty can of Diet Coke. She shook it mindlessly, the broken-off metal tab inside rattling its alarm.

Then she gasped. "I think it's—look! It's him." She raised the beacon of her soda can. But a second gasp followed, sharper. She covered her mouth with the bloodied Kleenex.

Jacob peered through the crowd and saw his brother, and then the reason for his mother's shock: Jonathan was wearing glasses.

Otherwise, he looked just as he had last fall when he greeted Jacob at Ben-Gurion: dark polyester slacks, white shirt, black shoes. His hair and beard were the same, the yarmulke still perched on his skull. But the glasses softened him. They were too wide for his face, gawky, like the oversized wingspan of some prehistoric bird. The gold frames accentuated his anemic skin.

Jacob's mother rushed to Jonathan. "Oh my God," she said. "What happened?" She lifted her hand to the edge of his glasses but did not quite touch the metal, as if, like a recently inflicted wound, it might be tender.

"What, 'What happened'?" Jonathan said. "What do you think? I wasn't seeing so clearly, so I got glasses."

"But your eyes were always perfect. You were always twenty/twenty."

Jonathan shrugged. "People's eyes go, Mom. It happens."

"Yes, but did you see a good doctor? These things can be misdiagnosed. We'll make an appointment tomorrow at Mass. Eye and Ear. I have a friend who—"

"Mom!" Jonathan clamped a hand on her shoulder. "I'm just a little nearsighted. I got glasses. I'm fine."

Like a beached fish conceding its inability to breathe, Jacob's mother stood with her mouth dumbly open. She lowered her eyes to her scabbing cuticles, dabbed at them once with the crusted Kleenex, then stuffed the tissue into the soda can's opening. Her thumb crushed a dimple in the aluminum.

"I'm sorry," she said. "Honey, I'm sorry. You have me so flustered, I didn't even give you a hug."

She reached around him and buried her face in his shoulder. When she disentangled herself, her cheeks were moist. "Now," she said, knuckling her eyes, "say hello to your brother."

As if waiting for Jacob to be pointed out in the crowd, Jonathan stood, staring vapidly. He seemed wrapped into himself, the way their father sometimes slipped away. But then, slowly, he extended his arm like a railroad crossing's warning gate. Jacob let his brother's hand hang empty for an instant before he grasped it with his own. There was the familiar, sticky sweat. Their thumbs bumped, interlocking gears.

From this close, Jonathan's lenses magnified his eyes. Jacob could see the pupils cowering against light, and immediately he wondered: Had Josef worn glasses? Was this their legacy? Would his own eyesight fail him now? Each passing year it was more difficult to tell which traits were inherited and which self-induced.

They dropped hands. Jonathan said, "You look well."

Jacob was so surprised by his brother's attempted goodwill that he forgot to say "Thanks" or "You too." They stepped apart, and only then did Jacob think of Ingrid. His aunt stood smiling, her hands loose at her sides. Jacob realized he was expected to introduce her.

"Jonathan, this is—God, this is funny. I still don't know what I'm supposed to call you. Aunt Ingrid?"

"Ingrid," she laughed. "Just Ingrid's fine."

"Okay. Jon, this is Ingrid."

Like a Japanese businessman, Jonathan clasped his hands and bowed in Ingrid's direction. "It's good to meet you," he said. "I only wish it were under happier circumstances."

Their mother placed her hand on the small of Jonathan's back, nudging him toward her. "Come on, Jon. You can at least shake her hand. There's no law against that. She's your aunt."

"No, no," Ingrid said. "If he wanted to, he would have put out his hand. I respect his choice."

Jonathan's face brightened with gratitude. He unclasped his hands and tilted forward, as if now he might greet her properly.

Most of the Jewish families had collected their respective passengers, and the area filled with people greeting the next arrival. Judging by the predominance of white-blond hair and sharp cheekbones, it must have been a Swissair flight.

"Well," Jacob's mother said. "Should we walk Ingrid over to her gate?"

"Sarah, you don't have to do that," Ingrid said. "Jonathan must be exhausted. It's past midnight his time."

"Honey? What do you think? Are you tired?"

Jonathan pushed his glasses to the bridge of his nose, the gesture as precise as a newly commissioned officer's salute. "Actually," he said, "what I'd like to do is daven."

Jacob's mother groaned. "Jon, honey. You've never even met your aunt. This is the only chance to see her before she leaves."

Jonathan's jaw tightened, as if physically restraining speech.

"What are you going to do?" his mother continued. "Start praying here? Right in front of everybody?"

"I'll stand over there," he said, "where it's a little private. Just five or ten minutes."

His mother smuggled Jacob a pleading look. *Do something*, she seemed to say. *Help me out*. But Jacob found himself unbothered by his brother's request. Maybe it was the shock of his glasses, or his travel-weariness, but Jonathan and his piety seemed innocuous. Jacob couldn't fathom a prayer so compelling that it needed to be uttered in Logan Airport, but if Jonathan did, what harm was there in indulging him?

Ingrid must have arrived at the same conclusion. "If he needs to pray," she said, "let him pray. Don't worry about me."

Jacob's mother held her hands up, a criminal acknowledging capture. "Fine. That's just fine. Then I'm going to take this opportunity to go to the ladies' room. You'll stay here?"

"Sure," Jacob said, and she turned away.

Jonathan removed a small black book from his shoulder bag and walked in the opposite direction.

"Well, that's my brother."

"Yes," Ingrid said. "The famous Jonathan."

"I know this will sound weird, but sometimes I can't believe he *is* my brother. You know? That we really grew up together?"

Ingrid glanced in the direction Jonathan had headed. "You must be glad, at least, that people can't confuse you anymore. Between the beard and the glasses and the yarmulke, you're not exactly identical."

Jacob laughed. "No, not exactly."

"On the other hand, I see the similarities. Both of you hold awfully tight to your convictions. But I'm glad you're both giving things a chance."

"I guess," Jacob said. "At least he shook my hand."

The people milling around them chattered, complaining about the incoming flight's delay. Announcements crackled over the PA system: baggage carousel numbers, parents paging misplaced children. The noise encased the two of them, an insulating scrim that amplified their own smaller sounds. Jacob could hear Ingrid's breath, the rub of fabric when she moved her arms.

She cleared her throat. "I'm afraid the next time I see you might be a funeral."

Jacob bit his lip, unable to greet the thought with words.

"I hope not," she added. "But we have to be realistic. I'm going to count on you to keep me posted, okay? You know you can always call collect."

"We can make a regular time," Jacob suggested.

"That would be fine. We'll work something out."

Sentences stampeded in Jacob's brain, a lifetime of questions left to ask. "Ingrid . . ." he began, but just her name stripped him bare. "There are a million things . . . I mean, stuff I want to . . ."

She caressed his hair, her fingers light and soothing as wind. "Don't worry," she said. "This isn't the end of anything."

"I don't think I could have made it without you."

"Of course you could. And you'll be fine. It won't be easy, but you'll be fine." Ingrid smoothed his hair where she had ruffled it. "Listen," she said, "there's something I want to give you, before the others come back. You know about the new Holocaust Museum, at the Smithsonian?"

"Yeah," Jacob said. "I saw something about it on TV last night." He had watched the news report in Nana Jenny's hospital room, looking to see if the words prompted any reaction, but his grandmother remained unreachable.

"The dedication is a week from tomorrow," Ingrid said. "Clinton will speak. And Elie Wiesel. Lots of survivors. David and I had been planning to go. But with my being out here these two weeks, and maybe having to come back if there's a funeral, it just doesn't make sense anymore."

She pulled a small white envelope from her purse.

"There are two tickets. I thought if you went down to Washington a day or two early you could go. You and Danny."

Jacob had told her about Danny two nights ago. She had congratulated him and asked the standard questions: How did they meet? What color were his eyes? Jacob was thrilled by the matter-of-factness of it all.

Ingrid pressed the envelope into his palm. "You know, there's never been anything for Josef. Nothing public. No memorial. I'd like to think his family was there for this."

Jacob couldn't tell her that he was still undecided about the trip to Washington. So much depended on how things went with Jonathan. He took the tickets and slid them into his pocket.

Ingrid's flight was boarding on the upper level. Jonathan had returned from his davening, and now their mother hurried back from the bathroom. They stood in a square around Ingrid's carry-on.

"Sarah," Ingrid said, "thanks for everything. Please let me know what I can do."

"You've already done so much," his mother said.

"Give my best to Eugene. And my apologies."

"I will. I'll tell him to call you."

They embraced and kissed on both cheeks, European-style. Ingrid turned then to Jonathan, who seemed energized by his interlude of prayer. Jacob remembered the way his brother had perked when they laid tefillin together at Etz Chaim.

"We've just barely met," Ingrid told him. "I shouldn't presume. But would you forgive me some advice from the Sages?"

"By all means," he said. "I'd be delighted."

"You may know the quote already. It's something your grand-mother used to tell me when I was a little girl. This is for you, too, Jacob. For both of you."

Jacob nodded to indicate his attention.

"The Sages said: 'Just as it is a mitzvah to say something that will be listened to, so it is a mitzvah to refrain from saying that which will not be listened to.' "

Ingrid paused, as if the words were stones cast into a pond, and she were watching their ripples circle outward.

"Now, don't make the mistake some people do, interpreting this that you should keep silent about difficult subjects. What the Sages mean, I think, is that you should find the *right* way to say everything. To make sure you always speak in a voice that can be listened to. *That*'s what you should be striving for."

Ingrid stopped, but her words seemed still to be sounding. She looked at Jonathan and Jacob together, somehow fitting both of them within her vision's scope.

Then she clapped her hands. "Ha! Listen to me. After all these years in the classroom I guess I can't help lecturing."

"No," Jonathan said, "it's a good passage. Very good. I'll look it up later when I unpack." He bowed as he had when they were introduced, but this time his distance was less standoffish than respectful. "Goodbye," he said. "I'm glad we had the chance to meet."

"Me too," Ingrid said. "Have a good visit."

Then Jacob stepped open-armed toward his aunt. He hugged her, hanging on to the strength of her back, wondering how he had ever survived without this strength. He wanted to say something to acknowledge the visceral kinship, but just as he was going to, Ingrid whispered in his ear a soothing "Shhh."

"All right," she said in full voice when they pulled apart. "I'm off. I'll be thinking of all of you." She shouldered her carry-on and strode away.

"Bye," they chorused after her. The crowd spilled between them like a wave erasing footprints in the sand.

Jacob took the backseat again. Jonathan sat pole-straight in the front, his yarmulke almost bumping the Honda's roof.

Their mother paid the dollar toll, and Jacob, ready to prove himself, gorged on his last dose of air before the Sumner Tunnel. It was really the same tunnel as the Callahan—the same piece of construction, running parallel beneath the polluted harbor—but in this direction it had a different name.

As they passed through the deepest point, Jacob's mother turned in her seat. "Well," she said, "I guess now it's just us."

Neither Jacob nor his brother responded. Jacob, concentrating, recirculated the dwindling breath in his lungs. Traffic hummed by in the other lane.

"Just the three of us," his mother continued. "Hey, you guys remember the time we were coming here for Chanukah, flying separate from Dad? Logan was fogged in so bad we had to land all the way in Portland, Maine. Remember that?"

Her voice was the cheerful banter of a camp counselor trying to convince shy cabinmates to mingle.

"I was sure it was going to be a total disaster. But it wound up being a lot of fun, didn't it? That crummy motel with no hot water anywhere except the Jacuzzi? Oh, that reminds me of something. Jon?"

Jonathan bent his neck slightly to show he'd heard.

"They didn't have a free room next to mine at the hotel. So I just had them bring in a cot. That should be fine, shouldn't it?"

Now Jonathan sat even straighter. His yarmulke brushed the car roof's fake felt, shifting on his skull.

"Well," he said, "after tonight I don't think I'll be staying in the hotel anyway. So for one night, sure, I guess it's fine."

Jacob, stunned, inched forward on his seat. Jonathan had spoken. He had breathed. He had lost the game.

"What do you mean?" Jacob's mother asked. "Where else would you be staying?"

"There are observant families," Jonathan said. "Jacob looked into it for me. It will make things much easier on all of us."

Now Jacob heard not just the fact of Jonathan's speech, but the content. This was almost an apology.

Jacob's mother shook her head. "Jon, honey, I haven't seen you in more than a year. And you want to rush off and stay with strangers? I'm your mother. Doesn't that count for anything?"

"Of course," he said. "But trust me, this will be better."

The roadway sloped upward. The tunnel's end yawned open in the distance, a widening shadowy maw. Jacob could see the green highway signs, just past the exit, but they didn't seem to move any closer. He rocked forward, as if that could make the car travel faster. His vision fuzzed with lack of oxygen.

Finally, they burst out and into evening's shade. His chest imploded. He breathed again.

A Trick of Fumes

Jacob waited for his brother on the front steps of Nana Jenny's building. Families returning from church nodded as they ambled past, young girls riding their father's necks like horses. Boys kicked stones along the sidewalk, scuffing their dress shoes, but nobody was in the mood to scold them.

Friday and Saturday had been drizzly, the entire city assuming the ashen complexion of a corpse. Aside from a visit to Nana Jenny's hospital room, and dinner Saturday with his mother, Jacob had not left his apartment. But this morning he had woken to a glinting, clarified brightness, as if during the night the earth had spiraled into a new orbit, miles closer to the sun. He and Danny walked through the lambent morning to the Kenmore Square IHOP for brunch. Then Danny headed home to Wilmington, and Jacob made his way up to his grandmother's.

As he sat waiting on the concrete stoop, the glare etched his skin like the focused beam beneath a child's magnifying glass, powerful enough to ignite paper. Tomorrow, he remembered, was Patriots' Day—the day of the Boston Marathon. This intense warmth that seemed special-ordered for Sunday strolls would be uncomfortable, potentially dangerous for the athletes.

The marathon route snaked down Beacon Street, three blocks from Nana Jenny's apartment. Shortly before two o'clock, the world's best runners would speed by on the pistons of their legs. Even more impressive, perhaps, were the amateurs who would follow: the first groups racing hard, faces stricken with the surprise of having come this far; and later, the cramp-clutching stragglers, lapsed to walking, but still pushing forward.

Since living in Boston, Jacob had managed to catch at least part of every marathon. He never quite planned on it, but always ended up somewhere along the route, lending his cheers to the weary competitors. Once he even found himself volunteering to hand out cups of water and replenishing orange slices. The runners' perseverance inspired him and at the same time, inexplicably, depressed him to his core.

Last year he had watched a man crawling on all fours, his piss-stained shorts sagging, tiny roses of blood blooming wherever his right knee touched the pavement. The man was miles from the finish. There was no way he could make it. But he could still move, he barked when people tried to stop him: "Don't touch me! I can still move."

By nightfall, Beacon Street would be relinquished to traffic. The only evidence of the almost inhuman physical achievements performed on this long asphalt stage would be the crumpled paper cups in drifts against the curb, and the discarded orange wedges, sucked dry of juice, like so many thousand collapsed smiles.

Pizzicato footsteps announced Jonathan's arrival. He stopped in front of Jacob, blocking the sun. Sweat studded his brow and spread like gray mold at his white shirt's underarms.

Jacob stood and brushed gravel from his pants. This was their first time alone, and he couldn't think of what to say, stymied by the same awkward apprehension as on a blind date. He had hoped three days' proximity would allow him a greater chance to decipher his brother, but like an object submerged in water, Jonathan remained inscrutable. It was impossible to tell which aspects were real and which merely tricks of refraction.

Jonathan hadn't mentioned anything about their calamitous parting in September. Nor had he explained his change of mind about accepting Jacob's help. Perhaps he was ready for some degree of reconciliation, but the clues could be construed just as easily otherwise. The uncertainty left Jacob poised like a sprinter in the blocks, every muscle tensed, waiting for an impossibly delayed crack of the starter's gun.

"Should we go up?" he asked. He hated the way his voice sounded, like an overfriendly real estate agent's.

Jonathan didn't seem to notice. "Might as well," he said.

They entered the foyer's cool darkness. Climbing the stairs, Jacob remembered how they used to race up the three flights, thighs burning, to the landing. In retrospect it seemed strange, given what awaited them, that they would have been so eager to reach the top. Now he followed his brother's even pace, their footsteps echoing like ticks of a giant clock.

Jacob unlocked the door and hesitantly cracked it open, the way he might enter a haunted house. The door shushed against the shag carpeting. He walked to the living room and sank into the couch, thinking perhaps they should sit a spell before starting. Jonathan hadn't been here in more than two years. He might need a chance to adjust to Nana Jenny's absence.

But his brother seemed prepared to dive right in. Like an interior decorator assessing the potential for remodeling, Jonathan marched to the center of the room. He lifted the china candy dish from the coffee table, eyed it, set it back down. He straight-armed the love seat, testing its springs. He fingered the frames of paintings, twisted lamp knobs to see if they worked.

With each article Jonathan handled, Jacob cringed. The candy dish shifted an inch when his brother replaced it, exposing a moon-sliver of clear glass in the coffee table's dust. Previously balanced paintings tilted on the wall. Jacob hadn't realized how much he had come to think of himself in these past weeks as guardian of Nana Jenny's apartment. Now he wanted to shout at Jonathan: *Don't touch! Keep your hands to yourself!* But Jonathan was only doing what they were here to do.

Their mother had told them they didn't need to document everything. They were only supposed to make a general survey of the apartment, so that if and when they moved Nana Jenny to the nursing home, the planning would be easier.

There were three categories: Move with Nana Jenny, Keep for the Family, and Sell/Give Away. Nobody had spoken about the subcategories within Keep for the Family, because nobody had to. They knew this was the chance to stake their claims.

Jonathan scribbled in the air with a pinched thumb and forefinger, as if summoning a waiter to bring the check. "Got any paper?" he asked. "Let's get this going."

"The hall desk," Jacob said. "Under the phone."

Jonathan found the pad and fished for a pen in the desk's top drawer. "Look or write?" he asked.

"What?"

"I figure one of us should look at everything and call out what it is, and the other can write it all down. Don't you think that'll be fastest?"

Jacob was shocked by his brother's pragmatism. Since when was Jonathan concerned with efficiency? But maybe being businesslike was the best approach, a relief from their simmering tensions. "Write," Jacob said. "If that's okay."

Jonathan handed him the pad and pen. "All right. I'll say an object, and which category, and if you disagree, say something. Ready?"

Jacob nodded.

"First thing: the couch. Mom said these nursing homes don't really have room for furniture. I'd say sell slash give away."

Jacob shrugged compliantly and wrote between the notebook paper's blue lines: *Big Couch. Sell/Give Away.*

"Love seat," Jonathan said. "Same thing: sell. Coffee table. Same."

Jonathan paced zealously across the room, gathering momentum. Would he auction off Nana Jenny's entire existence? Jacob tried to muster anger at his brother, but it was difficult to respond to such seeming lack of emotion.

Jonathan stopped at the painting on the far wall, the one he had knocked off-balance earlier. It was a Chagall print in shades of indigo. He cupped the corner of the frame the way an older relative chucks a toddler's chin, then tipped the picture back to horizontal. "The Chagall," he said. "Write down 'Move with Nana.' It would cheer up a room, don't you think?"

"Sure," Jacob said. "I think she'd want that." He pictured a nursing-home room, bare but for a bed and this lone piece of art.

Next, Jonathan stood at the rosewood bookcase. He xylophoned his fingernail along the row of clothbound volumes. "Do you have any interest in the *Encyclopedia Judaica?*"

A reflexive clenching in his stomach told Jacob not to give them away, not to give up anything. "Well," he began, trying to devise a reason he deserved the books. Then he stopped: What would he possibly do with them? "No," he admitted. "I guess not."

"All right. Then put 'Keep for Jonathan.' I'd really like to have them." He scanned the room. "That's it for here. How about the bedroom?"

Jacob followed his brother in a haze, a vague nausea still sapping his jaw. He didn't want any of these possessions, so why did he feel as though he were missing something? Maybe it was just Nana Jenny that he wanted. And for Jonathan to seem to care.

His brother walked straight to Nana Jenny's closet and slid the door aside. Three neat stacks of hats stood sentry on the wooden shelf. Hanging from a rod below were dress suits, arranged by color in a dull rainbow of tailored cloth.

Jacob stepped closer, drenching himself in the stale, old-lady potpourri: a mix of pressed wool and powders and other, more bodily elements. He could remember hugging Nana Jenny in this very place, when his head reached only the soft spot above her hip. He would hang on to her as long as he could get away with, his life preserver in the rough sea of their family.

"She couldn't possibly need all these," Jonathan said, "could she?" He poked the first pile of hats and the uppermost one toppled, the advance warning of an avalanche.

Jacob retrieved the hat. It was the same gray fedora Nana Jenny had worn when they visited the cemetery; a size too big, it had almost made her disappear.

"Let's keep half a dozen," Jonathan said, "and toss out the rest, okay?"

Jacob turned from the open closet. "I can't do this anymore."

"What, want me to write awhile?"

"No. This whole thing. I just can't."

"Well, it's not my favorite, either. But we have to. When else are we going to do it?"

Jacob massaged his temples, pushing away the encroaching ache. "I know," he said. "I know we have to. Listen, can we just take a little break? Are you hungry at all?"

Jonathan made a noncommittal gesture.

"Well, I am," Jacob said. "I'm starving."

*   *   *

Standing at the kitchen cabinet, Jonathan ticked his fingernail on a china bowl, its gray glaze lightly freckled, two blue lines painted around the rim.

"You *sure* this is milk?" he asked.

"Yes," Jacob said. "I'm sure. The white ones with the green flowers are meat."

Jonathan held the bowl to the light, as if examining a sheet of paper for the watermark. "I don't know. Maybe we should just order out. Is that kosher Chinese place still on Harvard Street?"

"Jon," Jacob said. "This is crazy. You'd trust some restaurant before you'd trust Nana Jenny?"

"It's not a question of trust. Of course I trust her. You just never know if something has been . . . used improperly."

"Oh, I get it," Jacob said. "You think we've defiled her dishes while she's been in the hospital? Jon, we didn't even touch anything except the Passover stuff."

Jacob grabbed his own bowl from the cabinet, half wanting to fling it at Jonathan's feet. It was just a bowl! What was the point of this ludicrous hair-splitting? But he thought of Ingrid's proverb, about the rightness of not saying some things. He was about to suggest they look for paper bowls and plates, hoping that might mollify Jonathan, when his brother opened the box of Mueslix and filled his china bowl. Maybe Jonathan had been thinking of Ingrid, too.

Jacob poured his own cereal and found the pint of skim milk on the refrigerator's top shelf. He sniffed it first just to be sure. A rancid, dead-animal smell stormed his nostrils.

"Guess we'll have to have it dry anyway," he said, feeling vindicated by the spoiled milk. Now it didn't matter which set of dishes they used. He poured the clotted liquid down the drain, running cold water to dilute the stink.

"We could do what Nana Jenny used to do," Jonathan said.

"What's that?"

"There was OJ in there, too, wasn't there?" Jonathan reopened the refrigerator and produced a small carton of Tropicana.

Jacob scrunched his nose. "Sick. You're not going to put *that* on cereal?"

"Don't you remember? It's how Nana Jenny ate it. I think it's a European thing."

"You're crazy. When did she ever do that?"

"When we stayed with them on the Cape. How could you forget?"

Jacob's throat pinched with anxiety. What else had he already forgotten? He let Jonathan drench the cereal in orange juice.

In the dining room, they took their traditional seats, facing across the table, separated by Papa Isaac's empty place. Jacob mined a spoonful of cereal from his bowl and had it halfway to his lips when he heard Jonathan mumbling. His brother's eyes were closed, his hands cupped above the Mueslix as if over a thawing fire. Jacob caught himself. He lowered his spoon.

Only when Jonathan had finished the blessing and opened his eyes did Jacob allow himself a bite. The juice tasted bitter at first, like the stomach acid that sometimes escaped up his throat in a burp, but the sweet cereal neutralized the sharpness. Jacob swallowed and dug into the bowl again.

Jonathan finished first. While Jacob still worked on the last soggy mouthfuls of Mueslix, his brother perused the dining room, making a quiet inventory. Eventually he stopped at the glass-doored breakfront, inside which the family of silver Kiddush cups was visible. There were Papa Isaac's cup and Nana Jenny's; one for each of Jacob's parents; then his and Jonathan's. Behind them all stood the tall chalice for Elijah.

Jacob wondered if there had once been cups for Josef and Ingrid, and if so, what had happened to them.

"Do you remember which was yours?" Jonathan asked, pulling out the two smallest cups and setting them on the table.

Of course Jacob remembered. Their cups were identical except for the color of the inset stones: his blue and Jonathan's green. Jacob pointed to the tiny hourglass shape on the left. "That one."

"I guess you should keep it," Jonathan said. "Here, might as well take it now." He maneuvered the cup in front of Jacob as though it were a chess piece.

Jacob, wary of an ambushing checkmate, hesitated to accept. "I don't know," he said. "Maybe we shouldn't separate them."

"What do you mean?"

"You know. They're like a set. They should stay in one place for when we all get together." Jacob realized as he said it that they might never "all" get together again. Ingrid was back in California; Jonathan would be returning to the yeshiva.

"Who would keep them?" Jonathan asked.

"I don't know. Dad, I guess."

His brother scoffed. "He won't want it. He hates this stuff."

"What about Ingrid, then?"

"Great, now she's suddenly the center of the family? Jake, we hardly even know her."

Jacob slapped the table. "She's Nana Jenny's daughter. She has as much right as Dad, or you and me."

A cold silence settled between them. It was true, Jacob thought; Ingrid was as deserving as any of them. But he knew the argument wasn't really about Ingrid, or their father, or the custody of Kiddush cups.

"Fine," Jonathan said. "Fine, I'll just put them back." He returned the two small cups to the breakfront, on either side of Papa Isaac's taller one.

When he shut the glass doors, the cabinet rattled like chattering teeth. Neither of them spoke or looked at the other, but they both understood where they had to go.

Jacob expected the door to stick, its hinges stubborn with rust or disuse. But with the hint of a push, it swung open.

Still standing in the hall, he hooked his arm around the frame and flipped the switch. The bare bulb flickered, shedding a dim, mucusy light over the room. Then it flashed brighter, as if after so many years of abandonment the filament were excited by the pulse of electricity.

He stepped in, and the smell was exactly as he remembered: cigar smoke trapped in furniture wax, the peppery must of old books. He thought of scientists who drill deep in the Antarctic ice cap, capturing millennia-old bubbles of air. That's what their grandfather's study was: a held breath, a prehistoric exhalation.

"It's so dusty," Jonathan whispered, entering after him.

"It always was," Jacob said.

"I know, but look." Jonathan ran his index finger along a bookshelf. A wave of grime collected on his fingernail. "Do you think Nana Jenny ever went in here?" he asked, wiping himself clean on his pant leg. "You know, after?"

"I don't know. It feels like she didn't even open the door."

Hebrew volumes peeked halfway out of shelves, jaundiced slips of paper still marking passages to be studied. The oak chair was pulled away from the desk, as if Papa Isaac had just gone to the kitchen for a cup of coffee, and would walk back through the door any second. In the corner, the old rocking chair balanced on its runners. Jacob pictured his grandfather sitting, limbs tensed with the effort of not rocking. He saw the pointed goatee, the unruly eyebrows, the hand slicing through the air on the count of three: *On your marks, set, go!*

And now began the weakening in his stomach, the feeling of his own insides dissolving like a sand castle devoured by rising tide. He knew Papa Isaac could not walk back through the door. His mind knew, but his body did not. His muscles remembered with animal clarity what this room meant. The burn of forearm and biceps. The heart-pounding rush.

Jonathan scoped the room, brushing dust, sniffing the air. For the first time all day he too seemed affected by their surroundings, his brash industriousness replaced by a tender curiosity. He approached the closet. "You think there's still—" he began, but as the door opened, his question answered itself. Like a row of limp criminals twisting on the gallows, the sports coats dangled from wooden hangers: some brown, some blue, otherwise the same.

Jonathan tried on a blue one. "Look," he said. "Why did I always think he was so big?"

Jacob eyed the fit. The sleeves were long, but by less than half an inch. The shoulders were actually tight. "I guess he was really just our height," he said. "Let me try."

Jonathan handed him a brown jacket and Jacob plunged his arms into the sleeves. The fit was identical.

Jonathan licked his thumb to shine one of his jacket's brass buttons. He straightened the lapels. Then he dipped his hand into the deep inside pocket, and for an instant, Jacob imagined his brother might give him something. A lemon drop, a peppermint, a shining silver dollar? His hand emerged empty.

Jonathan sat down in Papa Isaac's rocking chair, and the bent wood screeched against the weight. They had never been allowed to sit there, not even in play. Jonathan planted his feet on the floor, gripped the armrests with pincer fists. Jacob studied his brother in the chair, in the old sports coat, and his mind began to play tricks.

He whitened Jonathan's beard, trimmed it, added wrinkles to his face.

"It's amazing," he said. "You look just like him."

"Oh, please, don't say that."

"What? I thought that's what you wanted."

"Not yet. I'm not even twenty-five!"

Jacob was unnerved by his brother's rare flash of humor, unnerved and also ticklishly relieved. He went to return his jacket to its hanger, but was stopped by what he saw on the closet floor. The file box was tucked into the corner, hidden in the shadow of the dozen coats: a single metal drawer, the drab green of army fatigues. He had never seen it before.

He tugged the box into the light, then sank to the floor and pulled the drawer partway open. Hanging files were arranged alphabetically according to identification tabs typed in red: Automobile, Brookline Savings Bank, Cape House, Health Insurance. Jacob was surprised to think of Papa Isaac contending with these logistics; he had always imagined his grandfather exempted from such ordinariness.

Jonathan, joining him on the floor, reached over and pried out a folder marked "Correspondence (Sent)." He twisted himself Indian-style and opened the thick file in his lap.

Over Jonathan's shoulder, Jacob could see the handwritten letters, carbon copies on paper as thin and translucent as blister skin. The black script was botchy and gracelessly canted, as if the letters had been composed in the dark.

Jonathan flipped through the papers. "This is impossible," he complained. "I can't make out any of it." He lifted a pallid page close to his nose, then backed it away, adjusting focus. "Maybe it's these glasses. I'm still not used to them." He handed the open folder to Jacob.

It wasn't just his brother's eyes; the letters were indecipherable. Jacob picked out phrases here and there—"disappointed to learn," "in our best interest," "unworthy of attention"—but nothing that amounted to coherent meaning.

Examining the illegible scribbles, he realized he had never truly seen his grandfather's handwriting. Had Papa Isaac ever sent him a letter? Even when he and Jonathan had received birthday or Chanukah cards, the inscriptions were always in Nana Jenny's precise, unbroken script: "Wishing you G-d's blessing and guidance for another year, Your loving grandparents, Nana Jenny and"—and only then, in a fainter, back-slanted scrawl—"Papa Isaac."

Jacob considered Nana Jenny's final "and"—the fact that she had taken care of every word, every last letter, except for Papa Isaac's actual signature. Was she just being practical, knowing that his chicken scratch would be unreadable? Or did he force her to, an Old World husband with strict expectations of a wife? Maybe, Jacob thought as he replaced the stack of letters, she did it because she knew Papa Isaac's limitations. She knew this was all he was willing to grant them: his name.

The last folder in the cabinet was marked "Twins."

Jacob reached for the file, then stopped, his hand hovering above. What if it was like one of those land mines, submerged in a wheat field somewhere in France, that now, fifty years later, exploded in the face of the farmer who dared to plow too deep?

"Come on," Jonathan said. "Let's see." He elbowed in and yanked the folder. Then, as he hefted it in his palm, his face twisted sour. He returned the file to Jacob as though it were food he had tasted and decided he didn't like.

The file was paltry, much thinner than the bundle of letters Jacob had just sifted through. Inside were only a few documents: elementary-school and junior-high report cards; Xeroxed results from their yearly physicals; their birth certificates.

"This is it?" Jonathan said.

"I know," Jacob said. "It's weird."

"I mean, where's the rest of us? Where's our lives?"

Jacob whipped the folder closed and tossed it flat onto the open drawer.

Jonathan sat hunched into himself, their grandfather's sports coat straining at his shoulders. He rubbed his beard with bent knuckles, from Adam's apple to chin, over and over, as if trying to change the direction of the hairs. Behind his oversized glasses glinted the possibility of tears.

Across the distance of these last two years, across the width of ocean and the many time zones and their angry silence, Jonathan had seemed so menacing. But now, sitting beside him on the floor of Papa Isaac's study, Jacob could see his brother's utter fragility.

He could see Jonathan as the awkward kid he once had been, wanting so badly to be recognized by Papa Isaac, staking everything on a nod of the old man's head.

Who could understand this better than Jacob? Hadn't he wanted the very same thing?

"Do you think . . . ?" he asked. His voice vibrated strangely against the wood-paneled walls, wavering like a chord of black keys at a piano's low end. "Do you think he loved us?"

Jonathan breathed in through his nose, a long, steady inhalation that swelled his entire body. "Yes," he said, then sighed the air back out. "Yes. Of course he loved us."

"I don't know," Jacob said. "Sometimes, I think . . ."

What *did* he think? He knew there had been something like love, something as deep and volatile. He glanced at their slender file atop Papa Isaac's metal box—the meager accumulation of scores and evaluations—and it occurred to him there was nothing at all in the drawer for Josef, nothing for Ingrid, not even an empty folder. Could a man who had rejected his first son, his only daughter—could such a man be capable of love?

No, he thought, his grandfather's version of love was a limited resource, like wartime gasoline, perpetually hoarded in anticipation of impending crisis. His love was an endowment fund from which he might disburse token parcels of interest, but never touch the principal. This was not real love. Real love was boundless and could not be divided; it was an answer to which no questions pertained.

Jacob looked at his brother's face: a parallax view of his own; a photograph that had been printed from the same negative, with just a slightly different exposure. "If he loved us," Jacob said, "then how come he didn't want us to love each other?"

Jonathan opened his mouth as if to protest, but no sound emerged. He remained that way a long moment, caught between silence and speech, his mouth a murky wound.

"Sometimes . . ." he finally said. His voice was barely audible. "Sometimes I really hate him."

Jacob blinked twice, the closest thing his shocked body could summon to concurrence. He'd written Jonathan off as emotionless, his feelings subsumed to blind rule-following, but here was an admission balder than Jacob had ever dared.

Jonathan untwisted from his cross-legged position and pulled his knees to his chest, hugging himself. "I get so angry," he said. "I get so angry and I don't even know what I'm angry about. It's just this huge thing, this mountain, and every time I think I'm getting near the top, it gets bigger. You know how sometimes you wake up in the middle of the night and you're not sure where you are? Or you know where you are, but it's not the same place as where you went to sleep? *This* is where I always am. I wake up and I see this room. That desk. That rocking chair. I'm in my bed but I can feel *this* floor under me."

"I know," Jacob said. "Me too."

"I worried for a long time," Jonathan said. "You know, that what I'm doing with my life is because of him, just to please him or something. That's what everyone else seems to think."

"It's the same for me," Jacob said, "except the opposite. People think I'm only doing what I do to get back at him, or the family, or whatever. Dad's still convinced this is just some phase I'm going through."

Jonathan tapped a finger on his skull in some private Morse code. "Do you ever wonder? I mean, no matter how much you *know* what you're doing feels right, don't you find yourself sometimes doubting it? Is this really for me? Am I really doing it for *me*?"

His words entered Jacob like oxygen, essential and sweet. They hadn't spoken—hadn't *really* spoken—for so long, but this was a conversation Jacob could have with no one else. This was Jonathan: his own brain in a different body; his body around a different brain; his brother.

Jonathan continued, "When I start thinking like that, I remember what one of our teachers at Etz Chaim, Rabbi Saltzman, says. He says whatever you do in life, be happy. That's the greatest Jewish law. Even if you aren't observant, if you don't follow all the commandments, you should still obey that one."

"That doesn't sound very Orthodox," Jacob said. "It sounds kind of like hedonism."

"There's a difference between hedonism and happiness. You still *should* follow all the laws. Everybody should. But what good is it if you're not happy? What good is anything? Unhappiness dismisses Hashem's blessings. It's like saying the world He created isn't good enough."

Jacob inhaled the room's mustiness the way he might smell the air on a summer afternoon, trying to locate a coming thunderstorm. His pulse fluttered in his neck, in his temples, the insides of his thighs, like a swarm of moths beating against a screen.

He asked Jonathan, "Are *you* happy?"

His brother looked stunned, as if Jacob's question were an arrow aimed between his eyes. "Am I happy?" he repeated. "Do you mean in general, or right this very instant?"

"Either one, I guess," Jacob said.

"Right now?" Jonathan paused, stared straight at him. He leaned an inch closer. "Right now, I'd say I'm pretty happy."

Replacing the "Twins" folder, preparing to leave the room, Jacob saw what he had not seen earlier. Wedged in the back of the file drawer, to keep the thin folders from flopping, was a small, rectangular box. A char-black label branded the blond wood: a bullfighter standing next to a bull. *Te Amo Toro*, the burnt letters read. *100% Handmade Cigars. Imported. Long Filler.*

Jacob's gulp of breath must have given away his discovery.

"What?" Jonathan asked. "Is there something else?"

Jacob lifted the box and cradled it in his lap. He had always suspected their grandfather might have left a stash like this: a few telling photographs, a letter, a map to the buried treasure of their family.

"Go ahead," Jonathan said. "Open it."

Jacob cracked the lid, just an inch, and held it there, letting the box's air mingle with that of the room. Then, slowly, he tilted the lid the rest of the way. He peered inside with squinted eyes, as if afraid of a blinding light.

What he saw did not sear his vision. There were no photographs. There was no yellowed parchment of revelation.

"What is it?" Jonathan asked. "What's inside?"

Thick as Jacob's thumb, colored the dull green-brown of dried mud, the single cigar was wrapped in cellophane. A red band near the tip said *Te Amo*.

"You're kidding," Jonathan said. He plucked out the cigar and rolled it in his fingertips. "You've got to be kidding."

Jacob wasn't sure whether to scream or laugh. "I guess it's true," he said.

"What?"

"Sometimes a cigar box is just a cigar box."

Jonathan winced, but he couldn't help smiling. A laugh escaped through his nose. "You think these things get better with age?" he asked. "Like wine or cheese or something?"

"I can't imagine they get anything but raunchier." Jacob took the cigar from his brother and passed it beneath his nostrils. "It smells like"—the first thing that came to mind was the candied hickory of baked ham; Jacob needed a more kosher metaphor—"like hamster cages, maybe? Remember in fourth grade, when Miss Garrety kept them in the classroom? Like that. Wood shavings and piss all mixed together."

Jonathan licked his lips. "You should do cigar ads. You're very convincing."

Jacob balanced the cigar on his palm and held it halfway between himself and Jonathan. "Well?" he asked.

"Well what?"

"Do you want to do the honors, or should I?"

Jonathan raised his eyebrows. "You're not serious."

"What? It's not against the commandments or something?"

"No, it's just . . . I mean, I haven't really smoked since high school. And that wasn't cigars."

"Come on," Jacob said. "You were certainly proficient enough then. It's like riding a bicycle, right?"

Jonathan found matches and a pair of scissors in Papa Isaac's desk. He drilled a hole in the cigar with the pointed scissor tip, then struck a match and tempered the other end. He twirled it over the flame the way a glass blower would a molten vase.

"Here," he said, and blew out the match. He slipped off the cigar's red band and handed it to Jacob. Papa Isaac had given them these rings sometimes, flimsy scraps of paper they had cherished like heirloom jewelry. Back then, they had worn the rings on their thumbs. Now the band barely fit on Jacob's pinkie.

His brother poked the cigar into his mouth and lit another match. He puffed in short bursts until the end glowed uniformly orange. Then, after a longer draw, he spewed a gray mushroom cloud and gave Jacob the cigar.

"Don't inhale," Jonathan reminded him. "Just keep the smoke in your mouth."

The smoke stung Jacob's palate with the carbony bite of burnt toast. He felt as though the insides of his cheeks were being singed. "Whew," he said. "I didn't think it would be so harsh."

"You'll get used to it," Jonathan said. "Try again."

Jacob sucked more tentatively this time. The smoke was still acrid, but not as hot. He swirled it inside his cheeks like mouthwash, then spat it into the air.

"You're right," he said. "It's not quite so hideous the second time. Here, you go awhile." He took another quick puff and returned the cigar to Jonathan.

They smoked like that, passing the stogie back and forth, the only sounds the dry smack of their lips on the tightly rolled leaves and the rhythmic hiss of their exhalations. The overhead bulb flickered in its weary pattern. Dust swirled in the pasty light, settled, lifted again in the warmth of their nicotined breath. It had been so long since they had sat together like this, just sharing something. Jacob remembered the time they had climbed onto the roof at Cape Cod. It had ended badly, yes, but he didn't think of that part. He thought of the transcendent world that had been revealed on top of the pitched slope, the way everything looked so much clearer, the stars closer than stars were supposed to be. He remembered breathing the salt air with Jonathan, their bodies rising and falling in tandem like flotsam on a single wave. He remembered the way Jonathan shielded him from the nighttime breeze; the heat of his brother's flesh.

Jacob accepted the cigar again from Jonathan. With each exchange, it got more difficult to keep from touching fingers.

He pursed his lips around the pepper-tasting stub—this final, dwindling gift from Papa Isaac. The wrapped leaf was moist with Jonathan's spit, and with traces of his own. Maybe, he thought, this was as close as they could come: their saliva mingling on the stale tobacco. Or maybe, if they kept smoking, if they kept passing the cigar back and forth, back and forth until it disappeared in a trick of fumes, maybe then their lips would meet.

Monday was a holiday, but the Fenway was still open. Jacob reported to an office on the third floor.

On the bright yellow walls hung educational posters. One

depicted two young men, a blond and a brunet, naked except for the American flag draped around their waists. The blond looked like Danny, the same pouty lips and upturned nose. He held a condom like a communion wafer. The caption read: LIFE, LIBERTY, AND THE PURSUIT OF HAPPINESS.

The counselor's name was Tim. He wore a short-sleeved button-down shirt. His navy blue tie was unknotted. Jacob could see the scars on his face left by adolescent acne.

Tim reminded him that he was not obligated to find out his results. He could still walk out now; he never needed to know. Jacob said he understood, but that he wanted to find out. Tim asked if he had any questions. Any questions at all—about the possible results, about testing procedures, not just about HIV. Jacob answered no.

Then Tim pushed a piece of industrial-green paper across the desk, folded letter-style in thirds. He asked Jacob if he had brought his own slip of paper that documented his testing number. When Jacob replied that he had, Tim unfolded the top third of the green page. He asked Jacob to compare the numbers and to confirm that these were his results. The numbers matched.

Then, fingers fumbling as if he, too, were nervous, Tim unfolded the bottom third.

"There it is," he said. "Negative."

"Really?" Jacob said. "That's it?"

Tim smiled, shook his hand. "That's it."

Jacob walked out Haviland, up Mass. Ave., and was all the way to the corner of Boylston before he remembered to breathe. He removed the results from his pocket and located again the check mark that deemed him safe.

"Yes," he said out loud. "Yes!" He clenched an invisible trophy of air.

A cheer erupted from down the street, a collective roar like the rumble of distant engines. It sounded as though the whole world were applauding him. Could he be so drunk with relief that he imagined it?

He looked up and saw the old round-faced clock on the corner. Eight minutes after two. He remembered the marathon.

The leaders would just have turned onto Boylston, only blocks now from the finish line. In moments they would be greeted with TV cameras and laurel wreaths, bottles of water, foil blankets to protect their body temperature. They wouldn't have to run another step.

But other contestants were not yet at the halfway point. Some would never make it. Jacob thought of the man he'd seen last year, crawling bloody-kneed toward an impossible finish line.

He refolded the test results and stuffed them back into his pocket, deciding to turn left and avoid the crowd. Down Boylston, the roar swelled louder. Maybe it was a close race this year, he thought. Maybe two men, or three, were in contention, sprinting neck-and-neck for the tape. The crowd clapped and whistled its encouragement for runners he was too far away to see.

Across

Jacob had woken two or three times during the night, but in the untangled light of morning, it was again—still—a surprise to discover he was not alone. He rolled over gingerly, propping the covers so as not to disturb Danny by twisting them.

His neck was crimped, his shoulders knotted from sleeping in half his accustomed space. But like his stomach's pleasant soreness after a mammoth meal, this was a thoroughly enjoyable discomfort. He wouldn't have traded anything for last night's tiny traumas—the chill of tugged-away sheets, Danny's arm flopping across his chest—all the things that after months or years could become annoyances, but for these inaugural mornings were still thrilling in their awkward novelty.

Danny's nose was nestled into the pillow, close enough to draw the pillowcase with each steady inhalation. Some dreamy concern wrinkled his forehead. A violet scar, the size and shape of a golf ball's indentation, scored the skin just below his widow's peak. Danny had told him the story last night: a fight in fourth grade; a boy who accused Danny of blowing a tee-ball game with a bungled catch; a ballpoint pen stabbed into the skin.

With each passing day Jacob learned more of Danny's history; but it was not enough, it was never enough. He wanted to know everything: the dip above Danny's clavicle, the space between his toes. He aspired to identify him, as a mother cat does her kittens, by scent alone.

He lowered his face to within a scant inch of Danny's and sucked in the bewitching, alien staleness of his breath. It smelled like a car's steamed interior after a summer thunderstorm. Or the musty lining of a borrowed sleeping bag. Could he be imagining, or was there a sneezy hint of nutmeg?

Danny moaned something indecipherable through lips sticky with the paste of sleep. His jaw tried to yawn, hinged partway open, then abandoned the effort.

Jacob kissed his forehead scar. "Morning," he whispered.

Danny wrinkled his nose. His eyelids quivered, a tiny bird's wings shaking off dew.

Jacob spidered his hand and crawled it up Danny's chest, to the hollow at the base of his neck. "But, soft! What light through yonder window breaks? Time to get up, Juliet."

"Tickles," Danny protested. "Quit it."

Jacob persisted. He nibbled Danny's shoulder. He raked his fingers along the saw of Danny's spine.

Suddenly, Danny bucked and tossed off the covers. He swung his legs around, bounded off the futon, stretched half a jumping jack. "Come on," he said, hopping into a pair of shorts. "Get up already! It's seven o'clock."

That was one thing Jacob loved about Danny: zero to sixty in a second flat. Jonathan had been similar at that age, lolling around in a dopey haze when anything was asked of him, then rocketing into action when he wanted to. Jacob had always been more gradual. He remained in bed, speechless, watching.

Danny careened around the room like a dog let off his leash, collecting T-shirt and socks and shoes. He shook his hair into a semblance of order.

A minute later he returned to Jacob's side. "Don't just lay there," he said, charley-horsing Jacob's shoulder. "Get a move on. We've got a road to hit."

They were taking Mrs. Connell's car, a mud-brown Aries K with only half a muffler. But Jacob wasn't complaining. It was cheaper than flying or the bus, and there was a certain poetic justice in driving to the world's biggest gay gathering in your boyfriend's mother's suburban clunker.

They carried their duffels and, balanced between them, the

Coleman cooler Jacob had stocked with fruit and cold-cut sandwiches.

"It's like we're going to a Boy Scout jamboree," Danny said as they negotiated the stairway's narrow turn.

"Yeah," Jacob said, "emphasis on Boy."

"I still can't believe it. I mean, it's weird to, like, be conscious of this? But this is one of those things you're going to tell your kids about."

"That was fast," Jacob said. "We're dating three weeks, and already you're planning kids?"

Danny knocked the cooler into Jacob's thigh. "You know what I mean. I'm just psyched. Come on, get into the spirit."

They had reached the car. Jacob wanted to match Danny's enthusiasm—and he would, soon enough he would—but he was mindful of more sobering reasons for the trip. He lowered his side of the Coleman to the pavement. "I'll go get the panel," he said.

The cloth, folded delicately as a tissue-paper flower, was tucked into an old garment bag. Lifting it, Jacob was shocked by the lightness. This memorial they had worked so hard to finish, this final accumulation of Marty's life, weighed less than an airplane carry-on. But insubstantial as it was, it was something. Marty would never, like Josef, disappear.

When Jacob came outside again, Danny stood at the K-car's open trunk. He appeared to be talking to himself in the manner of a homeless person. He smiled, chuckled vigorously at a private joke.

Then he slammed the trunk, and as if a magician's cape had been whisked away, Chantelle's sun-sparked face was revealed.

"Chantelle!" Jacob said. "What are you doing here?" He walked around the car and planted a kiss on her cheek. "You didn't change your mind, did you? There's plenty of room in the back with Marty."

Jacob opened the door and laid the garment bag on the backseat. He resisted the urge to buckle it in with the safety belt.

"Actually, I considered it," Chantelle said. "The wedding isn't till Sunday, and I thought about hitching down with you guys to catch at least a day or two, then flying out of D.C. But Sherry called last night in a total panic. She wants me to come up early and take over the whole shebang."

"You?" Jacob said. "What does she think you know from weddings?"

Chantelle shrugged. "You know straight girls. They always want someone else to take control. I guess she figures better me than her yicky in-laws."

"Well, I'm sure you'll make a fine father-of-the-bride."

Danny pinged his knuckles on the car roof. "Hey," he said. "Look what Chantelle brought." He raised a large Tupperware container.

"Goodies?" Jacob asked.

Danny purred in confirmation.

"Well. How uncharacteristically maternal. First she's a wedding planner and now she's Fanny Farmer."

Chantelle jerked the Tupperware box as if she might rescind her generosity. "I know, it's not very PC to bring care packages to the boys going off to war. But in my family, nobody goes on a trip without a tin of brownies."

She pried a corner of the lid and showed Jacob the contents. He inhaled the moist, chocolatey scent. "Yum, these'll be great," he said. "You're a mensch if there ever was one."

"Coming from you," Chantelle said, "I'm not sure that's a compliment."

"Oh, it is. Believe me, it is."

Chantelle looked at the sky as if she could tell time from the sun's position. "Well, kids," she sighed, "some of us still have to work this week. I better get out of here."

"No, wait," Jacob said. "Wait. Stay right there." He ducked inside the car and fumbled in his duffel. Twenty seconds later he emerged brandishing a camera.

"Cool! Let me take it," Danny offered. "You and Chantelle with the Fens in the background."

"No," Jacob said, "I want all of us."

He set the camera on the car's hood, then paced ten feet and scuffed a mark on the pavement where Chantelle and Danny should stand. Back at the car, like a pool player leaning for a trick shot, he stretched across the hood and peered through the viewfinder. It didn't work; their heads were cut out of the frame. He instructed them to retreat two steps, but the angle was still wrong. The picture stopped at their chins.

"I have an idea," Danny said, digging in his pocket. "Here. Try this." He pulled out a Bic pen and poked it under the front of the camera. The camera skittered, slipping on the slanted hood, but Danny stabilized it. He let go, then held his cupped hands superstitiously over the tiny black box the way Jonathan had prayed over his bowl of Mueslix. The camera didn't move.

Danny rejoined Chantelle at the appointed spot, and Jacob checked the image again. This time the shot was perfect.

"Okay," he called, "everybody ready?"

"We're the ones who've *been* ready," Chantelle called.

Jacob pressed the button. He now had seven seconds to arrange himself. He dashed to his friends, dove between them, and wrapped his arms around their shoulders.

The camera shrilled its initial warning. A second's pause. Then another tone. Then another.

"Don't smile," Danny said, tickling Jacob's neck. "Don't smile! Look out! Here it comes!"

The camera's signal accelerated to a frenetic bleeping flurry. Jacob squeezed Chantelle and Danny closer, keeping his eyes wide, waiting for the shutter's click. He could already envision the developed photograph, displayed among the others on his bedside stand. He knew exactly where it belonged.

The route to Aish Ha-Torah would bring them within three blocks of Nana Jenny's apartment. Jacob directed Danny to take the detour.

Last night he had said goodbye to her at Beth Israel. Chances were she would still be there when he came back, still in her coma, still the same. But he would be away almost a week; anything could happen.

In his recent visits, Jacob had taken to chatting with his grandmother, imagining she absorbed everything he said. He had kept her posted about Ingrid and Jonathan, about their father's retreat to Washington. Now he told her about Danny and their plans for the march. He described Marty's Quilt panel: the photograph in the center, the laminated report card. He admitted the stitching was nowhere near what she used to do with her embroidered pillow covers. But it wasn't bad, he figured, for amateurs.

Then he mentioned the Holocaust Museum. And for the first

time since Ingrid had told him, Jacob spoke Josef's name out loud. The name sounded different in his voice, his American pronunciation, but he said it again into the quiet of Nana Jenny's room, and already the syllables were more comfortable on his tongue. He would be there for her, Jacob said. He would make sure her son was not forgotten.

Danny made the turn onto Park Street, and Jacob asked him to slow the car. As they coasted past his grandparents' building, Jacob gazed to the third floor's darkened windows, expecting the usual friction burn of incompletion. But he felt instead a satisfying exhaustion, like the hum of muscles after a decent workout. The apartment would still be here, he realized, when he returned; he would surely climb the familiar stairs again, breathe in the roasted-chicken air and the smoky dust of Papa Isaac's books. But for the first time, Jacob felt he didn't have to. He didn't have to revisit this place. If the building mysteriously vaporized, he would still know how to find everything he needed.

Danny double-parked in front of the synagogue.

"I'll wait here," he said, flipping on the hazards. "I don't think they'd appreciate, you know"—his hands drew a frame around his body.

"I'm not much better," Jacob said. He checked his own appearance: khaki shorts and a plain white T-shirt, sunglasses, black Converse high-tops.

"At least you've got the right color hair," Danny said.

"Yeah," Jacob said, "and the right nose." He removed his sunglasses and folded them on the dash. "Well, hang tight, I'll just be a couple minutes."

He uncorked himself from the car and climbed the steps to the synagogue's broad wooden door. When he tugged, the door stuck with a difference in air pressure, as though someone were fighting against him from the other side. He tried again, pulling harder, and when the seal popped he nearly lost his balance. He walked into the poorly lit foyer, the door whooshing shut behind him.

Just outside the sanctuary's entrance, a pile of yarmulkes nested in a wicker basket. Jacob hesitated—the beanie would be an absurd addition to his road-trip outfit—but he took one anyway and smoothed it onto his head.

The sanctuary was smaller than he'd expected, a third the size of Nana Jenny's synagogue. The Orthodox men blurred together in their dress shirts and identical striped tallises. Like a stand of trees worried by a whirlwind, they swayed in haphazard directions.

Then Jacob picked out his brother. Jonathan stood near the front, all the way to the side. His tallis was pulled in a tight kerchief around his head, his arms canted across his chest to hold the fabric in place. His eyes were shut, an intent but easy cast to his mouth. Jacob searched for some comparison, but he decided Jonathan looked only like himself: like Jonathan.

One square-jawed congregant, wearing thick black plastic glasses, turned and saw Jacob standing there. The man eyed him and began to approach, but Jacob reassured him with an I'll-wait gesture. He hovered at the back, self-conscious of his lack of tallis, his borrowed yarmulke, his bare legs.

When the service concluded, the serious pall that had swathed the room lifted like morning mist from a lake. The men milled about, chattering as they removed their ritual paraphernalia. On the pulpit, a white-haired man called for attention. "Please!" he shouted through the thicket of his untrimmed beard. "Please. Just one moment." When everyone quieted, he went on with his announcement. "I know many of you have to go to work. So do I. But today is an occasion. As of 3:24 this morning"—here he clapped his palm on a younger man's shoulders—"Abraham Cantor is a father! A healthy baby boy!"

There was a spirited chorus of "Mazel tov!," "Your Kaddish!," "Congratulations." Men migrated forward to shake the new father's hand.

"In honor of his blessing," the old man continued, "Abraham has brought a simple Kiddush. Some pastries and rolls here at the front. Please, come share with us."

In the excitement, no one perceived Jacob's incongruous presence. Like a kid crashing his parents' cocktail party, he wound his way through the men, ducking between their chummy back pats. He was halfway to the front when Jonathan noticed him.

His brother's mouth was full of pastry. He finished the last bite and with sugar-glazed fingers motioned for Jacob to meet him at the side.

"Jake," he said, when they reached each other. He licked his fingers clean and dried them on a handkerchief, then made a quick check of his watch. "I thought maybe you'd changed your mind."

"No," Jacob said, "we just got a slower start. I told you I'd stop by, and I am."

"Of course, of course. I wasn't accusing. Actually, it's the perfect time." Jonathan jerked his thumb toward the huddle of celebrating men. "You heard about the blessing?"

"Yeah. Convey my best wishes to the father."

"I will," Jonathan said. "He looks a bit overwhelmed right now, but I guess with a baby boy he should get used to that."

Jacob smiled. "At least it wasn't twins."

"Yes, you're right, he should be thankful for that." Jonathan smiled back, flashing his dimples. Jacob noticed that his cheeks had gained a faint tan.

"Well," he said. "I pretty much just wanted to say goodbye."

"Good," Jonathan said. "Good, I'm glad you did."

"You're all set with the place to stay and everything?"

"It's fine. The Kauffmans are being very generous. They said I can stay another week or more."

"And you'll . . ." Jacob hesitated; should he have to ask? "You'll check in on Nana Jenny?"

"Of course. I'm going right now, as soon as this is over."

The ease Jacob had felt driving past Nana Jenny's building returned to his body, a feathery decompression like stepping from a hot shower. "There was just one other thing," he said.

"Sure," Jonathan said. "Go ahead."

"Do you think you could light a yahrzeit candle for me? I mean, not for me, but kind of on my behalf?"

"This is for the friend you mentioned?" Jonathan asked. "The one who died last summer?"

Jacob shook his head. "No, somebody else."

"Because I could do it. But properly, it should be on the specific date a person died."

Jacob struggled to articulate an explanation, when so much was still left unexplained. "I don't know the date," he said. "Actually, I'm not completely positive this person even died. But in all likelihood."

Jonathan paused, eyebrows creased with consideration. Then he spoke with a teacher's calmly measured tone. "If you don't know the exact date, I believe it's acceptable to choose one. Then every year you honor that date as the yahrzeit."

"So could you light one?" Jacob said. "Tomorrow?"

"I'll light it this evening," Jonathan said, "and then it will burn all day tomorrow. Should I know who this person is, so I can say his name?"

Yes, Jacob thought, he should know; someday Jonathan should know of Josef and speak their uncle's name. But for now he said, "It's just someone who should be remembered."

They stood in their own eddy of silence, the synagogue's din swirling around them. Jacob observed his brother's face, the first scratchings of crow's-feet that forked from his eyes. He was getting older. They both were. Pretty soon, Jonathan might get married and have a kid, like the man being congratulated here this morning. Then Jacob himself would be an uncle.

"I guess I really should take off," he said. "Danny's waiting in the car."

Jonathan nodded, but otherwise didn't move.

Jacob, too, was reluctant to end this. "Listen," he said. "Why don't you come meet Danny? Just for a minute before we go."

Jonathan's face clouded with wariness. He raised his hand to protest, but before he could say anything, Jacob grasped his elbow. "Real quick," he said. "I'd really like you two to meet."

He steered his brother along the sanctuary's perimeter, around the empty pews, into the dim foyer. From this direction, the air pressure worked to his advantage; the door swung open easily. He stepped into the sunlight, holding the door, but Jonathan stopped, still inside the building.

"I can't," Jonathan said, planting his feet.

"What do you mean?" Jacob said. His fist clenched the door's handle like a weapon. The anger could still come on that fast.

"If I leave the building," Jonathan said, "then when I go back to the Kiddush I would have to make the blessings over food again. It's something we try to avoid."

Jacob looked into his brother's eyes, measuring. "Really?" he asked. "Are you sure that's all it is?"

"Yes, it's a technicality. Do you mind?"

"Stay there," Jacob said. He relaxed his grip. "I'll go down and get Danny to come here."

*   *   *

The car windows were up; Top 40 radio pulsed through the glass. Danny joggled in his seat, hair loosely flopping.

Jacob rapped on the window.

"Hey," Danny mouthed. Then, as he rolled down the glass, his words gained sound. "Ready to go?"

"In a sec," Jacob said. "First, come meet my brother."

Danny's eyes bugged. "Are you kidding?"

"No. I want you to meet him. He's already at the door."

"He hates me," Danny protested. "He doesn't want to meet me."

"Yes he does. Come on. It'll be fine."

He lugged Danny from the car and encouraged him with a kiss. A woman passing on the sidewalk stared at them, but Jacob kissed him again, more showily.

When they reached the door, Jacob yanked it open and propped it with his hip. Jonathan was there, waiting, his face sepia in the foyer's shadow. Danny stopped just outside, the morning light patterning his skin like coded messages flashed with a mirror.

There was a prolonged uncertainty, as though they were travelers in a foreign country, each pausing to determine if the other spoke his language. Neither one blinked. Neither spoke. Then, slowly, his forearm hair glinting red as it broke into the sun, Jonathan extended his hand across the threshold.

"Danny?" he said. "I'm Jonathan."

Danny met the hand. "Good to meet you."

Jonathan appraised Danny, glancing down and then back up his length. Jacob looked, too: the string-bean calves, the tiny waist, the shag of strawberry hair; all the parts he'd touched and memorized.

Jonathan released his grasp. "So," he said, "that's your car down there?"

Danny turned nervously to the street, as if to remind himself which car they'd driven. "My mom's," he said. "It's kind of on its last legs."

"Well, I hope you're not going to let Jacob drive. It's been a while, but as I remember, he's pretty reckless."

"Don't worry," Danny said. "I'll be watching him."

"Good. We expect him back in one piece."

They traded conspiratorial grins, then turned to Jacob as if waiting for a signal that they had fulfilled their obligation. Jacob wavered, overcome by the fact of Jonathan and Danny standing just a foot on either side of him, close enough to touch at the same time. He wanted to prolong this, to solder the exchange with meaningful words. But maybe this was as much as he could expect. Maybe for now this would have to be.

He gestured for Danny to take the door.

"Well," he said to Jonathan.

"I guess this is it," his brother said.

Emptiness for an instant. The blank cool of air between them. And then Jacob leaned into the absence. He found his brother's lanky form, and Jonathan, too, pulled him in. They hooked chins over each other's shoulders, a jigsaw puzzle fit. Jacob smelled a faint, familiar body sweat, but he couldn't tell which of them it came from.

"I'll be back Monday," he said when they pulled apart.

"Okay," Jonathan said, "I'll see you then?"

"Yeah. Monday. See you then."

Jonathan drifted back into the building's shadiness, and Danny let go the door, which sucked shut with an almost human sigh.

They walked down the wide concrete steps. Like a blind person following his guide, Jacob nestled his hand in the small of Danny's back. A gust of breeze shook the new leaves on nearby trees, and Jacob felt a fluttering on his skull.

Thinking to dart back into the synagogue and return the yarmulke, he reached up with his free hand and removed it. But something kept him pushing forward to the car. He caressed the cloth, slick and satiny in his fingertips, a black moon of fabric stamped with gold. He folded the yarmulke in half, then in half again, and tucked it deep inside his pocket.

This

Crossing the Tappan Zee Bridge, two minutes before noon, Jacob told Danny the story Nana Jenny told, the only time she ever spoke about the war.

It was Shabbos, or Chanukah, or some occasion. There was one of the usual arguments. Jacob couldn't recall the specifics, but he remembered his father and Papa Isaac shouting, neither listening to the other, neither trying. The force of their angry breath threatened to douse the holiday candle flames.

Jacob hunkered in his chair, trying to dodge the line of fire, and Jonathan did the same. Their mother wrung her napkin in silent impotence. She had given up trying to intervene.

Nana Jenny entered then from the kitchen, a bowl of chicken soup balanced in each outstretched hand. Her sudden presence absorbed sound and energy, demanding an end to the argument. Papa Isaac dropped his gaze to the tablecloth. Jacob's father halted mid-sentence and shut his mouth.

Through twists of steam, candlelight dappled Nana Jenny's face. Her skin deepened with previously hidden textures, like the moon viewed through a telescope. In the eerie hush, still clutching the soup, she spoke.

"It was one of the camps," she began. Her voice was soft, the brush of a feather on silk, but gradually it gained authority.

"The name doesn't matter. It could have been any one. Rations were scarce. Even if the guards had wanted to, there wasn't much to give. A tiny piece of bread each day. A bowl of soup made from potato skins.

"The prisoners had kept a calendar on the bunk post, notching with their fingernails, one mark for every day. They knew it was the fourteenth of Nisan. They knew this was the first night of Pesach.

"How they wanted to honor the holiday! They remembered the seders they used to have—serious times, yes, but also joyous—reenacting the liberation from bondage. But how could they possibly have a seder here? It's difficult enough keeping Pesach in the safety of your own home, let alone when you must struggle to stay alive. They had no matzah, no way of kashering. Their daily sliver of bread was the only hope against death.

"Some of the men wept; others had no strength even for this. Many shut their eyes, trying to forget. And in the dark chill of the barracks the rabbi rose. The Nazis had shaved his beard and his *payess*, but people remembered what he looked like before, chanting Torah in the synagogue. He was skinny now, almost too weak to stand. He held on to a bunk post for support.

"Into the dimness he lifted something up. It was a wedge of bread, no bigger than his fist. It was his own stale end of bread, saved from supper. The rabbi held the bread before his face. 'This,' he said, in what remained of his voice, 'this that you see. *This* is matzah.'

"He crushed the bread, making crumbs to pass from bunk to bunk. When every man had some, they recited the blessings, and so this was their seder. This was their Pesach."

Nana Jenny set down the soup, one helping at Jacob's place and one at Jonathan's, then turned back to the kitchen for more. Starving for the salty warmth, Jacob reached for his bowl. But when he touched the china his fingers jerked. Broth bloomed on the tablecloth. The bowl was burning hot.

ACKNOWLEDGMENTS

For their invaluable advice and support, I am especially indebted to Christopher Hogan, Michael Bronski, Vestal McIntyre, Scott Heim, Mitchell Waters, and Arnold Dolin; I am also deeply grateful to Susan Ackerman, James Ireland Baker, Brian Bouldrey, Bernard Cooper, Robert Drake, Jennifer Hengen, Julia Serebrinsky, Karen Iker, Linda Lowenthal, Jed Mattes, Jim Pines, and David Szanto.

Thanks to the New Hampshire State Council on the Arts for a timely fellowship.

I owe everything to my mother, Janet Lowenthal.

· A NOTE ON THE TYPE ·

The typeface used in this book, Transitional, is a digitized version of Fairfield, which was designed in 1937–40 by artist Rudolph Ruzicka (1883–1978), on a commission from Linotype. The assignment was the occasion for a well-known essay in the form of a letter from W. A. Dwiggins to Ruzicka, in response to the latter's request for advice. Dwiggins, who had recently designed Electra and Caledonia, relates that he would start by making very large scale drawings (10 and 64 times the size you are reading) and having test cuttings made, which were used to print on a variety of papers. "By looking at all these for two or three days I get an idea of how to go forward—or, if the result is a dud, how to start over again." At this stage he took parts of letters that satisfied him and made cardboard cutouts, which he then used to assemble other letters. This "template" method anticipated one that many contemporary computer type designers use.